The World Fantasy Awards:

Volume Two

Edited by

STUART DAVID SCHIFF
and
FRITZ LEIBER

DOUBLEDAY & COMPANY, INC.

GARDEN CITY, NEW YORK

1980

First Edition

ISBN: 0-385-15380-5
Library of Congress Catalog Card Number 79–8034
Copyright © 1980 by Stuart David Schiff
All Rights Reserved
Printed in the United States of America

Acknowledgments

"The Whimper of Whipped Dogs" by Harlan Ellison appeared in the Author's collection, *Deathbird Stories*. Copyright © 1973 by Harlan Ellison. Reprinted by arrangement with, and permission of, the Author and the Author's Agent, Robert P. Mills, Ltd.; New York.

"Jerusalem's Lot" Copyright © 1978 by Stephen King from *Night Shift* by Stephen King. Reprinted by permission of Doubleday & Company, Inc.

"The October Game" Copyright © 1948. Renewed 1975 by Ray Bradbury. Reprinted by permission of the Harold Matson Company, Inc.

"Smoke Ghost" Copyright © 1941. Copyright renewed 1968 by Fritz Leiber. Reprinted by permission of the author.

"Belsen Express" Copyright © 1975 by Fritz Leiber for *The Second Book of Fritz Leiber*. Reprinted by permission of the author.

"The King's Shadow Has No Limits" Copyright © 1975 by Stuart David Schiff for *Whispers* ⅝8. Reprinted by permission of the author's agent, Kirby McCauley, Ltd.

"The Ghastly Priest Doth Reign" Copyright © 1975 by Mercury Press Inc. Reprinted by permission of the author's agent, Kirby McCauley, Ltd.

Dedication

For the Cohan family, Cookie, Edward, Cindy, and Darren

Contents

ILLUSTRATIONS
Tim Kirk
From *Rime Isle*
Stephen Fabian
From *Whispers* magazine's "Nightmare" folio on William Hope Hodgson

Preface

Regardless of the method, there is *no* way to perfectly select the world's best. There are *always* flaws to be found in a selection process, *but* I believe that the World Fantasy Awards come as close to singling out that elusive champion as any system recognizing literary achievement. The World Fantasy Awards voting is not a static process but allows for growth and change in the voting scheme. Its current setup arrives at the nominees through input of *both* the fans and a select group of well-qualified members of the fantasy-horror literary community. The latter are then tasked with the imposing problem of determining the recipients of the World Fantasy Awards.

In the short history of the World Fantasy Awards, the judges have varied widely as have the nominees for the awards. There have been authors, critics, artists, editors, and publishers selecting winners from among revered professionals to devoted nonprofessionals. They have done an excellent job! The respect for the World Fantasy Award has already grown to the point that several books have appeared from professional publishers as a direct result of this new honor. In a publishing community where new is not necessarily equated with sales, that is in itself a great accolade.

Fritz Leiber and I have been given the honor of building this anthology to represent the winners and nominees from the Second and Third World Fantasy Award competitions. As with any book, certain rules had to be followed. These included both a finite length and budget. Nonetheless, we have been able to assemble a quality package that would make any editor proud. The thanks for this goes to the professionals appearing between these covers who have allowed us to use their work at reasonable fees. This love and respect for the genre and World Fantasy Awards is one of the big plusses our field regularly enjoys. It has made for this wonderfully exciting compilation that you readers are now invited to enjoy.

Stuart David Schiff
Box 1492-W Azalea Street,
Browns Mills, NJ 08015

Terror, Mystery, Wonder

by FRITZ LEIBER

The award stories in this book and the annual World Fantasy Convention which gave them (the first was held in 1975 in Providence, Rhode Island, honoring Howard Phillips Lovecraft; the award is a bust of that American master of the cosmic weird tale by Gahan Wilson) represent for me the culmination of a cycle which goes back to November 1936, when my twenty-five-year-old self began three terribly exciting months of correspondence with Lovecraft that ended with his death in March 1937 at the age of forty-six. At the start of that year I'd married Jonquil Stephens. That spring we'd driven out to Beverly Hills, California, and were temporarily living with my actor father and mother. I was supposed to be trying to get a job in the movies, but really I was trying unsuccessfully to write something—anything—for the magazine *Weird Tales*.

That brief but intense and *industrious* contact with a professional writer of weird stories strengthened in me a realization of the worth of the cosmic weird tale, the serious supernatural horror story, and set me an example of honesty, scholarship, and care in writing which has by fits and starts stuck with me.

About that *industrious:* There were many carefully written letters on both sides, considering the short time involved; he read and criticized a novella and some poems I'd written; we discussed his own works, problems of researching the Roman period for fictional purposes, and the controversial works of Charles Hoy Fort, all at considerable length; and I devised a splatter-stencil medium of silver star-fields on black paper and produced some illustrations for his stories which he praised; during the same time he corresponded productively also with my wife and my friend Harry Otto Fischer, all of us newcomers to his writing circle; my wife had been the first one to get in touch with him.

A great deal has happened over the intervening years besides the gradual growth of Lovecraft's literary reputation: chiefly the giant strides made by the sciences which inspired him, the travails of war and revolution and world growth, a sort of worldwide mistrust and disillusionment with all establishments—and a weary acceptance of them—replacing naïve and xenophobic nationalisms and socialistic and equalitarian faiths, and the proliferation with widening and diversifying media of the literary form to which he was devoted. As a matter of fact, Lovecraft himself foresaw much of what was coming, particularly in the literary and intellectual areas, when he wrote in the late 1920s in his "Supernatural Horror in Literature":

> For those who relish speculation regarding the future, the tale of supernatural horror provides an interesting field. Combated by a mounting wave of plodding realism, cynical flippancy, and sophisticated disillusionment, it is yet encouraged by a parallel tide of growing mysticism, as developed both through the fatigued reaction of "occultists" and religious fundamentalists against materialistic discovery and through the stimulation of wonder and fancy by such enlarged vistas and broken barriers as modern science has given us with its intra-atomic chemistry, advancing astrophysics, doctrines of relativity, and probings into biology and human thought.

Perusing that forecast today, I think of how the "mounting wave of realism" has been bloodily underlined for all by at least vicarious experiences of wars, concentration camps, the worlds of undergrounds and terrorism—the often violent "hazing" of America upon its graduation into a perhaps truer democracy and realization of world citizenship—and of how the disillusionment has become more than that of the sophisticated and the cynicism anything but flippant—there is the whole beat generation. In particular I think of how right Lovecraft was about "the tide of growing mysticism" and of how the reaction against materialistic discovery has expanded from that of the "occultists" and religious fundamentalists (whom he did *not* feel close to: note his quotation marks) to include that of the conservationists, the hippies, hosts of graduates of growingly respectable psychological and quasi-religious self-disciplines, and the many who though still may be called friends of science are certainly enemies of unregulated and unnecessary industrialism and of the doctrine of material progress for its own sake. (During a recent viewing of the 1936 H. G. Wells film, *Things to Come,* I was particularly struck by how repugnant to modern eyes is his ideal vision of a streamlined, cemented-over, cloverleafed, giant-airplane, laboratory-white world.) And finally, there are the huge and surely imagination-stimulating advances of space flight, atomic energy, electronic calculators and distance probes, and the wide-ranging explorations of inner space and of chemical influences upon it.

Another quotation from "Supernatural Horror in Literature" allows us to tie in this matter with the cosmic weird tale:

> The one test of the really weird is simply this—whether or not there be excited in the reader a profound sense of dread, and of contact with unknown spheres and powers; a subtle attitude of awed listening, as if for the beating of black wings and the scratching of outside shapes and entities on the known universe's utmost rim. And of course, the more completely and unifiedly a story conveys this atmosphere, the better it is as a work of art in the given medium.

Take that concern with "the known universe's utmost rim" and "unknown spheres and powers" and set it beside what he had to say about the way mysticism and the imagination are stimulated by science's "enlarged vistas and broken barriers . . . advancing astrophysics. . . ." (How he would have relished modern astronomy's black holes and radiogalaxies!) Think also of how an attitude of peering and listening for the subtlest unknown is at the heart of science itself. I believe you will then have strong confirmation that Lovecraft's chief contribution to the weird tale was his shaping of the materials of science and science fiction to it—that it chiefly was the cosmic of science he often talked about in this connection, not some cosmic of mysticism or religion. For him the cosmic—*his* cosmic—was a most important ingredient of the ideal weird tale. He wrote to me, "What I miss in Machen, James, Dunsany, de la Mare, Shiel, and even Blackwood and Poe, is a sense of the *cosmic*."

I think I can best get at several points which I wish to make if I now turn to the books of Charles Fort and various reactions to them.

Charles Fort was a writer of the first three decades of this century who rather derived from Dreiser, Ingersoll, Mark Twain, and the spirit of freewheeling then abroad in America: that a good man could tackle and write about anything (rather in the spirit that my own father built a summer home for us single-handed between acting seasons, and another off-season winterized it; later he put together his first Shakespearean company much in the same way). Fort chose to write about phenomena which science could not explain effectively or systematically: strange and errant planets and planetoids seen only once or observed a few times at odd intervals, falls from the heavens of materials other than meteorites; eerie and unusual sky sights of all sorts. Later he broadened his field to take in mysterious disappearances and appearances, impossible fires, and scares, crazes, and mysteries of every kind. He presented his findings in salty, picturesque, sardonic language with bursts of irreverent laughter rather reminiscent of Twain.

Fort was in a way the last of the nineteenth-century freethinkers and very much the H. L. Mencken of science and the scientists. He wasn't out to prove off-trail theories and occult visions of his own (his own personal encounters with the weird were very few and oddly prosaic) but to point out strange phenomena where they were reported to occur and to note how many such reports there were and to suggest most interestingly how reports of different sorts of weird phenomena could appear to be related to each other—strangely quiet fireballs low in the sky and religious revivals and the depredations of an escaped tame wolf, and mysterious fires indoors, that sort of thing. Today Fort's reports would be seized upon as evidence of flying saucers and other UFO phenomena, while the science-fiction minded might view his mysterious disappearances and appearances as hinting at possible dimensional doorways between parallel universes, but Fort regularly denied he had any stable pet theories of his own, only a bunch of provisional guesses and notions he threw out and as regularly discarded. When late in his life a zealous follower founded the Fortean Society he refused to join it, though following its doings with friendly interest; some years after his death the new man began to push the society into a fixed anti-establishment position, espousing various off-trail causes such as opposition to the fluoridation of water; that would not have been Fort's way, I believe.

(That's one of the commonest misapprehensions about Fort: that he had serious scientific theories of his own, or any sort of occult convictions, or underlying mystical certainties. Another is that he drew all his material from newspaper clippings, including silly-season stories from dubious tabloids. Not so. *The Book of the Damned* and *New Lands,* which are largely astronomical, depend chiefly on articles and letters in reputable American and British scientific journals; it was only in *Lo!* and *Wild Talents,* when he had broadened his interest to include phenomena of human and animal behavior, that he was forced to depend more on newspapers, which he scanned mostly in the reading rooms of the New York Public Library and the British Museum.)

Now when I was corresponding with Lovecraft I was very enthusiastic about Fort's books, and without thinking twice, I wrote him about how the man had brought to light facts that science had neglected or denied. Whereupon Lovecraft courteously explained to me how scientists cannot accept "new facts" on the basis of single or scattered reports, even by competent technicians and observers, and that experiments or observations must be repeatable—there must be general agreement—before they can become part of the body of scientific knowledge. And this is quite true, of course. Scientists don't arrive at the truth by inward certainty or by majority vote, but they do demonstrate it to each other (and to other men) by open and rational procedures. If an experiment or observation can't be repeated, it can't be accepted, no matter how great the reputation, scientific or otherwise, of the man who says he did it or saw it; the matter must then be tabled as an anecdote (perhaps an extremely interesting one) but unproven (it's very much like that Scottish criminal-law verdict) until new evidence comes in, if ever. (That's why, incidentally, there can't be a true science of history, or of artistic creation, or a lot of other things; you can't repeat the past to verify it; nor can you go back and rewrite *Hamlet* to check up.) Many of Fort's reports are cases of this sort—tabled, unproven, interesting scientific anecdotes; it's unfortunate that scientists, being human and fallible, should subsequently be apt to overstate the case on the side of authority, saying "So-and-so *must* have made a mistake . . . he *must* have been fooled by his apparatus, his instrument, etc.," rather than leaving the matter fully open (which is, admittedly, always an uncomfortably difficult thing to do).

But then Lovecraft went on to tell me that Fort's books were of course extremely exciting, stimulating, and suggestive reading and a grand source of material for weird fiction. There's this point, you see, about Fort's reports, that they have a very special sort of authenticity because you know he hasn't an ax to grind, he isn't trying to win you to some religious or occult theory of his own (which is, unfortunately, *not* so true for me when I read, say, even the great extrasensory-perception authority Rhine; I always suspect he has a weakness for proving immortality and the other world). No, Fort is a sort of pure aficionado of the weird, almost of strangeness for its own sake, you might say. Also there's the point that you know that for the materials he's discussing he's using the best authorities he can find. Finally, we should note that he was a down-to-earth realist in his writing. Dreiser was his mentor there. Fort never tried to play subtly on the emotions of his reader; his choppy, verbless sentences and other stylistic oddities were mere devices to catch interest, and his picturesque, even outrageous, metaphors were always clearly metaphors and nothing more. I'll leave this point now and return to it when I'm discussing weird literature—the terrible, mysterious, and wonderful that are collectively the chief subject of this essay.

Lovecraft himself, of course, was a complete agnostic and a scientific materialist—a scientific indifferentist, he'd say if you brought in ends and values—quite like Fort himself in some ways and very much the sort of reader Fort was addressing himself to. HPL wanted his weird kicks to be secular, you could put it, not religious or occult or even mystical. He viewed the universe as an intellectual thriller, a classic locked-room detective story alive with hints and clues pointing in all sorts of unexpected directions, where subtle speculations and deductions were everything and emotions almost nothing. That was living!—a mental thing, largely. He certainly didn't want his mind intruded upon by dynamic psychologies or consciousness-altering chemicals or techniques of any sort; he wanted that pure Sherlock Holmes reasoning apparatus working inside his skull (without the cocaine or morphine, of course!).

To be sure, there's the point that Lovecraft was a traditionalist, but that was to keep the world in decent order and the emotions and animal impulses properly under control. You weren't supposed to believe in the myths and traditions (what rational intellect could?) but you were supposed to act *as if* you believed in them—as if you were all a bunch of intellectual classical Roman and Greek aristocrats paying formal reverence to the Olympic gods to make sure the lower classes stayed afraid of them and didn't riot.

Fort had something of a Yankee contempt for the past with its stuffy pretenses, while Lovecraft was a New England traditionalist and a neoclassicist—that was their chief difference—the old Mark Twain versus Henry James contrast. (In a parallel way Fort sympathized quite strongly with the working man, the proletariat, while Lovecraft didn't.)

Lovecraft's own best and most characteristic stories, chiefly his later and longer ones, fit very well with the universe of the secular weird which Fort's books sketch out. In a very real sense he was one of the earliest and most successful Fortean authors, with each story's weird thrills and horrors springing from someone's attempt to correlate strange reports from very different areas of existence. In "The Call of Cthulhu" it is the dreams and nightmares of a lot of people, especially artistic and sensitive ones, which tie in with reports of outbursts of mania in mental hospitals and of native unrest in colonial countries, which in turn correlate with anthropologists' notes on religious practices in very savage tribes and instances of modern cult doings, all of this finally being paralled by evidence of seismic activity beneath the Pacific Ocean. Read this story and then read, say, Chapter 14 of *Lo!*, one of Fort's finest bursts of writing, the exposition of some events in England, 1904–5, stemming from the disappearance of a wolf belonging to

Captain Bains of Shotley Bridge (yes, it's the same tame wolf I
mentioned earlier), and see for yourself just how generally similar are the two writers' materials and approaches, though of
course Lovecraft perforce treats his fiction dead seriously, while
Fort gussies up his reports with sardonic humor and a lot of
Mark Twainish kidding of the British. In Lovecraft's "The Whis-
perer in Darkness," the correlated story elements are strange animal corpses glimpsed during a flood, reports of something rather
like Big Foot in lonely Vermont forested areas, shadowy night-
time fliers, old Indian myths and Puritan superstitions, the bark-
ing of dogs, and the discovery of the planet Pluto. The monsters
and gods in these tales are concocted by Lovecraft according to
what are essentially science-fiction methods; he goes to considerable pains to make sure their names are wholly alien. While his
invented books, such as the famed *Necronomicon,* are chiefly to
provide a suitable scholarly background and source for his expo-
sitions. I go into these matters more fully in my essays "Through
Hyperspace with Brown Jenkin" and "A Literary Copernicus."

My own fondness for secular weird thrills and the cosmic weird
tale were a long time developing and maturing. My childhood
mostly alternated between relatively short, exciting periods when
I was with my actor parents in or near the glittering and glamor-
ous world of the Shakespearean theater and generally longer, boring, lonely-seeming periods when I was going to school and living
with relatives in big-city apartments. I had a dread of the dark
that was a long time leaving me. (In contrast, I recall my own
son at the age of three racing about in circles outside for the first
time in the early night and crying out, "I'm in the dark! I'm in the
dark!" as though it were some sort of wonderful invisible water
he was thrashing through and with the delighted enthusiasm of
someone watching fireworks. Perhaps he was.) I don't recall
being interested in the dark at all myself—it was just frightening
stuff to be avoided. I wanted to be safe inside with my own people, my guardians, in my own lighted apartment. That was what
you might call the intrusive dark, that tried to get at you. There
was also the protective dark of bedclothes or shut eyes, that shut
off frightening sights—that was something else. I remember always taking an uneasy hour at least getting to sleep, especially
during my apartment and school periods. I had occasional bad

dreams and nightmares, though I wasn't steadily tormented with them as Lovecraft was. My worst ones came when I was trying to wake up and found myself in my familiar bed and room, with the creatures of my dreams still about me—clawed green hands reaching toward me out of secret panels and red-eyed skulls swooping about or peering at me from over the end of the bed. Now that I write these visions down, they seem to have a distinctly theatric, even melodramatic air. Did my dreams come from the stage? I'm not sure, though I do know *The Cat and the Canary* was responsible for some—it had secret panels. That was one trouble with safe apartments, incidentally—you never could be sure they didn't have secret panels, especially in the bedrooms behind the heads of the beds where they were hard to keep under observation.

I was not a very rapid or extremely voluminous reader. I imagine Poe's weird tales were the first I ran across: their concern with eerie and frightening things bothered me, but they were fascinating. Science fiction, which I first encountered in Edgar Rice Burroughs's Mars books, suited my imagination better, that and detective mystery stories, with the exploits of Craig Kennedy, Arthur B. Reeves's scientific detective, an acceptable way station between. I didn't cotton to the magazine *Weird Tales* when I first ran across it—too frightening, too much concerned with disease and death—nor to Sax Rohmer's Fu Manchu books—too many spiders and centipedes, of which I had a special dread. While the first time I encountered Lovecraft, in "The Colour Out of Space" in *Amazing Stories* where it was first published, its preoccupation with slow death and monstrous genetic transformations stemming from the fall of an unusual meteorite depressed me and haunted my mind uncomfortably for days.

No, it wasn't until I was in college and had made friends with a couple of chaps with a strong liking for the weird, and had begun to take night walks with them hunting for strange sights and eerie places (quite in the style of Poe's Dupin and his friend in Paris) that the darkness really began to glitter and sparkle for me, as it later did for my very young son. I think I really began to look at the dark then, to study it, not just avoid it with my eyes and cringe away. It was on the verge of becoming alluring. This initiation was sealed by my second encounter with Lovecraft in the form of a magazine tearsheet collection of a majority of his best tales. I read warily at first, then with increasing abandon, as I realized how they meshed with my own life. Most of his stories were set in and around universities (I was a junior at the University of Chicago.) and concerned the sciences, astronomy especially, with physics and chemistry not far behind. I was into those, quite enchanted by the mysteries and immensities of space and time, the various species of infinity, the relation of subjective and objective, inner and outer space, and the question of how we knew what we knew. His tales were about lonely scholarly people more interested in things than people; that fitted me too. And above all, although they had monsters and so-called gods in them, there was no religious stuffiness and emphasis on morality, nothing like that. In fact, it often seemed as if the gods were merely the biggest and worst of the alien monsters—which suited me too; I'd never had much religious indoctrination or pressuring, though I'd been sent to various Sunday schools; the relatives I stayed with had drifted away from churchgoing, as had my actor parents, who, though good people, didn't take religion very seriously.

Lovecraft's stories were about hunts for the weird and strange and mysterious, the wonderful and terrible, such as I had just got courage to participate in. These were the stories for me, all right! I wolfed them down.

Oh, what an elegant glitter those tales had for me on the occasion of that first reading! Terrors finely engraved in silver upon ebony, opalescently gleaming onyx mysteries, essence of black, star-spangled outer space! I wonder if the pattern of shifting tiny lights the eyes see in the absence of all light had anything to do with it—the random retinal firings that are so fascinating when we've developed the composure and sophistication to actually watch and study them. A couple of days ago the pupils of my eyes were chemically dilated for examination of the structures inside, and that night I was as always fascinated by the bright blurs and sunbursts automobile headlights and tail-lights became; this time when I studied them I noted that the spidery sunbursts had ten, eleven, or twelve legs each and that the patterns differed for right and left eye; such things endlessly fascinate me, somehow.

At any rate there's no questioning the supreme elegance of black trimmed with silver; you see it in all the eternally stylish evening dresses and uniforms; it is the style of the stars. Most recently I came across it in and on the June 1918 issue of an old San Francisco magazine called *Bohemia*. The cover depicted the gathering for a fox hunt; but the beautiful and mildly sinister woman standing among the red-coated huntsmen wore a black riding habit touched with white. Inside I discovered a short prose poem by Clark Ashton Smith, "The Black Lake," where, "in a land where weirdness and mystery had strangely leagued themselves with eternal desolation," a man climbs mountains to gaze down into a reputedly bottomless black lake after dawn but before the sun has risen above the crags.

> I was at length aware of certain small and scattered gleams of silver, apparently far under the surface. And fancying them the metal in some mysterious ledge, or the glints of long-sunken treasure, I bent closer in my eagerness, and finally perceived that what I saw was but the reflection of the stars, which, though the day was full upon the mountains and the lands without, were yet visible in the depth and darkness of that enshadowed place.

Really, the black and silver image is one we come upon again and again in the pursuit of wonder. It seems to bear repetition and so forms a fitting overture to our closer inspection of the roots of Terror, Mystery, and Wonder.

Terror first, if only because it is often our first reaction to the unknown. No question that dread, even the fear of death, can be stimulating to the imagination. Dr. Johnson said, "Depend upon it, sir, when a man knows he is to be hanged in a fortnight, it concentrates his mind wonderfully," and I am also reminded of the aphorism of Pythagoras: "Accept in your mind that anything which can happen can happen to you," and how *that* makes one think.

I know I wrote my own first two novels during the first twelve months after Pearl Harbor, when there were blackouts here on the Pacific Coast, while Japanese air raids, submarine shellings, invasion even, seemed not unlikely (you *knew* that because the price of homes dropped to a new low—some of these had belonged to citizens of Japanese ancestry, relocated in concentration camps, others to prudent persons who had fled to the relative safety of the Midwest or East. I had a nightmare about Jap bombers pursuing a refugee train across the Mojave Desert). Also, military service then seemed a distinct possibility for me. Decades later, I corresponded intensively with a young friend serving a year in Vietnam. During this period, when his life was always in danger, he absorbed an astonishing amount of music and reading material, wrote a great many voluminous, vividly reportorial letters, and composed two strong fantasy novellas and some shorter fictions; it was years before he equaled that output either in volume or intensity.

The mind seems to move so infinitely fast in fear, you know, as fast as light or even faster, fast as a crack crosses glass. Vistas and visions leap into being instantaneously, before, behind us, and to either side, above, below. It is like fireworks, or apparitions. We see things.

Certain it is when we are experiencing the fear of the unknown and at the same time the lure of the unknown that we are the most thrillingly alive. That's when excitement is greatest, all our senses straining for the faintest impressions, our mind at its keenest, our imagination at its peak, ready for anything (we hope). That sort of terror is truly a tonic—because it is mixed with what Lovecraft viewed as an aspect of the cosmic and described to me in one of his letters as "an outreaching toward a misty world of vari-colored wonders, transcended natural laws, limitless possibilities, delighted discoveries, and ceaseless adventurous expectancy" (which reminds me not so much of Viereck and Eldridge's "unendurable pleasure indefinitely prolonged" in their *My First Two Thousand Years* as of Duke Ferdinand's ridiculous and elegant dying boast in *The Duchess of Malfi:* "I will vaunt credit and affect high pleasures after death"). In short, there's always *wonder* along with the dread.

Shakespeare knew it when he had Horatio say of the Ghost, "It harrows me with fear and wonder."

No wonder without fear, no fear without wonder—that's the rule for the cosmic weird tale and also the compensation for the pains of fear, the jewel in the toad's head. It's also, incidentally, the reason many stories of white witchcraft and the benign occult are apt to be dull. It's not that such powers have to be wholly evil or malign; it is that deep down inside we know that whether they work for good or ill, they have to be *dangerous,* just as primitive man knew that the touch of a holy or taboo object could kill as surely as a lightning bolt. "And the Lord smote Uzza, because he put his hand to the ark: and there he died."

By now it is clear that the sort of fear we have in mind—cosmic terror—is not that engendered by the prospect of being tortured by the agents of a police state or locked in the same room with a homicidal maniac with razor-sharp butcher knife (no room for speculation or imagination's expansion there—you just feel sick), nor yet that (God help us!) produced by watching bloody death and morbid physical changes in a shocker-type film, but rather the sort that always carries a thrill with it, even when we know our lives may be at stake. In my novel *Our Lady of Darkness* this moved me to write, "What was the whole literature of supernatural horror but an essay to make Death itself exciting—wonder and strangeness to life's very end?"

Aristotle knew this when he pointed out that terror is one of the two elements in tragedy which freshen and renew the spirit.

Poe and Clark Ashton Smith knew it too, when they made death the chief topic of their tales.

And Lovecraft knew it when he wrote:

> The true weird tale has something more than secret murder, bloody bones, or a sheeted form clanking chains according to rule. A certain atmosphere of breathless and unexplainable dread of outer, unknown forces must be present; and there must be a hint, expressed with a seriousness and portentousness becoming its subject, of that most terrible conception of the human brain—a malign and particular suspension or defeat of those fixed laws of Nature which are our only safeguard against the assaults of chaos and the daemons of unplumbed space.

This statement, by the way, throws light on what can sometimes be the weakness of the horror story based too completely on insanity. We know it is the aberration of one individual. It lacks the cosmic touch.

Not "according to rule" and "something more"—those are the watchwords of the literature of supernatural dread, whether it take the form of *Macbeth,* where witches and the fates are most astutely blended, or of John Webster's Jacobean drama of black love, *The Duchess of Malfi,* Emily Brontë's epochal and haunting *Wuthering Heights,* Poe's "Fall of the House of Usher," Andreyev's chillingly monstrous *The Red Laugh,* Machen's superbly sinister fin de siècle melodrama, *The Three Imposters,* Hans Heinz Ewers's *Alraune,* the infinitely strange and lonely vision of mankind's eons-long future in Olaf Stapledon's *Last and First Men,* Herman Hesse's eerily illuminating *Steppenwolf,* William Sloane's novel of cosmic dread *To Walk the Night,* or the short stories of J. Sheridan LeFanu, "Vernon Lee" (Viola Paget), Ambrose Bierce, Algernon Blackwood, Walter de la Mare, M. R. James, H. Russell Wakefield, Ray Bradbury, and Robert Aickman.

It may be as simple as the gravestone inscription which gave Dorothy Sayers the cold grue—"It is Later Than You Think"— or as complex as Lovecraft's Cthulhu-Mythos extra-terrestrials (their black gloss of horror now rubbed somewhat dull, alas, by endless repetitious imitations).

"An unexplainable dread of outer, unknown forces"—that is essential . . . and also something that science has not done away with, nor will it ever do so. All that science has done is give man a dozen new sets of eyes with which to peer at frightening and wonderful and often most ambiguous and questionable things, as both Fort and Lovecraft realized very well.

To merit serious consideration, fiction of any sort must satisfy one pragmatic requirement (making due allowance for the time and place when it was written): Does it convince the reader?

In realistic fiction this means making the reader say, "Yes, this is what life is like" (or death, or joy, or poverty perhaps). Or in historical fiction: "This is what it was like to live then, at that particular time." Or in romance: "This is what love is like." (Or, more simply, "It makes me feel romantic.")

(And if all this sounds rather like asking, "Does it really entertain?" the answer is "Yes, that certainly is involved.")

In the literature of cosmic dread, or supernatural terror, the touchstone is: "This is what it is like to be face to face with the unknown." Or "I feel a thrill of terror." Or, "I feel frightened, yet at the same time filled with wonder."

We all know and can agree on such moments in masterworks of the weird, though they may come at slightly different times for different readers. Perhaps when Lady Macbeth, reading her husband's letter, comes to his statement descriptive of the Weird Sisters, "They have more in them than mortal knowledge," or earlier, when Banquo observes, "The earth hath bubbles, as the water hath." Or when the narrator in Poe's tale first perceives the tiny, wandering, roof-to-tarn crack that is to rive the House of Usher, or sees among the pictures in Roderick Usher's library one of a brilliantly lit, bare chamber that nevertheless seems far underground, or only later when he first hears distant sounds from far below while Usher reads aloud. Or when M. R. James's character in "Casting the Runes," reaching in the dark toward the pillow his head has just quitted, encounters a face or muzzle covered with bristly fur—or a bit earlier, when, opening his bedroom door, he finds nothing there but feels a hot draft moving past his bare legs. Or when in Lovecraft's "The Colour Out of Space," the professors gouging into the plastic-textured meteorite encounter a strangely colored globule or bubble and one of them strikes it smartly with his hammer "and it burst with a nervous little pop."

We may disagree as to exactly when such moments of eerie chill occur—it is a matter of individual mental chemistry, or speed of perception, or quickness to catch allusion—but we all agree they are there. As Lovecraft put it, "If the proper sensations are excited, such a 'high spot' must be admitted on its own merits as weird literature, no matter how prosaically it is later dragged down."

Is this as far as we can go in judging a tale of cosmic dread? By no means! True, Lovecraft also said, "All that a wonder story can ever be is a vivid picture of a certain type of human mood," but this is merely to say that stories are written by human beings and that he is a materialist and disbelieves in divine revelation. Clearly stories have structure, style, and scope, present various themes and materials, and how well they do this determines whether a story that satisfies the primary requirement of convincing the reader is merely competent or outstanding, even a masterpiece. One cannot judge the dinner by the appetizer alone.

It is helpful to liken the moment of authentic supernatural thrill to a lightning flash. The question then becomes, "What does the flash reveal? What, and how far can we see by it?" An instant of genuine cosmic dread inevitably creates in the reader a heightened awareness—the black doors to the unconscious and also to outer space have at least been set ajar. How does the writer then make use of this elevated sensitivity? What does he give it to feed on?

Lovecraft also wrote:

> The true function of fantasy is to give the imagination a ground for limitless expansion, and to satisfy aesthetically the sincere and burning curiosity and sense of awe which a sensitive minority of mankind feel toward the alluring and provocative abysses of unplumbed space and unguessed entity which press in upon the known world from unknown infinities and in unknown relationships of time, space, matter, force, dimensionality, and consciousness.

It is precisely and exactly this *ground* (of limitless imaginative expansion) which the lightning flash reveals to some degree—a whole new world of dread and wonder. What is the author able to show forth against this advantageous background—with the liberating, almost intoxicating effect of an ever increasing horizon that comes to someone mounting a hill, all sorts of unsuspected hidden areas laid bare and even more distant sights coming into view in all directions?

Fairly early in "The Shadow out of Time," Lovecraft achieves supernatural terror—perhaps when the narrator writes in Faustian mood, "I formed chimaerical notions about living in one age and casting one's mind all over eternity for knowledge of past and future ages." *Then* there comes a series of richly detailed visions, chilling and austere, heartbreakingly poignant and awesomely alien, of the past and future not only of mankind but also of other races and the entire solar system—visions that are certainly worth the lightning flash's candle:

> I talked with the mind of Yiang-Li, a philosopher from the cruel empire of Tsan-Chan, which is to come in 5,000 A.D.;

with that of a general of the great-headed brown people who held South Africa in 50,000 B.C.; with that of a twelfth-century Florentine monk named Bartolomeo Corsi; with that of a king of Lomar who had ruled that terrible polar land one hundred thousand years before the squat, yellow Inutos came from the west to engulf it.

I talked with the mind of Nug-Soth, a magician of the dark conquerors of 16,000 A.D.; with that of a Roman named Titus Sempronius Blaesus, who had been a quaestor in Sulla's time; with that of Khephnes, an Egyptian of the 14th Dynasty, who told me the hideous secret of Nyarlathotep; with that of a prince of Atlantis's middle kingdom; with that of a Suffolk gentleman of Cromwell's day, James Woodville; with that of a court astronomer of pre-Inca Peru; with that of the Australian physicist Nevil Kingston-Brown, who will die in 2,518 A.D.; with that of an archimage of vanished Yhe in the Pacific; with that of Theodotides, a Graeco-Bactrian official of 200 B.C.; with that of an aged Frenchman of Louis XIII's time named Pierre-Louis Montagny; with that of Crom-Ya, a Cimmerian chieftain of 15,000 B.C.; and with so many others that my brain cannot hold the shocking secrets and dizzying marvels I learned from them.

The foregoing is an excellent example of how the reader's imagination, guided by the writer's, ranges out across the vast, infinite-vistaed ground revealed in his weird, science-flavored story. The tale is quite similar in mood and giant time-landscape to Olaf Stapledon's *Last and First Men,* an especially favorite science-fiction novel of Lovecraft's which is like a great elegy on mankind's imagined two-billion-year career, passing through seventeen genetic transformations, three natural, fourteen artificially self-planned and self-inflicted, by turns a giant, a catlike creature, a giant brain, an artificial telepathic giant, even a flying batlike being, before his ultimate extinction. There are many chillingly eerie moments in this huge story, as when the Fifth Men set out to liberate and succor the buried, grief-drenched past by means of empathetic telepathic exploration, or when man, reduced to a spectrum of re-evolving beasts on Neptune, sometimes dimly remembers his former wide-minded greatness:

Certain strange vestiges of human mentality did indeed persist here and there, even as, in the fore-limbs of most species, there still remained buried the relics of man's once cunning fingers. . . . There were carnivora which, in the midst of the springtime fervour, would suddenly cease from love-making, fighting, and the daily routine of hunting, to sit alone in some high place day after day, night after night, watching, waiting; until at last hunger forced them into action.

William Hope Hodgson's *The Night Land* and *The House on the Borderland* provide other dark panoramas of the future which Lovecraft greatly admired. As he said in "Supernatural Horror in Literature," "Children will always be afraid of the dark, and men with minds sensitive to hereditary impulse will always tremble at the thought of the hidden and fathomless worlds of strange life which may pulsate in the gulfs beyond the stars, or press hideously upon our own globe in unholy dimensions which only the dead and the moon-struck can glimpse."

It has always seemed to me that great films are surely in part, and also a part of, great literature, particularly in those cases where the film-maker is both scenarist and director, and also creates an extended treatment or nontechnical shooting script, which can be, and sometimes is, published as a novella or novel in its own right. Examples: *Four Screenplays of Ingmar Bergman*, Simon and Schuster, 1960, and *Jean Cocteau: Three Screenplays* (*Orpheus, The Eternal Return, Beauty and the Beast*), Grossman, 1970. I have discussed the former at some length in my article, "Ingmar Bergman: Fantasy Novelist" in *The Second Book of Fritz Leiber*, DAW, 1975. Let us now look at Cocteau's *Orpheus*.

Orpheus is a development of the familiar legend of his descent into the Underworld (which Cocteau calls "the Zone") to rescue his wife Eurydice from Death. In the film Orpheus is the most famous and envied of modern poets. Death is personified by the Princess, a wealthy and beautiful patron of poets. She travels in a black Rolls-Royce limousine, chauffeured by her chief assistant, Heurtebise, an engaging suicide, with two black motorcyclists as outriders, who sometimes act as her agents of destruction. Orpheus witnesses their striking down of Cegestius, the Princess's protégé and Orpheus' youngest poetic rival, and is enlisted by her to help take the stricken youth to the hospital (actually a chalet that is a way station on a route to the Zone. Later Cegestius becomes her second assistant).

As a consequence of this encounter, the Princess breaks the rules under which she operates by falling in love with Orpheus and effecting the killing of his wife, Eurydice. Orpheus, with the crucial help of Heurtebise, achieves the familiar mythic rescue, and the powers-that-be in the Zone provisionally reprieve the Princess for her crime. Ultimately Orpheus dies, but is restored to life and Eurydice by the self-sacrifice of the Princess and Heurtebise, who thereafter await their doom in the Zone. (*Cegestius:* Madam, when one is arrested here, what happens? *Heurtebise:* It's not funny, I can assure you. *Cegestius:* It's not funny anywhere. *Heurtebise:* Least of all here.)

The function of mirrors is well described to Orpheus by *Heurtebise:* I will tell you the greatest secret . . . Mirrors are the doors through which Death comes and goes. Besides, look at yourself in the mirror throughout your life, and you will see Death at work like bees in a glass hive.

Later, in the Zone, they encounter a glazier carrying great panes of stuff in a wooden rack and crying out hauntingly, "Glass! New glass!"

I find the concept of the *Zone* so apt and the name itself so attractive that I am tempted to use it as synonymous with Lovecraft's *ground* (for the imagination's limitless expansion) revealed by the lightning flash of cosmic dread. (A not-unpleasant mnemonic for it is "Twilight Zone," that better-than-average early TV fantasy program.)

In his film Cocteau first suggests to us that the Princess, magnificently interpreted by Maria Casares, is in some sense Death, perhaps by the stroke of the black motorcyclists alone, perhaps when Orpheus touches Cegestius in the limousine on the way to the hospital and says, "But . . . he's dead," and she replies, "When will you learn to mind your own business?" (Understatement is the horror writer's surest tool.) Achieving another thrill of terror, Cocteau next convinces us that the Princess and her servants can pass through mirrors out of and into the Zone, which is no conventional supernatural half world, but "consists of the memories of men and the ruins of their habits" and is "a no-man's land between life and death," an area where space, time, and gravity work differently, even backward, a region of stark and ultimate reality having nothing to do with the fables by which we live our ordinary day-to-day lives.

Language itself is transformed in the Zone. When the Princess says to the knowing and knightly Heurtebise and the naïvely noble Cegestius while they are seeking to restore Orpheus to life, "Work! Work!" she is not speaking of everyday jobs and drudgery but of the passionate necessity to show forth your best to an utterly merciless cosmos and in the very face of death. This strong imperative is in her every frown and infrequent smile, as when at the end she says to Heurtebise only, "Thank you," and he replies, "It was nothing." (Understatement again.)

In *Macbeth,* Banquo's words to the witches, "If you can look into the seeds of time, and say which grain will grow and which will not," simultaneously thrill us eerily and catapult us to a vantage point from which we feel able to distinguish reality from mere potentiality or possibility. "The earth hath bubbles, as the water hath," maintains this lightning-etched mood, which is sounded forth in full register by Macbeth when he soliloquizes, "Present fears Are less than horrible imaginings: My thought, whose murder yet is but fantastical, shakes so my single state of man that function is smothered in surmise, and nothing is but what is not." This is Zone-language of the purest sort. Thereafter the steady lightning flashes keep us miraculously "upon this bank and shoal of time," while "Light thickens; and the crow makes wing to the rooky wood: Good things of day begin to droop and drowse; whiles night's black agents to their prey do rouse.——" and the vast dimensional pageantry finally recedes to "Tomorrow, and tomorrow, and tomorrow, creeps in this petty pace from day to day, to the last syllable of recorded time."

And when in Webster's *The Duchess of Malfi* the Duchess says, "What would it pleasure me to have my throat cut with diamonds? or to be smothèred with cassia? or to be shot to death with pearls? I know death hath ten thousand several doors for men to take their exits; and 'tis found they go on such strange geometrical hinges, you may open them both ways. . . ." and later when the dying Ferdinand says, "Whether we fall by ambition, blood, or lust, like diamonds we are cut with our own dust," they are talking Zone-language too.

And when in *Wuthering Heights* Catherine Linton rends a pillow in her frenzy and then, much as mad Ophelia with her flowers, childishly arranges the freed feathers, identifying them as turkey's, wild duck's, pigeon's, moor cock's, and precious lapwing's (but Catherine is not mad, only exalted), that is Zone-business, and wind-tormented, wind-named Wuthering Heights itself the Zone.

In *King Lear* another heath, a storm-beaten and lightning-riven one, is the Zone, where only fools and madmen are abroad—and tormented old kings and walking fires and all manner of fiends. It is from this dreadful and exalted vantage point that Shakespeare's imagination, by turns dark and lightning-stark, radiates out over the entire play. "Child Rowland to the dark tower came."

The Zone (Cocteau's concept is useful) necessarily takes surprisingly different forms in different weird fictions. In Ingmar Bergman's *The Hour of the Wolf* it is an area where the characters an artist creates become as real as living people and begin to order his life and the lives of those very close to him. (The Italian dramatist Pirandello discovered a similar area.) In Hesse's *Steppenwolf* it is THE MAGIC THEATER—FOR MADMEN ONLY! In Arthur Machen's eerie tales, it is the region where we may recognize the sexual, perverse, destructive, and orgiastic drives underlying human conduct—the modern reader must take into account that Machen's black and white novels and *The Great God Pan* were written for Victorians. In Clark Ashton Smith's literally macabre tales the Zone is the landscape where death is always present, always watching.

Now it can be argued that the Zone is just one more imaginary fictional world, usually of a demonic sort and filled with invented devilish and angelic presences (and in a sense it is), but there is a difference. To reach the Zone (any Zone), one must first feel cosmic dread—first the writer, then the reader. The touchstone that makes a story merit serious consideration also distinguishes and to a degree authenticates its Zone.

It is in the world of heightened awareness constituted by the Zone that the narrative of cosmic dread sets forth the insights and observations about life and character, love and death, the microcosm and the universe that set it rather above the story in which one or a few fast shocks are all the author tries for—we get a flash of fear but see nothing by it, and in a short story this may be sufficient.

At the start of his "Supernatural Horror in Literature," Lovecraft attempts to distinguish between stories of wonder and "tales of ordinary feelings and events," suggesting that the former are about cosmic phenomena, the latter about human character. But later, in discussing Emily Brontë's *Wuthering Heights* he is forced to admit that it is both a human novel and "a piece of terror literature"—that it bridges and denies the distinction he tried to create. "Though primarily a tale of life, and of human passions in agony and conflict, its epically cosmic setting affords room for horror of the most spiritual sort." His false divorcement of wonder from the commonplace impeded Lovecraft's own development as a creative writer, and in "The Thing on the Doorstep" he belatedly sought to bridge it by writing a terror tale that has character development and is a study of a marriage which is a struggle for dominance.

I think that what Lovecraft really wanted to keep out of the wonder story was "common sentimental distortions of ordinary feelings and events," as is shown by his reproof of Bulwer-Lytton's *Zanoni* for "a ponderous network of symbolic and didactic meanings" and the same writer's *A Strange Story* for "an atmosphere of homiletic pseudo-science designed to please the matter-of-fact and purposeful Victorian reader" and of William Hope Hodgson's *The Night Land* for "nauseously sticky romantic sentimentality," but as we have seen, sentimentality is the last thing one is apt to find in the hyper-real world of the Zone.

And as Lovecraft himself said:

> . . . much of the choicest weird work is unconscious; appearing in memorable fragments scattered through material whose massed effect may be of a very different cast. Atmosphere is the all-important thing, for the final criterion of authenticity is not the dovetailing of a plot but the creation of a given sensation. . . . such narratives often possess, in isolated sections, atmospheric touches which fulfill every condition of true supernatural horror-literature.

It is partly on these grounds, but also simply to give the fullest honest picture of the field, that I have given works like *Macbeth* and *King Lear* as examples of supernatural horror literature and tales of cosmic dread, whatever else they may be besides—and after all, systems of classification are nothing final or necessarily profound, they are merely for the most part pigeonholes into which to order and arrange things for purposes of easier discussion.

For example, I find it hard to understand why Ibsen's *Peer Gynt* and Melville's *Moby Dick* work so well without bringing in the matter of cosmic dread. Without the eeriness of the Great Boyg, shapeless but irresistible, and the green-dressed trolls and their grotesque revels in the Hall of the Mountain King, the former would never come fully alive—they crown Peer's own peculiar way of imagining and storytelling. Besides the touches of Death as a Button Molder and the Devil as a Pastor, possibly also a photographer, "A Thin Person" (understatement once again).

And as for *Moby Dick,* it seems clear to me that the drive of the tale and its ever-tightening grip on us depend on our mounting fear of the White Whale, so that it comes to seem to us that he must possess not only evil intelligence but also raw divinity of some kind—very much as we come to feel about the great white shark in the film *Jaws.* Moreover, there are gothic elements in the Melville book, particularly in the matter of the yellow crew of the captain's boat, who are mistaken for ghosts as they come aboard the *Pequod,* who remain mysteriously hidden in the hold, and who finally appear with the effect of phantoms as they emerge with their Parsee leader, Fedallah, to launch the captain's own boat—Fedallah, who dies roped to the breaching White Whale. Would *Moby Dick* work as well without this eeriness? I do not think so. And one might even say that here the sea, grand symbol of the unconscious, is the book's Zone. But it is unnecessary to go that far.

The World Fantasy Awards:

Volume Two

Harlan Ellison is one of the finest writers ever to have plied his craft. If the fantasy and science fiction field is ever to be judged against the rest of literature, we must hope that Harlan is ghettoized with us. His savage, brutal stories slice, rip, and rend their way to our darkest realities, our most indescribable fears. The following tale led off his World Fantasy Award-nominated *Deathbird Stories* and won an Edgar Award in 1974 from the Mystery Writers of America.

The Whimper of Whipped Dogs

by HARLAN ELLISON

On the night after the day she had stained the louvered window shutters of her new apartment on East 52nd Street, Beth saw a woman slowly and hideously knifed to death in the courtyard of her building. She was one of twenty-six witnesses to the ghoulish scene, and, like them, she did nothing to stop it.

She saw it all, every moment of it, without break and with no impediment to her view. Quite madly, the thought crossed her mind as she watched in horrified fascination, that she had the sort of marvelous line of observation Napoleon had sought when he caused to have constructed at the *Comédie-Française* theaters, a curtained box at the rear, so he could watch the audience as well as the stage. The night was clear, the moon was full, she had just turned off the 11:30 movie on channel 2 after the second commercial break, realizing she had already seen Robert Taylor in *Westward the Women,* and had disliked it the first time; and the apartment was quite dark.

She went to the window, to raise it six inches for the night's sleep, and she saw the woman stumble into the courtyard. She was sliding along the wall, clutching her left arm with her right hand. Con Ed had installed mercury-vapor lamps on the poles; there had been sixteen assaults in seven months; the courtyard was illuminated with a chill purple glow that made the blood streaming down the woman's left arm look black and shiny. Beth saw every detail with utter clarity, as though magnified a thousand power under a microscope, solarized as if it had been a television commercial.

The woman threw back her head, as if she were trying to scream, but there was no sound. Only the traffic on First Avenue, late cabs foraging for singles paired for the night at Maxwell's Plum and Friday's and Adam's Apple. But that was over there, beyond. Where *she* was, down there seven floors below, in the courtyard, everything seemed silently suspended in an invisible force-field.

Beth stood in the darkness of her apartment, and realized she had raised the window completely. A tiny balcony lay just over the low sill; now not even glass separated her from the sight; just the wrought-iron balcony railing and seven floors to the courtyard below.

The woman staggered away from the wall, her head still thrown back, and Beth could see she was in her mid-thirties, with dark hair cut in a shag; it was impossible to tell if she was pretty: terror had contorted her features and her mouth was a twisted black slash, opened but emitting no sound. Cords stood out in her neck. She had lost one shoe, and her steps were uneven, threatening to dump her to the pavement.

The man came around the corner of the building, into the courtyard. The knife he held was enormous—or perhaps it only seemed so: Beth remembered a bone-handled fish knife her father had used one summer at the lake in Maine: it folded back on itself and locked, revealing eight inches of serrated blade. The knife in the hand of the dark man in the courtyard seemed to be similar.

The woman saw him and tried to run, but he leaped across the distance between them and grabbed her by the hair and pulled her head back as though he would slash her throat in the next reaper-motion.

Then the woman screamed.

The sound skirled up into the courtyard like bats trapped in an echo chamber, unable to find a way out, driven mad. It went on and on. . . .

The man struggled with her and she drove her elbows into his sides and he tried to protect himself, spinning her around by her hair, the terrible scream going up and up and never stopping. She came loose and he was left with a fistful of hair torn out by the roots. As she spun out, he slashed straight across and opened her up just below the breasts. Blood sprayed through her clothing and the man was soaked; it seemed to drive him even more berserk. He went at her again, as she tried to hold herself together, the blood pouring down over her arms.

She tried to run, teetered against the wall, slid sidewise, and the man struck the brick surface. She was away, stumbling over a flower bed, falling, getting to her knees as he threw himself on her again. The knife came up in a flashing arc that illuminated the blade strangely with purple light. And still she screamed.

Lights came on in dozens of apartments and people appeared at windows.

He drove the knife to the hilt into her back, high on the right shoulder. He used both hands.

Beth caught it all in jagged flashes—the man, the woman, the knife, the blood, the expressions on the faces of those watching from the windows. Then lights clicked off in the windows, but they still stood there, watching.

She wanted to yell, to scream, "What are you doing to that woman?" But her throat was frozen, two iron hands that had been immersed in dry ice for ten thousand years clamped around her neck. She could feel the blade sliding into her own body.

Somehow—it seemed impossible but there it was down there, happening somehow—the woman struggled erect and *pulled* herself off the knife. Three steps, she took three steps and fell into the flower bed again. The man was howling now, like a great beast, the sounds inarticulate, bubbling up from his stomach. He fell on her and the knife went up and came down, then again, and again, and finally it was all a blur of motion, and her scream of lunatic bats went on till it faded off and was gone.

Beth stood in the darkness, trembling and crying, the sight filling her eyes with horror. And when she could no longer bear to look at what he was doing down there to the unmoving piece of meat over which he worked, she looked up and around at the windows of darkness where the others still stood—even as she stood—and somehow she could see their faces, bruise-purple with the dim light from the mercury lamps, and there was a universal sameness to their expressions. The women stood with their nails biting into the upper arms of their men, their tongues edging from the corners of their mouths; the men were wild-eyed and smiling. They all looked as though they were at cock fights. Breathing deeply. Drawing some sustenance from the grisly scene below. An exhalation of sound, deep, deep, as though from caverns beneath the earth. Flesh pale and moist.

And it was then that she realized the courtyard had grown foggy, as though mist off the East River had rolled up 52nd Street in a veil that would obscure the details of what the knife and the man were still doing . . . endlessly doing it . . . long after there was any joy in it . . . still doing it . . . again and again . . .

But the fog was unnatural, thick and gray and filled with tiny scintillas of light. She stared at it, rising up in the empty space of the courtyard. Bach in the cathedral, stardust in a vacuum chamber.

Beth saw eyes.

There, up there, at the ninth floor and higher, two great eyes, as surely as night and the moon, there were *eyes*. And—a face? Was that a face, could she be sure, was she imagining it . . . a face? In the roiling vapors of chill fog something lived, something brooding and patient and utterly malevolent had been summoned up to witness what was happening down there in the flower bed. Beth tried to look away, but could not. The eyes, those primal burning eyes, filled with an abysmal antiquity yet frighteningly bright and anxious like the eyes of a child; eyes filled with tomb depths, ancient and new, chasm-filled, burning, gigantic and deep as an abyss, holding her, compelling her. The shadow play was being staged not only for the tenants in their windows, watching and drinking of the scene, but for some *other*. Not on frigid tundra or waste moors, not in subterranean caverns or on some faraway world circling a dying sun, but here, in the city, here the eyes of that *other* watched.

Shaking with the effort, Beth wrenched her eyes from those burning depths up there beyond the ninth floor, only to see again the horror that had brought that *other*. And she was struck for the first time by the awfulness of what she was witnessing, she was released from the immobility that had held her like a coclacanth in shale, she was filled with the blood thunder pounding against the membranes of her mind: she had *stood* there! She had done nothing, nothing! A woman had been butchered and she had said nothing, done nothing. Tears had been useless, tremblings had been pointless, she *had done nothing!*

Then she heard hysterical sounds midway between laughter and giggling, and as she stared up into that great face rising in the fog and chimneysmoke of the night, she heard *herself* making those deranged gibbon noises and from the man below a pathetic, trapped sound, like the whimper of whipped dogs.

She was staring up into that face again. She hadn't wanted to see it again—ever. But she was locked with those smoldering eyes, overcome with the feeling that they were childlike, though she *knew* they were incalculably ancient.

Then the butcher below did an unspeakable thing and Beth reeled with dizziness and caught the edge of the window before she could tumble out onto the balcony; she steadied herself and fought for breath.

She felt herself being looked at, and for a long moment of frozen terror she feared she might have caught the attention of that face up there in the fog. She clung to the window, feeling everything growing faraway and dim, and stared straight across the court. She *was* being watched. Intently. By the young man in the seventh-floor window across from her own apartment. Steadily, he was looking at her. Through the strange fog with its burning eyes feasting on the sight below, he was staring at her.

As she felt herself blacking out, in the moment before unconsciousness, the thought flickered and fled that there was something terribly familiar about his face.

It rained the next day. East 52nd Street was slick and shining with the oil rainbows. The rain washed the dog turds into the gutters and nudged them down and down to the catch-basin openings. People bent against the slanting rain, hidden beneath umbrellas, looking like enormous, scurrying black mushrooms. Beth went out to get the newspapers after the police had come and gone.

The news reports dwelled with loving emphasis on the twenty-six tenants of the building who had watched in cold interest as Leona Ciarelli, 37, of 455 Fort Washington Avenue, Manhattan, had been systematically stabbed to death by Burton H. Wells, 41, an unemployed electrician, who had been subsequently shot to death by two off-duty police officers when he burst into Michael's Pub on 55th Street, covered with blood and brandishing a knife that authorities later identified as the murder weapon.

She had thrown up twice that day. Her stomach seemed incapable of retaining anything solid, and the taste of bile lay along the back of her tongue. She could not blot the scenes of the night before from her mind; she re-ran them again and again, every movement of that reaper arm playing over and over as though on a short loop of memory. The woman's head thrown back for silent screams. The blood. Those eyes in the fog.

She was drawn again and again to the window, to stare down into the courtyard and the street. She tried to superimpose over the bleak Manhattan concrete the view from her window in Swann House at Bennington: the little yard and another white, frame dormitory; the fantastic apple trees; and from the other window the rolling hills and gorgeous Vermont countryside; her memory skittered through the change of seasons. But there was always concrete and the rain-slick streets; the rain on the pavement was black and shiny as blood.

She tried to work, rolling up the tambour closure of the old rolltop desk she had bought on Lexington Avenue and hunching over the graph sheets of choreographer's charts. But Labanotation was merely a Jackson Pollock jumble of arcane hieroglyphics to her today, instead of the careful representation of eurhythmics she had studied four years to perfect. And before that, Farmington.

The phone rang. It was the secretary from the Taylor Dance Company, asking when she would be free. She had to beg off. She looked at her hand, lying on the graph sheets of figures Laban had devised, and she saw her fingers trembling. She had to beg off. Then she called Guzman at the Downtown Ballet Company, to tell him she would be late with the charts.

"My God, lady, I have ten dancers sitting around in a rehearsal hall getting their leotards sweaty! What do you expect me to do?"

She explained what had happened the night before. And as she told him, she realized the newspapers had been justified in holding that tone against the twenty-six witnesses to the death of Leona Ciarelli. Paschal Guzman listened, and when he spoke again, his voice was several octaves lower, and he spoke more slowly. He said he understood and she could take a little longer to prepare the charts. But there was a distance in his voice, and he hung up while she was thanking him.

She dressed in an argyle sweater vest in shades of dark purple, and a pair of fitted khaki gabardine trousers. She had to go out, to walk around. To do what? To think about other things. As she pulled on the Fred Braun chunky heels, she idly wondered if that heavy silver bracelet was still in the window of Georg Jensen's. In the elevator, the young man from the window across the court-yard stared at her. Beth felt her body begin to tremble again. She went deep into the corner of the box when he entered behind her.

Between the fifth and fourth floors, he hit the *off* switch and the elevator jerked to a halt.

Beth stared at him and he smiled innocently.

"Hi. My name's Gleeson, Ray Gleeson, I'm in 714."

She wanted to demand he turn the elevator back on, by what right did he pre*sume* to do such a thing, what did he mean by this, turn it on at once or suffer the consequences. That was what she *wanted* to do. Instead, from the same place she had heard the gibbering laughter the night before, she heard her voice, much smaller and much less possessed than she had trained it to be, saying, "Beth O'Neill, I live in 701."

The thing about it, was that *the elevator was stopped*. And she was frightened. But he leaned against the paneled wall, very well dressed, shoes polished, hair combed and probably blown dry with a hand drier, and he *talked* to her as if they were across a table at L'Argenteuil. "You just moved in, huh?"

"About two months ago."

"Where did you go to school? Bennington or Sarah Lawrence?"

"Bennington. How did you know?"

He laughed, and it was a nice laugh. "I'm an editor at a religious book publisher; every year we get half a dozen Bennington, Sarah Lawrence, Smith girls. They come hopping in like grasshoppers, ready to revolutionize the publishing industry."

"What's wrong with that? You sound like you don't care for them."

"Oh, I *love* them, they're marvelous. They think they know how to write better than the authors we publish. Had one darlin' little item who was given galleys of three books to proof, and she rewrote all three. I think she's working as a table-swabber in a Horn & Hardart's now."

She didn't reply to that. She would have pegged him as an antifeminist, ordinarily, if it had been anyone else speaking. But the eyes. There was something terribly familiar about his face. She was enjoying the conversation; she rather liked him.

"What's the nearest big city to Bennington?"

"Albany, New York. About sixty miles."

"How long does it take to drive there?"

"From Bennington? About an hour and a half."

"Must be a nice drive, that Vermont country, really pretty. They went coed, I understand. How's that working out?"

"I don't know, really."

"You don't know?"

"It happened around the time I was graduating."

"What did you major in?"

"I was a dance major, specializing in Labanotation. That's the way you write choreography."

"It's all electives, I gather. You don't have to take anything required, like sciences, for example." He didn't change tone as he said, "That was a terrible thing last night. I saw you watching. I guess a lot of us were watching. It was a really terrible thing."

She nodded dumbly. Fear came back.

"I understand the cops got him. Some nut, they don't even know why he killed her, or why he went charging into that bar. It was really an awful thing. I'd very much like to have dinner with you one night soon, if you're not attached."

"That would be all right."

"Maybe Wednesday. There's an Argentinian place I know. You might like it."

"That would be all right."

"Why don't you turn on the elevator, and we can go," he said, and smiled again. She did it, wondering why she had stopped the elevator in the first place.

On her third date with him, they had their first fight. It was at a party thrown by a director of television commercials. He lived on the ninth floor of their building. He had just done a series of spots for *Sesame Street* (the letters "U" for Underpass, "T" for Tunnel, lowercase "b" for boats, "C" for cars; the numbers 1 to 6 and the numbers 1 to 20; the words *light* and *dark*) and was celebrating his move from the arena of commercial tawdriness (and its attendant $75,000 a year) to the sweet fields of educational programing (and its accompanying descent into low-pay respectability). There was a logic in his joy Beth could not quite understand, and when she talked with him about it, in a far corner of the kitchen, his arguments didn't seem to parse. But he seemed happy, and his girlfriend, a long-legged ex-model from Philadelphia, continued to drift to him and away from him, like some exquisite undersea plant, touching his hair and kissing his neck, murmuring words of pride and barely submerged sexuality. Beth found it bewildering, though the celebrants were all bright and lively.

In the living room, Ray was sitting on the arm of the sofa, hustling a stewardess named Luanne. Beth could tell he was hustling; he was trying to look casual. When he *wasn't* hustling, he was always intense, about everything. She decided to ignore it, and wandered around the apartment, sipping at a Tanqueray and tonic.

There were framed prints of abstract shapes clipped from a calendar printed in Germany. They were in metal Bonniers frames.

In the dining room a huge door from a demolished building somewhere in the city had been handsomely stripped, teaked and refinished. It was now the dinner table.

A Lightolier fixture attached to the wall over the bed swung out, levered up and down, tipped, and its burnished globe-head revolved a full three hundred and sixty degrees.

She was standing in the bedroom, looking out the window,

when she realized *this* had been one of the rooms in which light had gone on, gone off; one of the rooms that had contained a silent watcher at the death of Leona Ciarelli.

When she returned to the living room, she looked around more carefully. With only three or four exceptions—the stewardess, a young married couple from the second floor, a stockbroker from Hemphill, Noyes—*everyone* at the party had been a witness to the slaying.

"I'd like to go," she told him.

"Why, aren't you having a good time?" asked the stewardess, a mocking smile crossing her perfect little face.

"Like all Bennington ladies," Ray said, answering for Beth, "she is enjoying herself most by not enjoying herself at all. It's a trait of the anal retentive. Being here in someone else's apartment, she can't empty ashtrays or rewind the toilet paper roll so it doesn't hang a tongue, and being tightassed, her nature demands we go.

"All right, Beth, let's say our goodbyes and take off. The Phantom Rectum strikes again."

She slapped him and the stewardess's eyes widened. But the smile remained frozen where it had appeared.

He grabbed her wrist before she could do it again. "Garbanzo beans, baby," he said, holding her wrist tighter than necessary.

They went back to her apartment, and after sparring silently with kitchen cabinet doors slammed and the television being tuned too loud, they got to her bed, and he tried to perpetuate the metaphor by fucking her in the ass. He had her on elbows and knees before she realized what he was doing; she struggled to turn over and he rode her bucking and tossing without a sound. And when it was clear to him that she would never permit it, he grabbed her breast from underneath and squeezed so hard she howled in pain. He dumped her on her back, rubbed himself between her legs a dozen times, and came on her stomach.

Beth lay with her eyes closed and an arm thrown across her face. She wanted to cry, but found she could not. Ray lay on her and said nothing. She wanted to rush to the bathroom and shower, but he did not move, till long after his semen had dried on their bodies.

"Who did you date at college?" he asked.

"I didn't date anyone very much." Sullen.

"No heavy makeouts with wealthy lads from Williams and Dartmouth . . . no Amherst intellectuals begging you to save them from creeping faggotry by permitting them to stick their carrots in your sticky little slit?"

"Stop it!"

"Come on, baby, it couldn't all have been knee socks and little round circle-pins. You don't expect me to believe you didn't get a little mouthful of cock from time to time. It's only, what? about fifteen miles to Williamstown? I'm sure the Williams werewolves were down burning the highway to your cunt on weekends; you can level with old Uncle Ray. . . ."

"Why are you like this?!" She started to move, to get away from him, and he grabbed her by the shoulder, forced her to lie down again. Then he rose up over her and said, "I'm like this because I'm a New Yorker, baby. Because I live in this fucking city every day. Because I have to play patty-cake with the ministers and other sanctified holy-joe assholes who want their goodness and lightness tracts published by the Blessed Sacrament Publishing and Storm Window Company of 277 Park Avenue, when what I *really* want to do is toss the stupid psalm-suckers out the thirty-seventh-floor window and listen to them quote chapter-and-worse all the way down. Because I've lived in this great big snapping dog of a city all my life and I'm mad as a mudfly, for chrissakes!"

She lay unable to move, breathing shallowly, filled with a sudden pity and affection for him. His face was white and strained, and she knew he was saying things to her that only a bit too much Almadén and exact timing would have let him say.

"What do you expect from me," he said, his voice softer now, but no less intense, "do you expect kindness and gentility and understanding and a hand on *your* hand when the smog burns your eyes? I can't do it, I haven't got it. No one has it in this cesspool of a city. Look around you; what do you think is happening here? They take rats and they put them in boxes and when there are too many of them, some of the little fuckers go out of their minds and start gnawing the rest to death. *It ain't no different here, baby!* It's rat time for everybody in this madhouse. You can't expect to jam as many people into this stone thing as we do, with buses and taxis and dogs shitting themselves scrawny and noise night and day and no money and not enough places to live and no place to go to have a decent think . . . you can't do it without making the time right for some godforsaken other kind of thing to be born! You can't hate everyone around you, and kick every beggar and nigger and *mestizo* shithead, you can't have cabbies stealing from you and taking tips they don't deserve, and then cursing you, you can't walk in the soot till your collar turns black, and your body stinks with the smell of flaking brick and decaying brains, you can't do it without calling up some kind of awful—"

He stopped.

His face bore the expression of a man who has just received brutal word of the death of a loved one. He suddenly lay down, rolled over, and turned off.

She lay beside him, trembling, trying desperately to remember where she had seen his face before.

He didn't call her again, after the night of the party. And when they met in the hall, he pointedly turned away, as though he had given her some obscure chance and she had refused to take it. Beth thought she understood: though Ray Gleeson had not been her first affair, he had been the first to reject her so completely. The first to put her not only out of his bed and his life, but even out of his world. It was as though she were invisible, not even beneath contempt, simply not there.

She busied herself with other things.

She took on three new charting jobs for Guzman and a new group that had formed on Staten Island, of all places. She worked furiously and they gave her new assignments; they even paid her.

She tried to decorate the apartment with a less precise touch. Huge poster blowups of Merce Cunningham and Martha Graham replaced the Brueghel prints that had reminded her of the view looking down the hill toward Williams. The tiny balcony outside her window, the balcony she had steadfastly refused to stand upon since the night of the slaughter, the night of the fog with eyes, that balcony she swept and set about with little flower boxes in which she planted geraniums, petunias, dwarf zinnias, and other hardy perennials. Then, closing the window, she went to give herself, to involve herself in this city to which she had brought her ordered life.

And the city responded to her overtures:

Seeing off an old friend from Bennington, at Kennedy International, she stopped at the terminal coffee shop to have a sandwich. The counter—like a moat—surrounded a center service island that had huge advertising cubes rising above it on burnished poles. The cubes proclaimed the delights of Fun City. *New York Is a Summer Festival,* they said, and *Joseph Papp Presents Shakespeare in Central Park* and *Visit the Bronx Zoo* and *You'll Adore Our Contentious but Lovable Cabbies.* The food emerged from a window far down the service area and moved slowly on a conveyor belt through the hordes of screaming waitresses who slathered the counter with redolent washcloths. The lunchroom had all the charm and dignity of a steel-rolling mill, and approximately the same noise level. Beth ordered a cheeseburger that cost a dollar and a quarter, and a glass of milk.

When it came, it was cold, the cheese unmelted, and the patty of meat resembling nothing so much as a dirty scouring pad. The bun was cold and untoasted. There was no lettuce under the patty.

Beth managed to catch the waitress's eye. The girl approached with an annoyed look. "Please toast the bun and may I have a piece of lettuce?" Beth said.

"We dun' do that," the waitress said, turned half away as though she would walk in a moment.

"You don't do what?"

"We dun' toass the bun here."

"Yes, but I *want* the bun toasted," Beth said firmly.

"An' you got to pay for extra lettuce."

"If I was asking for *extra* lettuce," Beth said, getting annoyed, "I would pay for it, but since there's *no* lettuce here, I don't think I should be charged extra for the first piece."

"We dun' do that."

The waitress started to walk away. "Hold it," Beth said, raising her voice just enough so the assembly-line eaters on either side stared at her. "You mean to tell me I have to pay a dollar and a quarter and I can't get a piece of lettuce or even get the bun toasted?"

"Ef you dun' like it . . ."

"Take it back."

"You gotta pay for it, you order it."

"I said take it back, I don't want the fucking thing!"

The waitress scratched it off the check. The milk cost 27¢ and tasted going-sour. It was the first time in her life that Beth had said *that* word aloud.

At the cashier's stand, Beth said to the sweating man with the felt-tip pens in his shirt pocket, "Just out of curiosity, are you interested in complaints?"

"No!" he said, snarling, quite literally snarling. He did not look up as he punched out 73¢ and it came rolling down the chute.

The city responded to her overtures:

It was raining again. She was trying to cross Second Avenue, with the light. She stepped off the curb and a car came sliding through the red and splashed her. "Hey!" she yelled.

"Eat shit, sister!" the driver yelled back, turning the corner.

Her boots, her legs and her overcoat were splattered with mud. She stood trembling on the curb.

The city responded to her overtures:

She emerged from the building at One Astor Place with her big briefcase full of Laban charts; she was adjusting her rain scarf about her head. A well-dressed man with an attaché case thrust the handle of his umbrella up between her legs from the rear. She gasped and dropped her case.

The city responded and responded and responded.

Her overtures altered quickly.

The old drunk with the stippled cheeks extended his hand and mumbled words. She cursed him and walked on up Broadway past the beaver film houses.

She crossed against the lights on Park Avenue, making hackies slam their brakes to avoid hitting her; she used *that* word frequently now.

When she found herself having a drink with a man who had elbowed up beside her in the singles' bar, she felt faint and knew she should go home.

But Vermont was so far away.

Nights later. She had come home from the Lincoln Center ballet, and gone straight to bed. Lying half-asleep in her bedroom, she heard an alien sound. One room away, in the living room, in the dark, there was a sound. She slipped out of bed and went to the door between the rooms. She fumbled silently for the switch on the lamp just inside the living room, and found it, and clicked it on. A black man in a leather car coat was trying to get *out* of the apartment. In that first flash of light filling the room she noticed the television set beside him on the floor as he struggled with the door, she noticed the police lock and bar had been broken in a new and clever manner *New York Magazine* had not yet reported in a feature article on apartment ripoffs, she noticed that he had gotten his foot tangled in the telephone cord that she had requested be extra-long so she could carry the instrument into the bathroom, I don't want to miss any business calls when the shower is running; she noticed all things in perspective and one thing with sharpest clarity: the expression on the burglar's face.

There was something familiar in that expression.

He almost had the door open, but now he closed it, and slipped the police lock. He took a step toward her.

Beth went back, into the darkened bedroom.

The city responded to her overtures.

She backed against the wall at the head of the bed. Her hand fumbled in the shadows for the telephone. His shape filled the doorway, light, all light behind him.

In silhouette it should not have been possible to tell, but somehow she knew he was wearing gloves and the only marks he would leave would be deep bruises, very blue, almost black, with the tinge under them of blood that had been stopped in its course.

He came for her, arms hanging casually at his sides. She tried to climb over the bed, and he grabbed her from behind, ripping her nightgown. Then he had a hand around her neck and he pulled her backward. She fell off the bed, landed at his feet and his hold was broken. She scuttled across the floor and for a moment she had the respite to feel terror. She was going to die, and she was frightened.

He trapped her in the corner between the closet and the bureau and kicked her. His foot caught her in the thigh as she folded tighter, smaller, drawing her legs up. She was cold.

Then he reached down with both hands and pulled her erect by her hair. He slammed her head against the wall. Everything slid up in her sight as though running off the edge of the world. He slammed her head against the wall again, and she felt something go soft over her right ear.

When he tried to slam her a third time she reached out blindly for his face and ripped down with her nails. He howled in pain and she hurled herself forward, arms wrapping themselves around his waist. He stumbled backward and in a tangle of thrashing arms and legs they fell out onto the little balcony.

Beth landed on the bottom, feeling the window boxes jammed up against her spine and legs. She fought to get to her feet, and her nails hooked into his shirt under the open jacket, ripping. Then she was on her feet again and they struggled silently.

He whirled her around, bent her backward across the wrought-iron railing. Her face was turned outward.

They were standing in their windows, watching.

Through the fog she could see them watching. Through the fog she recognized their expressions. Through the fog she heard them breathing in unison, bellows breathing of expectation and wonder. Through the fog.

And the black man punched her in the throat. She gagged and started to black out and could not draw air into her lungs. Back, back, he bent her further back and she was looking up, straight up, toward the ninth floor and higher. . . .

Up there: eyes.

The words Ray Gleeson had said in a moment filled with what he had become, with the utter hopelessness and finality of the choice the city had forced on him, the words came back. *You can't live in this city and survive unless you have protection . . . you can't live this way, like rats driven mad, without making the time right for some godforsaken other kind of thing to be born . . . you can't do it without calling up some kind of awful . . .*

God! A new God, an ancient God come again with the eyes and hunger of a child, a deranged blood God of fog and street violence. A God who needed worshipers and offered the choices of death as a victim or life as an eternal witness to the deaths of *other* chosen victims. A God to fit the times, a God of streets and people.

She tried to shriek, to appeal to Ray, to the director in the bedroom window of his ninth-floor apartment with his long-legged Philadelphia model beside him and his fingers inside her as they worshiped in their holiest of ways, to the others who had been at the party that had been Ray's offer of a chance to join their congregation. She wanted to be saved from having to make that choice.

But the black man had punched her in the throat, and now his hands were on her, one on her chest, the other in her face, the smell of leather filling her where the nausea could not. And she understood Ray had *cared,* had wanted her to take the chance offered; but she had come from a world of little white dormitories and Vermont countryside; it was not a real world. *This* was the real world and up there was the God who ruled this world, and she had rejected him, had said no to one of his priests and servitors. *Save me! Don't make me do it!*

She knew she had to call out, to make appeal, to try and win the approbation of that God. *I can't . . . save me!*

She struggled and made terrible little mewling sounds trying to summon the words to cry out, and suddenly she crossed a line, and screamed up into the echoing courtyard with a voice Leona Ciarelli had never known enough to use.

"Him! Take him! Not me! I'm yours, I love you, I'm yours! Take him, not me, please not me, take him, take him, I'm yours!"

And the black man was suddenly lifted away, wrenched off her, and off the balcony, whirled straight up into the fog-thick air in the courtyard, as Beth sank to her knees on the ruined flower boxes.

She was half-conscious, and could not be sure she saw it just that way, but up he went, end over end, whirling and spinning like a charred leaf.

And the form took firmer shape. Enormous paws with claws and shapes that no animal she had ever seen had ever possessed, and the burglar, black, poor, terrified, whimpering like a whipped dog, was stripped of his flesh. His body was opened with a thin incision, and there was a rush as all the blood poured from him like a sudden cloudburst, and yet he was still alive, twitching with the involuntary horror of a frog's leg shocked with an electric current. Twitched, and twitched again as he was torn piece by

piece to shreds. Pieces of flesh and bone and half a face with an
eye blinking furiously, cascaded down past Beth, and hit the cement below with sodden thuds. And still he was alive, as his or-
gans were squeezed and musculature and bile and shit and skin
were rubbed, sandpapered together and let fall. It went on and
on, as the death of Leona Ciarelli had gone on and on, and she
understood with the blood-knowledge of survivors *at any cost*
that the reason the witnesses to the death of Leona Ciarelli had
done nothing was not that they had been frozen with horror, that
they didn't want to get involved, or that they were inured to death
by years of television slaughter.

They were worshipers at a black mass the city had demanded
be staged; not once, but a thousand times a day in this insane asylum of steel and stone.

Now she was on her feet, standing half-naked in her ripped
nightgown, her hands tightening on the wrought-iron railing, begging to see more, to drink deeper.

Now she was one of them, as the pieces of the night's sacrifice
fell past her, bleeding and screaming.

Tomorrow the police would come again, and they would question her, and she would say how terrible it had been, that burglar,
and how she had fought, afraid he would rape her and kill her,
and how he had fallen, and she had no idea how he had been so
hideously mangled and ripped apart, but a seven-story fall, after
all . . .

Tomorrow she would not have to worry about walking in the
streets, because no harm could come to her. Tomorrow she could
even remove the police lock. Nothing in the city could do her any
further evil, because she had made the only choice. She was now
a dweller in the city, now wholly and richly a part of it. Now she
was taken to the bosom of her God.

She felt Ray beside her, standing beside her, holding her, pro-
tecting her, his hand on her naked backside, and she watched the
fog swirl up and fill the courtyard, fill the city, fill her eyes and
her soul and her heart with its power. As Ray's naked body
pressed tightly inside her, she drank deeply of the night, knowing
whatever voices she heard from this moment forward would be
the voices not of whipped dogs, but those of strong, meat-eating
beasts.

At last she was unafraid, and it was so good, so very good *not* to be afraid.

"When inward life dries up, when feeling decreases and apathy increases, when one cannot affect or even genuincly touch another person, violence flares up as a daimonic necessity for contact, a mad drive forcing touch in the most direct way possible."

—Rollo May, *Love and Will*

Stephen King is the most successful practitioner of horror fiction ever to have lived. His *Carrie, The Shining, Salem's Lot, The Stand,* and several yet-to-be-written volumes have earned him millions of dollars through book and motion picture sales. Still, he remains a craftsman and has not been overcome by his sudden wealth and fame (as evidenced by a recent teaching position at the University of Maine). King's *Salem's Lot* was nominated for a 1975 World Fantasy Award, but we feel that novel excerpts rarely work. Instead of such a fragment, we present a complete story, the prequel to that masterwork.

Jerusalem's Lot

by STEPHEN KING

Oct. 2, 1850.

DEAR BONES,

How good it was to step into the cold, draughty hall here at Chapelwaite, every bone in an ache from that abominable coach, in need of instant relief from my distended bladder—and to see a letter addressed in your own inimitable scrawl propped on the obscene little cherry-wood table beside the door! Be assured that I set to deciphering it as soon as the needs of the body were attended to (in a coldly ornate downstairs bathroom where I could see my breath rising before my eyes).

I'm glad to hear that you are recovered from the *miasma* that has so long set in your lungs, although I assure you that I do sympathize with the moral dilemma the cure has affected you with. An ailing abolitionist healed by the sunny climes of slave-struck Florida! Still and all, Bones, I ask you as a friend who has also walked in the valley of the shadow, *to take all care of yourself* and venture not back to Massachusetts until your body gives you leave. Your fine mind and incisive pen cannot serve us if you are clay, and if the Southern zone is a healing one, is there not poetic justice in that?

Yes, the house is quite as fine as I had been led to believe by my cousin's executors, but rather more sinister. It sits atop a huge and jutting point of land perhaps three miles north of Falmouth and nine miles north of Portland. Behind it are some four acres of grounds, gone back to the wild in the most formidable manner imaginable—junipers, scrub vines, bushes, and various forms of creeper climb wildly over the picturesque stone walls that separate the estate from the town domain. Awful imitations of Greek statuary peer blindly through the wrack from atop various hillocks—they seem, in most cases, about to lunge at the passer-by. My cousin Stephen's tastes seem to have run the gamut from the unacceptable to the downright horrific. There is an odd little summer house which has been nearly buried in scarlet sumac and a grotesque sundial in the midst of what must once have been a garden. It adds the final lunatic touch.

But the view from the parlour more than excuses this; I command a dizzying view of the rocks at the foot of Chapelwaite Head and the Atlantic itself. A huge, bellied bay window looks out on this, and a huge, toadlike secretary stands beside it. It will do nicely for the start of that novel which I have talked of so long [and no doubt tiresomely].

To-day has been gray with occasional splatters of rain. As I look out all seems to be a study in slate—the rocks, old and worn as Time itself, the sky, and of course the sea, which crashes against the granite fangs below with a sound which is not precisely sound but vibration—I can feel the waves with my feet even as I write. The sensation is not a wholly unpleasant one.

I know you disapprove my solitary habits, dear Bones, but I assure you that I am fine and happy. Calvin is with me, as practical, silent, and as dependable as ever, and by midweek I am sure that between the two of us we shall have straightened our affairs and made arrangement for necessary deliveries from town—and a company of cleaning women to begin blowing the dust from this place!

I will close—there are so many things as yet to be seen, rooms to explore, and doubtless a thousand pieces of execrable furniture to be viewed by these tender eyes. Once again, my thanks for the touch of familiar brought by your letter, and for your continuing regard.

Give my love to your wife, as you both have mine.

CHARLES.

Oct. 6, 1850.

DEAR BONES,

Such a place this is!

It continues to amaze me—as do the reactions of the townfolk in the closest village to my occupancy. That is a queer little place with the picturesque name of Preacher's Corners. It was there that Calvin contracted for the weekly provisions. The other errand, that of securing a sufficient supply of cordwood for the winter, was likewise taken care of. But Cal returned with gloomy countenance, and when I asked him what the trouble was, he replied grimly enough:

"They think you mad, Mr. Boone!"

I laughed and said that perhaps they had heard of the brain fever I suffered after my Sarah died—certainly I spoke madly enough at that time, as you could attest.

But Cal protested that no-one knew anything of me except through my cousin Stephen, who contracted for the same services as I have now made provision for. "What was said, sir, was that anyone who would live in Chapelwaite must be either a lunatic or run the risk of becoming one."

This left me utterly perplexed, as you may imagine, and I asked who had given him this amazing communication. He told me that he had been referred to a sullen and rather besotted pulp-logger named Thompson, who owns four hundred acres of pine, birch, and spruce, and who logs it with the help of his five sons, for sale to the mills in Portland and to householders in the immediate area.

When Cal, all unknowing of his queer prejudice, gave him the location to which the wood was to be brought, this Thompson stared at him with his mouth ajaw and said that he would send his sons with the wood, in the good light of the day, and by the sea road.

Calvin, apparently misreading my bemusement for distress hastened to say that the man reeked of cheap whiskey and that he had then lapsed into some kind of nonsense about a deserted village and cousin Stephen's relations—and worms! Calvin finished his business with one of Thompson's boys, who, I take it, was rather surly and none too sober or freshly-scented himself. I take it there has been some of this reaction in Preacher's Corners itself, at the general store where Cal spoke with the shop-keeper, although this was more of the gossipy, behind-the-hand type.

None of this has bothered me much; we know how rustics dearly love to enrich their lives with the smell of scandal and myth, and I suppose poor Stephen and his side of the family are fair game. As I told Cal, a man who has fallen to his death almost from his own front porch is more than likely to stir talk.

The house itself is a constant amazement. Twenty-three rooms, Bones! The wainscotting which panels the upper floors and the portrait gallery is mildewed but still stout. While I stood in my late cousin's upstairs bedroom I could hear the rats scuttering behind it, and big ones they must be, from the sound they make —almost like people walking there. I should hate to encounter one in the dark; or even in the light, for that matter. Still, I have noted neither holes nor droppings. Odd.

The upper gallery is lined with bad portraits in frames which must be worth a fortune. Some bear a resemblance to Stephen as I remember him. I believe I have correctly identified my Uncle Henry Boone and his wife Judith; the others are unfamiliar. I suppose one of them may be my own notorious grandfather, Robert. But Stephen's side of the family is all but unknown to me, for which I am heartily sorry. The same good humour that shone in Stephen's letters to Sarah and me, the same light of high intellect, shines in these portraits, bad as they are. For what foolish reasons families fall out! A rifled *escritoire,* hard words between brothers now dead three generations, and blameless descendants are needlessly estranged. I cannot help reflecting upon how fortunate it was that you and John Petty succeeded in contacting Stephen when it seemed I might follow my Sarah through the Gates—and upon how unfortunate it was that chance should have robbed us of a face-to-face meeting. How I would have loved to hear him defend the ancestral statuary and furnishings!

But do not let me denigrate the place to an extreme. Stephen's taste was not my own, true, but beneath the veneer of his additions there are pieces [a number of them shrouded by dust-covers in the upper chambers] which are true masterworks. There are beds, tables, and heavy, dark scrollings done in teak and mahogany, and many of the bedrooms and receiving chambers, the upper study and small parlour, hold a somber charm. The floors are rich pine that glow with an inner and secret light. There is dignity here; dignity and the weight of years. I cannot yet say I like it, but I do respect it. I am eager to watch it change as we revolve through the changes of this northern clime.

Lord, I run on! Write soon, Bones. Tell me what progress you make, and what news you hear from Petty and the rest. And please do not make the mistake of trying to persuade any new Southern acquaintances as to your views *too forcibly*—I understand that not all are content to answer merely with their mouths, as is our long-winded *friend*, Mr. Calhoun.

Yr. affectionate friend,
CHARLES.

Oct. 16, 1850.

DEAR RICHARD,

Hello, and how are you? I have thought about you often since I have taken up residence here at Chapelwaite, and had half-expected to hear from you—and now I receive a letter from Bones telling me that I'd forgotten to leave my address at the club! Rest assured that I would have written eventually anyway, as it sometimes seems that my true and loyal friends are all I have left in the world that is sure and completely normal. And, Lord, how spread we've become! You in Boston, writing faithfully for *The Liberator* [to which I have also sent my address, incidentally], Hanson in England on another of his confounded *jaunts*, and poor old Bones in the very *lions' lair*, recovering his lungs.

It goes as well as can be expected here, Dick, and be assured I will render you a full account when I am not quite as pressed by certain events which are extant here—I think your legal mind may be quite intrigued by certain happenings at Chapelwaite and in the area about it.

But in the meantime I have a favour to ask, if you will entertain it. Do you remember the historian you introduced me to at Mr. Clary's fund-raising dinner for the cause? I believe his name was Bigelow. At any rate, he mentioned that he made a hobby of collecting odd bits of historical lore which pertained to the very area in which I am now living. My favour, then, is this: Would you contact him and ask him what facts, bits of folklore, or *general rumour*—if any—he may be conversant with about a small, deserted village called *JERUSALEM'S LOT*, near a township called Preacher's Corners, on the Royal River? The stream itself is a tributary of the Androscoggin, and flows into that river approximately eleven miles above that river's emptying place near Chapelwaite. It would gratify me intensely, and, more important, may be a matter of some moment.

In looking over this letter I feel I have been a bit short with you, Dick, for which I am heartily sorry. But be assured I will explain myself shortly, and until that time I send my warmest regards to your wife, two fine sons, and, of course, to yourself.

Yr. affectionate friend,
CHARLES.

Oct. 16, 1850.

DEAR BONES,

I have a tale to tell you which seems a little strange [and even disquieting] to both Cal and me—see what you think. If nothing else, it may serve to amuse you while you battle the mosquitoes!

Two days after I mailed my last to you, a group of four young ladies arrived from the Corners under the supervision of an elderly lady of intimidatingly-competent visage named Mrs. Cloris, to set the place in order and to remove some of the dust that had been causing me to sneeze seemingly at every other step. They all seemed a little nervous as they went about their chores; indeed,

one flighty miss uttered a small screech when I entered the upstairs parlour as she dusted.

I asked Mrs. Cloris about this [she was dusting the downstairs
hall with grim determination that would have quite amazed you,
her hair done up in an old faded bandanna], and she turned to
me and said with an air of determination: "They don't like the
house, and I don't like the house, sir, because it has always been
a *bad* house."

My jaw dropped at this unexpected bit, and she went on in a
kindlier tone: "I do not mean to say that Stephen Boone was not
a fine man, for he was; I cleaned for him every second Thursday
all the time he was here, as I cleaned for his father, Mr. Ran-
dolph Boone, until he and his wife disappeared in eighteen and
sixteen. Mr. Stephen was a good and kindly man, and so you
seem, sir (if you will pardon my bluntness; I know no other way
to speak), but the house is *bad* and it always *has been,* and no
Boone has ever been happy here since your grandfather Robert
and his brother Philip fell out over stolen [and here she paused,
almost guiltily] items in seventeen and eighty-nine."

Such memories these folks have, Bones!

Mrs. Cloris continued: "The house was built in unhappiness,
has been lived in with unhappiness, there has been blood spilt on
its floors [as you may or may not know, Bones, my Uncle Ran-
dolph was involved in an accident on the cellar stairs which took
the life of his daughter Marcella; he then took his own life in a fit
of remorse. The incident is related in one of Stephen's letters to
me, on the sad occasion of his dead sister's birthday], there has
been disappearance and accident.

"I have worked here, Mr. Boone, and I am neither blind nor
deaf. I've heard awful sounds in the walls, sir, awful sounds—
thumpings and crashings and once a strange wailing that was
half-laughter. It fair made my blood curdle. It's a dark place, sir."
And there she halted, perhaps afraid she had spoken too much.

As for myself, I hardly knew whether to be offended or
amused, curious or merely matter-of-fact. I'm afraid that amusement won the day. "And what do you suspect, Mrs. Cloris?
Ghosts rattling chains?"

But she only looked at me oddly. "Ghosts there may be. But
it's not ghosts in the walls. It's not ghosts that wail and blubber

like the damned and crash and blunder away in the darkness. It's—"

"Come, Mrs. Cloris," I prompted her. "You've come this far. Now can you finish what you've begun?"

The strangest expression of terror, pique, and—I would swear to it—religious awe passed over her face. "Some die not," she whispered. "Some live in the twilight shadows Between to serve— Him!"

And that was the end. For some minutes I continued to tax her, but she grew only more obstinate and would say no more. At last I desisted, fearing she might gather herself up and quit the premises.

This is the end of one episode, but a second occurred the following evening. Calvin had laid a fire downstairs and I was sitting in the living-room, drowsing over a copy of *The Intelligencer* and listening to the sound of wind-driven rain on the large bay window. I felt comfortable as only one can on such a night, when all is miserable outside and all is warmth and comfort inside; but a moment later Cal appeared at the door, looking excited and a bit nervous.

"Are you awake, sir?" he asked.

"Barely," I said. "What is it?"

"I've found something upstairs I think you should see," he responded, with the same air of suppressed excitement.

I got up and followed him. As we climbed the wide stairs, Calvin said: "I was reading a book in the upstairs study—a rather strange one—when I heard a noise in the wall."

"Rats," I said. "Is that all?"

He paused on the landing, looking at me solemnly. The lamp he held cast weird, lurking shadows on the dark draperies and on the half-seen portraits that seemed now to leer rather than smile. Outside the wind rose to a brief scream and then subsided grudgingly.

"Not rats," Cal said. "There was a kind of blundering, thudding sound from behind the book-cases, and then a horrible gurgling—horrible, sir. And scratching, as if something were struggling to get out . . . to get at me!"

You can imagine my amazement, Bones. Calvin is not the type to give way to hysterical flights of imagination. It began to seem that there was a mystery here after all—and perhaps an ugly one indeed.

"What then?" I asked him. We had resumed down the hall, and I could see the light from the study spilling forth onto the floor of the gallery. I viewed it with some trepidation; the night seemed no longer comfortable.

"The scratching noise stopped. After a moment the thudding, shuffling sounds began again, this time moving away from me. It paused once, and I swear I heard a strange, almost inaudible laugh! I went to the book-case and began to push and pull, thinking there might be a partition, or a secret door."

"You found one?"

Cal paused at the door to the study. "No—but I found this!"

We stepped in and I saw a square black hole in the left case. The books at that point were nothing but dummies, and what Cal had found was a small hiding place. I flashed my lamp within it and saw nothing but a thick fall of dust, dust which must have been decades old.

"There was only this," Cal said quietly, and handed me a yellowed foolscap. The thing was a map, drawn in spider-thin strokes of black ink—the map of a town or village. There were perhaps seven buildings, and one, clearly marked with a steeple, bore this legend beneath it: *The Worm That Doth Corrupt*.

In the upper left corner, to what would have been the northwest of this little village, an arrow pointed. Inscribed beneath it: *Chapelwaite*.

Calvin said: "In town, sir, someone rather superstitiously mentioned a deserted village called Jerusalem's Lot. It's a place they steer clear of."

"But this?" I asked, fingering the odd legend below the steeple.

"I don't know."

A memory of Mrs. Cloris, adamant yet fearful, passed through my mind. "The Worm . . ." I muttered.

"Do you know something, Mr. Boone?"

"Perhaps . . . it might be amusing to have a look for this town tomorrow, do you think, Cal?"

He nodded, eyes lighting. We spent almost an hour after this looking for some breach in the wall behind the cubby-hole Cal had found, but with no success. Nor was there a recurrence of the noises Cal had described.

We retired with no further adventure that night.

On the following morning Calvin and I set out on our ramble through the woods. The rain of the night before had ceased, but the sky was somber and lowering. I could see Cal looking at me with some doubtfulness and I hastened to reassure him that should I tire, or the journey prove too far, I would not hesitate to call a halt to the affair. We had equipped ourselves with a picnic lunch, a fine Buckwhite compass, and, of course, the odd and ancient map of Jerusalem's Lot.

It was a strange and brooding day; not a bird seemed to sing nor an animal to move as we made our way through the great and gloomy stands of pine to the south and east. The only sounds were those of our own feet and the steady pound of the Atlantic against the headlands. The smell of the sea, almost preternaturally heavy, was our constant companion.

We had gone no more than two miles when we struck an overgrown road of what I believe were once called the "corduroy" variety; this tended in our general direction and we struck off along it, making brisk time. We spoke little. The day, with its still and ominous quality, weighed heavily on our spirits.

At about eleven o'clock we heard the sound of rushing water. The remnant of road took a hard turn to the left, and on the other side of a boiling, slaty little stream, like an apparition, was Jerusalem's Lot!

The stream was perhaps eight feet across, spanned by a moss-grown footbridge. On the far side, Bones, stood the most perfect little village you might imagine, understandably weathered, but amazingly preserved. Several houses, done in that austere yet commanding form for which the Puritans were justly famous, stood clustered near the steeply-sheared bank. Further beyond, along a weed-grown thoroughfare, stood three or four of what might have been primitive business establishments, and beyond that, the spire of the church marked on the map, rising up to the gray sky and looking grim beyond description with its peeled paint and tarnished, leaning cross.

"The town is well named," Cal said softly beside me.

We crossed to the town and began to poke through it—and this is where my story grows slightly amazing, Bones, so prepare yourself!

The air seemed leaden as we walked among the buildings; weighted, if you will. The edifices were in a state of decay—shutters torn off, roofs crumbled under the weight of heavy snows gone by, windows dusty and leering. Shadows from odd corners and warped angles seemed to sit in sinister pools.

We entered an old and rotting tavern first—somehow it did not seem right that we should invade any of those houses to which people had retired when they wished privacy. An old and weather-scrubbed sign above the splintered door announced that this had been the BOAR'S HEAD INN AND TAVERN. The door creaked hellishly on its one remaining hinge, and we stepped into the shadowed interior. The smell of rot and mould was vapourous and nearly overpowering. And beneath it seemed to lie an even deeper smell, a slimy and pestiferous smell, a smell of ages and the decay of ages. Such a stench as might issue from corrupt coffins or violated tombs. I held my handkerchief to my nose and Cal did likewise. We surveyed the place.

"My God, sir—" Cal said faintly.

"It's never been touched," I finished for him.

As indeed it had not. Tables and chairs stood about like ghostly guardians of the watch, dusty, warped by the extreme changes in temperature which the New England climate is known for, but otherwise perfect—as if they had waited through the silent, echoing decades for those long gone to enter once more, to call for a pint or a dram, to deal cards and light clay pipes. A small square mirror hung beside the rules of the tavern, *unbroken*. Do you see the significance, Bones? Small boys are noted for exploration and vandalism; there is not a "haunted" house which stands with windows intact, no matter how fearsome the eldritch inhabitants are rumoured to be; not a shadowy graveyard without at least one tombstone upended by young pranksters. Certainly there must be a score of young pranksters in Preacher's Corners, not two miles from Jerusalem's Lot. Yet the inn-keeper's glass [which must have cost him a nice sum] was intact—as were the other fragile items we found in our pokings. The only damage in Jerusalem's Lot has been done by impersonal Nature. The implication is obvious: Jerusalem's Lot is a shunned town. But why? I have a notion, but before I even dare hint at it, I must proceed to the unsettling conclusion of our visit.

We went up to the sleeping quarters and found beds made up, pewter water-pitchers neatly placed beside them. The kitchen was likewise untouched by anything save the dust of the years and that horrible, sunken stench of decay. The tavern alone would be an antiquarian's paradise; the wondrously queer kitchen stove alone would fetch a pretty price at Boston auction.

"What do you think, Cal?" I asked when we had emerged again into the uncertain daylight.

"I think it's bad business, Mr. Boone," he replied in his doleful way, "and that we must see more to know more."

We gave the other shops scant notice—there was a hostelry with mouldering leather goods still hung on rusted flatnails, a chandler's, a warehouse with oak and pine still stacked within, a smithy.

We entered two houses as we made our way toward the church at the center of the village. Both were perfectly in the Puritan mode, full of items a collector would give his arm for, both deserted and full of the same rotten scent.

Nothing seemed to live or move in all of this but ourselves. We saw no insects, no birds, not even a cobweb fashioned in a window corner. Only dust.

At last we reached the church. It reared above us, grim, uninviting, cold. Its windows were black with the shadows inside, and any Godliness or sanctity had departed from it long ago. Of that I am certain. We mounted the steps, and I placed my hand on the large iron door-pull. A set, dark look passed from myself to Calvin and back again. I opened the portal. How long since that door had been touched? I would say with confidence that mine was the first in fifty years; perhaps longer. Rust-clogged hinges screamed as I opened it. The smell of rot and decay which smote us was nearly palpable. Cal made a gagging sound in his throat and twisted his head involuntarily for clearer air.

"Sir," he asked, "are you sure that you are—?"

"I'm fine," I said calmly. But I did not feel calm, Bones, no more than I do now. I believe, with Moses, with Jereboam, with Increase Mather, and with our own Hanson [when he is in a philosophical *temperament*], that there are spiritually noxious places, buildings where the milk of the cosmos has become sour and rancid. This church is such a place; I would swear to it.

We stepped into a long vestibule equipped with a dusty coat rack and shelved hymnals. It was windowless. Oil-lamps stood in niches here and there. An unremarkable room, I thought, until I heard Calvin's sharp gasp and saw what he had already noticed.

It was an obscenity.

I daren't describe that elaborately-framed picture further than this: that it was done after the fleshy style of Rubens; that it contained a grotesque travesty of a madonna and child; that strange, half-shadowed creatures sported and crawled in the background.

"Lord," I whispered.

"There's no Lord here," Calvin said, and his words seemed to hang in the air. I opened the door leading into the church itself, and the odour became a miasma, nearly overpowering.

In the glimmering half-light of afternoon the pews stretched ghostlike to the altar. Above them was a high, oaken pulpit and a shadow-struck narthex from which gold glimmered.

With a half-sob Calvin, that devout Protestant, made the Holy Sign, and I followed suit. For the gold was a large, beautifully-wrought cross—but it was hung upside-down, symbol of Satan's Mass.

"We must be calm," I heard myself saying. "We must be calm, Calvin. We must be calm."

But a shadow had touched my heart, and I was afraid as I had never been. I have walked beneath death's umbrella and thought there was none darker. But there is. There is.

We walked down the aisle, our footfalls echoing above and around us. We left tracks in the dust. And at the altar there were other tenebrous *objets d'art*. I will not, cannot, let my mind dwell upon them.

I began to mount to the pulpit itself.

"Don't, Mr. Boone!" Cal cried suddenly. "I'm afraid—"

But I had gained it. A huge book lay open upon the stand, writ both in Latin and crabbed runes which looked, to my unpractised eye, either Druidic or pre-Celtic. I enclose a card with several of the symbols, redrawn from memory.

I closed the book and looked at the words stamped into the leather: *De Vermis Mysteriis*. My Latin is rusty, but serviceable enough to translate: *The Mysteries of the Worm*.

As I touched it, that accursed church and Calvin's white, up-turned face seemed to swim before me. It seemed that I heard low, chanting voices, full of hideous yet eager fear—and below that sound, another, filling the bowels of the earth. An hallucination, I doubt it not—but at the same moment, the church was filled with a very real sound, which I can only describe as a huge and macabre *turning* beneath my feet. The pulpit trembled beneath my fingers; the desecrated cross trembled on the wall.

We exited together, Cal and I, leaving the place to its own darkness, and neither of us dared look back until we had crossed the rude planks spanning the stream. I will not say we defiled the nineteen hundred years man has spent climbing upward from a hunkering and superstitious savage by actually running; but I would be a liar to say that we strolled.

That is my tale. You mustn't shadow your recovery by fearing that the fever has touched me again; Cal can attest to all in these pages, up to and including the hideous *noise*.

So I close, saying only that I wish I might see you [knowing that much of my bewilderment would drop away immediately], and that I remain your friend and admirer,

CHARLES.

Oct. 17, 1850.

DEAR GENTLEMEN:

In the most recent edition of your catalogue of household items (i.e., Summer, 1850), I noticed a preparation which is titled Rat's Bane. I should like to purchase one (1) 5-pound tin of this preparation at your stated price of thirty cents ($.30). I enclose return postage. Please mail to: Calvin McCann, Chapelwaite, Preacher's Corners, Cumberland County, Maine.

Thank you for your attention in this matter.

I remain, dear Gentlemen,
CALVIN MCCANN.

DEAR BONES,

Developments of a disquieting nature.

The noises in the house have intensified, and I am growing more to the conclusion that rats are not all that move within our walls. Calvin and I went on another search for hidden crannies or passages, but found nothing. How poorly we would fit into one of Mrs. Radcliffe's romances! Cal claims, however, that much of the sound emanates from the cellar, and it is there we intend to explore tomorrow. It makes me no easier to know that Cousin Stephen's sister met her unfortunate end there.

Her portrait, by the by, hangs in the upstairs gallery. Marcella Boone was a sadly pretty thing, if the artist got her right, and I do know she never married. At times I think that Mrs. Cloris was right, that it *is* a bad house. It has certainly held nothing but gloom for its past inhabitants.

But I have more to say of the redoubtable Mrs. Cloris, for I have had this day a second interview with her. As the most level-headed person from the Corners that I have met thus far, I sought her out this afternoon, after an unpleasant interview which I will relate.

The wood was to have been delivered this morning, and when noon came and passed and no wood with it, I decided to take my daily walk into the town itself. My object was to visit Thompson, the man with whom Cal did business.

It has been a lovely day, full of the crisp snap of bright autumn, and by the time I reached the Thompsons' homestead [Cal, who remained home to poke further through Uncle Stephen's library, gave me adequate directions] I felt in the best mood that these last few days have seen, and quite prepared to forgive Thompson's tardiness with the wood.

The place was a massive tangle of weeds and fallen-down buildings in need of paint; to the left of the barn a huge sow, ready for November butchering, grunted and wallowed in a muddy sty, and in the littered yard between house and out-buildings a woman in a tattered gingham dress was feeding chickens from her apron. When I hailed her, she turned a pale and vapid face toward me.

The sudden change in expression from utter, doltish emptiness to one of frenzied terror was quite wonderful to behold. I can only think she took me for Stephen himself, for she raised her hand in the prong-fingered sign of the evil eye and screamed. The chicken-feed scattered on the ground and the fowls fluttered away, squawking.

Before I could utter a sound, a huge, hulking figure of a man clad only in long-handled underwear lumbered out of the house with a squirrel-rifle in one hand and a jug in the other. From the red light in his eye and unsteady manner of walking, I judged that this was Thompson the Woodcutter himself.

"A Boone!" he roared. "G— d—n your eyes!" He dropped the jug a-rolling and also made the Sign.

"I've come," I said with as much equanimity as I could muster under the circumstances, "because the wood has not. According to the agreement you struck with my man—"

"G— d—n your man too, say I!" And for the first time I noticed that beneath his bluff and bluster he was deadly afraid. I began seriously to wonder if he mightn't actually use his rifle against me in his excitement.

I began carefully: "As a gesture of courtesy, you might—"

"G— d—n your courtesy!"

"Very well, then," I said with as much dignity as I could muster. "I bid you good day until you are more in control of yourself." And with this I turned away and began down the road to the village.

"Don'tchee come back!" he screamed after me. "Stick wi' your evil up there! Cursed! Cursed! Cursed!" He pelted a stone at me, which struck my shoulder. I would not give him the satisfaction of dodging.

So I sought out Mrs. Cloris, determined to solve the mystery of Thompson's enmity, at least. She is a widow [and none of your confounded *matchmaking,* Bones; she is easily fifteen years my senior, and I'll not see forty again] and lives by herself in a charming little cottage at the ocean's very doorstep. I found the lady hanging out her wash, and she seemed genuinely pleased to see me. I found this a great relief; it is vexing almost beyond words to be branded pariah for no understandable reason.

"Mr. Boone," said she, offering a half-curtsey. "If you've come about washing, I take none in past September. My rheumatiz pains me so that it's trouble enough to do my own."

"I wish laundry *was* the subject of my visit. I've come for help, Mrs. Cloris. I must know all you can tell me about Chapelwaite and Jerusalem's Lot and why the townfolk regard me with such fear and suspicion!"

"Jerusalem's Lot! You know about *that,* then."

"Yes," I replied, "and visited it with my companion a week ago."

"God!" She went pale as milk, and tottered. I put out a hand to steady her. Her eyes rolled horribly, and for a moment I was sure she would swoon.

"Mrs. Cloris, I am sorry if I have said anything to—"

"Come inside," she said. "You must know. Sweet Jesu, the evil days have come again!"

She would not speak more until she had brewed strong tea in her sunshiny kitchen. When it was before us, she looked pensively out at the ocean for a time. Inevitably, her eyes and mine were drawn to the jutting brow of Chapelwaite Head, where the house looked out over the water. The large bay window glittered in the rays of the westering sun like a diamond. The view was beautiful but strangely disturbing. She suddenly turned to me and declared vehemently:

"Mr. Boone, you must leave Chapelwaite immediately!"

I was flabbergasted.

"There has been an evil breath in the air since you took up residence. In the last week—since you set foot in the accursed place —there have been omens and portents. A caul over the face of the moon; flocks of whippoorwills which roost in the cemeteries; an unnatural birth. You *must* leave!"

When I found my tongue, I spoke as gently as I could. "Mrs. Cloris, these things are dreams. You must know that."

"Is it a dream that Barbara Brown gave birth to a child with no eyes? Or that Clifton Brockett found a flat, pressed trail five feet wide in the woods beyond Chapelwaite *where all had withered and gone white?* And can you, who have visited Jerusalem's Lot, say with truth that nothing still lives there?"

I could not answer; the scene in that hideous church sprang before my eyes.

She clamped her gnarled hands together in an effort to calm herself. "I know of these things only from my mother and her mother before her. Do you know the history of your family as it applies to Chapelwaite?"

"Vaguely," I said. "The house has been the home of Philip Boone's line since the 1780s; his brother Robert, my grandfather, located in Massachusetts after an argument over stolen papers. Of Philip's side I know little, except that an unhappy shadow fell over it, extending from father to son to grandchildren—Marcella died in a tragic accident and Stephen fell to his death. It was his wish that Chapelwaite become the home of me and mine, and that the family rift thus be mended."

"Never to be mended," she whispered. "You know nothing of the original quarrel?"

"Robert Boone was discovered rifling his brother's desk."

"Philip Boone was mad," she said. "A man who trafficked with the unholy. The thing which Robert Boone *attempted* to remove was a profane Bible writ in the old tongues—Latin, Druidic, others. A hell-book."

"De Vermis Mysteriis."

She recoiled as if struck. "You know of it?"

"I have seen it . . . touched it." It seemed again she might swoon. A hand went to her mouth as if to stifle an outcry. "Yes; in Jerusalem's Lot. On the pulpit of a corrupt and desecrated church."

"Still there; still there, then." She rocked in her chair. "I had hoped God in His wisdom had cast it into the pit of hell."

"What relation had Philip Boone to Jerusalem's Lot?"

"Blood relation," she said darkly. "The Mark of the Beast was on him, although he walked in the clothes of the Lamb. And on the night of October 31, 1789, Philip Boone disappeared . . . and the entire populace of that damned village with him."

She would say little more; in fact, seemed to know little more. She would only reiterate her pleas that I leave, giving as reason something about "blood calling to blood" and muttering about "those who *watch* and those who *guard*." As twilight drew on she seemed to grow more agitated rather than less, and to placate her I promised that her wishes would be taken under strong consideration.

I walked home through lengthening, gloomy shadows, my good mood quite dissipated and my head spinning with questions which still plague me. Cal greeted me with the news that our noises in the walls have grown worse still—as I can attest at this moment. I try to tell myself that I hear only rats, but then I see the terrified, earnest face of Mrs. Cloris.

The moon has risen over the sea, bloated, full, the colour of blood, staining the ocean with a noxious shade. My mind turns to that church again and

(here a line is struck out)

But you shall not see that, Bones. It is too mad. It is time I slept, I think. My thoughts go out to you.

Regards,
CHARLES.

(The following is from the pocket journal of Calvin McCann.)

Oct. 20, '50

Took the liberty this morning of forcing the lock which binds the book closed; did it before Mr. Boone arose. No help; it is all in cypher. A simple one, I believe. Perhaps I may break it as easily as the lock. A diary, I am certain, the hand oddly like Mr. Boone's own. Whose book, shelved in the most obscure corner of this library and locked across the pages? It seems old, but how to tell? The corrupting air has largely been kept from its pages. More later, if time; Mr. Boone set upon looking about the cellar. Am afraid these dreadful goings-on will be too much for his chancy health yet. I must try to persuade him—

But he comes.

Oct. 20, 1850.

BONES,

I can't write   I cant [*sic*] write of this yet   I   I   I

(From the pocket journal of Calvin McCann)

Oct. 20, '50

As I had feared, his health has broken—

Dear God, our Father Who art in Heaven!

Cannot bear to think of it; yet it is planted, burned on my brain like a tin-type; that horror in the cellar—!

Alone now; half-past eight o'clock; house silent but—

Found him swooned over his writing table; he still sleeps; yet for those few moments how nobly he acquitted himself while I stood paralyzed and shattered!

His skin is waxy, cool. Not the fever again, God be thanked. I daren't move him or leave him to go to the village. And if I did go, who would return with me to aid him? Who would come to this cursed house?

O, the cellar! The things in the cellar that have haunted our walls!

Oct. 22, 1850.

DEAR BONES,

I am myself again, although weak, after thirty-six hours of un-consciousness. Myself again . . . what a grim and bitter joke! I shall never be myself again, never. I have come face to face with an insanity and a horror beyond the limits of human expression. And the end is not yet.

If it were not for Cal, I believe I should end my life this min-ute. He is one island of sanity in all this madness.

You shall know it all.

We had equipped ourselves with candles for our cellar exploration, and they threw a strong glow that was quite adequate—hellishly adequate! Calvin tried to dissuade me, citing my recent illness, saying that the most we should probably find would be some healthy rats to mark for poisoning.

I remained determined, however; Calvin fetched a sigh and answered: "Have it as you must, then, Mr. Boone."

The entrance to the cellar is by means of a trap in the kitchen floor [which Cal assures me he has since stoutly boarded over], and we raised it only with a great deal of straining and lifting.

A foetid, overpowering smell came up out of the darkness, not unlike that which pervaded the deserted town across the Royal River. The candle I held shed its glow on a steeply-slanting flight of stairs leading down into darkness. They were in a terrible state of repair—in one place an entire riser missing, leaving only a black hole—and it was easy enough to see how the unfortunate Marcella might have come to her end there.

"Be careful, Mr. Boone!" Cal said; I told him I had no intention of being anything but, and we made the descent.

The floor was earthen, the walls of stout granite, and hardly wet. The place did not look like a rat haven at all, for there were none of the things rats like to make their nests in, such as old boxes, discarded furniture, piles of paper, and the like. We lifted our candles, gaining a small circle of light, but still able to see little. The floor had a gradual slope which seemed to run beneath the main living-room and the dining-room—i.e., to the west. It was in this direction we walked. All was in utter silence. The stench in the air grew steadily stronger, and the dark about us seemed to press like wool, as if jealous of the light which had temporarily deposed it after so many years of undisputed dominion.

At the far end, the granite walls gave way to a polished wood which seemed totally black and without reflective properties. Here the cellar ended, leaving what seemed to be an alcove off the main chamber. It was positioned at an angle which made inspection impossible without stepping around the corner.

Calvin and I did so.

It was as if a rotten spectre of this dwelling's sinister past had risen before us. A single chair stood in this alcove, and above it, fastened from a hook in one of the stout overhead beams, was a decayed noose of hemp.

"Then it was here that he hung himself," Cal muttered. "God!"

"Yes . . . with the corpse of his daughter lying at the foot of the stairs behind him."

Cal began to speak; then I saw his eyes jerked to a spot behind me; then his words became a scream.

How, Bones, can I describe the sight which fell upon our eyes? How can I tell you of the hideous tenants within our walls?

The far wall swung back, and from that darkness a face leered —a face with eyes as ebon as the Styx itself. Its mouth yawned in a toothless, agonized grin; one yellow, rotted hand stretched itself out to us. It made a hideous, mewling sound and took a shambling step forward. The light from my candle fell upon it—

And I saw the livid rope-burn about its neck!

From beyond it something else moved, something I shall dream of until the day when all dreams cease; a girl with a pallid, mouldering face and a corpse-grin; a girl whose head lolled at a lunatic angle.

They wanted us; I know it. And I know they would have drawn us into that darkness and made us their own, had I not thrown my candle directly at the thing in the partition, and followed it with the chair beneath that noose.

After that, all is confused darkness. My mind has drawn the curtain. I awoke, as I have said, in my room with Cal at my side.

If I could leave, I should fly from this house of horror with my nightdress flapping at my heels. But I cannot. I have become a pawn in a deeper, darker drama. Do not ask how I know; I only do. Mrs. Cloris was right when she spoke of blood calling to blood; and how horribly right when she spoke of those who *watch* and those who *guard*. I fear that I have wakened a Force which has slept in the tenebrous village of 'Salem's Lot for half a century, a Force which has slain my ancestors and taken them in unholy bondage as *nosferatu*—the Undead. And I have greater fears than these, Bones, but I still see only in part. If I knew . . . if I only knew all!

CHARLES.

Postscriptum—And of course I write this only for myself; we are isolated from Preacher's Corners. I daren't carry my taint there to post this, and Calvin will not leave me. Perhaps, if God is good, this will reach you in some manner.

C.

(From the pocket journal of Calvin McCann)

Oct. 23, '50

He is stronger to-day; we talked briefly of the *apparitions* in the cellar; agreed they were neither hallucinations or of an *ectoplasmic* origin, but *real*. Does Mr. Boone suspect, as I do, that they have gone? Perhaps; the noises are still; yet all is ominous yet, o'ercast with a dark pall. It seems we wait in the deceptive Eye of the Storm . . .

Have found a packet of papers in an upstairs bedroom, lying in the bottom drawer of an old roll-top desk. Some correspondence & receipted bills lead me to believe the room was Robert Boone's. Yet the most interesting document is a few jottings on the back of an advertisement for gentlemen's beaver hats. At the top is writ:

Blessed are the meek. ·

Below, the following apparent nonsense is writ:

b k e d s h d e r m t h e s   e a k
e l m s o e r a r e s h a m d e d

I believe 'tis the key of the locked and coded book in the library. The cypher above is certainly a rustic one used in the War for Independence known as the *Fence-Rail*. When one removes the "nulls" from the second bit of scribble, the following is obtained:

b e s d r t e e k
l s e a e h   m e

Read up and down rather than across, the result is the original quotation from the Beatitudes.

Before I dare show this to Mr. Boone, I must be sure of the book's contents . . .

Oct. 24, 1850.

DEAR BONES,

An amazing occurrence—Cal, always close-mouthed until absolutely sure of himself [a rare and admirable human trait!], has found the diary of my grandfather Robert. The document was in a code which Cal himself has broken. He modestly declares that the discovery was an accident, but I suspect that perseverance and hard work had rather more to do with it.

At any rate, what a somber light it sheds on our mysteries here! The first entry is dated June 1, 1789, the last October 27, 1789—four days before the cataclysmic disappearance of which Mrs. Cloris spoke. It tells a tale of deepening obsession—nay, of madness—and makes hideously clear the relationship between Great-uncle Philip, the town of Jerusalem's Lot, and the book which rests in that desecrated church.

The town itself, according to Robert Boone, pre-dates Chapelwaite (built in 1782) and Preacher's Corners (known in those days as Preacher's Rest and founded in 1741); it was founded by a splinter group of the Puritan faith in 1710, a sect headed by a dour religious fanatic named James Boon. What a start that name gave me! That this Boon bore relation to my family can hardly be doubted, I believe. Mrs. Cloris could not have been more right in her superstitious belief that familial blood-line is of crucial importance in this matter; and I recall with terror her answer to my question about Philip and *his* relationship to 'Salem's Lot. "Blood relation," said she, and I fear that it is so.

The town became a settled community built around the church where Boon preached—or held court. My grandfather intimates that he also held commerce with any number of ladies from the town, assuring them that this was God's way and will. As a result, the town became an anomaly which could only have existed in those isolated and queer days when belief in witches and the Virgin Birth existed hand in hand: an interbred, rather degenerate religious village controlled by a half-mad preacher whose twin gospels were the Bible and de Goudge's sinister *Demon Dwellings;* a community in which rites of exorcism were held regularly;

a community of incest and the insanity and physical defects which so often accompany that sin. I suspect [and believe Robert Boone must have also] that one of Boon's bastard offspring must have left [or have been spirited away from] Jerusalem's Lot to seek his fortune to the south—and thus founded our present lineage. I do know, by my own family reckoning, that our clan supposedly originated in that part of Massachusetts which has so lately become this Sovereign State of Maine. My great-grandfather, Kenneth Boone, became a rich man as a result of the then-flourishing fur trade. It was his money, increased by time and wise investment, which built this ancestral home long after his death in 1763. His sons, Philip and Robert, built Chapelwaite. *Blood calls to blood,* Mrs. Cloris said. Could it be that Kenneth was born of James Boon, fled the madness of his father and his father's town only to have his sons, all-unknowing, build the Boone home *not two miles from the Boon beginnings?* If 'tis true, does it not seem that some huge and invisible Hand has guided us?

According to Robert's diary, James Boon was ancient in 1789—and he must have been. Granting him an age of twenty-five in the year of the town's founding, he would have been one hundred and four, a prodigious age. The following is quoted direct from Robert Boone's diary:

August 4, 1789.

To-day for the first time I met this Man with whom my Brother has been so unhealthily taken; I must admit this Boon controls a strange Magnetism which upset me Greatly. He is a veritable Ancient, white-bearded, and dresses in a black Cassock which struck me as somehow obscene. More disturbing yet was the Fact that he was surrounded by Women, as a Sultan would be surrounded by his Harem; and P. assures me he is active yet, although at least an Octogenarian . . .

The Village itself I had visited only once before, and will not visit again; its Streets are silent and filled with the Fear the old Man inspires from his Pulpit: I fear also that Like has mated with Like, as so many of the Faces are similar. It seemed that each way I turned I beheld the old Man's Visage . . . all are so wan; they seem Lack-Luster, as if sucked dry

of all Vitality, I beheld Eyeless and Noseless Children,
Women who wept and gibbered and pointed at the Sky for
no Reason, and garbled talk from the Scriptures with talk of
Demons; . . .

P. wished me to stay for Services, but the thought of that sinister Ancient in the Pulpit before an Audience of this Town's
interbred Populace repulsed me and I made an Excuse . . .

The entries preceding and following this tell of Philip's growing
fascination with James Boon. On September 1, 1789, Philip was
baptized into Boon's church. His brother says: "I am aghast with
Amaze and Horror—my Brother has changed before my very
Eyes—he even seems to grow to resemble the wretched Man."

First mention of the book occurs on July 23. Robert's diary
records it only briefly: "P. returned from the smaller Village to-
night with, I thought, a rather wild Visage. Would not speak until
Bedtime, when he said that Boon had enquired after a Book titled
Mysteries of the Worm. To please P. I promised to write Johns &
Goodfellow a letter of enquiry; P. almost fawningly Grateful."

On August 12, this notation: "Rec'd two Letters in the Post
to-day . . . one from Johns & Goodfellow in Boston. They have
Note of the Tome in which P. has expressed an Interest. Only five
Copies extant in this Country. The Letter is rather cool; odd indeed. Have known Henry Goodfellow for Years."

August 13:
P. insanely excited by Goodfellow's letter; refuses to say
why. He would only say that Boon is *exceedingly anxious* to
obtain a Copy. Cannot think why, since by the Title it seems
only a harmless gardening Treatise . . .

Am worried for Philip; he grows stranger to me Daily. I wish
now we had not returned to Chapelwaite. The Summer is
hot, oppressive, and filled with Omens . . .

There are only two further mentions of the infamous book in
Robert's diary [he seems not to have realized the true importance
of it, even at the end]. From the entry of September 4:

I have petitioned Goodfellow to act as P.'s Agent in the matter of the Purchase, although my better Judgement cries against It. What use to demur? Has he not his own Money, should I refuse? And in return I have extracted a Promise from Philip to recant this noisome Baptism . . . yet he is so Hectic; nearly Feverish; I do not trust him. I am hopelessly *at Sea* in this Matter . . .

Finally, September 16:

The Book arrived to-day, with a note from Goodfellow saying he wishes no more of my Trade . . . P. was excited to an unnatural Degree; all but snatched the Book from my Hands. It is writ in bastard Latin and a Runic Script of which I can read Nothing. The Thing seemed almost warm to the Touch, and to vibrate in my Hands, as if it contained a huge Power . . . I reminded P. of his Promise to Recant and he only laughed in an ugly, crazed Fashion and waved that Book in my Face, crying over and over again: "We have it! We have it! The Worm! The Secret of the Worm!"
He is now fled, I suppose to his mad Benefactor, and I have not seen him more this Day . . .

Of the book there is no more, but I have made certain deductions which seem at least probable. First, that this book was, as Mrs. Cloris has said, the subject of the falling-out between Robert and Philip; second, that it is a repository of unholy incantation, possibly of Druidic origin [many of the Druidic blood-rituals were preserved in print by the Roman conquerors of Britain in the name of scholarship, and many of these infernal cook-books are among the world's forbidden literature]; third, that Boon and Philip intended to use the book for their own ends. Perhaps, in some twisted way, they intended good, but I do not believe it. I believe they had long before bound themselves over to whatever faceless powers exist beyond the rim of the Universe; powers which may exist beyond the very fabric of Time. The last entries of Robert Boone's diary lend a dim glow of approbation to these speculations, and I allow them to speak for themselves:

October 26, 1789

A terrific Babble in Preacher's Corners to-day; Frawley, the Blacksmith, seized my Arm and demanded to know "What your Brother and that mad Antichrist are into up there." Goody Randall claims there have been *Signs* in the Sky of *great impending Disaster*. A Cow has been born with two Heads.

As for Myself, I know not what impends; perhaps 'tis my Brother's Insanity. His Hair has gone Gray almost Overnight, his Eyes are great bloodshot Circles from which the pleasing light of Sanity seems to have departed. He grins and whispers, and, for some Reason of his Own, has begun to haunt our Cellar when not in Jerusalem's Lot.

The Whippoorwills congregate about the House and upon the Grass; their combined Calling from the Mist blends with the Sea into an unearthly Shriek that precludes all thought of Sleep.

October 27, 1789

Followed P. this Evening when he departed for Jerusalem's Lot, keeping a safe Distance to avoid Discovery. The cursed Whippoorwills flock through the Woods, filling all with a deathly, psycho-pompotic Chant. I dared not cross the Bridge; the Town all dark except for the Church, which was litten with a ghastly red Glare that seemed to transform the high, peak'd Windows into the Eyes of the Inferno. Voices rose and fell in a Devil's Litany, sometimes laughing, sometimes sobbing. The very Ground seem'd to swell and groan beneath me, as if it bore an awful Weight, and I fled, amaz'd and full of Terror, the hellish, screaming Cries of the Whippoorwills dinning in my ears as I ran through those shadow-riven Woods.

All tends to the Climax, yet unforeseen. I dare not sleep for the Dreams that come, yet not remain awake for what lunatic

Terrors may come. The night is full of awful Sounds and I
fear—
And yet I feel the urge to go again, to watch, to *see*. It
seems that Philip himself calls me, and the old Man.
The Birds
cursed cursed cursed

Here the diary of Robert Boone ends.

Yet you must notice, Bones, near the conclusion, that he claims
Philip himself seemed to call him. My final conclusion is formed
by these lines, by the talk of Mrs. Cloris and the others, but most
of all by those terrifying figures in the cellar, dead yet alive. Our
line is yet an unfortunate one, Bones. There is a curse over us
which refuses to be buried; it lives a hideous shadow-life in this
house and that town. And the culmination of the cycle is drawing
close again. I am the last of the Boone blood. I fear that something knows this, and that I am at the nexus of an evil endeavour
beyond all sane understanding. The anniversary is All Saints'
Eve, one week from today.

How shall I proceed? If only you were here to counsel me, to
help me! If only you were here!

I must know all; I must return to the shunned town. May God
support me!

CHARLES.

(From the pocket journal of Calvin McCann)

Oct. 25, '50

Mr. Boone has slept nearly all this day. His face is pallid and
much thinner. I fear recurrence of his fever is inevitable.

While refreshing his water carafe I caught sight of two un-
mailed letters to Mr. Granson in Florida. He plans to return to
Jerusalem's Lot; 'twill be the killing of him if I allow it. Dare I
steal away to Preacher's Corners and hire a buggy? I must, and
yet what if he wakes? If I should return and find him gone?

The noises have begun in our walls again. Thank God he still
sleeps! My mind shudders from the import of this.

Later

I brought him his dinner on a tray. He plans on rising later, and despite his evasions, I know what he plans; yet I go to Preacher's Corners. Several of the sleeping-powders prescribed to him during his late illness remained with my things; he drank one with his tea, all-unknowing. He sleeps again.

To leave him with the Things that shamble behind our walls terrifies me; to let him continue even one more day within these walls terrifies me even more greatly. I have locked him in.

God grant he should still be there, safe and sleeping, when I return with the buggy!

Still later

Stoned me! Stoned me like a wild and rabid dog! Monsters and fiends! These, that call themselves *men!* We are prisoners here—

The birds, the whippoorwills, have begun to gather.

October 26, 1850.

DEAR BONES,

It is nearly dusk, and I have just wakened, having slept nearly the last twenty-four hours away. Although Cal has said nothing, I suspect he put a sleeping-powder in my tea, having gleaned my intentions. He is a good and faithful friend, intending only the best, and I shall say nothing.

Yet my mind is set. Tomorrow is the day. I am calm, resolved, but also seem to feel the subtle onset of the fever again. If it is so, it *must* be tomorrow. Perhaps tonight would be better still; yet not even the fires of Hell itself could induce me to set foot in that village by shadowlight.

Should I write no more, may God bless and keep you, Bones.

CHARLES.

Postscriptum—The birds have set up their cry, and the horrible shuffling sounds have begun again. Cal does not think I hear, but I do.

C.

(From the pocket journal of Calvin McCann)

Oct. 27, '50
5 *AM*

He is impersuadable. Very well. I go with him.

November 4, 1850.

DEAR BONES,

Weak, yet lucid. I am not sure of the date, yet my almanac assures me by tide and sunset that it must be correct. I sit at my desk, where I sat when I first wrote you from Chapelwaite, and look out over the dark sea from which the last of the light is rapidly fading. I shall never see more. This night is my night; I leave it for whatever shadows be.

How it heaves itself at the rocks, this sea! It throws clouds of sea-foam at the darkling sky in banners, making the floor beneath me tremble. In the window-glass I see my reflection, pallid as any vampire's. I have been without nourishment since the twenty-seventh of October, and should have been without water, had not Calvin left the carafe beside my bed on that day.

O, Cal! He is no more, Bones. He is gone in my place, in the place of this wretch with his pipestem arms and skull face who I see reflected back in the darkened glass. And yet he may be the more fortunate; for no dreams haunt him as they have haunted me these last days—twisted shapes that lurk in the nightmare corridors of delirium. Even now my hands tremble; I have splotched the page with ink.

Calvin confronted me on that morning just as I was about to slip away—and I thinking I had been so crafty. I had told him that I had decided we must leave, and asked him if he would go to Tandrell, some ten miles distant, and hire a trap where we were less notorious. He agreed to make the hike and I watched him leave by the sea-road. When he was out of sight I quickly made myself ready, donning both coat and muffler [for the weather had turned frosty; the first touch of coming winter was on that morning's cutting breeze]. I wished briefly for a gun, then laughed at myself for the wish. What avails guns in such a matter?

I let myself out by the pantry-way, pausing for a last look at sea and sky; for the smell of the fresh air against the putrescence I knew I should smell soon enough; for the sight of a foraging gull wheeling below the clouds.

I turned—and there stood Calvin McCann.

"You shall not go alone," said he; and his face was as grim as ever I have seen it.

"But, Calvin—" I began.

"No, not a word! We go together and do what we must, or I return you bodily to the house. You are not well. You shall not go alone."

It is impossible to describe the conflicting emotions that swept over me: confusion, pique, gratefulness—yet the greatest of them was love.

We made our way silently past the summer house and the sundial, down the weed-covered verge and into the woods. All was dead still—not a bird sang nor a wood-cricket chirruped. The world seemed cupped in a silent pall. There was only the ever-present smell of salt, and from far away, the faint tang of wood-smoke. The woods were a blazoned riot of colour, but, to my eye, scarlet seemed to predominate all.

Soon the scent of salt passed, and another, more sinister odour took its place; that rottenness which I have mentioned. When we came to the leaning bridge which spanned the Royal, I expected Cal to ask me again to defer, but he did not. He paused, looked at that grim spire which seemed to mock the blue sky above it, and then looked at me. We went on.

We proceeded with quick yet dread footsteps to James Boon's church. The door still hung ajar from our latter exit, and the darkness within seemed to leer at us. As we mounted the steps, brass seemed to fill my heart; my hand trembled as it touched the door-handle and pulled it. The smell within was greater, more noxious than ever.

We stepped into the shadowy anteroom and, with no pause, into the main chamber.

It was a shambles.

Something vast had been at work in there, and a mighty destruction had taken place. Pews were overturned and heaped like jackstraws. The wicked cross lay against the east wall, and a jagged hole in the plaster above it testified to the force with which it had been hurled. The oil-lamps had been ripped from their high fixtures, and the reek of whale-oil mingled with the terrible stink which pervaded the town. And down the center aisle, like a ghastly bridal path, was a trail of black ichor, mingled with sinister tendrils of blood. Our eyes followed it to the pulpit—the only untouched thing in view. Atop it, staring at us with glazed eyes from across that blasphemous Book, was the butchered body of a lamb.

"God," Calvin whispered.

We approached, keeping clear of the slime on the floor. The room echoed back our footsteps and seemed to transmute them into the sound of gigantic laughter.

We mounted the narthex together. The lamb had not been torn or eaten; it appeared, rather, to have been *squeezed* until its blood-vessels had forcibly ruptured. Blood lay in thick and noisome puddles on the lectern itself, and about the base of it . . . *yet on the book it was transparent, and the crabbed runes could be read through it, as through coloured glass!*

"Must we touch it?" Cal asked, unfaltering.

"Yes. I must have it."

"What will you do?"

"What should have been done sixty years ago. I am going to destroy it."

We rolled the lamb's corpse away from the book; it struck the floor with a hideous, lolling thud. The blood-stained pages now seemed alive with a scarlet glow of their own.

My ears began to ring and hum; a low chant seemed to emanate from the walls themselves. From the twisted look on Cal's face I knew he heard the same. The floor beneath us trembled, as if the familiar which haunted this church came now unto us, to protect its own. The fabric of sane space and time seemed to twist and crack; the church seemed filled with spectres and litten with the hell-glow of eternal cold fire. It seemed that I saw James Boon, hideous and misshapen, cavorting around the supine body of a woman, and my Grand-uncle Philip behind him, an acolyte in a black, hooded cassock, who held a knife and a bowl.

"Deum vobiscum magna vermis—"

The words shuddered and writhed on the page before me, soaked in the blood of sacrifice, prize of a creature that shambles beyond the stars—

A blind, interbred congregation swaying in mindless, daemoniac praise; deformed faces filled with hungering, nameless anticipation—

And the Latin was replaced by an older tongue, ancient when Egypt was young and the Pyramids unbuilt, ancient when this Earth still hung in an unformed, boiling firmament of empty gas:

"Gyyagin vardar Yogsoggoth! Verminis! Gyyagin! Gyyagin! Gyyagin!"

The pulpit began to rend and split, pushing upward—

Calvin screamed and lifted an arm to shield his face. The narthex trembled with a huge, tenebrous motion like a ship wracked in a gale. I snatched up the book and held it away from me; it seemed filled with the heat of the sun and I felt that I should be cindered, blinded.

"Run!" Calvin screamed. "Run!"

But I stood frozen and the alien presence filled me like an ancient vessel that had waited for years—for generations!

"Gyyagin vardar!" I screamed. "Servant of Yogsoggoth, the Nameless One! The Worm from beyond Space! Star-Eater! Blinder of Time! Verminis! Now comes the Hour of Filling, the Time of Rending! Verminis! Alyah! Alyah! Gyyagin!"

Calvin pushed me and I tottered, the church whirling before me, and fell to the floor. My head crashed against the edge of an upturned pew, and red fire filled my head—yet seemed to clear it.

I groped for the sulphur matches I had brought.

Subterranean thunder filled the place. Plaster fell. The rusted bell in the steeple pealed a choked devil's carillon in sympathetic vibration.

My match flared. I touched it to the book just as the pulpit exploded upward in a rending explosion of wood. A huge black maw was discovered beneath; Cal tottered on the edge, his hands held out, his face distended in a wordless scream that I shall hear forever.

And then there was a huge surge of gray, vibrating flesh. The smell became a nightmare tide. It was a huge outpouring of a viscid, pustulant jelly, a huge and awful form that seemed to skyrocket from the very bowels of the ground. And yet, with a sudden horrible comprehension which no man can have known, I perceived *that it was but one ring, one segment, of a monster worm that had existed eyeless for years in the chambered darkness beneath that abominated church!*

The book flared alight in my hands, and the Thing seemed to scream soundlessly above me. Calvin was struck glancingly and flung the length of the church like a doll with a broken neck.

It subsided—the thing subsided, leaving only a huge and shattered hole surrounded with black slime, and a great screaming, mewling sound that seemed to fade through colossal distances and was gone.

I looked down. The book was ashes.

I began to laugh, then to howl like a struck beast.

All sanity left me, and I sat on the floor with blood streaming from my temple, screaming and gibbering into those unhallowed shadows while Calvin sprawled in the far corner, staring at me with glazing, horror-struck eyes.

I have no idea how long I existed in that state. It is beyond all telling. But when I came again to my faculties, shadows had drawn long paths around me and I sat in twilight. Movement had caught my eye, movement from the shattered hole in the narthex floor.

A hand groped its way over the riven floorboards.

My mad laughter choked in my throat. All hysteria melted into numb bloodlessness.

With terrible, vengeful slowness, a wracked figure pulled itself up from darkness, and a half-skull peered at me. Beetles crawled over the fleshless forehead. A rotted cassock clung to the askew hollows of mouldered collarbones. Only the eyes lived—red, insane pits that glared at me with more than lunacy; they glared with the empty life of the pathless wastes beyond the edges of the Universe.

It came to take me down to darkness.

That was when I fled, screeching, leaving the body of my lifelong friend unheeded in that place of dread. I ran until the air seemed to burst like magma in my lungs and brain. I ran until I had gained this possessed and tainted house again, and my room, where I collapsed and have lain like a dead man until to-day. I ran because even in my crazed state, and even in the shattered ruin of that dead-yet-animated shape, *I had seen the family resemblance.* Yet not of Philip or of Robert, whose likenesses hang in the upstairs gallery. *That rotted visage belonged to James Boon, Keeper of the Worm!*

He still lives somewhere in the twisted, lightless wanderings beneath Jerusalem's Lot and Chapelwaite—and *It* still lives. The burning of the book thwarted *It,* but there are other copies.

Yet I am the gateway, and I am the last of the Boone blood. For the good of all humanity I must die . . . and break the chain forever.

I go to the sea now, Bones. My journey, like my story, is at an end. May God rest you and grant you all peace.

CHARLES.

The odd series of papers above was eventually received by Mr. Everett Granson, to whom they had been addressed. It is assumed that a recurrence of the unfortunate brain fever which struck him originally following the death of his wife in 1848 caused Charles Boone to lose his sanity and murder his companion and longtime friend, Mr. Calvin McCann.

The entries in Mr. McCann's pocket journal are a fascinating exercise in forgery, undoubtedly perpetrated by Charles Boone in an effort to reinforce his own paranoid delusions.

In at least two particulars, however, Charles Boone is proved wrong. First, when the town of Jerusalem's Lot was "rediscovered" (I use the term historically, of course), the floor of the narthex, although rotted, showed no sign of explosion or huge damage. Although the ancient pews *were* overturned and several windows shattered, this can be assumed to be the work of vandals from neighboring towns over the years. Among the older residents of Preacher's Corners and Tandrell there is still some idle rumor about Jerusalem's Lot (perhaps, in his day, it was this kind of harmless folk legend which started Charles Boone's mind on its fatal course), but this seems hardly relevant.

Second, Charles Boone was not the last of his line. His grandfather, Robert Boone, sired at least two bastards. One died in infancy. The second took the Boone name and located in the town of Central Falls, Rhode Island. I am the final descendant of this offshoot of the Boone line; Charles Boone's second cousin, removed by three generations. These papers have been in my committal for ten years. I offer them for publication on the occasion of my residence in the Boone ancestral home, Chapelwaite, in the hope that the reader will find sympathy in his heart for Charles Boone's poor, misguided soul. So far as I can tell, he was correct about only one thing: this place badly needs the services of an exterminator.

There are some huge rats in the walls, by the sound.

Signed,
James Robert Boone
October 2, 1971.

Ray Bradbury's name is magic to the millions of people who have read his *The Martian Chronicles, Fahrenheit 451,* and *The Illustrated Man.* He has also written essays, poetry, screenplays, dramas, reviews, and cantatas, much more than "just" the fantasy and science fiction that most readers know and has sold more than *20,000,000* books! In 1977 Ray won the World Fantasy Award for Life Achievement and had his collection, *Long After Midnight,* nomimated for an award as well. From that book we have chosen an early Bradbury story, "The October Game." It has been previously anthologized in *Alfred Hitchcock Presents: Stories They Would Not Let Me Do on TV.* This neat little Halloween chiller was fittingly done as a reading at the First World Fantasy Convention held in Providence over Halloween weekend, 1975.

The October Game

by RAY BRADBURY

He put the gun back into the bureau drawer and shut the drawer. No, not that way. Louise wouldn't suffer that way. She would be dead and it would be over and she wouldn't suffer. It was very important that this thing have, above all, duration. Duration through imagination. How to prolong the suffering? How, first of all, to bring it about? Well.

The man standing before the bedroom mirror carefully fitted his cuff links together. He paused long enough to hear the children run by swiftly on the street below, outside this warm two-story house; like so many grey mice the children, like so many leaves.

By the sound of the children you knew the calendar day. By their screams you knew what evening it was. You knew it was very late in the year. October. The last day of October, with white bone masks and cut pumpkins and the smell of dropped candle fat.

No. Things hadn't been right for some time. October didn't help any. If anything it made things worse. He adjusted his black bow-tie. If this were spring, he nodded slowly, quietly, emotionlessly, at his image in the mirror, then there might be a chance. But tonight all the world was burning down into ruin. There was no green of spring, none of the freshness, none of the promise.

There was a soft running in the hall. "That's Marion," he told himself. "My little one. All eight quiet years of her. Never a word. Just her luminous blue eyes and her wondering little mouth." His daughter had been in and out all evening, trying on various masks, asking him which was most terrifying, most horrible. They had both finally decided on the skeleton mask. It was "just awful!" It would "scare the beans" from people!

Again he caught the long look of thought and deliberation he gave himself in the mirror. He had never liked October. Ever since he first lay in the autumn leaves before his grandmother's house many years ago and heard the wind and saw the empty trees. It had made him cry, without a reason. And a little of that sadness returned each year to him. It always went away with spring.

But it was different tonight. There was a feeling of autumn coming to last a million years.

There would be no spring.

He had been crying quietly all evening. It did not show, not a vestige of it, on his face. It was all somewhere hidden, but it wouldn't stop.

A rich syrupy smell of candy filled the bustling house. Louise had laid out apples in new skins of caramel; there were vast bowls of punch fresh-mixed, stringed apples in each door, scooped, vented pumpkins peering triangularly from each cold window. There was a waiting water tub in the center of the living room, waiting, with a sack of apples nearby, for bobbing to begin. All that was needed was the catalyst, the in-pouring of children, to start the apples bobbing, the stringed apples to penduluming in the crowded doors, the candy to vanish, the halls to echo with fright or delight, it was all the same.

Now, the house was silent with preparation. And just a little more than that.

Louise had managed to be in every other room save the room he was in today. It was her very fine way of intimating, Oh look, Mich, see how busy I am! So busy that when you walk into a room *I'm* in there's always something I need to do in *another* room! Just see how I dash about!

For a while he had played a little game with her, a nasty childish game. When she was in the kitchen then he came to the kitchen, saying, "I need a glass of water." After a moment, him standing, drinking water, she like a crystal witch over the caramel brew bubbling like a prehistoric mudpot on the stove, she said, "Oh, I must light the window pumpkins!" and she rushed to the living room to make the pumpkins smile with light. He came after her, smiling. "I must get my pipe." "Oh, the cider!" she had cried, running to the dining room. "I'll check the cider," he had said. But when he tried following she ran to the bathroom and locked the door.

He stood outside the bath door, laughing strangely and senselessly, his pipe gone cold in his mouth, and then, tired of the game, but stubborn, he waited another five minutes. There was not a sound from the bath. And lest she enjoy in any way knowing that he waited outside, irritated, he suddenly jerked about and walked upstairs, whistling merrily.

At the top of the stairs he had waited. Finally he had heard the bath door unlatch and she had come out and life below stairs had resumed, as life in a jungle must resume once a terror has passed on away and the antelope return to their spring.

Now, as he finished his bow-tie and put on his dark coat, there was a mouse-rustle in the hall. Marion appeared in the door, all skeletogenous in her disguise.

"How do I look, Papa?"

"Fine!"

From under the mask, blonde hair showed. From the skull sockets small blue eyes smiled. He sighed. Marion and Louise, the two silent denouncers of his virility, his dark power. What alchemy had there been in Louise that took the dark of a dark man and bleached and bleached the dark brown eyes and black black hair and washed and bleached the ingrown baby all during the period before birth until the child was born, Marion, blonde, blue-eyed, ruddy-cheeked. Sometimes he suspected that Louise had conceived the child as an idea, completely asexual, an immaculate conception of contemptuous mind and cell. As a firm rebuke to him she had produced a child in her *own* image, and, to top it, she had somehow *fixed* the doctor so he shook his head and said, "Sorry, Mr. Wilder, your wife will never have another child. This was the *last* one."

"And I wanted a boy," Mich had said, eight years ago.

He almost bent to take hold of Marion now, in her skull mask. He felt an inexplicable rush of pity for her because she had never had a father's love, only the crushing, holding love of a loveless mother. But most of all he pitied himself, that somehow he had not made the most of a bad birth, enjoyed his daughter for herself, regardless of her not being dark and a son and like himself. Somewhere he had missed out. Other things being equal, he would have loved the child. But Louise hadn't wanted a child anyway, in the first place. She had been frightened of the idea of birth. He had forced the child on her, and from that night, all through the year until the agony of the birth itself, Louise had lived in another part of the house. She had expected to die with the forced child. It had been very easy for Louise to hate this husband who so wanted a son that he gave his only wife over to the mortuary.

But—Louise had lived. And in triumph! Her eyes, the day he came to the hospital, were cold. I'm alive, they said. And I have a *blonde* daughter! Just look! And when he had put out a hand to touch, the mother had turned away to conspire with her new pink daughter-child—away from that dark forcing murderer. It had all been so beautifully ironic. His selfishness deserved it.

But now it was October again. There had been other Octobers, and when he thought of the long winter he had been filled with horror year after year to think of the endless months mortared into the house by an insane fall of snow, trapped with a woman and child, neither of whom loved him, for months on end. During the eight years there had been respites. In spring and summer you got out, walked, picnicked; these were desperate solutions to the desperate problem of a hated man.

But in winter the hikes and picnics and escapes fell away with the leaves. Life, like a tree, stood empty, the fruit picked, the sap run to earth. Yes, you invited people in, but people were hard to get in winter with blizzards and all. Once he had been clever enough to save for a Florida trip. They had gone south. He had walked in the open.

But now, the eighth winter coming, he knew things were finally at an end. He simply could not wear this one through. There was an acid walled off in him that slowly had eaten through tissue and tissue over the years, and now, tonight, it would reach the wild explosive in him and all would be over!

There was a mad ringing of the bell below. In the hall, Louise went to see. Marion, without a word, ran down to greet the first arrivals. There were shouts and hilarity.

He walked to the top of the stairs.

Louise was below, taking wraps. She was tall and slender and blonde to the point of whiteness, laughing down upon the new children.

He hesitated. What was all this? The years? The boredom of living? Where had it gone wrong? Certainly not with the birth of the child alone. But it had been a symbol of all their tensions, he imagined. His jealousies and his business failures and all the rotten rest of it. Why didn't he just turn, pack a suitcase and leave? No. Not without hurting Louise as much as she had hurt him. It was simple as that. Divorce wouldn't hurt her at all. It would simply be an end to numb indecision. If he thought divorce would give her pleasure in any way he would stay married the rest of his life to her, for damned spite. No, he must hurt her. Figure some way, perhaps, to take Marion away from her, legally. Yes. That was it. That would hurt most of all. To take Marion away.

"Hello down there!" He descended the stairs, beaming.

Louise didn't look up.

"Hi, Mr. Wilder!"

The children shouted, waved, as he came down.

By ten o'clock the doorbell had stopped ringing, the apples were bitten from stringed doors, the pink child faces were wiped dry from the apple bobbing, napkins were smeared with caramel and punch, and he, the husband, with pleasant efficiency had taken over. He took the party right out of Louise's hands. He ran about talking to the twenty children and the twelve parents who had come and were happy with the special spiked cider he had fixed them. He supervised *Pin the Tail on the Donkey, Spin the Bottle, Musical Chairs,* and all the rest, midst fits of shouting laughter. Then, in the triangular-eyed pumpkinshine, all house lights out, he cried, "Hush! Follow me!" he said, tiptoeing toward the cellar.

The parents, on the outer periphery of the costumed riot, commented to each other, nodding at the clever husband, speaking to the lucky wife. How *well* he got on with children, they said.

The children crowded after the husband, squealing.

"The cellar!" he cried. "The tomb of the witch!"

More squealing. He made a mock shiver. "Abandon hope all ye who enter here!"

The parents chuckled.

One by one the children slid down a slide which Mich had fixed up from lengths of table-section, into the dark cellar. He hissed and shouted ghastly utterances after them. A wonderful wailing filled the dark pumpkin-lighted house. Everybody talked at once. Everybody but Marion. She had gone through all the party with a minimum of sound or talk; it was all inside her, all the excitement and joy. What a little troll, he thought. With a shut mouth and shiny eyes she had watched her own party, like so many serpentines, thrown before her.

Now, the parents. With laughing reluctance they slid down the short incline, uproarious, while little Marion stood by, always wanting to see it all, to be last. Louise went down without his help. He moved to aid her, but she was gone even before he bent.

The upper house was empty and silent in the candleshine.

Marion stood by the slide. "Here we go," he said, and picked her up.

They sat in a vast circle in the cellar. Warmth came from the distant bulk of the furnace. The chairs stood in a long line down each wall, twenty squealing children, twelve rustling relatives, alternately spaced, with Louise down at the far end, Mich up at his end, near the stairs. He peered but saw nothing. They had all groped to their chairs, catch-as-you-can in the blackness. The entire program from here on was to be enacted in the dark, he as Mr. Interlocutor. There was a child scampering, a smell of damp cement, and the sound of the wind out in the October stars.

"Now!" cried the husband in the dark cellar. "Quiet!"

Everybody settled.

The room was black black. Not a light, not a shine, not a glint of an eye.

A scraping of crockery, a metal rattle.

"The witch is dead," intoned the husband.

"Eeeeeeeeeeeee," said the children.

"The witch is dead, she has been killed, and here is the knife she was killed with."

He handed over the knife. It was passed from hand to hand, down and around the circle, with chuckles and little odd cries and comments from the adults.

"The witch is dead, and this is her head," whispered the husband, and handed an item to the nearest person.

"Oh, I know how this game is played," some child cried happily in the dark "He gets some old chicken innards from the icebox and hands them around and says, 'These are her innards!' And he makes a clay head and passes it for her head, and passes a soup-bone for her arm. And he takes a marble and says, 'This is her eye!' And he takes some corn and says, 'This is her teeth!' And he takes a sack of plum pudding and gives that and says, 'This is her stomach!' I know how *this* is played!"

"Hush, you'll spoil everything," some girl said.

"The witch came to harm, and this is her arm," said Mich.

"Eeeee!"

The items were passed and passed, like hot potatoes, around the circle. Some children screamed, wouldn't touch them. Some ran from their chairs to stand in the center of the cellar until the grisly items had passed.

"Aw, it's only chicken insides," scoffed a boy "Come back, Helen!"

Shot from hand to hand, with small scream after scream, the items went down the line, down, down, to be followed by another and another.

"The witch cut apart, and this is her heart," said the husband.

Six or seven items moving at once through the laughing, trembling dark.

Louise spoke up. "Marion don't be afraid; it's only play."

Marion didn't say anything.

"Marion?" asked Louise. "Are you afraid?"

Marion didn't speak.

"She's all right," said the husband. "She's not afraid."

On and on the passing, the screams, the hilarity.

The autumn wind sighed about the house. And he, the husband, stood at the head of the dark cellar, intoning the words, handing out the items.

"Marion?" asked Louise again, from far across the cellar.

Everybody was talking.

"Marion?" called Louise.

Everybody quieted.

"Marion, answer me, are you afraid?"

Marion didn't answer.

The husband stood there, at the bottom of the cellar steps.

Louise called, "Marion, are you there?"

No answer. The room was silent.

"Where's Marion?" called Louise.

"She was here," said a boy.

"Maybe she's upstairs."

"Marion!"

No answer. It was quiet.

Louise cried out, "Marion, Marion!"

"Turn on the lights," said one of the adults.

The items stopped passing. The children and adults sat with the witch's items in their hands.

"No!" Louise gasped. There was a scraping of her chair, wildly, in the dark. "No! Don't turn on the lights, don't turn on the lights, oh God, God, God, don't turn them on, please, please *don't* turn on the lights, *don't!*" Louise was shrieking now. The entire cellar froze with the scream.

Nobody moved.

Everyone sat in the dark cellar, suspended in the suddenly frozen task of this October game; the wind blew outside, banging the house, the smell of pumpkins and apples filled the room with the smell of the objects in their fingers while one boy cried, "I'll go upstairs and look!" and he ran upstairs hopefully and out around the house, four times around the house, calling, "Marion, Marion, Marion!" over and over and at last coming slowly down the stairs into the waiting, breathing cellar and saying to the darkness, "I can't find her."

Then . . . some idiot turned on the lights.

Fritz Leiber could furnish a mansion with all the awards he has won. There are, among many, Hugos, Nebulas, and, of course, World Fantasy Awards. Harlan Ellison has noted that Leiber ". . . is one of the perhaps dozen writers in the history of literature whose command of the language, whose inventiveness, whose shining genius intimidates me." There was, as always, a standing ovation when Fritz won 1976's World Fantasy Award for Life Achievement, but our genre cannot hope to honor him any more than it already has. It is a shame the Nobel Prize judges are blind to this branch of literature. It would be an honor to have a Nobel Laureate in our midst!

Early in our correspondence, I asked Fritz what were his favorites from among his own stories. "Smoke Ghost" was at the top of that list. It is a dark gem from the 1940s and still relevant and chilling today. (SDS)

Smoke Ghost

by FRITZ LEIBER

Miss Millick wondered just what had happened to Mr. Wran. He kept making the strangest remarks when she took dictation. Just this morning he had quickly turned around and asked, "Have you ever seen a ghost, Miss Millick?" And she had tittered nervously and replied, "When I was a girl there was a thing in white that used to come out of the closet in the attic bedroom when I slept there, and moan. Of course it was just my imagination. I was frightened of lots of things." And he had said, "I don't mean that kind of ghost. I mean a ghost from the world today, with the soot of the factories on its face and the pounding of machinery in its soul. The kind that would haunt coal yards and slip around at night through deserted office buildings like this one. A real ghost. Not something out of books." And she hadn't known what to say.

He'd never been like this before. Of course he might be joking, but it didn't sound that way. Vaguely Miss Millick wondered whether he mightn't be seeking some sort of sympathy from her. Of course, Mr. Wran was married and had a little child, but that didn't prevent her from having daydreams. The daydreams were not very exciting, still they helped fill up her mind. But now he was asking her another of those unprecedented questions.

"Have you ever thought what a ghost of our times would look like, Miss Millick? Just picture it. A smoky composite face with the hungry anxiety of the unemployed, the neurotic restlessness of the person without purpose, the jerky tension of the high-pressure metropolitan worker, the uneasy resentment of the striker, the callous opportunism of the scab, the aggressive whine of the panhandler, the inhibited terror of the bombed civilian, and a thousand other twisted emotional patterns. Each one overlying and yet blending with the other, like a pile of semitransparent masks?"

Miss Millick gave a little self-conscious shiver and said, "That would be terrible. What an awful thing to think of."

She peered furtively across the desk. She remembered having heard that there had been something impressively abnormal about Mr. Wran's childhood, but she couldn't recall what it was. If only she could do something—laugh at his mood or ask him what was really wrong. She shifted the extra pencils in her left hand and mechanically traced over some of the shorthand curlicues in her notebook.

"Yet, that's just what such a ghost or vitalized projection would look like, Miss Millick," he continued, smiling in a tight way. "It would grow out of the real world. It would reflect the tangled, sordid, vicious things. All the loose ends. And it would be very grimy. I don't think it would seem white or wispy, or favor grave-yards. It wouldn't moan. But it would mutter unintelligibly, and twitch at your sleeve. Like a sick, surly ape. What would such a thing want from a person, Miss Millick? Sacrifice? Worship? Or just fear? What could you do to stop it from troubling you?"

Miss Millick giggled nervously. There was an expression beyond her powers of definition in Mr. Wran's ordinary, flat-cheeked, thirtyish face, silhouetted against the dusty window. He turned away and stared out into the gray downtown atmosphere that rolled in from the railroad yards and the mills. When he spoke again his voice sounded far away.

"Of course, being immaterial, it couldn't hurt you physically—at first. You'd have to be peculiarly sensitive to see it, or be aware of it at all. But it would begin to influence your actions. Make you do this. Stop you from doing that. Although only a projection, it would gradually get its hooks into the world of things as they are. Might even get control of suitably vacuous minds. Then it could hurt whomever it wanted."

Miss Millick squirmed and read back her shorthand, like the books said you should do when there was a pause. She became aware of the failing light and wished Mr. Wran would ask her to turn on the overhead. She felt scratchy, as if soot were sifting down on to her skin.

"It's a rotten world, Miss Millick," said Mr. Wran, talking at the window. "Fit for another morbid growth of superstition. It's time the ghosts, or whatever you call them, took over and began a rule of fear. They'd be no worse than men."

"But"—Miss Millick's diaphragm jerked, making her titter inanely—"of course, there aren't any such things as ghosts."

Mr. Wran turned around.

"Of course there aren't, Miss Millick," he said in a loud, patronizing voice, as if she had been doing the talking rather than he. "Science and common sense and psychiatry all go to prove it."

She hung her head and might even have blushed if she hadn't felt so all at sea. Her leg muscles twitched, making her stand up, although she hadn't intended to. She aimlessly rubbed her hand along the edge of the desk.

"Why, Mr. Wran, look what I got off your desk," she said, showing him a heavy smudge. There was a note of clumsily playful reproof in her voice. "No wonder the copy I bring you always gets so black. Somebody ought to talk to those scrubwomen. They're skimping on your room."

She wished he would make some normal joking reply. But instead he drew back and his face hardened.

"Well, to get back," he rapped out harshly, and began to dictate.

When she was gone, he jumped up, dabbed his finger experimentally at the smudged part of the desk, frowned worriedly at the almost inky smears. He jerked open a drawer, snatched out a rag, hastily swabbed off the desk, crumpled the rag into a ball and tossed it back. There were three or four other rags in the drawer, each impregnated with soot.

Then he went over to the window and peered out anxiously through the dusk, his eyes searching the panorama of roofs, fixing on each chimney and water tank.

"It's a neurosis. Must be. Compulsions. Hallucinations," he muttered to himself in a tired, distraught voice that would have made Miss Millick gasp. "It's that damned mental abnormality cropping up in a new form. Can't be any other explanation. But it's so damned real. Even the soot. Good thing I'm seeing the psychiatrist. I don't think I could force myself to get on the elevated tonight." His voice trailed off, he rubbed his eyes, and his memory automatically started to grind.

It had all begun on the elevated. There was a particular little sea of roofs he had grown into the habit of glancing at just as the packed car carrying him homeward lurched around a turn. A dingy, melancholy little world of tar-paper, tarred gravel and smoky brick. Rusty tin chimneys with odd conical hats suggested abandoned listening posts. There was a washed-out advertisement of some ancient patent medicine on the nearest wall. Superficially it was like ten thousand other drab city roofs. But he always saw it around dusk, either in the smoky half-light, or tinged with red by the flat rays of a dirty sunset, or covered by ghostly wind-blown white sheets of rain-splash, or patched with blackish snow; and it seemed unusually bleak and suggestive; almost beautifully ugly though in no sense picturesque; dreary, but meaningful. Unconsciously it came to symbolize for Catesby Wran certain disagreeable aspects of the frustrated, frightened century in which he lived, the jangled century of hate and heavy industry and total wars. The quick daily glance into the half darkness became an integral part of his life. Oddly, he never saw it in the morning, for it was then his habit to sit on the other side of the car, his head buried in the paper.

One evening toward winter he noticed what seemed to be a shapeless black sack lying on the third roof from the tracks. He did not think about it. It merely registered as an addition to the well-known scene and his memory stored away the impression for further reference. Next evening, however, he decided he had been mistaken in one detail. The object was a roof nearer than he had thought. Its color and texture, and the grimy stains around it, suggested that it was filled with coal dust, which was hardly reasonable. Then, too, the following evening it seemed to have been blown against a rusty ventilator by the wind—which could hardly have happened if it were at all heavy. Perhaps it was filled with leaves. Catesby was surprised to find himself anticipating his next daily glance with a minor note of apprehension. There was something unwholesome in the posture of the thing that stuck in his mind—a bulge in the sacking that suggested a misshaped head peering around the ventilator. And his apprehension was justified, for that evening the thing was on the nearest roof, though on the farther side, looking as if it had just flopped down over the low brick parapet.

Next evening the sack was gone. Catesby was annoyed at the momentary feeling of relief that went through him, because the whole matter seemed too unimportant to warrant feelings of any sort. What difference did it make if his imagination had played tricks on him, and he'd fancied that the object was slowly crawling and hitching itself closer across the roofs? That was the way any normal imagination worked. He deliberately chose to disregard the fact that there were reasons for thinking his imagination was by no means a normal one. As he walked home from the elevated, however, he found himself wondering whether the sack was really gone. He seemed to recall a vague, smudgy trail leading across the gravel to the nearer side of the roof, which was masked by a parapet. For an instant an unpleasant picture formed in his mind—that of an inky, humped creature crouched behind the parapet, waiting.

The next time he felt the familiar grating lurch of the car, he caught himself trying not to look out. That angered him. He turned his head quickly. When he turned it back, his compact face was definitely pale. There had been only time for a fleeting rearward glance at the escaping roof. Had he actually seen in silhouette the upper part of a head of some sort peering over the parapet? Nonsense, he told himself. And even if he had seen something, there were a thousand explanations which did not involve the supernatural or even true hallucination. Tomorrow he would take a good look and clear up the whole matter. If necessary, he would visit the roof personally, though he hardly knew where to find it and disliked in any case the idea of pampering a silly fear.

He did not relish the walk home from the elevated that evening, and visions of the thing disturbed his dreams, and were in and out of his mind all next day at the office. It was then that he first began to relieve his nerves by making jokingly serious remarks about the supernatural to Miss Millick, who seemed properly mystified. It was on the same day, too, that he became aware of a growing antipathy to grime and soot. Everything he touched seemed gritty, and he found himself mopping and wiping at his desk like an old lady with a morbid fear of germs. He reasoned that there was no real change in his office, and that he'd just now become sensitive to the dirt that had always been there, but there was no denying an increasing nervousness. Long before the car reached the curve, he was straining his eyes through the murky twilight, determined to take in every detail.

Afterward he realized he must have given a muffled cry of some sort, for the man beside him looked at him curiously, and the woman ahead gave him an unfavorable stare. Conscious of his own pallor and uncontrollable trembling, he stared back at them hungrily, trying to regain the feeling of security he had completely lost. They were the usual reassuringly wooden-faced people everyone rides home with on the elevated. But suppose he had pointed out to one of them what he had seen—that sodden, distorted face of sacking and coal dust, that boneless paw which waved back and forth, unmistakably in his direction, as if reminding him of a future appointment—he involuntarily shut his eyes tight. His thoughts were racing ahead to tomorrow evening. He pictured this same windowed oblong of light and packed humanity surging around the curve—then an opaque monstrous form leaping out from the roof in a parabolic swoop—an unmentionable face pressed close against the window, smearing it with wet coal dust—huge paws fumbling sloppily at the glass—

Somehow he managed to turn off his wife's anxious inquiries. Next morning he reached a decision and made an appointment for that evening with a psychiatrist a friend had told him about. It cost him a considerable effort, for Catesby had a well-grounded distaste for anything dealing with psychological abnormality. Visiting a psychiatrist meant raking up an episode in his past which he had never fully described even to his wife. Once he had made the decision, however, he felt considerably relieved. The psychiatrist, he told himself, would clear everything up. He could almost fancy him saying, "Merely a bad case of nerves. However, you must consult the oculist whose name I'm writing down for you, and you must take two of these pills in water every four hours," and so on. It was almost comforting, and made the coming revelation he would have to make seem less painful.

But as the smoky dusk rolled in, his nervousness had returned and he had let his joking mystification of Miss Millick run away with him until he had realized he wasn't frightening anyone but himself.

He would have to keep his imagination under better control, he told himself, as he continued to peer out restlessly at the massive, murky shapes of the downtown office buildings. Why, he had spent the whole afternoon building up a kind of neo-medieval cosmology of superstition. It wouldn't do. He realized then that he had been standing at the window much longer than he'd thought, for the glass panel in the door was dark and there was no noise coming from the outer office. Miss Millick and the rest must have gone home.

It was then he made the discovery that there would have been no special reason for dreading the swing around the curve that night. It was, as it happened, a horrible discovery. For, on the shadowed roof across the street and four stories below, he saw the thing huddle and roll across the gravel and, after one upward look of recognition, merge into the blackness beneath the water tank.

As he hurriedly collected his things and made for the elevator, fighting the panicky impulse to run, he began to think of hallucination and mild psychosis as very desirable conditions. For better or for worse, he pinned all his hopes on the psychiatrist.

"So you find yourself growing nervous and . . . er . . . jumpy, as you put it," said Dr. Trevethick, smiling with dignified geniality. "Do you notice any more definite physical symptoms? Pain? Headache? Indigestion?"

Catesby shook his head and wet his lips. "I'm especially nervous while riding in the elevated," he murmured swiftly.

"I see. We'll discuss that more fully. But I'd like you first to tell me about something you mentioned earlier. You said there was something about your childhood that might predispose you to nervous ailments. As you know, the early years are critical ones in the development of an individual's behavior pattern."

Catesby studied the yellow reflections of frosted globes in the dark surface of the desk. The palm of his left hand aimlessly rubbed the thick nap of the armchair. After a while he raised his head and looked straight into the doctor's small brown eyes.

"From perhaps my third to my ninth year," he began, choosing the words with care, "I was what you might call a sensory prodigy."

The doctor's expression did not change. "Yes?" he inquired politely.

"What I mean is that I was supposed to be able to see through walls, read letters through envelopes and books through their covers, fence and play ping-pong blindfolded, find things that were buried, read thoughts." The words tumbled out.

"And could you?" The doctor's voice was toneless.

"I don't know. I don't suppose so," answered Catesby, longlost emotions flooding back into his voice. "It's all confused now. I thought I could, but then they were always encouraging me. My mother . . . was . . . well . . . interested in psychic phenomena. I was . . . exhibited. I seem to remember seeing things other people couldn't. As if most opaque objects were transparent. But I was very young. I didn't have any scientific criteria for judgment."

He was reliving it now. The darkened rooms. The earnest assemblages of gawking, prying adults. Himself alone on a little platform, lost in a straight-backed wooden chair. The black silk handkerchief over his eyes. His mother's coaxing, insistent questions. The whispers. The gasps. His own hate of the whole business, mixed with hunger for the adulation of adults. Then the scientists from the university, the experiments, the big test. The reality of those memories engulfed him and momentarily made him forget the reason why he was disclosing them to a stranger.

"Do I understand that your mother tried to make use of you as a medium for communicating with the . . . er . . . other world?"

Catesby nodded eagerly.

"She tried to, but she couldn't. When it came to getting in touch with the dead, I was a complete failure. All I could do—or thought I could do—was see real, existing, three-dimensional objects beyond the vision of normal people. Objects anyone could have seen except for distance, obstruction, or darkness. It was always a disappointment to mother."

He could hear her sweetish, patient voice saying, "Try again, dear, just this once. Katie was your aunt. She loved you. Try to hear what she's saying." And he had answered, "I can see a woman in a blue dress standing on the other side of Dick's house." And she had replied, "Yes, I know, dear. But that's not Katie. Katie's a spirit. Try again. Just this once, dear." The doctor's voice gently jarred him back into the softly gleaming office.

"You mentioned scientific criteria for judgment, Mr. Wran. As far as you know, did anyone ever try to apply them to you?"

Catesby's nod was emphatic.

"They did. When I was eight, two young psychologists from the university got interested in me. I guess they did it for a joke at first, and I remember being very determined to show them I amounted to something. Even now I seem to recall how the note of polite superiority and amused sarcasm drained out of their voices. I suppose they decided at first that it was very clever trickery, but somehow they persuaded mother to let them try me out under controlled conditions. There were lots of tests that seemed very businesslike after mother's slipshod little exhibitions. They found I was clairvoyant—or so they thought. I got worked up and on edge. They were going to demonstrate my supernormal sensory powers to the university psychology faculty. For the first time I began to worry about whether I'd come through. Perhaps they kept me going at too hard a pace, I don't know. At any rate, when the test came, I couldn't do a thing. Everything became opaque. I got desperate and made things up out of my imagination. I lied. In the end I failed utterly, and I believe the two young psychologists got into a lot of hot water as a result."

He could hear the brusque, bearded man saying, "You've been taken in by a child, Flaxman, a mere child. I'm greatly disturbed. You've put yourself on the same plane as common charlatans. Gentlemen, I ask you to banish from your minds this whole sorry episode. It must never be referred to." He winced at the recollection of his feeling of guilt. But at the same time he was beginning to feel exhilarated and almost light-hearted. Unburdening his long-repressed memories had altered his whole viewpoint. The episodes on the elevated began to take on what seemed their proper proportions as merely the bizarre workings of overwrought nerves and an overly suggestible mind. The doctor, he anticipated confidently, would disentangle the obscure subconscious causes, whatever they might be. And the whole business would be finished off quickly, just as his childhood experience—which was beginning to seem a little ridiculous now—had been finished off.

"From that day on," he continued, "I never exhibited a trace of my supposed powers. My mother was frantic and tried to sue the university. I had something like a nervous breakdown. Then the divorce was granted, and my father got custody of me. He did his best to make me forget it. We went on long outdoor vacations and did a lot of athletics, associated with normal matter-of-fact people. I went to business college eventually. I'm in advertising now. But," Catesby paused, "now that I'm having nervous symptoms, I've wondered if there mightn't be a connection. It's not a question of whether I was really clairvoyant or not. Very likely my mother taught me a lot of unconscious deceptions, good enough to fool even young psychology instructors. But don't you think it may have some important bearing on my present condition?"

For several moments the doctor regarded him with a professional frown. Then he said quietly, "And is there some . . . er . . . more specific connection between your experiences then and now? Do you by any chance find that you are once again beginning to . . . er . . . see things?"

Catesby swallowed. He had felt an increasing eagerness to unburden himself of his fears, but it was not easy to make a beginning, and the doctor's shrewd question rattled him. He forced himself to concentrate. The thing he thought he had seen on the roof loomed up before his inner eye with unexpected vividness. Yet it did not frighten him. He groped for words.

Then he saw that the doctor was not looking at him but over his shoulder. Color was draining out of the doctor's face and his eyes did not seem so small. Then the doctor sprang to his feet, walked past Catesby, threw up the window and peered into the darkness.

As Catesby rose, the doctor slammed down the window and said in a voice whose smoothness was marred by a slight, persistent gasping, "I hope I haven't alarmed you. I saw the face of . . . er . . . a Negro prowler on the fire escape. I must have frightened him, for he seems to have gotten out of sight in a hurry. Don't give it another thought. Doctors are frequently bothered by *voyeurs* . . . er . . . Peeping Toms."

"A Negro?" asked Catesby, moistening his lips.

The doctor laughed nervously. "I imagine so, though my first odd impression was that it was a white man in blackface. You see, the color didn't seem to have any brown in it. It was dead-black."

Catesby moved toward the window. There were smudges on the glass. "It's quite all right, Mr. Wran." The doctor's voice had acquired a sharp note of impatience, as if he were trying hard to reassume his professional authority. "Let's continue our conversation. I was asking you if you were"—he made a face—"seeing things."

Catesby's whirling thoughts slowed down and locked into place. "No, I'm not seeing anything that other people don't see, too. And I think I'd better go now. I've been keeping you too long." He disregarded the doctor's half-hearted gesture of denial. "I'll phone you about the physical examination. In a way you've already taken a big load off my mind." He smiled woodenly. "Goodnight, Dr. Trevethick."

Catesby Wran's mental state was a peculiar one. His eyes searched every angular shadow, he glanced sideways down each chasm-like alley and barren basement passageway, and kept stealing looks at the irregular line of the roofs, yet he was hardly conscious of where he was going. He pushed away the thoughts that came into his mind, and kept moving. He became aware of a slight sense of security as he turned into a lighted street where there were people and high buildings and blinking signs. After a while he found himself in the dim lobby of the structure that housed his office. Then he realized why he couldn't go home, why he daren't go home—after what had happened at the office of Dr. Trevethick.

"Hello, Mr. Wran," said the night elevator man, a burly figure in overalls, sliding open the grille-work door to the old-fashioned cage. "I didn't know you were working nights now, too."

Catesby stepped in automatically. "Sudden rush of orders," he murmured inanely. "Some stuff that has to be gotten out."

The cage creaked to a stop at the top floor. "Be working very late, Mr. Wran?"

He nodded vaguely, watched the car slide out of sight, found his keys, swiftly crossed the outer office, and entered his own. His hand went out to the light switch, but then the thought occurred to him that the two lighted windows, standing out against the dark bulk of the building, would indicate his whereabouts and serve as a goal toward which something could crawl and climb. He moved his chair so that the back was against the wall and sat down in the semidarkness. He did not remove his overcoat.

For a long time he sat there motionless, listening to his own breathing and the faraway sounds from the streets below: the thin metallic surge of the crosstown streetcar, the farther one of the elevated, faint lonely cries and honkings, indistinct rumblings. Words he had spoken to Miss Millick in nervous jest came back to him with the bitter taste of truth. He found himself unable to reason critically or connectedly, but by their own volition thoughts rose up into his mind and gyrated slowly and rearranged themselves with the incvitable movement of planets.

Gradually his mental picture of the world was transformed. No longer a world of material atoms and empty space, but a world in which the bodiless existed and moved according to its own obscure laws or unpredictable impulses. The new picture illuminated with dreadful clarity certain general facts which had always bewildered and troubled him and from which he had tried to hide: the inevitability of hate and war, the diabolically timed mischances which wreck the best of human intentions, the walls of willful misunderstanding that divide one man from another, the eternal vitality of cruelty and ignorance and greed. They seemed appropriate now, necessary parts of the picture. And superstition only a kind of wisdom.

Then his thoughts returned to himself and the question he had asked Miss Millick, "What would such a thing want from a person? Sacrifices? Worship? Or just fear? What could you do to stop it from troubling you?" It had become a practical question.

With an explosive jangle, the phone began to ring. "Cate, I've been trying everywhere to get you," said his wife. "I never thought you'd be at the office. What are you doing? I've been worried."

He said something about work.

"You'll be home right away?" came the faint anxious question. "I'm a little frightened. Ronny just had a scare. It woke him up. He kept pointing to the window saying, 'Black man, black man.' Of course it's something he dreamed. But I'm frightened. You will be home? What's that, dear? Can't you hear me?"

"I will. Right away," he said. Then he was out of the office, buzzing the night bell and peering down the shaft.

He saw it peering up the shaft at him from the deep shadows three floors below, the sacking face pressed against the iron grillework. It started up the stair at a shockingly swift, shambling gait, vanishing temporarily from sight as it swung into the second corridor below.

Catesby clawed at the door to the office, realized he had not locked it, pushed it in, slammed and locked it behind him, retreated to the other side of the room, cowered between the filing cases and the wall. His teeth were clicking. He heard the groan of the rising cage. A silhouette darkened the frosted glass of the door, blotting out part of the grotesque reverse of the company name. After a little the door opened.

The big-globed overhead light flared on and, standing inside the door, her hand on the switch, was Miss Millick.

"Why, Mr. Wran," she stammered vacuously, "I didn't know

you were here. I'd just come in to do some extra typing after the movie. I didn't . . . but the lights weren't on. What were you—"

He stared at her. He wanted to shout in relief, grab hold of her, talk rapidly. He realized he was grinning hysterically.

"Why, Mr. Wran, what's happened to you?" she asked embarrassedly, ending with a stupid titter. "Are you feeling sick? Isn't there something I can do for you?"

He shook his head jerkily and managed to say, "No, I'm just leaving. I was doing some extra work myself."

"But you *look* sick," she insisted, and walked over toward him. He inconsequentially realized she must have stepped in mud, for her high-heeled shoes left neat black prints.

"Yes, I'm sure you must be sick. You're so terribly pale." She sounded like an enthusiastic, incompetent nurse. Her face brightened with a sudden inspiration. "I've got something in my bag, that'll fix you up right away," she said. "It's for indigestion."

She fumbled at her stuffed oblong purse. He noticed that she was absent-mindedly holding it shut with one hand while she tried to open it with the other. Then, under his very eyes, he saw her bend back the thick prongs of metal locking the purse as if they were tinfoil, or as if her fingers had became a pair of steel pliers.

Instantly his memory recited the words he had spoken to Miss Millick that afternoon. "It couldn't hurt you physically—at first . . . gradually get its hooks into the world . . . might even get control of suitably vacuous minds. Then it could hurt whomever it wanted." A sickish, cold feeling grew inside him. He began to edge toward the door.

But Miss Millick hurried ahead of him.

"You don't have to wait, Fred," she called. "Mr. Wran's decided to stay a while longer."

The door to the cage shut with a mechanical rattle. The cage creaked. Then she turned around in the door.

"Why, Mr. Wran," she gurgled reproachfully, "I just couldn't think of letting you go home now. I'm sure you're terribly unwell. Why, you might collapse in the street. You've just got to stay here until you feel different."

The creaking died away. He stood in the center of the office, motionless. His eyes traced the coal-black course of Miss Millick's footprints to where she stood blocking the door. Then a sound that was almost a scream was wrenched out of him, for it seemed to him that the blackness was creeping up her legs under the thin stockings.

"Why, Mr. Wran," she said, "you're acting as if you were crazy. You must lie down for a while. Here, I'll help you off with your coat."

The nauseously idiotic and rasping note was the same; only it had been intensified. As she came toward him he turned and ran through the storeroom, clattered a key desperately at the lock of the second door to the corridor.

"Why, Mr. Wran," he heard her call, "are you having some kind of a fit? You must let me help you."

The door came open and he plunged out into the corridor and up the stairs immediately ahead. It was only when he reached the top that he realized the heavy steel door in front of him led to the roof. He jerked up the catch.

"Why, Mr. Wran, you mustn't run away. I'm coming after you."

Then he was out on the gritty gravel of the roof. The night sky was clouded and murky, with a faint pinkish glow from the neon signs. From the distant mills rose a ghostly spurt of flame. He ran to the edge. The street lights glared dizzily upward. Two men were tiny round blobs of hat and shoulders. He swung around.

The thing was in the doorway. The voice was no longer solicitous but moronically playful, each sentence ending in a titter.

"Why, Mr. Wran, why have you come up here? We're all alone. Just think, I might push you off."

The thing came slowly toward him. He moved backward until his heels touched the low parapet. Without knowing why, or what he was going to do, he dropped to his knees. He dared not look at the face as it came nearer, a focus for the worst in the world, a gathering point for poisons from everywhere. Then the lucidity of terror took possession of his mind, and words formed on his lips.

"I will obey you. You are my god," he said. "You have supreme power over man and his animals and his machines. You rule this city and all others. I recognize that."

Again the titter, closer. "Why, Mr. Wran, you never talked like this before. Do you mean it?"

"The world is yours to do with as you will, save or tear to pieces," he answered fawningly, the words automatically fitting themselves together in vaguely liturgical patterns. "I recognize that. I will praise, I will sacrifice. In smoke and soot I will worship you for ever."

The voice did not answer. He looked up. There was only Miss Millick, deathly pale and swaying drunkenly. Her eyes were closed. He caught her as she wobbled toward him. His knees gave way under the added weight and they sank down together on the edge of the roof.

After a while she began to twitch. Small noises came from her throat and her eyelids edged open.

"Come on we'll go downstairs," he murmured jerkily, trying to draw her up. "You're feeling bad."

"I'm terribly dizzy," she whispered. "I must have fainted, I didn't eat enough. And then I'm so nervous lately, about the war and everything, I guess. Why, we're on the roof! Did you bring me up here to get some air? Or did I come up without knowing it? I'm awfully foolish. I used to walk in my sleep, my mother said."

As he helped her down the stairs, she turned and looked at him. "Why, Mr. Wran," she said, faintly, "you've got a big black smudge on your forehead. Here, let me get it off for you." Weakly she rubbed at it with her handkerchief. She started to sway again and he steadied her.

"No, I'll be all right," she said. "Only I feel cold. What happened, Mr. Wran? Did I have some sort of fainting spell?"

He told her it was something like that.

Later, riding home in the empty elevated car, he wondered how long he would be safe from the thing. It was a purely practical problem. He had no way of knowing, but instinct told him he had satisfied the brute for some time. Would it want more when it came again? Time enough to answer that question when it arose. It might be hard, he realized, to keep out of an insane asylum. With Helen and Ronny to protect, as well as himself, he would have to be careful and tightlipped. He began to speculate as to how many other men and women had seen the thing or things like it.

The elevated slowed and lurched in a familiar fashion. He looked at the roofs near the curve. They seemed very ordinary, as if what made them impressive had gone away for a while.

Fritz Leiber has won more World Fantasy Awards than any other writer. "Belsen Express" earned its honor as the Best Short Fiction of 1976. Winning awards seems to be a way of life for Fritz. With tales such as the following, it will be readily apparent to the reader why they keep coming his way. (SDS)

Belsen Express

by FRITZ LEIBER

George Simister watched the blue flames writhe beautifully in the grate, like dancing girls drenched with alcohol and set afire, and congratulated himself on having survived well through the middle of the Twentieth Century without getting involved in military service, world-saving, or any activities that interfered with the earning and enjoyment of money.

Outside rain dripped, a storm snarled at the city from the outskirts, and sudden gusts of wind produced in the chimney a sound like the mourning of doves. Simister shimmied himself a fraction of an inch deeper in his easy chair and took a slow sip of diluted scotch—he was sensitive to most cheaper liquors. Simister's physiology was on the delicate side; during his childhood certain tastes and odors, playing on an elusive heart weakness, had been known to make him faint.

The outspread newspaper started to slip from his knee. He detained it, let his glance rove across the next page, noted a headline about an uprising in Prague like that in Hungary in 1956 and murmured, "Damn Slavs," noted another about border fighting around Israel and muttered, "Damn Jews," and let the paper go.

He took another sip of his drink, yawned, and watched a virginal blue flame flutter frightenedly the length of the log before it turned to a white smoke ghost. There was a sharp *knock-knock*.

Simister jumped and then got up and hurried tight-lipped to the front door. Lately some of the neighborhood children had been trying to annoy him probably because his was the most respectable and best-kept house on the block. Doorbell ringing, obscene sprayed scrawls, that sort of thing. And hardly children—young rowdies rather, who needed rough handling and a trip to the police station. He was really angry by the time he reached the door and swung it wide. There was nothing but a big wet empty darkness. A chilly draft spattered a couple of cold drops on him. Maybe the noise had come from the fire. He shut the door and started back to the living room, but a small pile of books untidily nested in wrapping paper on the hall table caught his eye and he grimaced.

They constituted a blotchily addressed parcel which the postman had delivered by mistake a few mornings ago. Simister could probably have deciphered the address, for it was clearly on this street, and rectified the postman's error, but he did not choose to abet the activities of illiterates with leaky pens. And the delivery must have been a mistake for the top book was titled *The Scourge of the Swastika* and the other two had similar titles, and Simister had an acute distaste for books that insisted on digging up that satisfactorily buried historical incident known as Nazi Germany.

The reason for this distaste was a deeply hidden fear that George Simister shared with millions, but that he had never revealed even to his wife. It was a quite unrealistic and now completely anachronistic fear of the Gestapo.

It had begun years before the Second World War, with the first small reports from Germany of minority persecutions and organized hoodlumism—the sense of something reaching out across the dark Atlantic to threaten his life, his security, and his confidence that he would never have to suffer pain except in a hospital.

Of course it had never got at all close to Simister, but it had exercised an evil tyranny over his imagination. There was one nightmarish series of scenes that had slowly grown in his mind and then had kept bothering him for a long time. It began with a thunderous knocking, of boots and rifle butts rather than fists, and a shouted demand: "Open up! It's the Gestapo." Next he would find himself in a stream of frantic people being driven toward a portal where a division was made between those reprieved and those slated for immediate extinction. Last he would be inside a closed motor van jammed so tightly with people that it was impossible to move. After a long time the van would stop, but the motor would keep running, and from the floor, leisurely seeking the crevices between the packed bodies, the entrapped exhaust fumes would begin to mount.

Now in the shadowy hall the same horrid movie had a belated showing. Simister shook his head sharply, as if he could shake the scenes out, reminding himself that the Gestapo was dead and done with for more than ten years. He felt the angry impulse to throw in the fire the books responsible for the return of his waking nightmare. But he remembered that books are hard to burn. He stared at them uneasily, excited by thoughts of torture and confinement, concentration and death camps, but knowing the nasty aftermath they left in his mind. Again he felt a sudden impulse, this time to bundle the books together and throw them in the trash can. But that would mean getting wet, it could wait until tomorrow. He put the screen in front of the fire, which had died and was smoking like a crematory, and went up to bed.

Some hours later he waked with the memory of a thunderous knocking.

He started up, exclaiming, "Those damned kids!" The drawn shades seemed abnormally dark—probably they'd thrown a stone through the street lamp.

He put one foot on the chilly floor. It was now profoundly still. The storm had gone off like a roving cat. Simister strained his ears. Beside him his wife breathed with irritating evenness. He wanted to wake her and explain about the young delinquents. It was criminal that they were permitted to roam the streets at this hour. Girls with them too, likely as not.

The knocking was not repeated. Simister listened for footsteps going away, or for the creaking of boards that would betray a lurking presence on the porch.

After awhile he began to wonder if the knocking might not

have been part of a dream, or perhaps a final rumble of actual thunder. He lay down and pulled the blankets up to his neck. Eventually his muscles relaxed and he got to sleep.

At breakfast he told his wife about it.

"George, it may have been burglars," she said.

"Don't be stupid, Joan. Burglars don't knock. If it was anything it was those damned kids."

"Whatever it was, I wish you'd put a bigger bolt on the front door."

"Nonsense. If I'd known you were going to act this way I wouldn't have said anything. I told you it was probably just the thunder."

But next night at about the same hour it happened again.

This time there could be little question of dreaming. The knocking still reverberated in his ears. And there had been words mixed with it, some sort of yapping in a foreign language. Probably the children of some of those European refugees who had settled in the neighborhood.

Last night they'd fooled him by keeping perfectly still after banging on the door, but tonight he knew what to do. He tiptoed across the bedroom and went down the stairs rapidly, but quietly because of his bare feet. In the hall he snatched up something to hit them with, then in one motion unlocked and jerked open the door.

There was no one.

He stood looking at the darkness. He was puzzled as to how they could have got away so quickly and silently. He shut the door and switched on the light. Then he felt the thing in his hand. It was one of the books. With a feeling of disgust he dropped it on the others. He must remember to throw them out first thing tomorrow.

But he overslept and had to rush. The feeling of disgust or annoyance, or something akin, must have lingered, however, for he found himself sensitive to things he wouldn't ordinarily have noticed. People especially. The swollen-handed man seemed deliberately surly as he counted Simister's pennies and handed him the paper. The tight-lipped woman at the gate hesitated suspiciously, as if he were trying to pass off a last month's ticket.

And when he was hurrying up the stairs in response to an approaching rumble, he brushed against a little man in an oversize coat and received in return a glance that gave him a positive shock.

Simister vaguely remembered having seen the little man several times before. He had the thin nose, narrow-set eyes and receding chin that is by a stretch of the imagination described as "rat-faced." In the movies he'd have played a stool pigeon. The flapping overcoat was rather comic.

But there seemed to be something at once so venomous and sly, so time-bidingly vindictive, in the glance he gave Simister that the latter was taken aback and almost missed the train.

He just managed to squeeze through the automatically closing door of the smoker after the barest squint at the sign to assure himself that the train was an express. His heart was pounding in a way that another time would have worried him, but now he was immersed in a savage pleasure at having thwarted the man in the oversize coat. The latter hadn't hurried fast enough and Simister had made no effort to hold open the door for him.

As a smooth surge of electric power sent them sliding away from the station Simister pushed his way from the vestibule into the car and snagged a strap. From the next one already swayed his chief commuting acquaintance, a beefy, suspiciously red-nosed, irritating man named Holstrom, now reading a folded newspaper one-handed. He shoved a headline in Simister's face. The latter knew what to expect.

"Atomic Weapons for West Germany," he read tonelessly. Holstrom was always trying to get him into outworn arguments about totalitarianism, Nazi Germany, racial prejudice and the like. "Well, what about it?"

Holstrom shrugged. "It's a natural enough step, I suppose, but it started me thinking about the top Nazis and whether we really got all of them."

"Of course," Simister snapped.

"I'm not so sure," Holstrom said. "I imagine quite a few of them got away and are still hiding out somewhere."

But Simister refused the bait. The question bored him. Who talked about the Nazis any more? For that matter, the whole trip this morning was boring; the smoker was overcrowded; and when they finally piled out at the downtown terminus, the rude jostling increased his irritation.

The crowd was approaching an iron fence that arbitrarily split the stream of hurrying people into two sections which reunited a few steps farther on. Beside the fence a new guard was standing, or perhaps Simister hadn't noticed him before. A cocky-looking young fellow with close-cropped blonde hair and cold blue eyes.

Suddenly it occurred to Simister that he habitually passed to the right of the fence, but that this morning he was being edged over toward the left. This trifling circumstance, coming on top of everything else, made him boil. He deliberately pushed across the stream, despite angry murmurs and the hard stare of the guard.

He had intended to walk the rest of the way, but his anger made him forgetful and before he realized it he had climbed aboard a bus. He soon regretted it. The bus was even more crowded than the smoker and the standees were morose and lumpy in their heavy overcoats. He was tempted to get off and waste his fare, but he was trapped in the extreme rear and moreover shrank from giving the impression of a man who didn't know his own mind.

Soon another annoyance was added to the ones already plaguing him—a trace of exhaust fumes was seeping up from the motor at the rear. He immediately began to feel ill. He looked around indignantly, but the others did not seem to notice the odor, or else accepted it fatalistically.

In a couple of blocks the fumes had become so bad that Simister decided he must get off at the next stop. But as he started to push past her, a fat woman beside him gave him such a strangely apathetic stare that Simister, whose mind was perhaps a little clouded by nausea, felt almost hypnotized by it, so that it was several seconds before he recalled and carried out his intention.

Ridiculous, but the woman's face stuck in his mind all day.

In the evening he stopped at a hardware store. After supper his wife noticed him working in the front hall.

"Oh, you're putting on a bolt," she said.

"Well, you asked me to, didn't you?"

"Yes, but I didn't think you'd do it."

"I decided I might as well." He gave the screw a final turn and stepped back to survey the job. "Anything to give you a feeling of security."

Then he remembered the stuff he had been meaning to throw out that morning. The hall table was bare.

"What did you do with them?" he asked.

"What?"

"Those fool books."

"Oh, those. I wrapped them up again and gave them to the postman."

"Now why did you do that? There wasn't any return address and I might have wanted to look at them."

"But you said they weren't addressed to us and you hate all that war stuff."

"I know, but—" he said and then stopped, hopeless of making her understand why he particularly wanted to feel he had got rid of that package himself, and by throwing it in the trash can. For that matter, he didn't quite understand his feelings himself. He began to poke around the hall.

"I did return the package," his wife said sharply. "I'm not losing my memory."

"Oh, all right!" he said and started for bed.

That night no knocking awakened him, but rather a loud crashing and rending of wood along with a harsh metallic *ping* like a lock giving.

In a moment he was out of bed, his sleep-sodden nerves jangling with anger. Those hoodlums! Rowdy pranks were perhaps one thing, deliberate destruction of property certainly another. He was halfway down the stairs before it occurred to him that the sound he had heard had a distinctly menacing aspect. Juvenile delinquents who broke down doors would hardly panic at the appearance of an unarmed householder.

But just then he saw that the front door was intact.

Considerably puzzled and apprehensive, he searched the first floor and even ventured into the basement, racking his brains as to just what could have caused such a noise. The water heater? Weight of the coal bursting a side of the bin? Those objects were intact. But perhaps the porch trellis giving way?

That last notion kept him peering out of the front window several moments. When he turned around there was someone behind him.

"I didn't mean to startle you," his wife said. "What's the matter, George?"

"I don't know. I thought I heard a sound. Something being smashed."

He expected that would send her into one of her burglar panics, but instead she kept looking at him.

"Don't stand there all night," he said. "Come on to bed."

"George, is something worrying you? Something you haven't told me about?"

"Of course not. Come on."

Next morning Holstrom was on the platform when Simister got there and they exchanged guesses as to whether the dark rain-clouds would burst before they got downtown. Simister noticed the man in the oversize coat loitering about, but he paid no attention to him.

Since it was a bank holiday there were empty seats in the smoker and he and Holstrom secured one. As usual the latter had his newspaper. Simister waited for him to start his ideological snipping—a little uneasily for once; usually he was secure in his prejudices, but this morning he felt strangely vulnerable.

It came. Holstrom shook his head. "That's a bad business in Czechoslovakia. Maybe we were a little too hard on the Nazis."

To his surprise Simister found himself replying with both nervous hypocrisy and uncharacteristic vehemence. "Don't be ridiculous! Those rats deserved a lot worse than they got!"

As Holstrom turned toward him saying, "Oh, so you've changed your mind about the Nazis." Simister thought he heard someone just behind him say at the same time in a low, distinct, pitiless voice: "I heard you."

He glanced around quickly. Leaning forward a little, but with his face turned sharply away as if he had just become interested in something passing the window, was the man in the oversize coat.

"What's wrong?" Holstrom asked.

"What do you mean?"

"You've turned pale. You look sick."

"I don't feel that way."

"Sure? You know, at our age we've got to begin to watch out. Didn't you once tell me something about your heart?"

Simister managed to laugh that off, but when they parted just outside the train he was conscious that Holstrom was still eying him rather closely.

As he slowly walked through the terminus his face began to assume an abstracted look. In fact he was lost in thought to such a degree that when he approached the iron fence, he started to pass it on the left. Luckily the crowd was thin and he was able to cut across to the right without difficulty. The blonde young guard looked at him closely—perhaps he remembered yesterday morning.

Simister had told himself that he wouldn't again under any circumstances take the bus, but when he got outside it was raining torrents. After a moment's hesitation he climbed aboard. It seemed even more crowded than yesterday, if that were possible, with more of the same miserable people, and the damp air made the exhaust odor particularly offensive.

The abstracted look clung to his face all day long. His secretary noticed, but did not comment. His wife did, however, when she found him poking around in the hall after supper.

"Are you still looking for that package, George?" Her tone was flat.

"Of course not," he said quickly, shutting the table drawer he'd opened.

She waited. "Are you sure you didn't order those books?"

"What gave you that idea?" he demanded. "You know I didn't."

"I'm glad," she said. "I looked through them. There were pictures. They were nasty."

"You think I'm the sort of person who'd buy books for the sake of nasty pictures?"

"Of course not, dear, but I thought you might have seen them and they were what had depressed you."

"Have I been depressed?"

"Yes. Your heart hasn't been bothering you, has it?"

"No."

"Well, what is it then?"

"I don't know." Then with considerable effort he said, "I've been thinking about war and things."

"War! No wonder you're depressed. You shouldn't think about things you don't like, especially when they aren't happening. What started you?"

"Oh, Holstrom keeps talking to me on the train."

"Well, don't listen to him."

"I won't."

"Well, cheer up then."

"I will."

"And don't let anyone make you look at morbid pictures. There was one of some people who had been gassed in a motor van and then laid out—"

"Please, Joan! Is it any better to tell me about them than to have me look at them?"

"Of course not, dear. That was silly of me. But do cheer up."

"Yes."

The puzzled, uneasy look was still in her eyes as she watched him go down the front walk next morning. It was foolish, but she had the feeling that his gray suit was really black—and he had whimpered in his sleep. With a shiver at her fancy she stepped inside.

That morning George Simister created a minor disturbance in the smoker, it was remembered afterwards, though Holstrom did not witness the beginning of it. It seems that Simister had run to catch the express and had almost missed it, due to a collision with a small man in a large overcoat. Someone recalled that trifling prelude because of the amusing circumstance that the small man, although he had been thrown to his knees and the collision was chiefly Simister's fault, was still anxiously begging Simister's pardon after the latter had dashed on.

Simister just managed to squeeze through the closing door while taking a quick squint at the sign. It was then that his queer behavior started. He instantly turned around and unsuccessfully tried to force his way out again, even inserting his hands in the crevice between the door frame and the rubber edge of the sliding door and yanking violently.

Apparently as soon as he noticed the train was in motion, he turned away from the door, his face pale and set, and roughly pushed his way into the interior of the car.

There he made a beeline for the little box in the wall containing the identifying signs of the train and the miniature window which showed in reverse the one now in use, which read simply EXPRESS. He stared at it as if he couldn't believe his eyes and then started to turn the crank, exposing in turn all the other white signs on the roll of black cloth. He scanned each one intently, oblivious to the puzzled or outraged looks of those around him.

He had been through all the signs once and was starting through them again before the conductor noticed what was happening and came hurrying. Ignoring his expostulations, Simister asked him loudly if this was really the express. Upon receiving a curt affirmative, Simister went on to assert that he had in the moment of squeezing aboard glimpsed another sign in the window—and he mentioned a strange name. He seemed both very positive and very agitated about it, the conductor said. The latter asked Simister to spell the name. Simister haltingly complied:

"B . . . E . . L . . . S . . . E . . N . . ."

The conductor shook his head, then his eyes widened and he demanded, "Say, are you trying to kid me? That was one of those Nazi death camps." Simister slunk toward the other end of the car.

It was there that Holstrom saw him, looking "as if he'd just got a terrible shock." Holstrom was alarmed—and as it happened felt a special private guilt—but could hardly get a word out of him, though he made several attempts to start a conversation, choosing uncharacteristically neutral topics. Once, he remembered, Simister looked up and said, "Do you suppose there are some things a man simply can't escape, no matter how quietly he lives or how carefully he plans?" But his face immediately showed he had realized there was at least one very obvious answer to this question, and Holstrom didn't know what to say. Another time he suddenly remarked, "I wish we were like the British and didn't have standing in buses," but he subsided as quickly. As they neared the downtown terminus Simister seemed to brace up a little, but Holstrom was still worried about him to such a degree that he went out of his way to follow him through the terminus. "I was afraid something would happen to him, I don't know what," Holstrom said. "I would have stayed right beside him except he seemed to resent my presence."

Holstrom's private guilt, which intensified his anxiety and doubtless accounted for his feeling that Simister resented him, was due to the fact that ten days ago, cumulatively irritated by Simister's smug prejudices and blinkered narrow-mindedness, he had anonymously mailed him three books recounting with uncompromising realism and documentation some of the least pleasant aspects of the Nazi tyranny. Now he couldn't but feel they might have helped to shake Simister up in a way he hadn't intended, and he was ashamedly glad that he had been in such a condition when he sent the package that it had been addressed in a drunken scrawl. He never discussed this matter afterwards, except occasionally to make strangely feelingful remarks about "What little things can unseat a spring in a man's clockworks!"

So, continuing Holstrom's story, he followed Simister at a distance as the latter dejectedly shuffled across the busy terminus. "Terminus?" Holstrom once interrupted his story to remark. "He's a god of endings, isn't he?—and of human rights. Does that mean anything?"

When Simister was nearing an iron fence a puzzling episode occurred. He was about to pass it to the right, when someone just ahead of him lurched or stumbled. Simister almost fell himself, veering toward the fence. A nearby guard reached out and in steadying him pulled him around the fence to the left.

Then, Holstrom maintains, Simister turned for a moment and Holstrom caught a glimpse of his face. There must have been something peculiarly frightening about that backward look, something perhaps that Holstrom cannot adequately describe, for he instantly forgot any idea of surveillance at a distance and made every effort to catch up.

But the crowd from another commuters' express enveloped Holstrom. When he got outside the terminus it was some moments before he spotted Simister in the midst of a group jamming their way aboard an already crowded bus across the street. This perplexed Holstrom, for he knew Simister didn't have to take the bus and he recalled his recent complaint.

Heavy traffic kept Holstrom from crossing. He says he shouted, but Simister did not seem to hear him. He got the impression that Simister was making feeble efforts to get out of the crowd that was forcing him onto the bus, but, "They were all jammed together like cattle."

The best testimony to Holstrom's anxiety about Simister is that as soon as the traffic thinned a trifle he darted across the street, skipping between the cars. But by then the bus had started. He was in time only for a whiff of particularly obnoxious exhaust fumes.

As soon as he got to his office he phoned Simister. He got Simister's secretary and what she had to say relieved his worries, which is ironic in view of what happened a little later.

What happened a little later is best described by the same girl. She said, "I never saw him come in looking so cheerful, the old grouch—excuse me. But anyway he came in all smiles, like he'd just got some bad news about somebody else, and right away he started to talk and kid with everyone, so that it was awfully funny when that man called up worried about him. I guess maybe, now I think back, he did seem a bit shaken underneath, like a person who's just had a narrow squeak and is very thankful to be alive.

"Well, he kept it up all morning. Then just as he was throwing his head back to laugh at one of his own jokes, he grabbed his chest, let out an awful scream, doubled up and fell on the floor. Afterwards I couldn't believe he was dead, because his lips stayed so red and there were bright spots of color on his cheeks, like rouge. Of course it was his heart, though you can't believe what a scare that stupid first doctor gave us when he came in and looked at him."

Of course, as she said, it must have been Simister's heart, one way or the other. And it is undeniable that the doctor in question was an ancient, possibly incompetent dispenser of penicillin, morphine and snap diagnoses swifter that Charcot's. They only called him because his office was in the same building. When Simister's own doctor arrived and pronounced it heart failure, which was what they'd thought all along, everyone was much relieved and inclined to be severely critical of the first doctor for having said something that sent them all scurrying to open the windows.

For when the first doctor had come in, he had taken one look at Simister and rasped, "Heart failure? Nonsense! Look at the color of his face. Cherry red. That man died of carbon monoxide poisoning."

SPECIAL AWARD—
PROFESSIONAL

DONALD M. GRANT

All of Donald M. Grant's adult years and a goodly number of his adolescent ones were spent with books and book publishing. That is a *very* long time for anybody to be hooked by a dream quest. Publishing is like a fatal malady; once it settles into one's blood it is most difficult to escape. We suppose there is a vampiric tenaciousness in its so gentle kiss.

Grant has been "booking it" since the mid-1940s when, as a high school student, he knew he wanted to go into publishing. And did. The techniques were quite different in those days: typed pages; small presses—printed two pages at a time; hand-collated; folding until fingers were sore and bloody. Dark years, one might say, but hard and honest years that were a learning process and an inspiration for the magnificent techniques to come: typography— the magic of a computer typesetter; paper—tints and textures from a fantasy world; and color—that bright and glittering jewel out of one of Robert E. Howard's forgotten and haunted tombs.

Although Grant was a partner in other important publishing ventures, he is most proud of his post-1960 work. He has published more than *fifty* hardcovers in that time. That is not too bad an output for a *one-man* house. Of those titles, he has a lot of good feelings, a lot of favorites: *Red Shadows,* with its initial adventure into interior color art; *Black God's Shadow; Red Nails; King —of the Khyber Rifles;* art books by Virgil Finlay, Joseph Clement Coll, Alicia Austin, and George Barr; bibliographies of Edgar Rice Burroughs, Robert E. Howard, and Clark Ashton Smith; and who can forget Roy Krenkel's memorable association with Robert E. Howard in *The Sowers of the Thunder?*

The Future for Donald M. Grant is very bright indeed. Having developed a large and devoted following, he can experiment a bit more, knowing that a certain amount of his costs are always going to be covered. His fantastic book of more than fifty color plates by George Barr was an incredible risk for a relatively small publisher, but the book has sold out its entire 2,500-copy press-run. Don has said his quest "is for the perfect book—the ideal marriage of text and illustration living in the dream house that is design." It is like the quest for a lost city; getting there is a good part of the fun. We in the fantasy-horror field have long been privileged to share and enjoy Don's quixotic journey. It *has* been fun and we hope to continue with Don and enter with him that lost city of the perfect book. As a marker along the way, Donald M. Grant was awarded 1976's Special World Fantasy Award, Professional category.

ALTERNATE WORLD
RECORDING, INC.

Shelley and Roy Torgeson's Alternate World Recording, Inc. won 1977's Special World Fantasy Award in the Professional category. Their company is dedicated to bringing a unique record series of literary readings and dramatizations from the masterworks of fantasy and science fiction. Their offerings are handsomely packaged in jackets featuring fine original artwork by the likes of Gahan Wilson, Ed Emsh, Jeff Jones, George Barr, and Tom Barber. The records are produced under professional studio standards and with quality materials. They are the first recording company to ever dedicate itself entirely to the fantasy and science fiction field. The results are spectacular additions to the fantasy-horror genre.

Of major interest were discs by Harlan Ellison, Robert Bloch, Ugo Toppo (reading Robert E. Howard), Theodore Sturgeon, and Brian Aldiss. A magnificent double album, *Blood! The Life and Future Times of Jack the Ripper,* may be their finest achievement. It features *both* Harlan Ellison and Robert Bloch reading three of their stunning and chilling tributes to the legend of Jack the Ripper. Alternate World Recording has also produced: *Gravely, Robert Bloch,* a reading by Bloch; *Gonna Roll the Bones,* read by Fritz Leiber; *Frankenstein Unbound,* performed by Brian Aldiss; and several other important records. We are certainly not alone in looking forward to their renewed production in years to come.

Avram Davidson has won both Hugo and Edgar Awards but still does not enjoy the fame and fortune his talents deserve; 1976 saw him add a World Fantasy Award to his trophy shelf for *The Enquiries of Dr. Eszterhazy* as Best Collection. The final story in that book follows this introduction and first appeared in the pages of *Whispers* magazine. It takes us to a mythical Balkan kingdom just prior to the First World War.

The King's Shadow Has No Limits

by AVRAM DAVIDSON

The Late Renascence historian known as Pannonicus had written that "The names of nations are often changed; the names of rivers, never." Had he contented himself with observing that the names of nations changed more often than those of rivers, his comment would have been more correct. The name of Triune Monarchy of Scythia-Pannonia-Transbalkania had been officially adopted only in the fifth year of the Reign of the present Monarch; the name of the Ister is found upon the earliest maps; the so-called *Addendum to Procopius* quotes a Fragment of Tacitus, now lost, to the effect that *"The river of the Galans flows into the Ister,"* and so forth. Gaul, Gael, Galan, Galicia, Gallego, Galatia, all mark the marches of that once-widespread people whose languages are now spoken only upon the highlands, and islands of the misty Atlantic. The lesser of the two streams on whose banks came into being the great City of Bella still bears, officially, the name of Galants . . . but to every non-scholar in the Capital of the Triune Monarchy it is and only is The Little Ister.

For a long time the lower part of this stream, particularly where it flowed through the South Ward, had been little better than an open sewer: now, however, it was announced, "The Council and Corporation of the City of Bella"—a phrase which lacked, somehow, quite the majesty of, say, *Senatus populusque Romanum*—was going to embark upon a twofold program of flood control and beautification in regard to the lesser river: and this project was to be dedicated as a birthday present to His Royal and Imperial Majesty, Ignats Louis. With a certain degree of caution, it had not been made entirely clear *which* birthday it was going to commemorate. The King-Emperor, in no great period of time, would be eighty-two.

Some alteration to adjoining property was, of course, inevitable; and one property owner, a parvenu brewer, had been gauche enough to protest. The law books had been opened wide enough to acquaint him with the law of eminent domain, and then slapped shut in his face, so to speak; whilst the slap was still echoing, the Court of First Jurisdiction had seen fit to add, perhaps as *obiter dicta,* the old saying, *"The King's shadow has no limits. . . ."*

Doctor Eszterhazy, one fairly fine day, thought that he would go and have a look at the work in progress. He did not take any of his carriages, and neither did he take the steam runabout—the last time he had taken his steam runabout into the South Ward an aggressive drunkard had staggered up and insisted on being supplied with twopennyworth of roasted chestnuts. Eszterhazy took the tram.

The rains that spring had been less than usual, and this portended trouble for the farmers' crops, and, eventually, for the poor, to whom even a rise of . . . say, two pennies . . . in the price of a commodity meant tragedy. But even this much drought made work on the Little Ister easier: a series of dams had, first reduced the flow to a trickle, and then—the last one—cut it off entirely. Where the old stream had in freshet inundated slums and junkyards, an enormous excavation was now preparing the way for a tree-lined pool. Exactly how much the poor would appreciate this park was not yet certain, but certainly they must have appreciated the great increase in employment which the project afforded. It would have been most ungrateful if they had not, for this did more than merely supply them with wages, it helped

"dissipate unrest," as the *Gazette* newspaper reminded its readers
. . . few of whom were likely to be seeking employment on the
project, however.

Eszterhazy, more or less by osmosis, progressed through the
crowd over the Swedish Bridge (it had once been crossed by
Charles XII, fleeing the Turks, among whom he had found brief
refuge after fleeing the Russians), and eventually found a place
on the railing. He seemed to be looking down upon an anthill
which had been roughly broken open.

"Unrest" there certainly was in more than usual quantity. The
Royal Pannonian Government had again refused Slovatchko-lan-
guage rights to the Slovatchko minority in the schools of Avar-
Ister, capital of Pannonia, whilst vigorously insisting upon an ex-
tension of Avar-language rights for the Avar-speaking minority in
the schools of Bella: the Serbians, as usual, had been far from
slow in pointing out that such a situation would never arise in a
(projected) Kingdom of the Serbians, Slovatchkoes, and Dalma-
tians. The Roumanou had revived their old practice of driving
swine to market through the Turkish and Tartar sections of the
towns; the regular routes would have been shorter, but it would
not have been as much fun. The Concordat with the Vatican was
shortly due for its quinquennial confirmation, and the Byzantine
delegates in the Diet were again announcing that, if it were
confirmed, they would vote against the Budget. The grain mer-
chants, in anticipation of a shortage, had already begun to hoard
supplies. And the Hyperboreans were again refusing to pay their
head tax.

Long lines of men reached from the bottom of the excavation
to its top, and were passing up leathern buckets of dirt from hand
to hand. Steam-shovels would have been quicker, but there were
only a dozen or so of these smoking monsters in all of Bella,
whereas the number of the underemployed was beyond count.
Some of the workers, had they belonged to a class higher in the
social scale, would have been still in school. Others must certainly have had wives and children to support. A surprising number were quite on in years, and one of these for some reason kept
repeatedly attracting Eszterhazy's attention: an old, old man,
white-haired and -bearded, clad in tatters, who moved slowly to
receive his bucket of dirt, strained to maintain it, slowly turned to

pass it on. Again and again the eyes of the watcher returned to this single figure, though he could not have said why.

It took less time to withdraw from the railings of the bridge than it had to get to them. Eszterhazy crossed over to the south side, wandered a while through the mazy little streets where the fishwives were forever slapping herring on the chopping-blocks and hoarsely shouting, "A penny off! A penny off!" and came back again within sight of the work. Slowly, slowly, the sides of the great pit were being peeled back at an angle, the dirt tossed down into a huge heap. The heap itself was in constant flux, shovels moving it continually to several points, whence by buckets it slowly moved to the top and into the wagons which carried it off, he did not know where. The men in the bucket-brigade swayed to and fro, from side to side. The leathern containers moved up, up, up. When they had been emptied, they were tossed down into the pit again.

Eszterhazy's eyes were seeking something . . . someone . . . He had not realized whom until he found him once again. He was nearer, this time, and in a moment or two, he realized what it was about the ragged old man which had been attracting his gaze.

For some reason, the old toiler reminded him of the old Emperor. And this brought him a recollection of some words of Augustine about astrology: of two men known to him, whose births, having occurred upon an estate "where even the birth of puppies were recorded," were known to have been under the same sign at the same hour and minute—yet one grew up to inherit the estate, and the other toiled on "without the yoke of bondage being lifted for a moment. . . ." The reflection disturbed him. Had the old man been near, he would have given him alms; as it was—

He boarded the tram which had taken him to the South Ward, but—on impulse—got off quite a ways before his home stop. He had seen a crowd where crowds were not usually to be seen, and he walked across the street and into the square where it was. He saw an old, neglected-looking church and the high iron palings and tottering tombstones of a neglected churchyard. People were swarming in and out. An old woman, her bosom covered with a tattered sack, hurried past him, one hand clutched tightly upward as though to contain and protect; behind her another old woman, and an old man, and a youngish woman, and a child—all in sackcloth and all with expressions of great wonder and all with a clutched fist.

"What is it that you all have there, Mother?" he asked one. She shot him a look of resentful astonishment, and said, as she hurried by, "Dust of Saint Dominik. . . ."

"Ahhh . . ." he murmured. All was now clear. He made his way through the church and into the churchyard. The throng was clustered around a tomb of incredibly antique design; it had been whitewashed, and a number of priests were standing next to it. One was scraping the side of the tomb with a short knife of exactly the sort which painters use to remove old paint before putting on a fresh coat. A second priest gathered the powder in a paper, and, when the first paused, transferred it to a bowl, whence a third spooned it up, tiny spoon by tiny spoon—the fourth and last priest stood a slight bit apart, reading aloud from the Psalter.

Two men, evidently the verger and the sexton, allowed the pilgrims to approach the tomb one by one, each knelt, and (presumably) prayed a moment, arose, held out a hand, received a tiny spoonful of dust, withdrew. This, then, was the somewhat famous tomb of Saint Domenicus Paleologus, a younger son of a cadet branch of the Imperial House of Byzantium. His missionary labors had included the free treatment of the sick; so great his reputation, that his very tomb had repeatedly been, and literally, torn to pieces in order that the hallowed fragments might prove medically utile. At length the ecclesiastical authorities had fenced and walled the saint's last resting-place: the present ceremony was already hundreds of years old, once a year the dust was scraped from the tomb and distributed. Doubtless the ceremony had been fashionable, but not for long years now, those clustering here and straining for the puissant dust were all from the poor.

The pious rich had other places.

The bell began to ring in the church tower, a flock of doves wheeled up and around, the crowd set up a melancholy howl, pressed closer around the priests at the tomb, who began to move faster and faster. The ceremony was coming to its conclusion. In front of Eszterhazy was an old man dressed in blue canvas, worn soft, worn full of holes, scarcely in any better condition than the remnant of a sack which he had about his back and shoulders. The aged supplicant knelt, received his bit of dust, hastily spooned out, had begun to hobble away—when a heavy old woman, perhaps a fishwife by the sound and smell of her, hurrying so as not to miss out, fell full against him. The hand he had clenched fell out, fell open, in a second was empty.

The old man gazed at his empty hand, still lightly covered by the dust of lime, with stupefaction. He hooted once, twice, in grief and senile disbelief, turned as though to return for another portion, was pushed back, pushed aside. Tears ran from his rufous eyes into his snowy beard. Then, with a sudden and unexpected movement, he plunged his head forward, tongue out, and licked the dust adhering to his hand. Then he tottered away, and Eszterhazy tried to follow after him. But the press was too great.

The last toll of the bell echoed in the air, the last spoon of dust was distributed from the bowl, the priest with full deliberateness lifted the bowl and smashed it, and the unsatisfied remnant of the crowd gave voice to one more howl of sorrow—

The ceremony was over.

As fast as he could, as soon as he could, Eszterhazy scuttled from the churchyard, his eyes darting everywhere around the square. He darted, first up one street, then back to the square and then up another—all, all in vain. The old man was not to be seen, was nowhere to be seen.

Old man whose face was the face of the old man who was Emperor.

Eszterhazy at last sat down in a low dram-shop, ordered cognac. The rough, pale spirit in the dirty glass had never been to France, had been nowhere near France. No matter. He sipped, then he gulped. Then he coughed, choked. Then he made himself be calm and still, and he made himself reflect, there in the stifling room with the rough concrete walls and the flies and the stench from the privy in the nearby yard.

First he forced himself to consider what might have been the state of his own mind, to have created this sudden obsession that every white-bearded old man he saw had the Emperor's face . . . then he reproached himself for the exaggeration. Still: two, in little over an hour's time. . . . Briefly, he considered protesting this last ceremony to the Cardinal-Archbishop, to the Minister of Cults; decided not to; in the six centuries which had passed since the death of St. Domenicus Paleologus (himself close kin to an Emperor) the ceremony had been repeatedly—and uselessly—forbidden: now, at least, it was reduced to one hour, once a year; no one nowadays was injured . . . and, perhaps, he thought wryly, the lime content of the dust might be of some mild use to the body! . . .

But, back to his own state of mind—certainly, he had been increasingly, if somewhat unconsciously, uneasy about the state of the nation. And to him, as to almost everyone else, the Emperor *was* the nation. Had he not been uneasy, too, about the state of the aged Emperor's health? Did not every report of even a cold send ripples of uneasiness throughout the land, cause prayers, most of them genuine, to be offered for old Bobbo's health? So it was perhaps not a completely unreasonable thing if he had seen his Sovereign's face in the face of other old men who suffered. . . . He suddenly sat up. Suppose (his heart thumped) supposed it was *not* an illusion! Suppose—could it be possible!—that it *was* Ignats Louis himself whom he had seen? The first old man, laboring in the pit, no, that was impossible, he could not have had the strength, that one had been too far off for him to have been sure. But this other, this second one? The pouched, protruding and reddened eyes, the bifurcated beard, the long nose, the very stoop and gait . . . Could the Emperor have suddenly taken a notion to play Haroun al-Rashid and go about incognito to take the pulse of the city, so to speak? This pilgrimage just now over, for instance . . .

For although the King-Emperor reigned and lived in an age of telephones and gramophones and motorcars, he had been born in an age when the steamboat was only a toy on a pond. Born to an obscure princeling in a house—not even a castle—on the Gothic-Slovatchko border marches, deep in the forests, raised in infancy and early childhood not by nannies, mademoiselles, Fräuleins, but according to antique custom by his wetnurse in her own cottage. What tales of ages even earlier yet had he heard day after day and night after night? He had already had his first beard when destiny, in the form of a court circle alarmed at the growing insanity of the then emperor, had plucked him from the hunting-

TIM KIRK From *Rime Isle*

TIM KIRK From *Rime Isle*

STEPHEN FABIAN From *Whispers* magazine's "Nightmare" folio on William Hope Hodgson

STEPHEN FABIAN From *Whispers* magazine's "Nightmare" folio on
William Hope Hodgson

lodge and the wilderness and sent him to military school—their idea and their only idea of how to fit the Heir for the heavy task ahead.

Small wonder that religious eccentrics of all sorts, not to say outright charlatans, were able to find access, increasingly as his hearing diminished, to his ancient ear; yes, it just might be possible that he had of his own mere whim and fancy decided to participate in the now-brief pilgrimage for the Dust of Saint Dominik. One might find out.

One would *have* to. . . .

He had by this time left the dram-shop and, wandering about in a deep study, marked not his steps, and, looking up, found himself, as the bells tolled noon, at another of the scenes continued from ancient ages: the distribution of the Beggars' Dole. Only a single arch of heavy masonry remained to mark the location of the City Gates. Down to the early years of the present Reign the Imperial Capital had remained a walled city, its gates literally locked at sunset, the keys ceremonially handed over to the Emperor to keep till shortly before dawn. The city had since spread far and wide, the walls for the most part demolished. But the City Gates remained, or, at any rate, one of the arches of the Main Gate still remained. And at this spot, where once assembled the lame, the halt, the blind, the pauper and the leper, to beg for alms, at this same place forever commemorated in living legend and in folklore, each noon the ancient beneficence of bread and milk was still distributed.

Slowly the line of recipients moved forward. Doubtless there were no longer any lepers among them. Even the standards of raggedness had improved. There were a few more old women than old men, shuffling forward to accept the mug of milk and the chunk of bread from the "one friar, one sister, and one knight" traditionally charged with the duty. The "knight" was usually a very junior member of the Household, Eszterhazy did not know him, today. Eszterhazy drew near. The two policemen on duty looked at him, indifferently, yawned. Eszterhazy examined the recipients one by one. Why? Absurd! What did it matter? Ahah, a Tartar, few to be seen nowadays. . . . This next one still in fragments of the old-style costume of the sailing-bargees . . . this one a Goth . . . the next—

So. Yes. In shapeless coat, rags wrapped about shuffling feet, cap torn in two places, bread in one hand and milk in the other, with dim purpose heading for the worn old steps at the side to sit and eat and drink: if this was not Himself the King-Emperor, it was no one else. Only a sudden flash of memory of the fatal identification of Louis and Marie Antoinette by the innocent priest at Varennes, some dim caution flaring up, prevented Eszterhazy from bowing, from kneeling. But he was sufficiently taller than the sunken, shrunken figure to justify bending, and he made of this merely physical motion an act of homage; he inclined his head as he said, softly, "Sire."

The old eyes, rheumy and filmed, looked at him. The old head nodded twice. The old hands started to dip the bread in the milk, paused. The old man slowly crossed himself. Once again the bread went toward the mug, once again it stopped.

"Long, long ago," he said, in his high, now somewhat tremulous voice, "a delegation of the Jewish notables came to see me, to thank me for something or other. And I, may God forgive me, I was young then, there was a rabbi among them, and I said to him, jovial, I said, 'And is your Messiah here?' God forgive me, God forgive me. . . . And he looked at me, this old man who had looked as it were on Pharaoh, and this is what he said, 'Do not seek him here. Seek him among the sickly beggars at the City Gate.'" Again the bread went toward the milk, this time it went in, came up dripping, and with dexterous haste he caught the sop and took it in his mouth before, sodden, it could fall.

Eszterhazy said nothing. The old man munched and sucked and swallowed. It did not take him long to be done with the refreshment. Then he said, "God has given this weary old body such length of days so that this Empire and its many nations might have some few more years of peace, you see. What did the old France say? He said, 'After him the deluge. . . . And the Deluge swept away his House.' But, now, after me, after me . . . what? Tell me, learned fellow, what was the name of that old empire which in olden days sank beneath the sea?"

"Sire: Atlantis."

"Yes, so. After me, this Empire will sink like Atlantis, and the children of these children," he gestured to a few boys and girls playing near off, "will look for it upon the maps in vain." He was long silent. Then, in a whisper of a whisper, *"Sed Dea spes mea."*

When Eszterhazy raised his head, the place beside him was empty.

Up and down and back and forth through the ancient-most quarters of the City, Eszterhazy sought his Sovereign: what his Sovereign was seeking, he did not know.

A voice close by said, "Watch!" He looked up, started, stopped. There had been no great danger, indeed, the caution may have been less to prevent his walking into the horse and hearse than to adjure him to take off his hat: which he now did. There was but one horse, there were no carriages of mourners to mark the sad bobbing of the jet-black ostrich plumes. Alongside and behind this modern version of the death-cart walked a half-dozen figures in the robes and the hoods of the Penitential Brotherhood who had once been charged with burying the victims of the Plague and were still charged with conducting the funerals of paupers. If equality existed anywhere in the many nations of the Triune Monarchy it existed in the ranks of the Penitential Brotherhood. The knight of many quarterings might be found therein, and therein, too, the convict on ticket-of-leave. He did not know the one who called out, as the hearse rattled and creaked over the stone blocks and the tram tracks, *"Thou too, thou too!"* nor did he know the one who echoed this call with another, *"Pray for him and pray for us. . . ."* He recognized none of the faces beneath the hoods of those who bore lighted candles, till one of them casually half-glanced in his direction: and so again he saw the bloodless, weary countenance of his Emperor.

The day wore to its close; he found his way to his home. A while he spent in thought, then he thought to send a message, then he got up and went to his telephone. The number he announced was one of two digits and below fifty: the call went through immediately.

"The Equerries' Room," a voice said. What emotions could he imagine in the voice? Best to imagine none.

"Pray ask Count Kristofr Eszterhazy if he will speak with his cousin, Doctor Engelbert."

Almost at once the familiar voice, "Yes, Engli, what? . . ."

"Kristi, forgive the presumption, but . . . but, how is it with The Presence?"

A short silence, heavy breathing, then, "Engli, you frighten me, how *could* you have known?"

He felt his heart swell. "What? What?" he mumbled.

"We thought he had fainted, he was unconscious for most of the day, he seemed to be saying something from time to time, it made no sense, ever; things like, oh, 'How heavy is the dirt,' maybe—or, 'Quick, quick, the dust,' or, 'The dole,' and 'Is he here?' But he was mostly silent—*all day long!* We feared the worst, no one but the doctors were allowed in, and of course no one was allowed out. But about an hour ago he suddenly regained consciousness. The doctors say that he is as well now as he was yesterday. So we must say: Thank God."

The call was soon ended.

—What had happened? Was it possible? Had he, Engelbert Eszterhazy, suffered and shared in suffering a hallucination of the most fantastic kind conceivable? Dreamed, constructed an entire phantasm out of the depths of his own mind—a phantasm which . . . somehow, somehow . . . in some way seemed to fit in with the phantasm of this other and so much older man, lying motionless on his hard bed halfway across the City? Incredible as this was, still, it was the likeliest explanation. The likeliest—which may not have been the best and truest. . . .

. . . Or had some . . . some *aspect* of the aged Monarch left its fleshly mansion, and, as the Kaffirs of Africa said, gone wandering about whilst the body slept . . . or . . . or what?

Long, long he pondered the matter, pacing back and forth in his study, back and forth.

At length, longing for fresher air, he went up to the roof of his house. It stood on no great hill, but stand upon a hill it did: all, all about him, on every side, the Imperial Capital lay spread out to his view, gas and electric lamps in streets and houses; and with naphtha and acetylene flares as well, where the markets were: necklaces and pendants and clusters, a coffer full of jewels spread out before him. And above, every tower and crenelation and door and gate of the Castle on the bluffs above the glittering, reflective Ister was illuminated.

He heard, over and over again, in his mind, as though even now spoken next his ear, the words which either the aged Sovereign or else his very simulacrum or Doppelgänger had said. *After me, this Empire will sink like Atlantis, and the children of these children will look for it upon the maps in vain. . . ."*

And he asked himself again and again: Could these words be true? Dare he even think they might be true?

Below, all about, the lights dwindled. Above, the stars wheeled. And then came the mists from the river. And then the cold wind.

Manly Wade Wellman is a giant of a man both physically and literarily. His non-fiction has been nominated for a Pulitzer Prize, his fantasy collection, *Worse Things Waiting*, won the first World Fantasy Award for Best Collection, and Governor Jim Hunt recently presented him with the North Carolina Literary Award. Wellman is best identified with his tales of the southern mountain folk he knows and loves so well. "The Ghastly Priest Doth Reign" is from that canon and was nominated for a 1976 World Fantasy Award.

The Ghastly Priest Doth Reign

by MANLY WADE WELLMAN

The jury found Jack Bowdry not guilty of murder. All anybody could testify was that he'd cursed and damned Kib Wordin for a witch-man and gave him twenty-four hours to leave the Sawback Mountain country, and twenty-five hours later Kib Wordin lay dead under the creepy tree in his cabin yard with a homemade silver bullet in his head. Come to think, a witch-man had died at that red-painted cabin thirty years back, and another witch-man years before that.

Anyway, Jack's neighbors helped him fetch his stuff from the county jail and rejoiced him up Walnut Creek to his home place next to Hosea's Hollow. They'd shucked his corn for him, handed and hung his tobacco in the curing barn. All vowed he'd done a good thing about Kib Wordin, whatever the jury couldn't decide, and at sundown that pretty fall day they good-byed him at his door.

Tolly Paradine, the schoolmaster's daughter, waited with him, making him feel almighty big because she was so little, with her pale-gold hair and rosy-gold cheeks. He stood a foot over her and near about a foot broader, with his brickbat jaw and big hands dangling from his blue shirtsleeves, with gray-threaded black hair, with thirty-four years to Tolly's twenty.

"I redded your place up for you," she said. "Jack, I'm proud you'll neighbor us again. And glad Kib Wordin won't pester me no more to come live with him."

He stared up slope to the ridge. "Better haste to catch up you daddy yonder," he said. "I'll come visit tomorrow if you say I can."

"Well you know you can, Jack." She upped to kiss his rough cheek, then ran after her folks. Jack looked again at what he'd seen to make him hurry her off from there.

Against the soft evening sky at ridge top stood a squatty man, with a long, ashy-pale coat down to his ankles. As Jack looked, the fellow slid away into some brushy trees.

"Huh," said Jack Bowdry, deep in his deep chest, and faced toward his notch-logged cabin with its lime-painted clay chinking. He pushed the door open and set foot on the sill. Then he scowled down at what he'd near about stepped on. A gold coin, big as a half dollar, a double eagle such as was still round when Roosevelt started being President. It looked put there for him to pick up.

He glowered back to where that long-coated somebody had been. Then he toed the coin down into the yard and kicked it away in a twinkle of light into the bushes and went inside.

His cabin was just the one long room. The plank floor was swept. On the fireplace crane hung a kettle of stewed chicken, dumplings, carrots, the things Tolly knew he relished most. Jack built a fire under the kettle and put the match to the wick of his lamp. It let him see his bed at the far end, made up with a brown blanket and a white pillow, more of Tolly's doing. A smile creased the corners of Jack's wide mouth as he set the lamp on the fireboard, under his rifle and shotgun on the deer horns up there, and next to the row of books he'd read over and over.

Grandma Cutshaw's Bible; *Amateur Builder's Handbook;* Macaulay's poems that Jack almost knew by heart; *Guide to Rocks and Minerals; Jack Ranger's School Days; Robinson Crusoe;* Hill's *Manual of Social and Business Forms,* how to make a will, figure interest, all like that; and—

But he had only seven books. What was this one with the white paper cover at the end of the row?

He took it down. *Albertus Magnus, or White and Black Magic for Man and Beast.* Jack had heard tell of it, that you couldn't throw or give it away or burn it, you must bury it and say a funeral over it like for a dead man. Tolly had never left that here for him, nor either that gold eagle on the door log. The book flopped open in his hand:

> . . . in the red forest there is a red church, and in the red church stands a red altar, and upon the red altar there lies a red knife; take the red knife and cut red bread.

Jack slammed it shut and put it back on the shelf. Tomorrow he'd show it to Tolly's educated father. He took down the Macaulay and opened it to wash away the taste of the other book. Here was *The Battle of Lake Regillus:*

> Those trees in whose dim shadow
> The ghastly priest doth reign,
> The priest who slew the slayer,
> And shall himself be slain.

Now, what in hell might that mean? He shoved the Macaulay back, too, and spooned out a plateful of chicken stew and carried it to his table. Tasty, the stew was. He was glad to find himself enjoying to eat, proving to himself that he wasn't pestered by all these funny happenings. Even after two big helps, enough was left in the kettle to hot up for noon dinner tomorrow. Jack lighted his corncob pipe and went yet again for a book. Better be the Bible this time. He carried it and the lamp to the table.

Grandma used to cast signs, open the Bible anywhere and put a finger on whatever text is there. Do that three times and figure out the meaning. Jack opened the Bible midway and stabbed down his big finger.

. . . preparest a table for me in the presence of mine enemies.

The Twenty-third Psalm. Tolly had prepared Jack a mighty good table. But the presence of enemies, now. He opened farther along, pointed again.

. . . cried out, Great is Diana of the Ephesians.

Book of Acts that time, and Saint Paul getting hollered at, scolded. One more time, the very last page, a verse at the end of Revelation.

. . . Without are dogs, and sorcerers . . .

Just then, a scrabbling at the door.

Jack sailed out of his chair, dropping the Bible and snatching his double-bitted ax from beside the fireplace. He ran and grabbed the latch string and yanked the door inward. "What's going out here?" he roared.

A half-cowering shape backed off down the path toward the road.

"Where did you come from?" Jack yelled at it.

It stood up then, in a drench of moonlight, in its long pale coat, lifting its hands toward him. Not a dog, after all. Jack charged, ax lifted, and the shape scuttled away among the trees. Jack stood alone in the moon-bright road. Something else hurried at him from down slope. Again he whirled up the ax.

"Jack!" cried Tolly Paradine's voice.

He caught her wrist. "I thought you were that other one yonder."

"No, I came to tell you—"

"Inside, quick." He whirled her along the path and into the cabin and slammed the door behind them. Tolly looked at him with big scared eyes, and her golden skin was as pale as her hair.

"How come you to be out?" Jack demanded.

"Daddy was reading in a book he's got," she quavered. "It's *The Golden Bough,* somebody named Frazer wrote it."

"Ain't never heard tell of it." He cracked the door open, peered out, then shut them in again. "What's a book got to do with it?"

"Daddy says there's some kind of old worship." She dropped into his chair. "Long time ago, over the sea, somewhere near Rome. But longer ago than Rome." She trembled her lips. "Folks worshiped Diana."

"Just so happens I was reading in the Bible about Diana," Jack told her. "Wasn't she the hunting goddess, goddess of the moon? I recollect that from a book in school."

"Daddy says she was all kinds of goddess. They worshiped her with fire; sometimes they killed people for a sacrifice. Why, Daddy says some scholars think the whole witch business comes down from old worship of Diana. Like Kib Wordin's witch stuff."

"There's another tale about Diana," remembered Jack, leaning against the fireboard. "A man was out hunting and he seen her in swimming, naked as a jaybird. It was just a happen-so, but she flung water on him and turned him into a buck deer for his own dogs to pull down and kill. Ain't what sounds like a good goddess to worship."

"In those old days, the chief priest lived under a sacred tree," Tolly pattered on. "And when somebody killed him, that fellow got to be the priest, till another killed *him,* and—"

She fell quiet. Jack frowned.

"What sort of tree is it got to be?" he asked her.

"Daddy never said that." Her eyes got wider. "You're thinking on that tree at Kib Wordin's place. Maybe one like that. No telling what a tree can get to be, over thousands of years, no more than what worship can get to be."

"And before Kib Wordin, a witch-man died up there," Jack reminded. "And before him, another one."

"And now—" she began, but again she stopped.

"And now, you aim to say, it's me," he finished for her. He shook his head, and his black hair stirred. "All right, what if old Jack Bowdry just ain't accepting the nomination? What if I just ain't having it, no way?"

"Daddy explained me about it," she stammered. "A branch from that old witch tree could be planted and grow to a witch tree itself, and be their worship place." She looked near about ready to cry. "You don't believe it's so," she half accused.

"Yes, I do. Stuff tonight makes me to believe."

He told her about the man in the long gray coat, the gold coin, the messages from the books.

"What man was it?" asked Tolly. "I don't call to mind anybody with a coat like that."

"I doubt if he wore it to be known," said Jack. "Anyway, it's like he was here to threaten me, and the money to buy me, and this here book to teach me."

He took down *Albertus Magnus*. "No, Tolly, don't touch it. Anyway, I've seen that tree at Wordin's place, far off. Maybe it's what's grown up to cause this witch business."

"Kib Wordin read to me out of that book one time," she said. "Told me he'd put a spell on me so I couldn't refuse him."

"But you refused him."

"It was just about then when you—" She broke off. "You know."

"Sure enough I know. I put that silver bullet right back of his ear."

"You killed the priest, and that makes you the new one," said Tolly. "It's in Daddy's books. If you say no, they'll kill you, whoever they are."

"Ain't I a sitting duck to be killed?" he cried out. "Whoever wants that priest job next, won't he kill me if he can?"

"But when you see what's happening—"

"Stop rooting against me, Tolly!" he yelled, and she shrank down in the chair. "Whatever happens, I still ain't their man."

He glared at the book in his hand and walked to the door.

"What are you going to do?" Tolly squeaked behind him.

"A couple things needing to be done. The first of them won't take but two-three minutes."

He dragged the door open and stepped out into the night. Scraps of moonlight flitted among the trees as he walked to the road. He knelt and groped with his free hand until he found soft earth. Powerfully he scooped out great clods. He pushed *Albertus*

Magnus into the hole, dragged the loosened earth back over it and rammed it down hard.

Still kneeling, he tried to think of the burial service. "Ashes to ashes, dust to dust," he said aloud, and the night round him was as still as stone. "Until the day break and the shadows flee away," he recollected a few more words to say. Then he got up. There was Tolly, standing beside him.

"Get back inside," he grumbled.

"Not with you out here."

He took her arm and pulled her to the door and inside. "Sit," he ordered her, pointing to the chair. "Don't you leave out of here till I get back."

"What you aiming to do, Jack?"

"I've kindly got it in mind that that witch tree up yonder's been growing long enough."

"If you don't come back—"

"Just start pestering about that when I don't."

He rolled his shirtsleeves back from his corded arms and took the double-bitted ax again. Out he tramped, slamming the door behind him.

Out to the road, past the grave where he'd buried *Albertus Magnus,* up slope. He moved between bunches of big trees he'd once reckoned he knew as friends, oaks and walnuts and tall watching pines, with sooty shadows amongst them. They stared at him from both sides; they seemed to hold their breath. He heard only his own dull footsteps until, before he knew it, he was where the path turned off to the red-painted cabin where once he'd sneaked up on Kib Wordin.

There was light through the trees there; not the moon glow on the road, but a dull red light. Jack stole along the path. Now he saw the slumpy-roofed cabin where three witch-men had lived and died, with its sneaky look like a hungry beast waiting, waiting. The red light soaked out through curtains at the windows. Who was inside there now? Doing what?

He decided not to knock and find out. He took careful steps into the yard, and he was right under the tree he'd come to find.

Never had he relished the look of that tree, even from far off, and he didn't relish its look now. It seemed to move or shiver in the dull red light. Its coaly black trunk might could be a foot and a half thick above roots that clutched deep down among rocks. Just above Jack's head the branches kinked this way and that way, like nothing so much as snakes. They wiggled, or maybe it was just the stir of lean, ugly leaves.

He walked all the way round, bending his head under the snaky branches, studying the trunk. Finally he set his booted feet just so on the damp-feeling earth. He shifted his grip on the ax helve and hiked it high. If whoever or whatever was in yonder with the red light heard him chop and came out, he'd be ready, ax in hand. Hard and deep he drove down the blade just above the roots.

Sound rose round him, soft to hear but scary to feel. It was like an echoed cry of pain, as if the wood he chopped was living flesh. He ripped the ax loose and raised it, and knew without looking up that those branches sure enough squirmed. A whisper sneaked in the air, like an angry voice. Again he swung the ax. A big chip sailed loose, showing white wood that glowed with its own pale, sick light.

Jack recollected the old Cherokee who'd said that trees felt when they were chopped, and it hadn't made him like to cut timber any right much. But this tree was different, it was an enemy tree. He looked toward the cabin. Not a stir from there. He slashed and slashed at the blackness of the trunk, every blow flinging white chips away. Sweat popped out on him. The murmur kept murmuring, but it didn't slow him up a hooter. Another six or seven chops at the right place, and that tree would fall. It would slap down right on the pulpy shingles of that red-lighted cabin. Once more he heaved up his ax.

And something grabbed onto it and held it on high.

At once he was fighting to get the ax back, but he couldn't. They crawled and struggled above him, those snaky branches, winding the ax helve, sliding twigs round his right arm like a basket weaving itself there. He let go the ax to fight that grip on him. His feet came clear of the ground with the effort, and the branches bent with his weight. Powerfully he fought his way round the trunk, the twigs still netting his arm. His hand and wrist tingled as if they were being bitten, sucked.

His free left hand hustled his great big clasp knife out of his pants pocket. He yanked the longest blade open with his teeth and slashed at those snaring twigs.

They parted under the edge that was as sharp as a whetrock could make it. As his right hand came free, more twigs scrambled down to spiral his left arm. He whipped the knife over to his right hand to hack and chop those new tethers. Free for a second, he tried to flounder away, but he slipped on soggy earth and fell to his knees. The branches grabbed and tied him again.

He started to curse, but saved his breath. He slashed with the knife, passing it from hand to hand. He cleared the twigs from wrists and arms, but a thicker branch wound him, tying his right arm to his side. It squeezed tighter than the strongest wrestler he'd ever tried holds with; he sawed at it, and it was hard to cut through. He got it whittled free of him, just as a bigger branch snapped a loop on his ankle and flung him full length.

"If I knew where your heart was," he panted as if the tree could hear, and maybe it did. Twenty twigs scraped and felt for new holds on him, wove and twisted round him, made it harder for him to cut at them. The cut ends kept crawling back, thicker, harder to slice away. He wished he had his ax, flung down yonder out of reach.

He turned himself over, and over again. He was as strong as any man in the Sawback Mountain country, and the surge of his turning broke some twigs, not all of them. Hacking at the ones still at him, he saw the cabin door open and somebody stepping out in the red light.

Hunched, wearing a long pale coat, it must be the one who'd spied at his homecoming. Close it came. A hand lifted a dark-shining blade, a big corn knife, just over him.

"Stay right there," said the quiet, cold voice of Tolly, from just beyond them.

The fellow froze, the corn knife drooped.

"Put that thing to Jack and I'll shoot you," Tolly said, as quiet as if she was saying the time of day. "I've got Jack's shotgun here, and a bunch of silver dimes wadded down both barrels on top of the buckshot."

The corn knife sank and pointed to the ground.

"You want to kill Jack and be the priest," Tolly said. "Then what if I killed you and got to be priestess? What if I used that witch book to witch your soul right down to the floor of hell?"

The fellow spun round and scurried off. Jack heard the long coat whip, heard a crash among dark trees. Tolly ran close.

"Look out," Jack wheezed.

But she stood right over him, laid the shotgun muzzles to that pallid wound he'd cut in the trunk, and slammed loose with both barrels. Flame flashed, the two shots howled like two claps of thunder, and something screamed a death scream. All those holds on Jack turned weak and fell away. With one floundering, scrambling try he ripped free of them and came to his feet beside Tolly.

The tree blazed up like fat meat where the blasts had driven into it. Jack pulled Tolly clear as the whole thing fell away from them, fell right on the roof of the cabin. The flames ran up into the branches and caught the shingles, burning blood red and sick white. Still holding to Tolly, Jack started her away at a run to the road and down the mountain.

Once they looked back. Flames jumped high and bright into the high darkness against the stars, gobbling that tree and that cabin, putting an end to both of them.

Tolly and Jack got married Thanksgiving week. Before that, the neighbor folks built a bedroom to Jack's cabin at the left, a lean-to kitchen at the right. Before that, too, half a dozen sorry men and women left out of the Sawback Mountain country. Nobody knew where they went, or even for dead sure which was the one who wore the long coat. All anybody was certain sure of was that you could live another sight better there without that half dozen people and whatever they'd been up to.

Frank Belknap Long may eventually be best remembered as the closest friend of literary giant Howard Phillips Lovecraft. This will be unfortunate because Long's fiction is quite good. The quality was considered high enough to earn him 1978's World Fantasy Award for Life Achievement. A superb Doubleday volume, *The Early Long,* mixed Frank's own reminiscences with the best of his horror fiction. The book received a 1976 World Fantasy Award nomination. Rather than use from that volume his classic (and oft-reprinted) "The Hounds of Tindalos" or "The Space Eaters," we have decided to use this quiet little chiller, a favorite of his and ours.

A Visitor from Egypt

by FRANK BELKNAP LONG

On a dismal rainy afternoon in August a tall, very thin gentleman tapped timidly on the frosted glass window of the curator's office in a certain New England museum. He wore a dark blue Chinchilla overcoat, olive-green Homburg hat with high tapering crown, yellow gloves, and spats. A blue silk muffler with white dots encircled his neck and entirely concealed the lower portion of his face and virtually all of his nose. Only a small expanse of pink and very wrinkled flesh was visible above the muffler and below his forehead, but as this exposed portion of his physiognomy contained his eyes it was as arresting as it was meager. So arresting indeed was it that it commanded instant respect, and the attendants, who were granted liberal weekly emoluments for merely putting yards of red tape between the main entrance and the narrow corridor that led to the curator's office, waived all of their habitual and asinine inquiries and conducted the muffled gentleman straight to what a Victorian novelist would have called the sacred precincts.

Having tapped, the gentleman waited. He waited patiently, but something in his manner suggested that he was extremely nervous and perturbed and decidedly on edge to talk to the curator. And yet when the door of the office at last swung open, and the curator peered out fastidiously from behind gold-rimmed spectacles, he merely coughed and extended a visiting-card.

The card was conservatively fashionable in size and exquisitely engraved, and as soon as the curator perused it his countenance underwent an extraordinary alteration. He was ordinarily a supremely reticent individual with long, pale face and lugubrious, condescending eyes, but he suddenly became preposterously friendly and greeted his visitor with an effusiveness that was almost hysterical. He seized his visitor's somewhat flabby gloved hand and gave it a Babbittesque squeeze. He nodded and bowed and smirked and seemed almost beside himself with gratification.

"If only I had known, Sir Richard, that you were in America! The papers were unusually silent—outrageously silent, you know. I cannot imagine how you managed to elude the reporters. They are usually so persistent, so indecently curious. I really cannot imagine how you achieved it!"

"I did not wish to talk to idiotic old women, to lecture before mattoids, to have my photo reproduced in your absurd papers." Sir Richard's voice was oddly high-pitched, almost effeminate, and it quivered with the intensity of his emotion. "I *detest* publicity, and I regret that I am not utterly unknown in this—er— region."

"I quite understand, Sir Richard," murmured the curator soothingly. "You naturally desired leisure for research, for discussion. You were not interested in what the vulgar would say or think about you. A commendable and eminently scholarly attitude to take, Sir Richard! A splendid attitude! I quite understand and sympathize. We Americans have to be polite to the press occasionally, but you have no idea how it cramps our style, if I may use an expressive but exceedingly coarse colloquialism. It really does, Sir Richard. You have no idea—but do come in. Come in, by all means. We are honored immeasurably by the visit of so eminent a scholar."

Sir Richard bowed stiffly and preceded the curator into the office. He selected the most comfortable of the five leather-backed chairs that encircled the curator's desk and sank into it with a faintly audible sigh. He neither removed his hat nor withdrew the muffler from his pinkish visage.

The curator selected a seat on the opposite side of the table and politely extended a box of Havana panatelas. "Extremely mild," he murmured. "Won't you try one, Sir Richard?"

Sir Richard shook his head. "I have never smoked," he said, and coughed.

There ensued a silence. Then Sir Richard apologized for the muffler. "I had an unfortunate accident on the ship," he explained. "I stumbled in one of the deck games and cut my face rather badly. It's in a positively unpresentable condition. I know you'll pardon me if I don't remove this muffler."

The curator gasped. "How horrible, Sir Richard! I can sympathize, believe me. I hope that it will not leave a scar. One should have the most expert advice in such matters. I hope—Sir Richard, have you consulted a specialist, may I ask?"

Sir Richard nodded. "The wounds are not deep—nothing serious, I assure you. And now, Mr. Buzzby, I should like to discuss with you the mission that has brought me to Boston. Are the predynastic remains from Luxor on exhibition?"

The curator was a trifle disconcerted. He had placed the Luxor remains on exhibition that very morning, but he had not as yet arranged them to his satisfaction, and he would have preferred that his distinguished guest should view them at a later date. But he very clearly perceived that Sir Richard was so intensely interested that nothing that he could say would induce him to wait, and he *was* proud of the remains and flattered that England's ablest Egyptologist should have come to the city expressly to see them. So he nodded amiably and confessed that the bones were on exhibition, and he added that he would be delighted and honored if Sir Richard would view them.

"They are truly marvelous," he explained. "The pure Egyptian type—dolichocephalic, with relatively primitive features. And they date—Sir Richard, they date from at least 8,000 B.C."

"Are the bones tinted?"

"I should say so, Sir Richard! They are wonderfully tinted, and the original colors have scarcely faded at all. Blue and red, Sir Richard, with red predominating."

"Hm. A most absurd custom," murmured Sir Richard.

Mr. Buzzby smiled. "I have always considered it pathetic, Sir Richard. Infinitely amusing, but pathetic. They thought that by painting the bones they could preserve the vitality of the corruptible body. Corruption putting on incorruption, as it were."

"It was blasphemous!" Sir Richard had arisen from his chair. His face, above the muffler, was curiously white, and there was a hard, metallic glitter in his small dark eyes. "They sought to cheat Osiris! They had no conception of hyperphysical realities!"

The curator stared curiously. "Precisely what do you mean, Sir Richard?"

Sir Richard started a trifle at the question, as though he were awakening from some strange nightmare, and his emotion ebbed as rapidly as it had arisen. The glitter died out of his eyes and he sank listlessly back in his chair. "I—I was merely amused by your comment. As though by merely painting their mummies they could restore the circulation of the blood!"

"But that, as you know, Sir Richard, would occur in the other world. It was one of the most distinctive prerogatives of Osiris. He alone could restore the dead."

"Yes, I know," murmured Sir Richard. "They counted a good deal on Osiris. It is curious that it never occurred to them that the god might be offended by their presumptions."

"You are forgetting the Book of the Dead, Sir Richard. The promises in that are very definite. And it is an inconceivably ancient book. I am strongly convinced that it was in existence in 10,000 B.C. You have read my brochure on the subject?"

Sir Richard nodded. "A very scholarly work. But I believe that the Book of the Dead as we know it was a forgery!"

"Sir Richard!"

"Parts of it are undoubtedly predynastic, but I believe that the Judgment of the Dead, which defines the judicial prerogatives of

Osiris, was inserted by some meddling priest as late as the historical period. It is a deliberate attempt to modify the relentless character of Egypt's supreme deity. Osiris does not judge, he *takes*."

"He takes, Sir Richard?"

"Precisely. Do you imagine any one can ever cheat death? Do you imagine that, Mr. Buzzby? Do you imagine for one moment that Osiris would restore to life the fools that returned to him?"

Mr. Buzzby colored. It was difficult to believe that Sir Richard was really in earnest. "Then you honestly believe that the character of Osiris as we know it is—"

"A myth, yes. A deliberate and childish evasion. No man can ever comprehend the character of Osiris. He is the Dark God. *But he treasures his own.*"

"Eh?" Mr. Buzzby was genuinely startled by the tone of ferocity in which the last remark was uttered. "What did you say, Sir Richard?"

"Nothing." Sir Richard had risen and was standing before a small revolving bookcase in the center of the room. "Nothing, Mr. Buzzby. But your taste in fiction interests me extremely. I had no idea you read young Finchley!"

Mr. Buzzby blushed and looked genuinely distressed. "I don't ordinarily," he said. "I despise fiction ordinarily. And young Finchley's romances are unutterably silly. He isn't even a passable scholar. But that book has—well, there are a few good things in it. I was reading it this morning on the train and put it with the other books temporarily because I had no other place to put it. You understand, Sir Richard? We all have our little foibles, eh? A work of fiction now and then is sometimes—er—well, suggestive. And H. E. Finchley is rather suggestive occasionally."

"He is, indeed. His Egyptian redactions are imaginative masterpieces!"

"You amaze me, Sir Richard. Imagination in a scholar is to be deplored. But of course, as I said, H. E. Finchley is not a scholar and his work is occasionally illuminating if one doesn't take it too seriously."

"He knows his Egypt."

"Sir Richard, I can't believe you really approve of him. A mere fictionist—"

Sir Richard had removed the book and opened it casually. "May I ask, Mr. Buzzby, if you are familiar with Chapter 13, *The Transfiguration of Osiris?*"

"Bless me, Sir Richard, I am not. I skipped that portion. Such purely grotesque rubbish repelled me."

"Did it, Mr. Buzzby? But the repellent is usually arresting. Just listen to this:

"It is beyond dispute that Osiris made his worshipers dream strange things of him, and that he possessed their bodies and souls forever. There is a devilish wrath against mankind with which Osiris was for Death's sake inspired. In the cool of the evening he walked among men, and upon his head was the Crown of Upper Egypt, and his cheeks were inflated with a wind that slew. His face was veiled so that no man could see it, but assuredly it was an old face, very old and dead and dry, for the world was young when tall Osiris died."

Sir Richard snapped the book shut and replaced it in the shelf. "What do you think of that, Mr. Buzzby?" he inquired.

"Rot," murmured the curator. "Sheer, unadulterated rot."

"Of course, of course. Mr. Buzzby, did it ever occur to you that a god may live, figuratively, a dog's life?"

"Eh?"

"Gods are transfigured, you know. They go up in smoke, as it were. In smoke and flame. They become pure flame, pure spirit, creatures with no visible body."

"Dear, dear, Sir Richard, that had not occurred to me." The curator laughed and nudged Sir Richard's arm. "Beastly sense of humor," he murmured, to himself. "The man is unutterably silly."

"It would be dreadful, for example," continued Sir Richard, "if the god had no control over his transfiguration; if the change occurred frequently and unexpectedly; if he shared, as it were, the ghastly fate of a Dr. Jekyll and Mr. Hyde."

Sir Richard was advancing toward the door. He moved with a curious, shuffling gait and his shoes scraped peculiarly upon the floor. Mr. Buzzby was instantly at his elbow. "What is the matter, Sir Richard? What has happened?"

"Nothing!" Sir Richard's voice rose in hysterical denial. "Nothing. Where is the lavatory, Mr. Buzzby?"

"Down one flight of stairs on your left as you leave the corridor," muttered Mr. Buzzby. "Are—are you ill?"

"It is nothing, nothing," murmured Sir Richard. "I must have a drink of water, that is all. The injury has—er—affected my throat. When it becomes too dry it pains dreadfully."

"Good heavens!" murmured the curator. "I can send for water, Sir Richard. I can indeed. I beg you not to disturb yourself."

"No, no, I insist that you do not. I shall return immediately. Please do not send for anything."

Before the curator could renew his protestations Sir Richard had passed through the door and disappeared down the corridor.

Mr. Buzzby shrugged his shoulders and returned to his desk. "A most extraordinary person," he muttered. "Erudite and original, but queer. Decidedly queer. Still, it is pleasant to reflect that he has read my brochure. A scholar of his distinction might very pardonably have overlooked it. He called it a scholarly work. A scholarly work. Hmm. Very gratifying, I'm sure."

Mr. Buzzby clipped and lit a cigar.

"Of course he is wrong about the Book of the Dead," he mused. "Osiris was a most benevolent god. It is true that the Egyptians feared him, but only because he was supposed to judge the dead. There was nothing essentially evil or cruel about him. Sir Richard is quite wrong about that. It is curious that a man so eminent could go so sensationally astray. I can use no other phrase. Sensationally astray. I really believe that my arguments impressed him, though. I could see that he was impressed."

The curator's pleasant reflections were coarsely and unexpectedly interrupted by a shout in the corridor. "Get them extinguishers down! Quick, you bastard!"

The curator gasped and rose hastily to his feet. Profanity violated all the rules of the museum and he had always firmly insisted that the rules should be obeyed. Striding quickly to the door he threw it open and stared incredulously down the corridor.

"What was that?" he cried. "Did any one call?"

He heard hurried steps and the sound of someone shouting, and then an attendant appeared at the end of the corridor. "Come quickly, sir!" he exclaimed. "There's fire and smoke comin' out of the basement!"

Mr. Buzzby groaned. What a dreadful thing to happen when he had such a distinguished guest! He raced down the corridor and seized the attendant angrily by the arm. "Did Sir Richard get out?" he demanded. "Answer me! Is Sir Richard down there now?"

"Who?" gasped the attendant.

"The gentleman who went down a few minutes ago, you idiot. A tall gentleman wearing a blue coat?"

"I dunno, sir. I didn't see nobody come up."

"Good God!" Mr. Buzzby was frantic. "We must get him out immediately. I believe that he was ill. He's probably fainted."

He strode to the end of the corridor and stared down the smoke-filled staircase leading to the lavatory. Immediately beneath him three attendants were cautiously advancing. Wet handkerchiefs, bound securely about their faces, protected them from the acrid fumes, and each held at arm's length a cylindrical fire extinguisher. As they descended the stairs they squirted the liquid contents of the extinguishers into the rapidly rising spirals of lethal blue smoke.

"It was much worse a minute ago," exclaimed the attendant at Mr. Buzzby's elbow. "The smoke was thicker and had a most awful smell. Like them dinosaur eggs smelt when you first unpacked 'em last spring, sir."

The attendants had now reached the base of the staircase and were peering cautiously into the lavatory. For a moment they peered in silence, and then one of them shouted up at Mr. Buzzby. "The smoke's dreadfully dense here, sir. We can't see any flames. Shall we go in, sir?"

"Yes, do!" Mr. Buzzby's voice was tragically shrill. "Do all you can. Please!"

The attendants disappeared into the lavatory and the curator waited with an agonized and expectant ear. His heart was wrung at the thought of the fate which had in all probability overtaken his distinguished guest, but he could not think of anything further to do. Sinister forebodings crowded into his mind, but he was powerless to act.

Then it was that the shrieks commenced. From whatever cause arising they were truly ghastly, but they began so suddenly, so unexpectedly, that at first the curator could form no theory as to what had caused them. They issued so horribly and suddenly from the lavatory, echoing and re-echoing through the empty corridors, that the curator could only stare and gasp.

But when they became fairly coherent, when the screams of affright turned to appeals for mercy, for pity, and when the language in which they found grim expression changed too, becoming familiar to the curator but incomprehensible to the man beside him, a dreadful incident occurred which the latter has never been able to consign to a merciful mnemonic oblivion.

The curator fell upon his knees, literally went down upon his knees at the head of the staircase and raised both arms in an unmistakable gesture of supplication. And then from his ashen lips there poured a torrent of grotesque gibberish:

"sdmw stn Osiris! sdmw stn Osiris! sdmw stn Osiris! sdm-f Osiris! Oh, sdm-f Osiris! sdmw stn Osiris!"

"Fool!" A muffled form emerged from the lavatory and ponderously ascended the stairs. "Fool! You—you have sinned irretrievably!" The voice was guttural, harsh, remote, and seemed to come from an immeasurable distance.

"Sir Richard! Sir Richard!" The curator got stumblingly to his feet and staggered toward the ascending figure. "Protect me, Sir Richard. There's something unspeakable down there. I thought— for a moment I thought—Sir Richard, did you *see* it? Did you hear anything? those shrieks—"

But Sir Richard did not reply. He did not even look at the curator. He brushed past the unfortunate man as though he were a mere meddling fool, and grimly began to climb the stairs that led to the Hall of Egyptian Antiquities. He ascended so rapidly that the curator could not catch up with him, and before the frightened man had reached the half-way landing his steps were resounding on the tiled floor above.

"Wait, Sir Richard!" shrieked Buzzby. "Wait, please! I am sure that you can explain everything. I am afraid. Please wait for me!"

A spasm of coughing seized him, and at that moment there ensued a most dreadful crash. Fragments of broken glass tinkled suggestively upon the stone floor, and awoke ominous echoes in the corridor and up and down the winding stairway. Mr. Buzzby clung to the banisters and moaned. His face was purplish and distorted with fear and beads of sweat glistened on his high forehead. For a moment he remained thus cowering and whimpering on the staircase. Then, miraculously, his courage returned. He ascended the last flight three steps at a time and dashed wildly forward.

An intolerable thought had abruptly been born in the poor, bewildered brain of Mr. Buzzby. It had suddenly occurred to him that Sir Richard was an impostor, a murderous madman intent only upon destruction, and that his collections were in immediate danger. Whatever Mr. Buzzby's human deficiencies, in his professional capacity he was conscientious and aggressive to an almost abnormal degree. And the crash had been unmistakable and susceptible of only one explanation. Mr. Buzzby completely forgot his fear in his concern for his precious collections. Sir Richard had smashed one of the cases and was extracting its contents! There was little doubt in Mr. Buzzby's mind as to which of the cases Sir Richard had smashed. "The Luxor remains can never be duplicated," he moaned. "I have been horribly duped!"

Suddenly he stopped, and stared. At the very entrance to the Hall lay an assortment of garments which he instantly recognized. There was the blue Chinchilla coat and the Alpine Homburg with its high tapering crown, and the blue silk muffler that had concealed so effectively the face of his visitor. And on the very top of the heap lay a pair of yellow suede gloves.

"Good God!" muttered Mr. Buzzby. "The man has shed all of his clothes!"

He stood there for a moment staring in utter bewilderment and then with long, hysterical strides he advanced into the hall. "A hopeless maniac," he muttered, under his breath. "A sheer, raving lunatic. Why did I not—"

Then, abruptly, he ceased to reproach himself. He forgot entirely his folly, the heap of clothes, and the smashed case. Everything that had up to that moment occupied his mind was instantly extruded and he shriveled and shrank with fear. Never had the unwilling gaze of Mr. Buzzby encountered such a sight.

Mr. Buzzby's visitor was bending over the shattered case and only his back was visible. But it was not an ordinary back. In a lucid, unemotional moment Mr. Buzzby would have called it a nasty, malignant back, but in juxtaposition with the crown that topped it there is no Aryan polysyllable suggestive enough to describe it. For the crown was very tall and ponderous with jewels and unspeakably luminous, and it accentuated the vileness of the back. It was a green back. *Sapless* was the word that ran through Mr. Buzzby's mind as he stood and stared at it. And it was wrinkled, too, horribly wrinkled, all crisscrossed with centuried grooves.

Mr. Buzzby did not even notice his visitor's neck, which glistened and was as thin as a beanpole, nor the small round scaly head that bobbed and nodded ominously. He saw only the hideous back, and the unbelievably awesome crown. The crown shed a fiery radiance upon the reddish tiles of the dim, vast hall, and the starkly nude body twisted and turned and writhed shockingly.

Black horror clutched at Mr. Buzzby's throat, and his lips trembled as though he were about to cry out. But he spoke no word. He had staggered back against the wall and was making curious futile gestures with his arms, as though he sought to embrace the darkness, to wrap the darkness in the hall about him, to make himself as inconspicuous as possible and invisible to the thing that was bending over the case. But apparently he soon found to his infinite dismay that the thing was aware of his presence, and as it turned slowly toward him he made no further attempt to obliterate himself, but went down on his knees and screamed and screamed and screamed.

Silently the figure advanced toward him. It seemed to glide rather than to walk, and in its terribly lean arms it held a queer assortment of brilliant scarlet bones. And it cackled loathsomely as it advanced.

And then it was that Mr. Buzzby's sanity departed utterly. He groveled and gibbered and dragged himself along the floor like a man in the grip of an instantaneous catalepsy. And all the while he murmured incoherently about how spotless he was and would Osiris spare him and how he longed to reconcile himself with Osiris.

But the figure, when it got to him, merely stooped and breathed on him. Three times it breathed on his ashen face and one could almost see the face shrivel and blacken beneath its warm breath. For some time it remained in a stooping posture, glaring glassily, and when it arose Mr. Buzzby made no effort to detain it. Holding the scarlet bones very firmly in its horribly thin arms it glided rapidly away in the direction of the stairs. The attendants did not see it descend. No one ever saw it again.

And when the coroner, arriving in response to the tardy summons of an attendant, examined Mr. Buzzby's body, the conclusion was unavoidable that the curator had been dead for a long, long time.

Dennis Etchison appears to be normal enough when you meet him, but anybody capable of rendering so clearly the horrors of the psyche and our world cannot be that normal. He evokes extraordinarily chilling moods and terrors in the tradition of Beaumont, Matheson, and Bradbury. This haunting was one of three 1976 World Fantasy Award nominees from Kirby McCauley's 1976 World Fantasy Award-winning *Frights*. The horror introduced makes the specter of a gasoline shortage a bit more palatable.

It Only Comes Out at Night

by DENNIS ETCHISON

If you leave L.A. by way of San Bernardino, headed for Route 66 and points east, you must cross the Mojave Desert.

Even after Needles and the border, however, there is no relief; the dry air only thins further as the long, relentless climb continues in earnest. Flagstaff is still almost two hundred miles, and Winslow, Gallup, and Albuquerque are too many hours away to think of making without food, rest and, mercifully, sleep.

It is like this: the car runs hot, hotter than it ever has before, the plies of the tires expand and contract until the sidewalls begin to shimmy slightly as they spin on over the miserable Arizona roads, giving up a faint odor like burning hair from between the treads, as the windshield colors over with essence of honeybee, wasp, dragonfly, mayfly, June bug, ladybug and the like, and the radiator, clotted with the bodies of countless Kamikaze insects, hisses like a moribund lizard in the sun. . . .

All of which means, of course, that if you are traveling that way between May and September, you move by night.

Only by night.

For there are, after all, dawn check-in motels, Do Not Disturb signs for bungalow doorknobs; there are diners for midafternoon breakfasts, coffee by the carton; there are twenty-four-hour filling stations bright as dreams—Whiting Brothers, Conoco, Terrible Herbst—their flags as unfamiliar as their names, with ice machines, soda machines, candy machines; and there are the sudden, unexpected Rest Areas, just off the highway, with brick bathrooms and showers and electrical outlets, constructed especially for those who are weary, out of money, behind schedule. . . .

So McClay had had to learn, the hard way.

He slid his hands to the bottom of the steering wheel and peered ahead into the darkness, trying to relax. But the wheel stuck to his fingers like warm candy. Off somewhere to his left, the horizon flickered with pearly luminescence, then faded again to black. This time he did not bother to look. Sometimes, though, he wondered just how far away the lightning was striking; not once during the night had the sound of its thunder reached him here in the car.

In the back seat, his wife moaned.

The trip out had turned all but unbearable for her. Four days it had taken, instead of the expected two and a half; he made a great effort not to think of it, but the memory hung over the car like a thunderhead.

It had been a blur, a fever dream. Once, on the second day, he had been passed by a churning bus, its silver sides blinding him until he noticed a Mexican woman in one of the window seats. She was not looking at him. She was holding a swooning infant to the glass, squeezing water onto its head from a plastic baby bottle to keep it from passing out.

McClay sighed and fingered the buttons on the car radio.

He knew he would get nothing from the AM or FM bands, not out here, but he clicked it on anyway. He left the volume and tone controls down, so as not to wake Evvie. Then he punched the seldom-used middle button, the shortwave band, and raised the gain carefully until he could barely hear the radio over the hum of the tires.

Static.

Slowly he swept the tuner across the bandwidth, but there was only white noise. It reminded him a little of the summer rain yesterday, starting back, the way it had sounded bouncing off the windows.

He was about to give up when he caught a voice, crackling, drifting in and out. He worked the knob like a safe-cracker, zeroing in on the signal.

A few bars of music. A tone, then the voice again. ". . . Greenwich Mean Time." Then the station ID.

It was the Voice of America Overseas Broadcast.

He grunted disconsolately and killed it.

His wife stirred.

"Why'd you turn it off?" she murmured. "I was listening to that. Good. Program."

"Take it easy," he said, "easy, you're still asleep. We'll be stopping soon."

". . . Only comes out at night," he heard her say, and then she was lost again in the blankets.

He pressed the glove compartment, took out one of the Automobile Club guides. It was already clipped open. McClay flipped on the overhead light and drove with one hand, reading over—for the hundredth time?—the list of motels that lay ahead. He knew the list by heart, but seeing the names again reassured him somehow. Besides, it helped to break the monotony.

It was the kind of place you never expect to find in the middle of a long night, a bright place with buildings (a building, at least) and cars, other cars drawn off the highway to be together in the protective circle of light.

A Rest Area.

He would have spotted it without the sign. Elevated sodium vapor lighting bathed the scene in an almost peach-colored glow, strikingly different from the cold blue-white sentinels of the Interstate Highway. He had seen other Rest Area signs on the way out, probably even this one. But in daylight the signs had meant nothing more to him than Frontage Road or Business District Next Right. He wondered if it was the peculiar warmth of light that made the small island of blacktop appear so inviting.

McClay decelerated, downshifted, and left Interstate 40.

The car dipped and bumped, and he was aware of the new level of sound from the engine as it geared down for the first time in hours.

He eased in next to a Pontiac Firebird, toed the emergency brake, and cut the ignition.

He allowed his eyes to close and his head to sink back into the headrest. At last.

The first thing he noticed was the quiet.

It was deafening. His ears literally began to ring, with the high-pitched whine of a late-night TV test pattern.

The second thing he noticed was a tingling at the tip of his tongue.

It brought to mind a picture of a snake's tongue. Picking up electricity from the air, he thought.

The third was the rustling awake of his wife, in back.

She pulled herself up. "Are we sleeping now? Why are the lights . . . ?"

He saw the outline of her head in the mirror. "It's just a rest stop, hon. I—the car needs a break." Well, it was true, wasn't it? "You want the rest room? There's one back there, see it?"

"Oh my God."

"What's the matter now?"

"Leg's asleep. Listen, are we or are we not going to get a—"

"There's a motel coming up." He didn't say that they wouldn't hit the one he had marked in the book for another couple of hours; he didn't want to argue. He knew she needed the rest—he needed it too, didn't he? "Think I'll have some more of that coffee, though," he said.

"Isn't any more," she yawned.

The door slammed.

Now he was able to recognize the ringing in his ears for what it was: the sound of his own blood. It almost succeeded in replacing the steady drone of the car.

He twisted around, fishing over the back of the seat for the ice chest.

There should be a couple of Cokes left, at least.

His fingers brushed the basket next to the chest, riffling the edges of maps and tour books, by now reshuffled haphazardly over the first-aid kit he had packed himself (tourniquet, forceps, scissors, ammonia inhalants, Merthiolate, triangular bandage, compress, adhesive bandages, tannic acid) and the fire extinguisher, the extra carton of cigarettes, the remainder of a half-gallon of drinking water, the thermos (which Evvie said was empty, and why would she lie?).

He popped the top of a can.

Through the side window he saw Evvie disappearing around the corner of the building. She was wrapped to the gills in her blanket.

He opened the door and slid out, his back aching.

He stood there blankly, the unnatural light washing over him.

He took a long, sweet pull from the can. Then he started walking.

The Firebird was empty.

And the next car, and the next.

Each car he passed looked like the one before it, which seemed crazy until he realized that it must be the work of the light. It cast an even, eerie tan over the baked metal tops, like orange sunlight through air thick with suspended particles. Even the windshields appeared to be filmed over with a thin layer of settled dust. It made him think of country roads, sundowns.

He walked on.

He heard his footsteps echo with surprising clarity, resounding down the staggered line of parked vehicles. Finally it dawned on him (and now he knew how tired he really was) that the cars must actually have people in them—sleeping people. Of course. Well, hell, he thought, watching his step, I wouldn't want to wake anyone. The poor devils.

Besides the sound of his footsteps, there was only the distant *swish* of an occasional, very occasional car on the highway; from here, even that was only a distant hush, growing and then subsiding like waves on a nearby shore.

He reached the end of the line, turned back.

Out of the corner of his eye he saw, or thought he saw, a movement by the building.

It would be Evvie, shuffling back.

He heard the car door slam.

He recalled something he had seen in one of the tourist towns in New Mexico: circling the park—in Taos, that was where they had been—he had glimpsed an ageless Indian, wrapped in typical blanket, ducking out of sight into the doorway of a gift shop; with the blanket over his head that way, the Indian had somehow resembled an Arab, or so it had seemed to him at the time.

He heard another car door slam.

That was the same day—was it only last week?—that she had noticed the locals driving with their headlights on (in honor of something or other, some regional election, perhaps: " 'My face speaks for itself,' drawled Herman J. 'Fashio' Trujillo, Candidate for Sheriff"); she had insisted at first that it must be a funeral procession, though for whom she could not guess.

McClay came to the car, stretched a last time and crawled back in.

Evvie was bundled safely again in the back seat.

He lit a quick cigarette, expecting to hear her voice any second, complaining, demanding that he roll down the windows, at least, and so forth. But, as it turned out, he was able to sit undisturbed as he smoked it down almost to the filter.

Paguate. Bluewater. Thoreau.

He blinked.

Klagetoh. Joseph City. Ash Fork.

He blinked and tried to focus his eyes from the taillights a half-mile ahead to the bug-spattered glass, then back again.

Petrified Forest National Park.

He blinked, refocusing. But it did no good.

A twitch started on the side of his face, close by the corner of his eye.

Rehoboth.

He strained at a road sign, the names and mileages, but instead a seemingly endless list of past and future stops and detours shimmered before his mind's eye.

I've had it, he thought. Now, suddenly, it was catching up with him, the hours of repressed fatigue; he felt a rushing out of something from his chest. No way to make that motel—hell, I can't even remember the name of it now. Check the book. But it doesn't matter. The eyes. *Can't control my eyes anymore.*

(He had already begun to hallucinate things like tree trunks and cows and mack trucks speeding toward him on the highway. The cow had been straddling the broken line; in the last few minutes its lowing, deep and regular, had become almost inviting.)

Well, he could try for *any* motel. Whatever turned up next.

But how much farther would that be?

He ground his teeth together, feeling the pulsing at his temples. He struggled to remember the last sign.

The next town. It might be a mile. Five miles. Fifty.

Think! He said it, he thought it, he didn't know which.

If he could just pull over, pull over right now and lie down for a few minutes—

He seemed to see clear ground ahead. No rocks, no ditch. The shoulder, just ahead.

Without thinking he dropped into neutral and coasted, aiming for it.

The car glided to a stop.

God, he thought.

He forced himself to turn, reach into the back seat.

The lid to the chest was already off. He dipped his fingers into the ice and retrieved two half-melted cubes, lifted them into the front seat, and began rubbing them over his forehead.

He let his eyes close, seeing dull lights fire as he daubed at the lids, the rest of his face, the forehead again. As he slipped the ice into his mouth and chewed, it broke apart as easily as snow.

He took a deep breath. He opened his eyes again.

At that moment a huge tanker roared past, slamming an aftershock of air into the side of the car. The car rocked like a boat at sea.

No. It was no good.

So. So he could always turn back, couldn't he? And why not? The Rest Area was only twenty, twenty-five minutes behind him. (Was that all?) He could pull out and hang a U and turn back, just like that. And then sleep. It would be safer there. With luck, Evvie wouldn't even know. An hour's rest, maybe two; that was all he would need.

Unless—was there another Rest Area ahead?

How soon?

He knew that the second wind he felt now wouldn't last, not for more than a few minutes. No, it wasn't worth the chance.

He glanced in the rearview mirror.

Evvie was still down, a lumpen mound of blanket and hair.

Above her body, beyond the rear window, the raised headlights of another monstrous truck, closing ground fast.

He made the decision.

He slid into first and swung out in a wide arc, well ahead of the blast of the truck, and worked up to fourth gear. He was thinking about the warm, friendly lights he had left behind.

He angled in next to the Firebird and cut the lights.

He started to reach for a pillow from the back, but why bother? It would probably wake Evvie, anyway.

He wadded up his jacket, jammed it against the passenger armrest, and lay down.

First he crossed his arms over his chest. Then behind his head. Then he gripped his hands between his knees. Then he was on his back again, his hands at his sides, his feet cramped against the opposite door.

His eyes were wide open.

He lay there, watching chain lightning flash on the horizon.

Finally he let out a breath that sounded like all the breaths he had ever taken going out at once, and drew himself up.

He got out and walked over to the rest room.

Inside, white tiles and bare lights. His eyes felt raw, peeled. Finished, he washed his hands but not his face; that would only make sleep more difficult.

Outside again and feeling desperately out of synch, he listened to his shoes falling hollowly on the cement.

"Next week we've got to get organized. . . ."

He said this, he was sure, because he heard his voice coming back to him, though with a peculiar empty resonance. Well, this time tomorrow night he would be home. As unlikely as that seemed now.

He stopped, bent for a drink from the water fountain.

The footsteps did not stop.

Now wait, he thought, I'm pretty far gone, but—

He swallowed, his ears popping.

The footsteps stopped.

Hell, he thought, I've been pushing too hard. We. She. No, it was my fault, my plan this time. To drive nights, sleep days. Just so. As long as you *can* sleep.

Easy, take it easy.

He started walking again, around the corner and back to the lot.

At the corner, he thought he saw something move at the edge of his vision.

He turned quickly to the right, in time for a fleeting glimpse of something—someone—hurrying out of sight into the shadows.

Well, the other side of the building housed the women's rest room. Maybe it was Evvie.

He glanced toward the car, but it was blocked from view.

He walked on.

Now the parking area resembled an oasis lit by firelight. Or a western camp, the cars rimming the lot on three sides in the manner of wagons gathered against the night.

Strength in numbers, he thought.

Again, each car he passed looked at first like every other. It was the flat light, of course. And of course they were the same cars he had seen a half-hour ago. And the light still gave them a dusty, abandoned look.

He touched a fender.

It *was* dusty.

But why shouldn't it be? His own car had probably taken on quite a layer of grime after so long on these roads.

He touched the next car, the next.

Each was so dirty that he could have carved his name without scratching the paint.

He had an image of himself passing this way again—God forbid—a year from now, say, and finding the same cars parked here. The *same* ones.

What if, he wondered tiredly, what if some of these cars had been abandoned? Overheated, exploded, broken down one fine midday and left here by owners who simply never returned? Who would ever know? Did the Highway Patrol, did anyone bother to check? Would an automobile be preserved here for months, years by the elements, like a snakeskin shed beside the highway?

It was a thought, anyway.

His head was buzzing.

He leaned back and inhaled deeply, as deeply as he could at this altitude.

But he did hear something. A faint tapping. It reminded him of running feet, until he noticed the lamp overhead:

There were hundreds of moths beating against the high fixture, their soft bodies tapping as they struck and circled and returned again and again to the lens; the light made their wings translucent.

He took another deep breath and went on to his car.

He could hear it ticking, cooling down, before he got there. Idly he rested a hand on the hood. Warm, of course. The tires? He touched the left front. It was taut, hot as a loaf from the oven. When he took his hand away, the color of the rubber came off on his palm like burned skin.

He reached for the door handle.

A moth fluttered down onto the fender. He flicked it off, his finger leaving a streak on the enamel.

He looked closer and saw a wavy, mottled pattern covering his unwashed car, and then he remembered. The rain, yesterday afternoon. The rain had left blotches in the dust, marking the finish as if with dirty fingerprints.

He glanced over at the next car.

It, too, had the imprint of dried raindrops—but, close up, he saw that the marks were superimposed in layers, over and over again.

The Firebird had been through a great many rains.

He touched the hood.

Cold.

He removed his hand, and a dead moth clung to his thumb. He tried to brush it off on the hood, but other moth bodies stuck in its place. Then he saw countless shriveled, mummified moths pasted over the hood and top like peeling chips of paint. His fingers were coated with the powder from their wings.

He looked up.

High above, backed by banks of roiling cumulous clouds, the swarm of moths vibrated about the bright, protective light.

So the Firebird had been here a very long time.

He wanted to forget it, to let it go. He wanted to get back in the car. He wanted to lie down, lock it out, everything. He wanted to got to sleep and wake up in Los Angeles.

He couldn't.

He inched around the Firebird until he was facing the line of cars. He hesitated a beat, then started moving.

A LeSabre.

A Cougar.

A Chevy van.

A Corvair.

A Ford.

A Mustang.

And every one was overlaid with grit.

He paused by the Mustang. Once—how long ago?—it had been a luminous candy-apple red; probably belonged to a teenager. Now the windshield was opaque, the body dulled to a peculiar shade he could not quite place.

Feeling like a voyeur at a drive-in movie theater, McClay crept to the driver's window.

Dimly he perceived two large outlines in the front seat.

He raised his hand.

Wait.

What if there were two people sitting there on the other side of the window, watching him?

He put it out of his mind. Using three fingers, he cut a swath through the scum on the glass and pressed close.

The shapes were there. Two headrests.

He started to pull away.

And happened to glance into the back seat.

He saw a long, uneven form.

A leg, the back of a thigh. Blond hair, streaked with shadows. The collar of a coat.

And, delicate and silvery, a spider web, spun between the hair and collar.

He jumped back.

His leg struck the old Ford. He spun around, his arms straight. The blood was pounding in his ears.

He rubbed out a spot on the window of the Ford and scanned the inside.

The figure of a man, slumped on the front seat.

The man's head lay on a jacket. No, it was not a jacket. It was a large, formless stain. In the filtered light, McClay could see that it had dried to a dark brown.

It came from the man's mouth.

No, not from the mouth.

The throat had a long, thin slash across it, reaching nearly to the ear.

He stood there stiffly, his back almost arched, his eyes jerking, trying to close, trying not to close. The lot, the even light reflecting thinly from each windshield, the Corvair, the van, the Cougar, the LeSabre, the suggestion of a shape within each one.

The pulse in his ears muffled and finally blotted out the distant gearing of a truck up on the highway, the death-rattle of the moths against the seductive lights.

He reeled.

He seemed to be hearing again the breaking open of doors and the scurrying of padded feet across paved spaces.

He remembered the first time. He remembered the sound of a second door slamming in a place where no new car but his own had arrived.

Or—had it been the door to his car slamming a second time, after Evvie had gotten back in?

If so, how? Why?

And there had been the sight of someone moving, trying to slip away.

And for some reason now he remembered the Indian in the tourist town, slipping out of sight in the doorway of that gift shop. He held his eyelids down until he saw the shop again, the window full of kachinas and tin gods and tapestries woven in a secret language.

At last he remembered it clearly: the Indian had not been entering the store. *He had been stealing away.*

McClay did not yet understand what it meant, but he opened his eyes, as if for the first time in centuries, and began to run toward his car.

If I could only catch my goddamn breath, he thought.

He tried to hold on. He tried not to think of her, of what might have happened the first time, of what he might have been carrying in the back seat ever since.

He had to find out.

He fought his way back to the car, against a rising tide of fear he could not stem.

He told himself to think of other things, of things he knew he could control: mileages and motel bills, time zones and weather reports, spare tires and flares and tubeless repair tools, hydraulic jack and Windex and paper towels and tire iron and socket wrench and waffle cushion and traveler's checks and credit cards and Dopp Kit (toothbrush and paste, deodorant, shaver, safety blade, brushless cream) and sunglasses and Sight Savers and tear-gas pen and fiber-tip pens and portable radio and alkaline batteries and fire extinguisher and desert water bag and tire gauge and motor oil and his money belt with identification sealed in plastic—

In the back of his car, under the quilt, nothing moved, not even when he finally lost his control and his mind in a thick, warm scream.

David Drake is the assistant editor of *Whispers* magazine and a writer of powerful heroic fantasy, horror, and science fiction. His stories are often brutal, no room for laughter or games. People venture forth, quest, do battle, and generally meet horrible deaths. His tales have long been making annual appearances in Jerry Page's *Year's Best Horror* volumes, and this original from the pages of *Whispers* magazine earned David a 1976 World Fantasy Award nomination.

The Barrow Troll

by DAVID DRAKE

Playfully, Ulf Womanslayer twitched the cord bound to his saddle horn. "Awake, priest? Soon you can get to work."

"My work is saving souls, not being dragged into the wilderness by madmen," Johann muttered under his breath. The other end of the cord was around his neck, not that of his horse. A trickle of blood oozed into his cassock from the reopened scab, but he was afraid to loosen the knot. Ulf might look back. Johann had already seen his captor go into a berserk rage. Over the Northerner's right shoulder rode his ax, a heavy hooked blade on a four-foot shaft. Ulf had swung it like a willow-wand when three Christian traders in Schleswig had seen the priest and tried to free him. The memory of the last man in three pieces as head and sword arm sprang from his spouting torso was still enough to roil Johann's stomach.

"We'll have a clear night with a moon, priest; a good night for our business." Ulf stretched and laughed aloud, setting a raven on a fir knot to squawking back at him. The berserker was following a ridge line that divided wooded slopes with a spine too thin-soiled to bear trees. The flanking forests still loomed above the riders. In three days now, Johann had seen no man but his captor, nor even a tendril of smoke from a lone cabin. Even the route they were taking to Parmavale was no mantrack but an accident of nature.

"So lonely," the priest said aloud.

Ulf hunched hugely in his bearskin and replied, "You soft folk in the south, you live too close anyway. Is it your Christ-god, do you think?"

"Hedeby's a city," the German priest protested, his fingers toying with his torn robe, "and my brother trades to Uppsala. . . . But why bring me to this manless waste?"

"Oh, there were men once, so the tale goes," Ulf said. Here in the empty forest he was more willing for conversation than he had been the first few days of their ride north. "Few enough, and long enough ago. But there were farms in Parmavale, and a lordling of sorts who went a-viking against the Irish. But then the troll came and the men went, and there was nothing left to draw others. So they thought."

"You Northerners believe in trolls, so my brother tells me," said the priest.

"Ay, long before the gold I'd heard of the Parma troll," the berserker agreed. "Ox-broad and stronger than ten men, shaggy as a denned bear."

"Like you," Johann said, in a voice more normal than caution would have dictated.

Blood fury glared in Ulf's eyes and he gave a savage jerk on the cord. "You'll think me a troll, priestling, if you don't do just as I say. I'll drink your blood hot if you cross me."

Johann, gagging, could not speak nor wished to.

With the miles the sky became a darker blue, the trees a blacker green. Ulf again broke the hoof-pummeled silence, saying, "No, I knew nothing of the gold until Thora told me."

The priest coughed to clear his throat. "Thora is your wife?" he asked.

"Wife? Ho!" Ulf brayed, his raucous laughter ringing like a demon's. "Wife? She was Hallstein's wife, and I killed her with all her house about her! But before that, she told me of the troll's horde, indeed she did. Would you hear that story?"

Johann nodded, his smile fixed. He was learning to recognize death as it bantered under the axhead.

"So," the huge Northerner began. "There was a bonder, Hallstein Kari's son, who followed the king to war but left his wife, that was Thora, behind to manage the stead. The first day I came by and took a sheep from the herdsman. I told him if he misliked it to send his master to me."

"Why did you do that?" the fat priest asked in surprise.

"Why? Because I'm Ulf, because I wanted the sheep. A woman acting a man's part, it's unnatural anyway.

"The next day I went back to Hallstein's stead, and the flocks had already been driven in. I went into the garth around the buildings and called for the master to come out and fetch me a sheep." The berserker's teeth ground audibly as he remembered. Johann saw his knuckles whiten on the ax helve and stiffened in terror.

"Ho!" Ulf shouted, bringing his left hand down on the shield slung at his horse's flank. The copper boss rang like thunder in the clouds. "She came out," Ulf grated, "and her hair was red. 'All our sheep are penned,' says she, 'but you're in good time for the butchering.' And from out the hall came her three brothers and the men of the stead, ten in all. They were in full armor and their swords were in their hands. And they would have slain me, Ulf Otgeir's son, *me,* at a woman's word. Forced me to run from a woman!"

The berserker was snarling his words to the forest. Johann knew he watched a scene that had been played a score of times with only the trees to witness. The rage of disgrace burned in Ulf like pitch in a pine faggot, and his mind was lost to everything except the past.

"But I came back," he continued, "in the darkness, when all feasted within the hall and drank their ale to victory. Behind the hall burned a log fire to roast a sheep. I killed the two there, and I thrust one of the logs half burnt up under the eaves. Then at the door I waited until those within noticed the heat and Thora looked outside.

" 'Greetings, Thora,' I said. 'You would not give me mutton, so

I must roast men tonight.' She asked me for speech. I knew she
was fey, so I listened to her. And she told me of the Parma lord
and the treasure he brought back from Ireland, gold and gems.
And she said it was cursed that a troll should guard it, and that I
must needs have a mass priest, for the troll could not cross a
Christian's fire and I should slay him then."

"Didn't you spare her for that?" Johann quavered, more fearful
of silence than he was of misspeaking.

"Spare her? No, nor any of her house," Ulf thundered back.
"She might better have asked the flames for mercy, as she knew.
The fire was at her hair. I struck her, and never was women better made for an ax to bite—she cleft like a waxen doll, and I
threw the pieces back. Her brothers came then, but one and one
and one through the doorway, and I killed each in his turn. No
more came. When the roof fell, I left them with the ash for a
headstone and went my way to find a mass priest—to find you,
priestling." Ulf, restored to good humor by the climax of his own
tale, tweaked the lead cord again.

Johann choked onto his horse's neck, nauseated as much by the
story as by the noose. At last he said, thick-voiced, "Why do you
trust her tale if she knew you would kill her with it or not?"

"She was fey," Ulf chuckled, as if that explained everything.
"Who knows what a man will do when his death is upon him? Or
a woman," he added more thoughtfully.

They rode on in growing darkness. With no breath of wind to
stir them, the trees stood as dead as the rocks underfoot.

"Will you know the place?" the German asked suddenly.
"Shouldn't we camp now and go on in the morning?"

"I'll know it," Ulf grunted. "We're not far now—we're going
down hill, can't you feel?" He tossed his bare haystack of hair,
silvered into a false sheen of age by the moon. He continued,
"The Parma lord sacked a dozen churches, so they say, and then
one more with more of gold than the twelve besides, but also the
curse. And he brought it back with him to Parma, and there it
rests in his barrow, the troll guarding it. That I have on Thora's
word."

"But she hated you!"

"She was fey."

They were into the trees, and looking to either side Johann

could see hill slopes rising away from them. They were in a valley, Parma or another. Scraps of wattle and daub, the remains of a house or a garth fence, thrust up to the right. The first that had grown through it were generations old. Johann's stubbled tonsure crawled in the night air.

"She said there was a clearing," the berserker muttered, more to himself than his companion. Johann's horse stumbled. The priest clutched the cord reflexively as it tightened. When he looked up at his captor, he saw the huge Northerner fumbling at his shield's fastenings. For the first time that evening, a breeze stirred. It stank of death.

"Others have been here before us," said Ulf needlessly.

A row of skulls, at least a score of them, stared blank-eyed from atop stakes rammed through their spinal openings. To one, dried sinew still held the lower jaw in a ghastly rictus; the others had fallen away into the general scatter of bones whitening the ground. All of them were human or could have been. They were mixed with occasional glimmers of buttons and rust smears. The freshest of the grisly trophies was very old, perhaps decades old. Too old to explain the reek of decay.

Ulf wrapped his left fist around the twin handles of his shield. It was a heavy circle of linden wood, faced with leather. Its rim and central boss were of copper, and rivets of bronze and copper decorated the face in a serpent pattern.

"Good that the moon is full," Ulf said, glancing at the bright orb still tangled in the fir branches. "I fight best in the moonlight. We'll let her rise the rest of the way, I think."

Johann was trembling. He joined his hands about his saddle horn to keep from falling off the horse. He knew Ulf might let him jerk and strangle there, even after dragging him across half the northlands. The humor of the idea might strike him. Johann's rosary, his crucifix—everything he had brought from Germany or purchased in Schleswig save his robe—had been left behind in Hedeby when the berserker awakened him in his bed. Ulf had jerked a noose to near-lethal tautness and whispered that he needed a priest, that this one would do, but that there were others should this one prefer to feed crows. The disinterested bloodlust in Ulf's tone had been more terrifying than the threat itself.

Johann had followed in silence to the waiting horses. In despair, he wondered again if a quick death would not have been better than this lingering one that had ridden for weeks a mood away from him.

"It looks like a palisade for a house," the priest said aloud in what he pretended was a normal voice.

"That's right," Ulf replied, giving his ax an exploratory heft that sent shivers of moonlight across the blade. "There was a hall here, a big one. Did it burn, do you think?" His knees sent his roan gelding forward in a shambling walk past the line of skulls. Johann followed of necessity.

"No, rotted away," the berserker said, bending over to study the postholes.

"You said it was deserted a long time," the priest commented. His eyes were fixed straight forward. One of the skulls was level with his waist and close enough to bite him, could it turn on its stake.

"There was time for the house to fall in; the ground is damp," Ulf agreed. "But the stakes, then, have been replaced. Our troll keeps his front fence new, priestling."

Johann swallowed, said nothing.

Ulf gestured briefly. "Come on, you have to get your fire ready. I want it really holy."

"But we don't sacrifice with fires. I don't know how—"

"Then learn!" the berserker snarled with a vicious yank that drew blood and a gasp from the German. "I've seen how you Christ-shouters love to bless things. You'll bless me a fire, that's all. And if anything goes wrong and the troll spares you—I won't, priestling. I'll rive you apart if I have to come off a stake to do it!"

The horses walked slowly forward through brush and soggy rubble that had been a hall. The odor of decay grew stronger. The priest himself tried to ignore it, but his horse began to balk. The second time he was too slow with a heel to its ribs, and the cord nearly decapitated him. "Wait!" he wheezed. "Let me get down."

Ulf looked back at him, flat-eyed. At last he gave a brief crow-peck nod and swung himself out of the saddle. He looped both sets of reins on a small fir. Then, while Johann dismounted clumsily, he loosed the cord from his saddle and took it in his ax hand. The men walked forward without speaking.

"There, . . ." Ulf breathed.

The barrow was only a black-mouthed swell in the ground, its size denied by its lack of features. Such trees as had tried to grow on it had been broken off short over a period of years. Some of the stumps had wasted into crumbling depressions, while from others the wood fibers still twisted raggedly. Only when Johann matched the trees on the other side of the tomb to those beside him did he realize the scale on which the barrow was built: its entrance tunnel would pass a man walking upright, even a man Ulf's height.

"Lay your fire at the tunnel mouth," the berserker said, his voice subdued. "He'll be inside."

"You'll have to let me go—"

"I'll have to nothing!" Ulf was breathing hard. "We'll go closer, you and I, and you'll make a fire of the dead trees from the ground. Yes. . . ."

The Northerner slid forward in a pace that was cat-soft and never left the ground a finger's breadth. Strewn about them as if flung idly from the barrow mouth were scraps and gobbets of animals, the source of the fetid reek that filled the clearing. As his captor paused for a moment, Johann toed one of the bits over with his sandal. It was the hide and paws of something chiseltoothed, whether rabbit or other was impossible to say in the moonlight and state of decay. The skin was in tendrils, and the skull had been opened to empty the brains. Most of the other bits seemed of the same sort, little beasts, although a rank blotch on the mound's slope could have been a wolf hide. Whatever killed and feasted here was not fastidious.

"He stays close to hunt," Ulf rumbled. Then he added, "The long bones by the fence; they were cracked."

"Umm?"

"For marrow."

Quivering, the priest began gathering broken-off trees, none of them over a few feet high. They had been twisted off near the ground, save for a few whose roots lay bare in wizened fists. The crisp scales cut Johann's hands. He did not mind the pain. Under his breath he was praying that God would punish him, would torture him, but at least would save him free of this horrid demon that had snatched him away.

"Pile it there," Ulf directed, his axhead nodding toward the stone lip of the barrow. The entrance was corbeled out of heavy stones, then covered over with dirt and sods. Like the beast fragments around it, the opening was dead and stinking. Biting his tongue, Johann dumped his pile of brush and scurried back.

"There's light back down there," he whispered.

"Fire?"

"No, look—it's pale, it's moonlight. There's a hole in the roof of the tomb."

"Light for me to kill by," Ulf said with a stark grin. He looked over the low fireset, then knelt. His steel sparked into a nest of dry moss. When the tinder was properly alight, he touched a pitchy faggot to it. He dropped his end of the cord. The torchlight glinted from his face, white and coarse-pored where the tangles of hair and beard did not cover it. "Bless the fire, mass-priest," the berserker ordered in a quiet, terrible voice.

Stiff-featured and unblinking, Johann crossed the brushwood and said, "In nomine Patris, et Filii, et Spiritus Sancti, Amen."

"Don't light it yet," Ulf said. He handed Johann the torch. "It may be," the berserker added, "that you think to run if you get the chance. There is no Hell so deep that I will not come for you from it."

The priest nodded, white-lipped.

Ulf shrugged his shoulders to loosen his muscles and the bear hide that clothed them. Ax and shield rose and dipped like ships in a high sea.

"Ho! Troll! Barrow fouler! Corpse licker! Come and fight me, troll!"

There was no sound from the tomb.

Ulf's eyes began to glaze. He slashed his ax twice across the empty air and shouted again, "Troll! I'll spit on your corpse, I'll lay with your dog mother. Come and fight me, troll, or I'll wall you up like a rat with your filth!"

Johann stood frozen, oblivious even to the drop of pitch that sizzled on the web of his hand. The berserker bellowed again, wordlessly, gnashing at the rim of his shield so that the sound bubbled and boomed in the night.

And the tomb roared back to the challenge, a thunderous BAR BAR BAR even deeper than Ulf's.

Berserk, the Northerner leaped the brush pile and ran down the tunnel, his ax thrust out in front of him to clear the stone arches.

The tunnel sloped for a dozen paces into a timber-vaulted chamber too broad to leap across. Moonlight spilled through a circular opening onto flags slimy with damp and liquescence. Ulf, maddened, chopped high at the light. The ax burred inanely beneath the timbers.

Swinging a pair of swords, the troll leaped at Ulf. It was the size of a bear, grizzled in the moonlight. Its eyes burned red.

"Hi!" shouted Ulf and blocked the first sword in a shower of sparks on his axhead. The second blade bit into the shield rim, shaving a hand's length of copper and a curl of yellow linden from beneath it. Ulf thrust straight-armed, a blow that would have smashed like a battering ram had the troll not darted back. Both the combatants were shouting; their voices were dreadful in the circular chamber.

The troll jumped backward again. Ulf sprang toward him and only the song of the blades scissoring from either side warned him. The berserker threw himself down. The troll had leaped onto a rotting chest along the wall of the tomb and cut unexpectedly from above Ulf's shield. The big man's boots flew out from under him and he struck the floor on his back. His shield still covered his body.

The troll hurtled down splay-legged with a cry of triumph. Both bare feet slammed on Ulf's shield. The troll was even heavier than Ulf. Shrieking, the berserker pistoned his shield arm upward. The monster flew off, smashing against the timbered ceiling and caroming down into another of the chests. The rotted wood exploded under the weight in a flash of shimmering gold. The berserker rolled to his feet and struck overarm in the same motion. His lunge carried the axhead too far, into the rock wall in a flower of blue sparks.

The troll was up. The two killers eyed each other, edging sideways in the dimness. Ulf's right arm was numb to the shoulder. He did not realize it. The shaggy monster leaped with another double flashing and the ax moved too slowly to counter. Both edges spat chunks of linden as they withdrew. Ulf frowned, backed a step. His boot trod on an ewer that spun away from him. As he cried out, the troll grinned and hacked again like Death the Reaper. The shield-orb flattened as the top third of it split away. Ulf snarled and chopped at the troll's knees. It leaped above the steel and cut left-handed, its blade nocking the shaft an inch from Ulf's hand.

The berserker flung the useless remainder of his shield in the troll's face and ran. Johann's torch was an orange pulse in the triangular opening. Behind Ulf, a swordedge went *sring!* as it danced on the corbels. Ulf jumped the brush and whirled. "Now!" he cried to the priest, and Johann hurled his torch into the resin-jeweled wood.

The needles crackled up in the troll's face like a net of orange silk. The flames bellied out at the creature's rush but licked back caressingly over its mats of hair. The troll's swords cut at the fire. A shower of coals spit and crackled and made the beast howl.

"Burn, dog-spew!" Ulf shouted. "Burn, fish-guts!"

The troll's blades rang together once and again. For a moment it stood, a hillock of stained gray, as broad as the tunnel arches. Then it strode forward into the white heart of the blaze. The fire bloomed up, its roar leaping over the troll's shriek of agony. Ulf stepped forward. He held his ax with both hands. The flames sucked down from the motionless troll, and as they did, the shimmering arc of the axhead chopped into the beast's collarbone. One sword dropped and the left arm slumped loose.

The berserker's ax was buried to the helve in the troll's shoulder. The faggots were scattered, but the troll's hair was burning all over its body. Ulf pulled at his ax. The troll staggered, moaning. Its remaining sword pointed down at the ground. Ulf yanked again at his weapon and it slurped free. A thick velvet curtain of blood followed it. Ulf raised his dripping ax for another blow, but the troll tilted toward the withdrawn weapon, leaning forward, a smoldering rock. The body hit the ground, then flopped so that it lay on its back. The right arm was flung out at an angle.

"It was a man," Johann was whispering. He caught up a brand and held it close to the troll's face. "Look, look!" he demanded excitedly, "it's just an old man in bearskin. Just a man."

Ulf sagged over his ax as if it were a stake impaling him. His frame shuddered as he dragged air into it. Neither of the troll's swords had touched him, but reaction had left him weak as one death-wounded. "Go in," he wheezed. "Get a torch and lead me in."

"But . . . why—" the priest said, in sudden fear. His eyes met the berserker's and he swallowed back the rest of his protest. The torch threw highlights on the walls and flags as he trotted down the tunnel. Ulf's boots were ominous behind him.

The central chamber was austerely simple and furnished only with the six chests lining the back of it. There was no corpse, nor even a slab for one. The floor was gelatinous with decades' accumulation of foulness. The skidding tracks left by the recent combat marked paving long undisturbed. Only from the entrance to the chests was a path, black against the slime of decay, worn. It was toward the broken container and the objects which had spilled from it that the priest's eyes arrowed.

"Gold," he murmured. Then, "Gold! There must—the others— in God's name, there are five more and perhaps all of them—"

"Gold," Ulf grated terribly.

Johann ran to the nearest chest and opened it one-handed. The lid sagged wetly, but frequent use had kept it from swelling tight to the side panels. "Look at this crucifix!" the priest marveled. "And the torque, it must weigh pounds. And Lord in heaven, this—"

"Gold," the berserker repeated.

Johann saw the ax as it started to swing. He was turning with a chalice ornamented in enamel and pink gold. It hung in the air as he darted for safety. His scream and the dull belling of the cup as the ax divided it were simultaneous, but the priest was clear and Ulf was off balance. The berserker backhanded with force enough to drive the peen of his axhead through a sapling. His strength was too great for his footing. His feet skidded, and this time his head rang on the wall of the tomb.

Groggy, the huge berserker staggered upright. The priest was a scurrying blur against the tunnel entrance. "Priest!" Ulf shouted at the suddenly empty moonlight. He thudded up the flags of the tunnel. "Priest!" he shouted again.

The clearing was empty except for the corpse. Nearby, Ulf heard his roan whicker. He started for it, then paused. The priest—he could still be hiding in the darkness. While Ulf searched for him, he could be rifling the barrow, carrying off the gold behind his back. "Gold," Ulf said again. No one must take his gold. No one ever must find it unguarded.

"I'll kill you!" he screamed into the night. "I'll kill you all!"

He turned back to his barrow. At the entrance, still smoking, waited the body of what had been the troll.

SPECIAL AWARD— NON-PROFESSIONAL

CARCOSA

One of the unfortunate aspects of the recent boom in amateur presses is that fan publishers have concentrated on a few famous writers, Lovecraft and Howard as a rule, while other excellent fantasy writers of the period have been ignored. Carcosa was founded with the goal of saving such writers and their best work from a pulp graveyard. The concept of Carcosa was to collect the best fantasy stories of this genre's best, albeit less well known, authors, and to showcase these in mammoth deluxe limited editions, lavishly illustrated by major fantasy artists—in short, the type of book that collectors dream about but that no major publisher will attempt today—and to offer these books at the lowest possible price. It seemed an impossible dream.

The dreamer was Karl Edward Wagner. A writer in this field himself, Wagner had been reading and collecting science-fiction and fantasy since the mid-1950s and owns one of the major pulp collections in the world. As such, Wagner was aware of the wealth of first-rate fantasy fiction that languished in these crumbling pages. Further, a close friendship with *Weird Tales* great Manly Wade Wellman, precisely the sort of writer whose work had been unjustly neglected, made Wagner all the more determined to see that writers such as Wellman should receive the recognition they so deserved—and receive it *during* their lifetimes.

An admirer of the works of Robert W. Chambers, Wagner chose to call his publishing project *Carcosa,* after the haunted city mentioned by Chambers and Ambrose Bierce. Earlier, in the fan press boom of the late 1940s, there had existed a short-lived (one book) fan-publishing venture in Los Angeles called Carcosa House. To secure use of the name, Wagner contacted the four Carcosa House partners—William L. Crawford, Ted E. Dikty, Russell Hodgkins, and Frederick Shroyer—and received their permission, good will, and advice: Dikty went so far as to act as production manager for the first book.

There remained the problem of financing the project; at the time, Wagner was completing medical school, and Carcosa promised to be an expensive hobby. Fortunately, Wagner was quick to find backers in James Groce, a roommate and classmate at UNC School of Medicine, and in David Drake, who was finishing law school at nearby Duke University. Groce was also a fan and had a fondness for reckless ventures such as this promised to be. Drake was a writer as well as a fan of this genre. With Wagner as editor, the three men formed a partnership, and in 1972 Carcosa was born.

The first book from Carcosa was to be *Worse Things Waiting,* a collection of Manly Wade Wellman's best fantasy stories. This book had rather a fantastic history in itself: it was originally to have been published in the 1930s, but its publisher was a victim of the Depression; shortly after World War II, Arkham House listed *Worse Things Waiting* as a forthcoming title, but the project was shelved after Wellman and editor August Derleth had a disagreement. The Carcosa edition, with contents selected by Wagner, was a far more ambitious volume than either of the earlier attempts. In another bit of good fortune, longtime pulp dealer and collector Richard Minter was able to put Wagner in touch with Lee Brown Coye, an artist whose distinctive and macabre drawings had chilled readers of *Weird Tales* during the 1940s. Coye illustrated Carcosa's initial volume, and it was immediately evident that he had perfected his unique grotesqueries in his years of near obscurity.

Of the problems and delays in production encountered by Carcosa with its first volume, only another who has dabbled in amateur publishing may comprehend and sympathize. Biting bullets and tranquilizers, the three owners pressed onward in the face of all odds and logic. Finally, after a year in production, *Worse Things Waiting* was published. Fan response was extremely favorable, and at the First World Fantasy Convention in Providence, *Worse Things Waiting* won a World Fantasy Award as Best Collection, while Lee Brown Coye won the same award as Best Artist.

Fans asked for an encore. Carcosa returned two years later with *Far Lands Other Days,* a six hundred-page shelf-bender of the best fantasy and adventure stories of E. Hoffmann Price. To illustrate this collection, Carcosa sought out George Evans. Evans, who had done horror illustration in the comics for E.C., had for some years drawn the famous comic strip *Terry and the Pirates,* which made him admirably suited to create a series of pulp-style illustrations for both fantasy and adventure tales. Again, the book was well received, and *Far Lands Other Days* was a runner-up for the World Fantasy Award in its year.

Lee Brown Coye returned with Carcosa's third book, *Murgunstrumm & Others,* by Hugh B. Cave. This was a thick volume of Grand Guignol horror thrillers, which inspired Coye to the best work of his career. Fans, most of whom had never even heard of Hugh B. Cave, were treated to a feast of pulp-gothic horrors and Coye fiends. In a repeat performance, Coye won his second World Fantasy Award, while *Murgunstrumm & Others* carried off the same award in the Best Collection category.

Amateur publishing is no hobby for the faint of spirit, as anyone who has attempted the same will tell you. To produce books such as those Carcosa has published increases the problems involved tremendously. The Carcosa partners often wonder if the project is really worth all the effort it demands. Praise from the fans is gratifying, but applause soon dies away. Awards are a coveted tribute to success, but trophies gather dust on shelves. The final test is the accomplishment itself. As to that, Carcosa has thus far produced three volumes that any reader would be proud to own. But more than that, it has showcased the talents of authors and artists whose work would otherwise have been left to oblivion. And most important, the interest in their work engendered by Carcosa has encouraged these rare talents to create *new* tales and drawings in the fantasy genre.

To Carcosa, the struggle is worth it. Their fourth volume, *Lonely Vigils,* by Manly Wade Wellman, with illustrations by George Evans, is currently in production, and a fifth, *Death*

Stalks the Night, by Hugh B. Cave, incorporating the final drawings of Lee Brown Coye, is scheduled to follow.

STUART DAVID SCHIFF—*WHISPERS*

Whispers magazine was founded in 1973 to generate new fiction and art in the fantasy-horror field. The journal borrowed its name from an imaginary horror pulp mentioned in Howard Phillips Lovecraft's "The Unnameable." The real *Whispers*'s early issues presented original material by E. Hoffmann Price, Joseph Payne Brennan, Brian Lumley, Lee Brown Coye, Frank Utpatel, Steve Fabian, Fritz Leiber, Karl Edward Wagner, David Drake, Dirk Mosig, and many others. These especially talented people helped *Whispers* earn its first World Fantasy Award for 1973–74.

During the following years, more new stories and graphics were stimulated by this little magazine. New contributors included Manly Wade Wellman, Carl Jacobi, Avram Davidson, Hugh B. Cave, Gahan Wilson, Frank Belknap Long, Ramsey Campbell, Vincent Di Fate, William Nolan, Robert Bloch, and other equally talented people. With support such as that, it was not surprising that *Whispers* won the 1977 Special World Fantasy Award for itself and its editor-publisher, Stuart David Schiff.

It should also be noted that *Whispers* magazine became the *first* non-professional literary magazine ever to have its fiction gathered for professional publication when *Whispers I* was published in 1977. Jove reprinted that anthology in early 1979 and *Whispers II* was published by Doubleday in late 1979. *Whispers III* is scheduled for early 1981.

Karl Edward Wagner, M.D., is a gentleman of varied talents. His anti-hero, Kane, has already brought him legendary status as the heroic fantasy field's brightest new star. His acclaim as editor of Robert E. Howard's Conan stories is rivaled only by the excellence of his own Conan novel, *The Road of Kings*. Yet Karl's horror fiction has spawned "Sticks," an already classic original from the pages of *Whispers* magazine. That beauty won the August Derleth Award as Best Short Fiction of 1974 and also garnered a 1975 World Fantasy Award nomination. "Two Suns Setting" features his Kane and was a 1976 nominee for the World Fantasy Award.

Two Suns Setting

by KARL EDWARD WAGNER

I

ALONE WITH THE NIGHT WINDS

Sullen red disc, the sun was burying itself beneath a monotonous horizon of rolling gravel waste that stretched behind him miles uncounted—and possibly untrod save by his horse's hoofs. Long before the sunlight failed, its warmth was snuffed out in the empty lifelessness of the desert, so that in its last hour the sun shone cheerless as the rising moon. Crimson as it climbed, the full moon seemed a false dawn to mock the dying sun, arriving prematurely, disrespectful as a greedy heir pacing in eager impatience before the master's deathbed. For a space the limitless skies of twilight displayed two rubrous globes low on either horizon, so that Kane mused as to whether his long journey across the desert might not have led him to some strange dusk world where two ancient suns smoldered in the heavens. The region seemed unearthly in its chill desolation—and certainly an aura of unguessable antiquity hung as a gray shadow over each tumbled bit of stone.

Kane had left Carsultyal with no particular destination or goal other than to ride far beyond that city's influence. There were those who said that Kane was driven from Carsultyal, his power there broken at last by fellow sorcerers jealous of his long-held prestige—and alarmed by the bizarrely alien direction his studies had taken in recent years. Kane himself considered his departure more or less voluntary, albeit precipitous, arguing privately that had he really wanted, he could have fended off the attack of his former colleagues—even though he owed allegiance to neither god nor demon from whom he might have sought intercession. Rather, mankind's first great city had grown stagnant over the last century. The spirit of discovery, of renaissance that had drawn him to Carsultyal in its earliest years was burned out now, so that boredom, his nemesis, had overtaken Kane once more. To be sure, he had been restless, his thoughts drawn more and more to the world beyond Carsultyal—lands yet to know the presence of man. But that he returned to his pathless wandering without much forethought could be judged in that Kane had left the city with little more than a few supplies, a double handful of gold coins, a fast horse, and a sword of tempered Carsultyal steel. Those who sought to seize his relinquished power may have regretted their inheritance, but this minor vindication seemed pointless now.

With dusk, the wind began to rise, a whining, chill breath from the mountains whose rusted peaks still burned with the final rays of the sun, now vanished beneath the opposite horizon. Kane shivered and drew his russet cloak closer about his massive shoulders, regretting the warm furs that scavengers now snarled over in Carsultyal. The Herratlonai was a cold, empty waste, where nights dropped to freezing. With the mountain wind, his outfit of green wool shirt, dark leather vest and pants was less than adequate for the night.

The previous day he had eaten the last hoarded chips of dried fruit and jerky—after short rations for a week or more. Of water there luckily was yet half a bag; he had filled the skins to bursting before entering the desert, and a waterhole had providentially appeared along the ghost of a trail he followed. Or thought he followed. The gravel waste southeast of Carsultyal's domains was reputed to border on one of the prehuman realms of lost antiquity. There were tales of cities impossibly ancient buried beneath the gravel dunes. Kane had come upon what he hoped might be traces of a forgotten path across the desert to the fabled mountains of the eastern continent. He determined to follow this, and at times he discovered sentinel boulders whose all but effaced hieroglyphs might resemble those glimpsed in books of elder world lore—or might be the deluding artistry of wind and ice. Beyond this tantalization, Kane found nothing further to disrupt the monotonous desolation but stray patches of sparse scrub and gorgeous columns of agatized wood. The grass his mount cropped; for himself Kane had not seen even a lizard in days. Perhaps it had been rash to attempt traverse of a desert whose limits no man had knowledge of, at least without a pack train of provisions. But Kane had not embarked under the brightest of circumstances, nor had the years dulled his reckless whim. Philosophically he congratulated himself on riding a course no enemy would care to follow.

Then the mountains had broken through the thin haze of the eastern horizon like a row of worn and discolored teeth. Their presence gave some cause for optimism—at least he was across the desert—but this hope was clouded when the late afternoon sun revealed the hills to be merely a more vertical variation on the present terrain. Dry slopes of gravel and crumbling bluffs appeared lifeless except for dark blotches of twisted underbrush. From the talus gleamed iridescent flashes of sunlight, colored then flung back by mammoth slabs of petrified wood, strewn about like a giant's plundered jewel hoard.

But with darkness had also come the startling smell of wood smoke in the mountain wind—a familiar scent uncanny in this stark desolation. Kane brushed smooth the grimy beard that hung like rust over coarse features, thumbed a few blowing strands of red hair back beneath a leather headband sewn with plaques of lapis lazuli—sniffing the night wind in disbelief. His mount paced onward, the night deepened, and against the foot of the mountains ahead beckoned the light of a campfire. No, simply the light of a fire, he mused—there was no reason to be more specific. At this distance it must be a good-sized blaze.

He guided his horse closer, picking his way carefully over the gravel in the moonlight. With a twisting ache in his belly, Kane recognized the odor of roasting meat within the smoke, and there was no longer any doubt. Calculatingly he studied the still distant campfire. He had seen no evidence of habitation against the slope, and in this emptiness such would seem an impossibility. Not that it seemed any more probable, but indications were that he had chanced upon some other wanderer. As to who or what might be camped beside the ridge, or what circumstances had brought about his presence, Kane was at loss to conjecture. Nothing was known of those who might dwell beyond the settled northwestern crescent of the Great Southern Continent, and in the dawn world more races than mankind walked the Earth.

Whoever had built the fire ate his meat cooked and so could not be hopelessly alien. From the size of the campfire, Kane guessed it was a small party of nomads or savages—likely someone from whatever lay beyond the mountains. The significant point was the roasting meat. Licking dry lips, Kane unfastened his sword from saddle and buckled it across his back, so that the familiar hilt protruded reassuringly over his right shoulder. The scabbard tip he left untied, so that it would pivot freely on its shoulder swivel when he grasped the hilt. Cautiously he approached the campfire.

II

TWO WHO MET BY FIRELIGHT

His keen nostrils caught an animal smell, sour beneath the pungency of wood smoke and cooked flesh. At first the crackling firelight screened the shape crouched beyond, so that Kane warily nudged his steed toward another angle of vision to confirm his dawning suspicion. His face tightened at recognition. Only one man squatted beside the blaze—if a giant might be termed "man."

Kane had seen, had spoken with giants in the course of his wanderings, although in recent decades they were seldom encountered. A proudly aloof, taciturn race he knew them to be. Few in number and scornful of mankind's emerging civilization, they lived a semibarbaric existence in lands unfrequented by man. True, there abounded gruesome tales of individual giants who terrorized isolated human settlements, but these were outlaws to their own race—or more often the monstrous hybrid ogres.

This particular individual did not appear threatening. While he obviously had heard the clash of shod hoofs on stone, his attitude seemed curious rather than hostile as Kane approached. Not that someone his stature need display an aggressive front at the appearance of a single horse and rider. In comfortable reach lay a hooked ax whose bronze head could serve as ship's anchor. Kane realized that from the other's higher vantage point, his approach had been observed beyond the ring of firelight. Still the giant showed no sinister action. Spitted over sputtering flames turned an entire carcass of what looked to be goat. Hot, succulent meat . . .

Hunger overpowered caution. Poised to wheel and gallop away at the first sign of danger, Kane boldly rode up to the fringe of firelit circle and halted.

"Good evening," he greeted levelly, speaking the language of the giant's race with complete fluency. "Your campfire was visible at some distance. I wondered if I might join you."

The giant grunted and shielded his eyes with a hand larger than a spade. "Well, what's this here. A human who speaks the Old Tongue. Out of nowhere too—and in a land that even ghosts have abandoned. This sort of novelty can't be ignored. Come on into the light, manling. We'll share hospitality of the trail." His voice, though loud as a man's shout, had an even bass timbre.

Kane muttered thanks and dismounted, deciding to gamble on the giant's apparent goodwill. As he stepped before the fire, he and his host exchanged curious inspection. At a bit over six feet and carrying past three hundred pounds of bone, sinew, and muscle, Kane was seldom physically overawed. This night he stood alone in the desert before one who could overpower him as if he were a weakling child.

He estimated the giant's height somewhere around fifteen feet. It was difficult to tell, since he sat crouched on the ground, knees drawn up, enswathed in a cloak of bearskins like a misshapen, hairy tent. Disregarding the matter of size, the giant's appearance was human enough—his proportions were those of a man in his prime, though he seemed somewhat lanky from a slightly disproportionate length of limb. He was broadly muscled, and his weight must be enormous. He wore rough boots the size of panniers, and under the cloak a crudely stitched tunic and leggings of hide. Calves and arms were matted with coarse bristles. Perhaps too bony to be called craggy, his features were not displeasing; his beard was shaggy, brown hair drawn back in a short braid at the nape. Brown also were his eyes, set wide beneath an intelligent brow.

Looking him over as a man might size up a stray dog, the giant glanced at Kane's face, and gave an interested grunt. He gazed thoughtfully into Kane's cold blue eyes for a moment—something few cared to do. "You're Kane, aren't you," he commented.

Kane started, then smiled bitterly. "A thousand miles from the cities of man, and a giant calls me by name."

The giant seemed amused. "Oh, you'll have to wander far if you really seek anonymity. We giants have watched the frantic history of your race. We recall when mankind aborted from its womb, pretending to be adult instead of misbegotten fetus. To man these few centuries are time immemorial; to our race a nostalgic yesterday. We remember well the Curse of Kane and still recognize his mark."

"That history is already garbled and distorted," Kane murmured, eyes for a moment focused beyond. "Kane is becoming misty legend in the old homes of man—and lost in obscurity in the new lands. Already I've traveled through lands where men did not know me for who I am."

"And you kept wandering, too—because they soon learned to dread the name of Kane," concluded the giant. "Well, Kane—my name is Dwassllir, and I'm pleased to find a legend joining me at my lonely fire."

Kane shrugged an ironic acknowledgment. "What's that roasting in your lonely fire?" He looked hungrily at the grease-dripping carcass.

"A mountain goat I dropped this afternoon—good game is scarce around here, I've found. Hey, give that spit a nudge, will you."

Kane heaved the spit to the rarest side. "You going to eat all of it?" he asked bluntly, too hungry for pride.

Dwassllir might well have done so otherwise, but the giant seemed glad for the companionship, and tore off a generous side of ribs that taxed even Kane's voracity. Again the image of stray dog occurred to Kane, but the growling in his belly claimed first place in his thoughts. The goat was tough, stringy, half raw and gamy in taste; it was ecstasy to devour. One eye still watching the giant warily, he gnawed on the ribs with gusto, washing down the greasy flesh with mouthfuls of stale water from Dwassllir's canteen.

With a belch that fanned the flames, Dwassllir stood and stretched—licked his fingers, wiped face with hands, then scrubbed his hands with loose gravel. When the giant was erect, Kane realized that his height was closer to eighteen feet. Leisurely Dwassllir picked over the remains of the goat. "Want any more?" he inquired. Kane shook his head, still struggling with the ribs. A short tug wrenched loose the remaining hind leg, and the giant settled back with a contented sigh to gnaw the joint.

"Game is hard to run across in this range," he reflected, gesturing with the tattered femur. "Doubt if you'd find anything in that stretch of desert yonder. Likely that horse will be the only meat you'll find until you get into the plains east of here."

"I thought about eating him," Kane conceded. "But on foot I'd stand little chance of crossing this waste."

Dwassllir snorted disparagingly. Because of their enormous size, giants looked upon a horse as only another game animal. "The frailty of your race! Strip man of his crutches, and he's helpless to stand against his world."

"Don't oversimplify," Kane objected. "Mankind will be master of this world. In only a few centuries I've seen our civilization grow from a sterile paradise, from scattered barbaric tribes to a vast and expanding empire of cities, villages and farms. Ours is the fastest-rising civilization ever to burst upon this world."

"Only because man has stolen his civilization from the ruins of better races who preceded him. Human civilization is parasitic—a gaudy fungus that owes its vitality to the dead genius upon whose corpse it flourishes!"

"Wiser races, I'll grant you," Kane pointed out. "But it is mankind who has survived, not Earth's elder races. It is a measure of man's resourcefulness that he can salvage from prehuman civilizations knowledge that is invaluable to the advance of his own race. Carsultyal has risen thus from a fishing village to the greatest city in the known world. Her rediscovered knowledge has shaped the emergence of mankind to our present civilization."

Dwassllir snapped the femur explosively and sucked at its marrow. "Civilization! You boast that as man's major accomplishment! It is nothing—only an outgrowth of human weakness! Man is too frail, too unworthy a creature to live within his environment. He must instead prop himself up with his civilization, his learning. My race learned to live in the real world—to merge with our environment. We need no civilization. Man is a cripple who flaunts his infirmity, boasts of his crutches. You retreat into the walls of your civilization because you are too weak to stand before nature as part of the natural environment. Instead of living as partner to nature, man hides behind his civilization, curses and defies true life, distorts his environment to accommodate his own failings. Beware that your environment does not strike back from all your blasphemies, for that day mankind shall be snuffed out like the unnatural freak man is!

"Even you, Kane—you who are reviled as the most dangerous man of your race, without your horse, your clothes, your weapons —could you have crossed that desert alive as you have just barely done? One of my race could!

"My race is older than yours. We had grown to maturity while a mad god was playing his idiot game of shaping mankind from the bestial filth that skulked where shadow lay deepest. Had man walked the Earth of my race's youth, his civilization would have protected him no better than an eggshell. That Earth was more feral than this world man knows. My ancestors defied storms, glaciers, catastrophes that would have swept away your cities like dry leaves before the wind! They stood naked before beasts more savage than any man has known—grappled and conquered the sabre-tooth, the great sloth, the cave bear, the woolly mammoth, and other creatures whose strength and ferocity are unknown in this tame age! Could man have survived in that heroic age? I doubt that all his cunning and trickery could have saved him!"

"Perhaps not, but then your race has considerable physical advantage," argued Kane, wondering how wise it might be to provoke the other. "If my stride were long as yours, then I wouldn't need a horse to cross a desert—although I think your disdain might not exist, if there were a steed great enough for a giant to straddle. Nor would I need my sword if I were huge enough to crush a lion as if it were only a jackal. Your boast is founded on the fact that your size makes you physically superior to the dangers of your environment, which is a boast that any large and powerful animal could echo. Who is braver—one of your ancestors who barehanded throttled a cave bear close to him in size, or a man with a spear who kills a tiger many times his superior in physical power?"

He paused, waiting to see if the giant had taken offense. However, Dwassllir was not of volatile temper. Belly full and feet warm, he was in a pleasant mood for fireside debate with his diminutive companion.

"True, yours is an older race, and mankind an arrogant youth," Kane continued. "But what are the accomplishments of your race? If you scorn to build cities, to sail ships, to settle the wilderness, to master the secrets of prehuman knowledge—then what have you achieved? Art, poetry, philosophy, spiritualism—are these fields your race has mastered?"

"Our achievement has been to live at peace with our environment—to live as a part of the natural world, instead of waging war with nature," declared Dwassllir steadily.

"All right then, I'll accept that," Kane persisted. "Perhaps you have found fulfillment in your rather primitive life style. However, the measure of a race's attainments must finally be its ability to flourish within its chosen role. If your race has done this so well, why then do your numbers diminish, while mankind spreads over the Earth? Never has your race been a populous one, and today man encounters giant only rarely. Will your race then fade away with the passing years—until one day the giants will be known only in legend along with the fierce creatures your ancestors fought? What then will survive your passing? What will remain to tell of your vanished glory?"

Dwassllir became sadly pensive, so that Kane regretted having pursued the argument. "You humans seem too content to measure achievement in terms of numbers," he answered. "But I can't make full refutation of your logic. Our numbers have been declining for centuries, and I can't really tell you why. Our lives are long—I'm not as much your junior in years as you may suppose, Kane. We are slow to mate and raise children, but this was always so. Our natural enemies have all passed into extinction or retreated to the most obscure reaches. Our simple medicines are sufficient to nurse us through whatever disease or injury might strike us. No, our deaths have not increased.

"I think our race has grown old, tired. Perhaps we should have followed the giant beasts of the savage past into the realm of shadow. At least our old enemies gave life adventure! It is as if my race has lived beyond its era, and now we perish from boredom. We're like one of your kings who has conquered all his enemies and now has only a dull old age to endure.

"My race rose in a heroic age, Kane! It was truly a day of giants in that era! But that age is dead. Gone are the great beasts. Vanished the elder races whose wars rocked the roots of mountains. Earth has been inherited by the insignificant scavenger. Man crawls about the ruins of the great age, and proclaims himself to be Earth's new master! Perhaps man will survive to accomplish his insolent usurpation—more likely he will destroy himself in seeking to command mysteries the elder races found too awesome for even their powers to control!

"But when the day comes that man will be master of the Earth, my race will hopefully not be present to endure that humiliation! We are a race of heroes who have outlived the age of heroes! Can you blame us if we tire of existence in this age of boastful pigmies!"

Kane fell silent. "I understand your sentiments," he finally said. "But to abandon yourself to despair, to brood upon vanished glory doesn't impress me as heroic."

He stopped, not wishing to deepen the shadow of melancholy that had gathered over their thoughts. "May I ask what brings you to this lost wilderness of dead rock?" he asked, thinking to change subject. "Or do these nameless mountains border on the lands of your people?"

Dwassllir shook himself and tossed an uprooted shrub into the fire. The leaves hissed shrilly, then whipped loose from blackened stems to rise like red stars fading into the night. "What I seek is no secret," he replied. "Although it may seem pointless to you as it has to some of my friends.

"Centuries ago, before this region was stripped barren of soil and hence of life, there were villages of my race along these mountains—which are not nameless, but are called the Antamareesi range. Under these hills lie immense caverns, which my ancestors used for shelter in days before they raised houses, then later mined for the veins of metal they discovered within. The climate was warmer, the land was green, game was plentiful—it was a good region to settle and to look upon in that age.

"Those were the great days! Life in that age was an ever challenging struggle between the savagery of the ancient Earth and the unyielding strength of my race! Can you imagine the tremendous energy of those people! They stood chest to chest against a ferociously hostile world, and they conquered whatever enemy they faced! Their gods were Fire and Ice—the implacable opposites that were the ruling forces of their age! And their enemies were not only the forces of nature, or the great beasts—some of the elder races challenged the ascendency of my race as well!

"Perhaps it was their sorcery that left this region lifeless and barren. Our legends tell of battles with strange races and stranger weapons in the dawn world—and my ancestors were victorious over these enemies too. The hero of one legendary battle, King Brotemllain, whose name you may know as the greatest king of my race, ruled over these mountains. His body was laid to rest within one of these caverns, and upon his brow remains the ancestral crown of my people—ancient even then, and given to him after death because of the undying greatness of his rule."

Dwassllir was afire now, his momentary depression seared away by intense fervor. He considered Kane thoughtfully, made a decision, and spoke earnestly, "I've been searching for Brotemllain's legendary burial place. And from certain signs, I think I'm about to discover it. I mean to recover his crown! King Brotemllain's crown is emblematic of my race's ancient glory. Although our wars and our kings are all past now, I believe that resurrection of this legendary symbol might unlock some of the old energy and vitality of my people. Perhaps the idea brands me a fool and dreamer as many have scoffed, but I mean to do this thing! Surely this relic from an age of heroes could serve to spark some new flame of glory to my race even in these gray days!

"I wouldn't suggest this to another of your race, Kane—but because you are who you are, I'll offer both an invitation and a challenge. If you'd care to come along with me on this search, Kane, I'd welcome your company. It may be that you will understand my race better if you follow me into the shadow of that age of lost glory."

"Thank you for the invitation—and the challenge," declared Kane solemnly. The venture intrigued him, and the giant seemed to eat well. "I'll be proud to make that journey with you."

III

DEAD GIANT'S CROWN

The trees grew less far apart here, though still dwarfed and tortured by the chill breeze. Two days had Kane followed Dwassllir about the crumbling ridges—his horse matching the giant's restless stride. Now on the third day Dwassllir's whoop chorused by a hundred echoes announced the termination of his search.

The discovery seemed unimpressive. They had entered a deep valley and traced a course to its gorgelike head, where Kane glanced uneasily at the boulder-strewn slopes enclosing them overhead. At times Dwassllir had eagerly pointed out some rounded monument whose carvings the winds of time had all but obliterated. Again he would pause to examine some unprepossessing mound, where the drifting gravel nestled upon blocks of hewn stone and perhaps a shard of ceramic, a smear of charcoal fragments, or a lump of dried wood so ancient that it seemed more lifeless than the stones.

"There stands the entrance to the tomb of King Brotemllain," Dwassllir proclaimed, and he gestured to a rubble-choked patch of darkness that burrowed into the valley wall. The opening had been about twenty-five feet high and half as broad, although several feet were now filled in by debris. Evidence of masonry framed the entrance, along with great chunks of shredded wood, some whose blackened splinters were conglomerate with verdigris—all that remained of portals at last fallen to time itself.

"I'm certain this is the valley described in our legends," the giant rumbled jubilantly. "The passage leads into a vast system of caverns. It was a natural opening my ancestors enlarged to enter a major side branch as it passes close to the surface. Beyond these ruins of the ancient monument should lie the domed natural chamber where Brotemllain's corpse was enthroned for the ages."

Kane frowned at the dark opening doubtfully, a whisper of unease drifting through his thoughts. "I wouldn't count on finding much in there but bats and dust. Time and decay generally devour the leavings of less hallowed thieves. Or does this tomb have its unseen guardians? It would seem unusual with so renowned a tenant and so legendary a treasure, if this tomb were not guarded by some still vigilant spell."

With a shrug Dwassllir dismissed Kane's foreboding. "Unusual for your race, maybe. But this was a shrine most sacred to my race. Besides, who would dare pilfer the grave of a giant? Come on, we'll take torches and see if King Brotemllain still holds court."

While Kane struck fire, the giant scoured about for a supply of resiniferous wood. He returned with a dead tree as thick as Kane's thigh. Taking several shorn branches, Kane accompanied Dwassllir into the cave—the latter wielding a section of trunk.

Their progress was quickly interrupted. Blocking the passage but for a narrow crevice interposed a jumble of broken rock. A segment of the passage wall had collapsed.

Dwassllir examined the barrier thoughtfully. "It's going to take some time to dig through this," he concluded sourly.

"Assuming your efforts didn't bring down the rest of the mountain," was Kane's ominous comment. "There's a fault in the rock here, or this slide would not have broken through. If the caverns run as extensively as you say, there must be flaws undermining this entire range. The centuries have spread the cracks and further weakened the rock, so it's solid as a rotted tooth. It's a wonder these mountains haven't tumbled flat before now."

Jabbing out his torch, the giant craned his neck to peer along the crevice. "Passage opens up again, and just beyond I think I can make out where it opens into the main cavern." He glowered at the obstruction helplessly for a moment, then gazed down at the man.

"You know, you could squeeze through that crack, Kane," he told him. "You could get past and see what's beyond. If there's nothing to be found, then there's nothing lost. But if this is King Brotemllain's tomb, then you can learn if his crown still lies within."

Kane considered the crevice, face noncommittal. "It can be done," he pronounced. Casually, not wishing to show his nerve less steady than the giant's: "I'll go look for your bones on my own then."

The crack was inches too narrow for one of Kane's massive build, so that his clothing scuffed and flesh scraped as he wriggled through the tightest portion. But the wall had not collapsed in a solid thrust; rather splintered chunks of stone had broken through in a disordered array, and the occlusion was spread like stubby fingers instead of a compact fist. Then his thrusting torch shone clear of the rubble, and Kane edged into unobstructed passage-way. Quickly he rebuckled his scabbard across his back, but the bare blade stayed in his left fist.

A short way beyond he found the cavern. A pair of steps too high for human stride completed the passage's gentle descent. Kane lifted the torch and looked about, his senses strained to catch any hint of danger. There was nothing to detect, but the obscure sense of menace persisted. Waving the brand to fan its light, he was unable to discern the cavern's boundaries, although this chamber seemed to extend for hundreds of feet. Stalactites hung from ceiling far above, making a monstrous multifanged jaw with stalagmite tusks below. "I've just walked down the beast's tongue," mumbled Kane, clambering over the steps. Thin dust sifted over the stone; this cavern was long dead too.

"What do you see, Kane!" roared Dwassllir from the crevice. High above the curtain of bats stirred fitfully.

Despite his familiarity with the giant's deafening tone, Kane started and nervously glanced toward the distant ceiling. The torch flared in his hand as he crossed the chamber, sword poised for whatever laired within the darkness.

Then he froze—a thrill tingling through his body as he gazed at what waited at the torchlight's perimeter.

"Dwassllir!" he shouted, in his excitement heedless of the booming echoes. "He's here! You've found the tomb! King Brotemllain's here on his throne, and his crown rests on his skull!"

Revealed in the torchlight jutted an immense throne of hewn stone, upon which its skeletal king still reposed in sepulchral majesty. In the cool aridity of the cavern, the lich had outlasted centuries. Tatters of desiccated flesh held the skeleton together in leathery articulation. Bare bone gleamed dully through chinks in the clinging mail of muscle and sinew, shrunken to ironlike texture. Throne arms were yet gripped by fingers like gnarled oak roots, while about the base was gathered a moldering drift of disintegrating furs. The gaunt skull retained sufficient shreds of flesh to half mask its death's-head grin with lines of sternness— forming a grimace suggesting laughter muffled by set lips. The eyes were sunken circles of darkness whose shadowy depths eluded Kane's torch. Not so the orbs that brooded from above the brow.

Red as setting suns in the torchlight, a pair of fist-sized rubies blazed from King Brotemllain's crown. Kane swore softly, impressed by the wealth he witnessed almost as deeply as he stood in awe of its grisly majesty. The circle of gold could belt a dancing girl's waist, and patterned about the two great stones were another ten or more rough-cut gems of walnut size. Ancient treasure from the giant's plutonian harvested hoard.

Thinking of the kingdom encircled in the riches of King Brotemllain's crown, Kane bitterly regretted his shout of discovery. Had he reported the cavern empty, there might have been a chance to smuggle the crown past the giant—or return for it later. But now Dwassllir knew of the crown, and Dwassllir waited at the only exit to the tomb. To attempt to find egress through some hypothetical interpassage into the network of caverns said to run under the mountains would be suicidal—slightly less so than to challenge the giant for possession. Kane ruefully studied the treasure. Unless chance presented for stealthy murder . . .

"Kane!" The giant's bellow concluded his musing. "You all right in there, Kane? Is it really King Brotemllain?"

"Can't do anything else, Dwassllir!" Kane yelled back, echoes garbling his words. "It's just like your legends told! There's a colossal throne of stone in the cavern's center! About twenty feet of moldy skeleton's sitting on it, and on his skull there's a golden crown with two enormous rubies! Just a minute and I'll climb up and get it for you!"

"No! Leave it there!" Eagerness shook the giant's shout. "I

want to see this for myself!" From the barrier sounded groan and rattle of shifting rubble.

"Wait, damn it all!" Kane howled, scrambling back to the passage. "You're going to bring the whole damn mountain down on us! I'll get your crown for you!"

"Leave it! This isn't just a treasure hunt! It's more than just recovering Brotemllain's crown!" puffed the giant, straining to roll back a boulder. "I've dreamed for more years than you can guess of standing before King Brotemllain's throne! Of standing where no giant has entered since the heroic age of my race! Of calling upon his shade for the strength to lead my race back to its lost glory! So I'll stand before King Brotemllain, and I'll lift his crown from his brow with my own hands! And when I return, my people will see and listen and know that the tales of our ancient greatness are history, not myth!

"Now come on and help me widen this crevice, will you? You can clear away this smaller stuff. This cavern's stood for millennia; we can risk another few minutes."

Kane cursed and joined him at the barrier—reflecting that it was useless arguing with a fanatical giant. Grimly he hauled back on a boulder jammed against the inner face of the blockage.

Sudden tearing groan and Dwassllir's gasp of dismay gave him barely enough warning. Kane catapulted backward just as the unbalanced rock slide protested their trespass. Like the irresistible fist of doom, the rock shelf burst from the wall and smashed against the opposite side.

Deafened by the concussion, pelted by splintered fragments, Kane twisted frantically to roll clear. He fell in a bruised huddle past the foot of the steps. For a moment of dazed confusion it seemed that the entire cavern rocked and bucked with a crescendo repercussion of the collapsed passageway.

When the last slamming echo had lost its note, the final chunk of cracked stone bounced past, Kane groggily sat up to lick his wounds. Sore, but no bones broken, a long gash down his left shoulder. His sword arm was numb where a rock splinter had struck, and it would need bandaging to staunch the trickle of blood. Relatively unscathed, he decided, considering he had nearly been crushed deader than King Brotemllain.

His sword was still sheathed, but the torch had been lost as he leapt away, and the chamber was as dark as a tomb could get. Kane did not need a torch to learn the worst; the absence of any ray of light told him that. King Brotemllain's tomb was also sealed as thoroughly as any tomb need be.

IV

A FINAL CORONATION

Gloomily he felt his way back along the passage and pushed against the intervening wall of rock. There were boulders as wide as he was tall, and the spaces between were packed solid with lesser rubble. Given slaves and equipment enough, he might clear out another crevice. Dwassllir could perhaps burrow through, but the giant was probably a mangled keystone in the barrier right now.

Burned pitch stung his groping fingers, and Kane tugged the extinguished torch out from under some debris. Since there seemed little else to do, he sat down and struck a fire. The torch alight once more, the rockslide appeared no less substantial. Angrily Kane kicked at a toppled boulder.

Air fanned the torch flame, however, pointing a yellow, beckoning finger back into the burial cavern. Remembering this cave was a branch of a greater plexus, Kane eagerly sought to trace the faint stir of wind.

As he crossed the chamber, Kane saw the effects of the rockslide within the cavern. The sudden grinding force had sent a shudder through the tired stone, so that stalactites had plummeted like crystal lightning bolts from their eternally dark heaven. One had missed spearing Brotemllain by scant yards.

A sighing wind breathed corpse-breath through a gaping pit many yards across at the cavern's one end. The explosive concussions that rocked the stone had not been fantasy of a head blow then. Evidently in the chain-reaction shock wave which the slide had drummed through the brittle stone, a large section of rock from the high ceiling had struck here. Its impact had driven through the chamber floor to reveal another cavern beneath this one. The network of caves must bore through the mountains like the tortuous course of a feasting worm, thought Kane, peering into the pit.

Wind gusted faintly through the hole, bringing a sick smell of dampness—a stale, unclean, animal smell that intrigued Kane. It seemed he could hear the rush of unseen waters. An underground river probably—deep underground it must be too. The wind stole in through rotted chinks in the mountains' shell most likely. At least Kane hoped his deductions were correct.

The floor of this new cavern appeared to be about seventy-five feet below him. The collapsing stone had made a chaotic incline down which progress seemed possible. "I've found another road to Hell," Kane muttered aloud.

A rustle beyond him made him look to its source; then he knew he was on the threshold of Hell. At the edge of light danced a cockroach—incredibly, a bone-white cockroach nearly a yard in length. With chitinous concentration, it was nuzzling a dead bat, and it waved its antennae querulously at the offending light. In disbelief Kane tossed a rock in its direction, and the roach scuttled off chuckling into the darkness.

Fascinated, Kane returned to the pit and thrust his torch out over the aperture. Near the incline's base two white-furred creatures raised blind eyes to the light and slunk away squealing in fear. And Kane recognized them be to rats the size of jackals.

Understanding came to him. Water, air—the caverns below held life. But an obscenely distorted form of life it was. Probably these outsized creatures had evolved from cave dwellers who somehow were trapped beneath the surface ages ago—or maybe retreated there from choice when the land became desert. In primeval night, without seasons, without light, they had mutated to grotesque, primitive forms—adapted to the demented savagery of their environment. Falling stone had crushed bats as well as other nameless things, and now the scent of blood was luring the monstrous cave creatures to this area.

And what else dwells below? wondered Kane uneasily. He drew away from the pit, deciding that so certain a path to Hell could rest untrod until all other chances of escape were eliminated. Digging out through the passage even seemed a brighter prospect.

As he returned to the rock fall, he caught the sound of stone grating on stone. For a moment he feared the slide was shifting, but as he watched tensely he saw this was not so. Excitement cutting through despondency, Kane quickly stepped to the barrier and rhythmically pounded against a boulder with a chunk of rock.

After a pause, his tapping was dimly echoed from the opposite side. So the giant had escaped the avalanche. His strength could clear the passage if it were at all possible.

Eagerly Kane began to dig into his side of the barrier. Not daring to contemplate another slide, he strained his powerful back to roll away small boulders, tore his fingers scrabbling doglike through the chipped stone. Luckily, it was a bed of broken rock that had slid into the passage, rather than a solid stone shelf.

Time crawled immeasurably, marked only by the dwindling torch and the deepening excavation. Kane's hands were raw and blistered when a sudden wrenching of stone tore open a patch of daylight. Filtered by distance and dust, the ray of sunlight seemed of blinding brilliance to his eyes.

"Dwassllir!" shouted Kane, peering through the chink in the barrier. A shaft perhaps the size of a man's head had been formed between the angle of two boulders, although several feet of debris yet blocked the passage.

A huge brown eye squinted back at him. "Kane?" The giant sounded pleasantly surprised. "So you dodged the slide, manling! You're as hard to kill as legend tells!"

"Can you get me out of here?"

"Can if I'm going to get myself in!" Dwassllir returned stubbornly. "I think I can prop up these boulders so we can dig out space enough for me to crawl through."

"One of the characteristics of higher life forms is the ability to learn by experience," grumbled Kane, bending his back to dislodge a portion of rubble. But the giant's determination was as unyielding as the rock about them.

Slowly the crevice began to reappear, and with freedom outlined in an ever broadening patch of light, the grueling work seemed less fatiguing. Only a precariously balanced jumble of boulders remained.

But this time warning came too late.

A sudden shriek of rasping stone as Dwassllir recklessly hauled back on one of the piled boulders. Released from pressure, a second slab of rock plunged forward like a catapult missile. Kane yelled and tried to dodge. He had been unbalanced with effort, and even his blurring speed was too slow to evade the tumbling projectile.

Thunder as it struck, the slab caromed crazily upon the piled boulders, spun about and smashed against the wall where Kane stood. Kane hissed in pain. At the last instant he had twisted behind a sheltering boulder. This had absorbed the impact of the falling slab, but the explosive force had jammed the intervening rock against his thighs, pinning him to the wall.

Blood oozed from torn skin, trickled into his boots. Grimacing in pain as he tried to wriggle free, Kane discovered he had escaped crushed bones by the smallest fraction.

Miraculously, the rest of the pile had held stable. Dwassllir was cautiously poking at the opening. "Kane? Damn! You're harder to kill than a snake! Can you squeeze out of there?"

"I can't!" grunted Kane, straining to slide the rock. "Lot of rock fragments all jammed together—holding it in place! My feet are pinned in!" He cursed and writhed against his pillory, scraping off more skin as the only evident result.

"Well, I'll pull you out as I dig through," boomed Dwassllir reassuringly, and he once more attacked the rockslide.

But Kane heard sounds of grating rock not turned by Dwassllir's hand. From within the burial cavern he could hear a heavy body climbing over loose stone.

Teeth bared in defiant snarl, Kane stared wild-eyed into the funeral chamber.

At first he thought the corpse of King Brotemllain had risen on skeletal limbs—for wavering in the darkness he could discern two ruby coals throwing back the torchlight. But the crown had not moved, still made sullen glow above the throne.

These were truly eyes he saw—eyes that held him in a baleful glare. Climbing from the aperture in the cavern floor came a creature from beneath the abyss of night.

Sabre-tooth! Or nightmare spawn of sabre-tooth tiger and stygian darkness. The gargantuan creature that shambled forth from the timeless caverns of night was as demented progeny of its natural forebears as were the other grotesque cave beasts Kane had seen. Rock crunched beneath taloned tread as it stalked from the gaping pit, an albino behemoth more than double the stature of its fearsome ancestor. Dripping jaws yawned hungrily in a cough of challenge—sabre-toothed jaws that could close upon Kane as a cat snaps up a rat.

Lord Tloluvin alone might know what fantastic demons stalked the unlighted caverns that crawled down into his hellish realm, what depraved savagery in their nighted netherworld bred the cave beasts to grotesque giantism. Drawn by the noise and the scent of blood, this monster had left its sunless lair to hunt on the threshold of a land barred to its demonic kin for uncounted centuries.

It sensed its prey.

Unable to squirm free, Kane drew his sword for a hopeless defense. The cave creature had located him—in the darkness its hunting senses must be preternaturally keen—but it hesitated to spring. Seemingly it was confused by the wan rays of sunlight trespassing upon its realm.

The torch lay thrust between rocks almost within Kane's reach. By a series of desperate lunges he succeeded in spearing it on his sword tip and drawing it to him. Answering the sabre-tooth's growl, he swung the brand to flaring brilliance. The cat retreated somewhat, still intent on its trapped prey, but uncertain how to cope with this blazing light that seared its all but sightless eyes.

"Dwassllir! Can you break through!" The torch had burned through much of its length, so that the dwindling flame stung Kane's fingers.

The giant groaned with frantic effort. "There's a slab of rock midway I can't shift without bringing down the whole slide! If I had a beam I could use for bracing, I could grub out the boulders holding it up and crawl through! Not enough room through there otherwise!"

The sabre-tooth coughed angrily and advanced a step, stubby tail twitching. Its hunger would soon overwhelm its caution, Kane realized in sick dread, as the cat drew its mammoth bulk into a crouch. In a minute its spring would crush him against the stone.

Eyes blazing feral hatred, Kane steadied his sword. There would be time for only one hopeless thrust as the cat's irresistible spring splintered his chest to pulpy ruin, but Kane meant for his slayer to feel his steel.

"I'll try for his throat when he leaps!" Kane shouted grimly. "Wound him bad as I'm able! Go back and hunt up a log to brace with, Dwassllir. If my sword thrusts deep enough to cripple, there's a chance you can kill this beast with your ax. Brotemllain's crown waits there for you, and when you return to your people you can tell them the price of its winning!"

Dwassllir was tearing away rubble furiously, though Kane did not risk a glance to note his progress. "Keep the cat back as long as you can, Kane!" His voice came muffled. "It was my doing got you into this, and I'll not abandon you like a slinking coward!"

The torch was sputtering, moments of life remained for both flame and wielder. Came a low rumble of shifting stone, but Kane glared unwaveringly into the cat's wrathful eyes. The tiger started, spat in sudden bafflement. Kane braced himself to meet its deadly lunge, then saw in amazement that the sabre-tooth was edging away.

A flaming length of trunkwood slithered across the stones, propelled by a bass roar from down low. Turning in disbelief, Kane saw Dwassllir's grimy face grinning triumphantly up at him from beneath a jutting shelf of rock.

"Made it, by damn!" the giant bellowed. He grunted breathlessly as he wriggled his colossal frame through the burrow he had dug. "Used my ax to shore up that main slab! She creaked some, but her haft's seasoned hickory, and she'll likely hold till we're out of here!"

At the sudden appearance of a creature rivaling its own awesome bulk, the sabre-tooth had retreated into the darkness of the cavern. Dwassllir shoved his torch farther down the passage, then bent to Kane. A heave of his mighty shoulders drew back the imprisoning stone.

Kane pitched forward. Biting his lips against the agony, he slithered out of the crevice to freedom.

"Can you walk, manling?"

Wincing, Kane took a few unsteady strides. "Yeah, though I'd rather ride."

The giant hefted the torch. "I'll see King Brotemllain now," he declared.

"Don't be a fool, Dwassllir!" Kane protested. "Without your ax you're no match for that monster! You haven't driven it off—it's still prowling in the cavern! We'll be lucky to crawl out before it decides to attack!" The giant brushed him aside.

"Look, at least let's draw back and give that cat a chance to leave! We can find timber to shore up the ledge, and free your ax! Then we'll try for the crown!"

"Not enough time!" Dwassllir's face was resolute. "I never really expected that ax to hold. It'll give way any second, and this shaft will be sealed forever! Can't even risk trying to wrench it free! The torch will keep the beast at bay long enough to get the crown. Besides, he won't be the only demon to crawl up from the pit. You don't need to stay though."

Kane swore and limped after him.

"Ha! Sabre-tooth!" roared Dwassllir, scooping up a broken section of stalactite. A growl answered him from the cavern's echoing recesses. "Sabre-tooth! Do you know me! My ancestors were your enemy! We fought your forebears in ages past and made necklaces for our women from your pretty fangs! Hear me, sabre-tooth! Though you're three times the size of your tawny ancestor, I've no fear of you! I am Dwassllir—last true son of the blood of the old kings! I've come for my crown! Hide in your hole, sabre-tooth—or I'll have a white fur cloak to wear with my royal crown!"

The giant's challenge echoed through the cavern, rolled back by the sabre-tooth's angry snarl. Somewhere in the shadows the cat paced stiff-legged—but the cacophony of echoes made its position uncertain. Bats swooped in panic; dust and bits of stone trickled over them. Kane shifted his sword uneasily, not caring to think what silent blow might strike his back.

"King Brotemllain! The legends of my race do not lie!"

breathed Dwassllir in awe. Reverently he stood before the throne of the ages dead hero—his face aglow with vision of ancient glory. Reflected in his eyes was crimson brightness from the ruby crown.

The giant discarded the stalactite club, stretched to touch the dead king's crown. With gentle strength he broke it free from its encrusted setting. "Grandsire, your children have need of this . . ."

Avalanche of ivory fanged terror, the sabre-tooth bolted from the darkness. Shattering silence with its killing scream, it leapt for the giant's unprotected back. Off guard, Dwassllir pivoted at the final instant to half evade the cat's full rush. Its crushing impact hurled giant and cave beast against the throne and onto the cavern floor.

Jaws locked in Dwassllir's shoulder, the tiger raked furiously against his back, talons tearing deep gashes. Kane limped in, sword flashing. But his movements were clumsy, and at first slash a blow of the creature's paw spun him away. He fell heavily at the foot of the throne, shook his head dully to clear vision.

Dwassllir howled and lurched to his knees, huge hands clawing desperately to dislodge the murderous fangs. His flailing arm touched the fallen torch, and he seized it instantly, smashing its blazing end into the monster's face. Seared by the blinding heat, the sabre-tooth released its death grip with an enraged shriek— and the giant's punishing kick flung them apart.

Smoke hung over the cat's gory maw. Gouts of scarlet spurted from the giant's deeply gouged shoulder. "Face to face, sabre-tooth!" roared Dwassllir wildly. "Skulker in shadow! Slinking coward! Dare now to attack your master face to face!"

Even as the tiger crouched to spring, Dwassllir leapt upon it, crippled left arm brandishing the torch. They grappled in midair, and the cavern seemed to quake at their collision. Over and over they rolled, torch flung wide, while Kane groggily tried to regain his feet. The giant struggled grimly to stave off those awful fangs, to writhe atop the sabre-tooth's greater bulk. Fearsome jaws champed on emptiness as they fought, but its slashing claws were goring horrible wounds through the giant's flesh.

Stoically enduring the agony, Dwassllir threw all his leviathan strength into tightening his grip on the cat's head. He bellowed insanely—curses of pain, of fury—locked his teeth in the beast's ear and ripped away its stump with taunting laughter. Life blood poured over his limbs, made a slippery mat of scarlet-sodden white fur. Still he howled and jeered, chanted snatches of ancient verse—sagas of his race—pounded the sabre-tooth's skull against stone.

With a sudden wrench, Dwassllir hauled himself astride the cat's back. "Now die, sabre-tooth!" he roared. "Die knowing defeat as did your scrawny grandsires!"

He dug his knees into the creature's ribs, clamped heels together beneath its belly. The cat tried to roll, to dislodge him—but it could not. Great fists knotted over frothed fangs, arms locked champing jaws apart—Dwassllir bunched his shoulders and heaved backward. Gasping, coughing breath snorted from the cat's nostrils; its struggle was no longer to attack. For the first time in centuries, a sabre-tooth knew fear.

Blood gleamed a rippling pattern across the straining muscles of the giant's broad back. Irresistibly his hold tightened. Inexorably the tiger's spine bowed backward. An abrupt, explosive snap as vertebrae and sinew surrendered.

Laughing, Dwassllir twisted the sabre-tooth's head completely around. He spat into its dying eyes.

"Now then, King Brotemllain's crown!" he gasped, and staggered away from the twitching body. The giant reeled, but stood erect. His fur garments were shredded, dark and sticky. Blood flowed so freely as to shroud the depth and extent of his wounds; flaps of flesh hung ragged, and bone glistened yellow as he moved.

He groaned as he reached the throne and slumped down with his back braced against it. Kane found his senses clear enough to stand and knelt beside the stricken giant. Deftly his hands explored the other's wounds, sought vainly to staunch the bright, spurting blood from the sabre gouges. But Kane was veteran of too many battles not to know his wounds were mortal.

Dwassllir grinned gamely, his face pale beneath splashed gore. "That, Kane, is how my ancestors overcame the great beasts of Earth's dawn."

"No giant ever fought a creature like this," Kane swore, "nor killed it barehanded!"

The giant shrugged weakly. "You think not, manling? But you don't know the legends of our race, Kane. And the legends are truth, I know that now! Fire and Ice! Those were heroic days!"

Kane looked about the cavern, then bent to retrieve a fallen circle of gold. The rubies gleamed like Dwassllir's life blood; the crown was heavy in his hands. And though there was a fortune in his grasp, Kane no longer wanted King Brotemllain's crown.

"This is yours now," he muttered, and placed the crown upon Dwassllir's nodding brow.

The giant's head came erect again, and there was fierce pride in his face—and sadness. "I might have led them back to those lost days of glory!" he whispered. Then: "But there'll be another of my race, perhaps—another who will share my vision of the great age!"

He signed for Kane to leave him. Already his eyes looked upon things beyond this lonely cavern in a desolate waste. "That was an age to live in!" he breathed hoarsely. "An age of heroes!"

Kane somberly rose to his feet. "A great race, a heroic age—it's true," he acknowledged softly. "But I think the last of its heroes has passed."

Britisher Ramsey Campbell won a World Fantasy Award in 1978 for his "The Chimney" (appearing in Doubleday's *Whispers I*); however, 1976's "The Companion" was one of several Campbell items previously nominated for a World Fantasy Award. Stephen King uncompromisingly called this tale ". . . the best postwar story of supernatural horror I have ever read." It takes place in an amusement park although it is anything but amusing.

The Companion

by RAMSEY CAMPBELL

When Stone reached the fairground, having been misdirected twice, he thought it looked more like a gigantic amusement arcade. A couple of paper cups tumbled and rattled on the shore beneath the promenade, and the cold, insinuating October wind scooped the Mersey across the slabs of red rock that formed the beach and over the tyres and broken bottles. Beneath the stubby white protrusions of the long fairground façade were tucked souvenir shops and fish and chips; among them, in the fairground entrances, scraps of paper whirled.

Stone almost walked away. This wasn't his best holiday. One fairground in Wales had been closed, and this one certainly wasn't what he'd expected. The guidebook had made it sound like a genuine fairground, sideshows you must stride among, not looking in case their barkers lured you in, the sudden shock of waterfalls cascading down what looked like painted cardboard, the familiar sensations which were almost always there and for which welcome surged through him: the shots and bells and wooden concussion of sideshows, the girls' shrieks overhead, the slippery armour and juicy crunch of toffee-apples, the illuminations hanging against a darkening sky. But at least, he thought, he had· chosen his time well. Few people were about, and if he went in now he might have the funfair almost to himself.

As he approached an entrance he saw his mother eating fish and chips from a paper tray in the shop. No, rubbish. Besides, she would never have eaten standing up in public—"like a horse," as she used to say. As he passed the shop, she hurried onto the promenade, face averted from him and the wind. He picked at the image gingerly, anxious not to awaken its implications. Of course, it had been the way she ate, with little snatching motions of her fork and mouth. He pushed the incident to the side of his mind in the hope that it would fall away, and hurried through the entrance.

Noise and colour collided with him. Beneath the iron girders of a roof like that of a railway station, the sirens and simulated whistling jets and groaning metal and gnashing gears fused with their echoes in a single roaring, almost indistinguishable mass of sound, while panels of illuminated plastic, bright pink, pale green, sour orange, and yellow, spun and changed and fluttered on Stone's eyes. He retreated a step. Then, since none of the sensations diminished and he would have had to turn and run to reduce them, he strode forward.

Once he'd adjusted to its excesses, the fairground looked and felt dusty. The machines—a great disc rimmed with seats, that lifted roofward and tilted on its axis as it spun, dangling a lone couple over its gears; a looped caterpillar of seats that undulated brutally and trapped its passengers beneath a canvas canopy; a kind of roundabout whose independently rotating seats were given sudden violent jerks and spun helplessly—seemed grimy, as if just removed from a cupboard where they'd been left for years. With so few people in sight it seemed almost that the machines, frustrated by inaction, were operating themselves. For a moment Stone had the impression of being shut in a dusty room where the toys, as in childhood tales, had come to life. He shrugged vaguely and turned to leave. He wondered whether he had to drive to the fairground at Southport; it was a good few miles across the Mersey. His holiday was dwindling rapidly. He wondered how they were managing at the tax office this year in his absence. Slower as usual, no doubt.

Then he saw the roundabout. It was like a toy forgotten by another child and left here, or handed down the generations. Beneath its ornate scrolled canopy the horses rose on poles toward their reflexions in a ring of mirrors. The horses were white wood or wood painted white, their bodies dappled with purple, red and green, and some of their sketched faces too. From the hub, above a large notice MADE IN AMSTERDAM, an organ piped to itself. On the hub Stone saw carved fish, mermen, zephyrs, a head and shoulders smoking a pipe in a frame, a landscape of hills and lake and unfurling perched hawk. "Oh yes," Stone said.

He clambered onto the platform. He felt a hint of embarrassment and glanced about, but nobody was watching. "Can you pay me," said the head in the frame. "My boy's gone for a minute."

The man's hair was the colour of the smoke from his pipe, and his lips puckered on the stem and smiled. "It's a good roundabout," Stone said.

"You know about them, do you?"

"Well, a little." The man looked disappointed; Stone hurried on. "I know a good deal about fairgrounds. They're my holiday, you see, every year. Each year I cover a different area. I may write a book." At least, the idea had occasionally tempted him; but he hadn't taken notes, and he had ten years to retirement, for which the book had suggested itself as an activity.

"You go alone every year?"

"It has its merits. Less expensive, for one thing. I'm saving. Before I retire I intend to see Disneyland and Vienna." He thought of the Big Wheel, Harry Lime, the earth falling away beneath. "I'll get on," he said.

He patted the unyielding shoulders of the horse beneath him. He remembered a childhood friend who'd had a rocking horse in his bedroom. Stone had ridden it a few times, more and more wildly as the time to go home approached; his friend's bedroom was brighter and better lit than his, and as he clung to the wooden shoulders he was clutching the friendly room too. Fancy thinking of that now, he thought. Because I haven't been on a real roundabout for years, I suppose.

The roundabout shifted and the horse rose bearing him and sank. As they moved forward, slowly gathering momentum, Stone saw a crowd surging through one of the entrances and spreading through the funfair. He grimaced: it had been his fairground for a while, they needn't have arrived just as he was enjoying his roundabout.

The crowd swung away. A jangle of pinball machines sailed by. Amid the dodgems a giant with a barrel body spun, limp arms flapping, a red electric cigar thrust in its blankly grinning face and throbbing like an arrested balloon of slow, thick laughter. The roundabout was rotating faster and the fairground flashed on Stone's eyes like the images of a thaumatrope. Perhaps it was because he hadn't eaten for a while, saving himself for the toffee-apples, but he was becoming dizzy. It felt like the whirling, blurring shot of the fair in *Saturday Night and Sunday Morning,* a fair he hadn't liked, because it was too grim. Give him *Strangers on a Train, Some Came Running,* even the fairground murder in *Horrors of the Black Museum.* He shook his head to try to control his pouring thoughts.

A howling wind mixed with screams whipped by. It was looped on a tape inside the Ghost Train. The roundabout completed a quickening turn, and Stone's eyes fixed for a moment on the crowd standing beneath the beckoning green corpse. They were staring at him. No, he realized the next time they came round, they were staring at the roundabout. He was just something that kept reappearing as they watched. At the back of the crowd, staring and poking around inside his nostrils, stood Stone's father.

Stone gripped the horse's neck as he began to fall. The man had already been incorporated into the retreating crowd. Why was his mind so traitorous today? It wouldn't be so bad if the comparisons it was making weren't so repulsive. Why, he'd never met a man or woman since his parents to compare with them. Admired people, yes, but not in the same way. Not since the two polished boxes had been lowered into holes and hidden. Noise and colour spun about him and inside him. Why wasn't he allowing himself to think about his parents' death? He knew why he was blocking and that should be his salvation. At the age of ten he'd suffered death and hell every night.

The memories tumbled over him as he clung to the wood in the whirlpool. His father had denied him a nightlight and his mother had nodded, saying "Yes, I think it's time." He'd lain in bed terrified to move in case he betrayed his presence to the darkness, mouthing "Please God, don't let it" over and over. He lay so that he could see the faint grey rectangle of the window between the parted curtains in the far distance, but even that light seemed to be receding. He knew that death and hell would be like this. Sometimes, as he began to blur with sleep and the room grew larger and the shapes dark against the darkness awoke, he couldn't tell that he hadn't already died.

He sat back as the horse slowed and he began to slip forward across its neck. What then? Well, of course he'd seen through the self-perpetuating trap of religious guilt, of hell, of not daring not to believe in it because then it would get you. For a while he'd been vaguely uneasy in dark places, but not sufficiently so to track down the feeling and conquer it. After a while it had dissipated, along with his parents' overt disapproval of his atheism. Yes, he thought as his memories and the roundabout slowed, I was happiest then, lying in bed hearing them, no, feeling them and the house around me. Then, when he was thirty, a telephone call had summoned him to the hole in the road. There'd been a moment of sheer vertiginous terror at the sight of the car like a black beetle thrust nose first into the hole and suffocated. Then it was over. His parents had gone into darkness. That was enough. It was the one almost religious observance he imposed upon himself. Think no more.

And there was no reason to do so now. He staggered away from the roundabout, toward the pinball arcade that occupied most of one side of the funfair. He remembered how, when he lay mouthing soundlessly in bed, he would sometimes stop and think of what he'd read about dreams: that they might last for hours but in reality occupied only a split second. Was the same true of thoughts? And prayers, when you had nothing but darkness by which to tell the time? Besides defending him, his prayers were counting off the moments before dawn. Perhaps he had used up only a minute, only a second of darkness. Death and hell. What strange ideas I used to have, he thought. Especially for a ten-year-old. I wonder where they went. Away to be replaced by my ability with figures, of course.

Three boys of about twelve were crowded round a pinball machine. As the screen of their bodies parted for a moment he saw that they were trying to trigger it with a coin on a piece of wire. He took a stride toward them and opened his mouth, but restrained the sound. Everyone in the funfair must be half deafened; if the boys set about him, pulled him down and kicked him, his shouts wouldn't be heard. There was no sign of an attendant. Stone hurried back to the roundabout. Several little girls were mounting horses. Well, let them, he'd finished with it. "Those boys are up to no good," he said to the man in the frame.

"You! Yes, you! I've seen you before, don't let me see you again," the man shouted. They dispersed, swaggering.

"It didn't use to be like this," Stone said, breathing hard with relief. "I suppose your roundabout is all that's left of the old fairground."

"The old one?" the man said. "No, this didn't come from there."

"I thought it must have been taken over by this."

"No, it's still there, what's left of it," the man said. "You want to see it? Through that exit and just keep going. You'll come to the side entrance in five minutes, if it's still open."

The moon had risen. It glided along the rooftops as Stone emerged from the back of the funfair and hurried along the terraced street. Its light lingered on the tips of chimneys and on the highest edges of the roofs. Inside the houses, above slivers of earth or stone between the garden wall and the buildings, Stone saw faces silvered by television.

He reached the end of the street. Opposite, across a wider road, an alley paralleled a side street. Just keep going. Avoiding the alley and its connotations of someone else's domestic familiarity, Stone made for the street. As he entered it he glimpsed a group of boys emerging from the street he'd just left and running into the alley.

Anxiety impelled him as he wondered whether to turn back. His car was on the promenade, he could reach it in five minutes. They must be the boys he had seen in the pinball arcade, out for revenge. Quite possibly they had knives or broken bottles, no doubt they knew how to use them from the television. His heels clacked in the silence. Exits from the alley gaped between the houses. He tried to set his feet down gently as he ran. The boys were making no sound at all, at least none that reached him. If they managed to overbalance him they could smash his bones while he struggled to rise. At his age that could be worse than dangerous. He passed another dark exit. The houses looked threatening in their weight and impassivity. He must stay on his feet whatever happened. If two of them got hold of his arms he could only shout and yell. The houses leapt away as the street bent at a corner, and their opposite numbers loomed closer. In front of him, beyond a wall of corrugated tin, lay the old fairground.

He halted panting, trying to quell his breath before it blotted out any sounds in the alley. Both sides of the street ended as if lopped, and the road was blocked by the wall of tin. In the middle, however, the tin had been prised back like a lid, and a jagged entrance gaped among the sharp shadows and moonlit inscriptions. The fairground was closed and deserted.

As he realized that the last exit from the alley was back beyond the corner of the street, Stone stepped through the gap in the tin. He stared down the street, which was empty of pursuit, in fact of everything except scattered fragments of brick and glass. It occurred to him that they might not have been the same boys after all. He pulled the tin to behind him and looked around.

The circular booths, the long target galleries, the low roller coaster, the ark and crazy house draped shadow over each other and merged with the colour of the paths between. Even the roundabout was hooded by darkness hanging from its canopy. Such wood as he could see in the moonlight looked ragged, the paint patchy. But between the silent machines and stalls one ride was faintly illuminated: the Ghost Train.

He walked toward it. Its front was emitting a pale green glow which at first sight looked like moonlight, but which was brighter than the white tinge the moon imparted to the adjoining rides. Stone could see one empty car on the rails, close to the entrance to the ride. As he approached, he glimpsed from the corner of his eye a group of men, stallholders presumably, talking and gesticulating in the shadows between two stalls. So the fairground wasn't entirely deserted. He hurried toward the Ghost Train. They might be about to close, but perhaps they would allow him one ride, seeing that the Ghost Train was still lit. He hoped they hadn't seen him using the vandals' entrance.

As he reached the ride and realized that the glow came from a coat of luminous paint, liberally applied but now rather dull and threadbare, he heard a loud clang from the tin wall. It might have been someone throwing a brick, or it might have been the reopening of the torn door; the stalls obstructed his view. His gaze darted about for another exit but found none. He might run into a dead end. It was best to stay where he was. He couldn't trust the stallholders; they might live nearby, they might know the boys or even be their parents. As a child he'd once run to someone who had proved to be his attacker's unhelpful father. He climbed into the Ghost Train car.

Nothing happened. Nobody was attending the ride. Stone strained his ears. Neither the boys, if they were there, nor the attendant seemed to be approaching. If he called out the boys would hear him. Instead, frustrated and furious, he began to kick the metal inside the nose of the car.

Immediately the car trundled forward over the lip of an incline in the track and plunged through the Ghost Train doors into darkness.

As he swung around an unseen clattering curve, surrounded by noise and darkness, Stone felt as if he had suddenly become the victim of delirium. He remembered his storm-wracked childhood bed and the teeming darkness pouring into him. Why on earth had he come on this ride? He'd never liked ghost trains as a child, and as he grew up had instinctively avoided them. He'd allowed his panic to trap him. The boys might be waiting when he emerged. Well, in that case he would appeal to whoever was operating the ride. He sat back, gripping the wooden seat beneath him with both hands, and gave himself up to the straining and abrupt swoops of the car, and the darkness.

Then, as his anxiety about the outcome of the ride diminished, another impression began to trickle back. As the car had swung round the first curve he had glimpsed an illuminated shape, two illuminated shapes, withdrawn so swiftly that he'd had no time to glance up at them. He had the impression that they had been the faces of a man and a woman, gazing down at him. At once they had vanished into the darkness or been swept away by it. It seemed to him for some reason very important to remember their expressions.

Before he could pursue this, however, he saw a greyish glow ahead of him. He felt an unreasoning hope that it would be a window, which might give him an idea of the extent of the darkness. But already he could see that its shape was too irregular. A little closer and he could make it out. It was a large stuffed grey rabbit with huge glass or plastic eyes, squatting upright in an alcove with its front paws extended before it. Not a dead rabbit, of course: a toy. Beneath him the car was clattering and shaking, yet he had the odd conviction that this was a deliberate effect, that in fact the car had halted and the rabbit was approaching or growing. Rubbish, he thought. It was a pretty feeble ghost, anyway. Childish. His hands pulled at splinters on the wooden seat. The rabbit rushed toward him as the track descended a slight slope. One of its eyes was loose, and white stuffing hung down its cheek from the opening. It was at least four feet tall. As the car almost collided with it before whipping away around a curve, the rabbit toppled toward him and the light which illuminated it went out.

Stone gasped and clutched his chest. He'd twisted round to look behind him at the darkness where he judged the rabbit to have been, until a spasm wrenched him frontward again. Light tickling drifted over his face. He shuddered, then relaxed. Of course they always had threads hanging down for cobwebs, his friends had told him that. But no wonder the fairground was deserted if this was the best they could do. Giant toys lit up, indeed. Not only cheap but liable to give children nightmares.

The car coursed up a slight incline and down again before shaking itself in a frenzy around several curves. Trying to soften you up before the next shock, Stone thought. Not me, thank you. He lay back in his seat and sighed loudly with boredom. The sound hung on his ears like muffs. Why did I do that? he wondered. It's not as if the operator can hear me. Then who can?

Having spent its energy on the curves, the car was slowing. Stone peered ahead, trying to anticipate. Obviously he was meant to relax before the car startled him with a sudden jerk. As he peered, he found his eyes were adjusting to the darkness. At least, he could make out a few feet ahead at the side of the track a squat and bulky grey shape. He squinted as the car coasted toward it. It was a large armchair.

The car came abreast of it and halted. Stone peered at the chair. In the dim, hectic flecked light, which seemed to attract and outline all the restless discs on his eyes, the chair somehow looked larger than he. Perhaps it was farther away than he'd thought. Some clothes thrown over the back of the chair looked diminished by it, but they could be a child's clothes. If nothing else, Stone thought, it's instructive to watch my mind working. Now let's get on.

Then he noticed that the almost invisible light was flickering. Either that, which was possible although he couldn't determine the source of the light, or the clothes were shifting: very gradually but nonetheless definitely, as if something hidden by them on the seat of the chair were lifting them to peer out, perhaps preparatory to emerging. Stone leaned toward the chair. Let's see what it is, let's get it over with. But the light was far too dim and the chair too distant. Probably he would be unable to see it even when it emerged, the way the light had been allowed to run down, unless he left the car and went closer. He had one hand on the side of the car when he realized that if the car moved off while he was out of it, he would be left to grope his way through the darkness. He slumped back and at that moment glimpsed a violent movement among the clothes near the seat of the chair. He glanced toward it. Before his eyes could focus, the dim grey light was extinguished.

Stone sat for a moment, all of him concentrating on the silence, the blind darkness. Then he began to kick frantically at the nose of the car. The car shook a little with his attack, then jerked forward.

When the car nosed its way around the next curve, slowing as if sniffing the track ahead, and the clacking and rumbling ceased, Stone heard a muted thud and creak of wood. It came from in front of him. The sort of thing you hear in a house at night, he thought. Soon be out now.

Without warning a face came speeding toward him out of the darkness a few feet ahead. It jerked forward as he did. Of course it would, he thought with a grimace, sinking back and watching

his face recede briefly in the mirror. He realized that he and the
car were surrounded by a faint light, which extended as far as the
wooden frame of the mirror. Must be the end of the ride. They
can't get any more obvious than that. Effective in its way, I suppose.

He watched himself in the mirror as the car followed the curve
past. The light had fallen behind, but his silhouette loomed on it.
Suddenly he frowned. His silhouette was moving independent of
the movement of the car. It was beginning to swing out of the
limits of the mirror. Then he remembered the wardrobe which
had stood at the foot of his bed in his childhood, and understood.
The mirror was set into a door, which was opening.

Stone pressed himself against the opposite side of the car,
which had slowed almost to a halt. No, no, he thought, it mustn't.
Don't. He heard a grinding of gears beneath him. Unmeshed
metal shrieked. He threw his body forward against the nose of the
car. In the darkness to his left he heard the creak of the door and
a soft thud. The car moved a little, then caught the gears and
ground forward.

As the light went out behind him, Stone felt a weight fall beside
him on the seat.

He cried out. Or tried to, for as he gulped in air it seemed to
draw darkness into his lungs, darkness that swelled and poured
into his heart and brain. There was a moment at which he knew
nothing, as if he'd become darkness and silence and the memory
of suffering. Then the car was rattling on, the darkness was
sweeping over him and by, and the nose of the car banged open
the doors and plunged out into the night.

As the car swung onto the length of track outside the Ghost
Train, Stone caught sight of the gap between the stalls where he
had noted the stallholders. A welling moonlight showed him that
between the stalls stood a pile of sacks, nodding and gesticulating
in the wind. Then the seat beside him emerged from the shadow,
and he looked down.

Next to him on the seat was a shrunken hooded figure. It wore
a faded jacket and trousers striped and patched in various
colours, indistinguishable in the receding moonlight. The head almost reached his shoulder. Its arms hung slack at its sides, and its
feet drummed laxly on the metal beneath the seat. Shrinking

back, Stone reached for the front of the car to pull himself up, and the figure's head fell back.

Stone closed his eyes. When he opened them he saw within the hood an oval of white cloth upon which, black crosses for eyes and nose, a barred crescent for a mouth, a grinning face was stitched.

As he had suddenly realized that the car hadn't halted nor even slowed down before plunging down the incline back into the Ghost Train, Stone did not immediately notice that the figure had taken his hand.

BEST ARTIST

FRANK FRAZETTA

Artwork has always been an important facet of the publishing business, but only the past several years have regularly seen major volumes of art brought out by prestigious publishers as highly successful trade books. Some of these gatherings have sold enough copies to have made national best-seller lists, and two artists receiving such recognition are Frank Frazetta and Roger Dean.

Frank Frazetta is one of the field's few artists whose work guarantees sales for a book. It has been said that some publishers set out to find a book for his art rather than have him illustrate the book. Frazetta is a free spirit in the finest sense of the word. His art is rarely planned in detail. It is conceived and executed directly on the masonite or wood he works on. His paintings are anything but realistic. They are action dramas, brilliant excursions into his fertile imagination. His art vibrates with energy, his figures demand to move. There are no Frazetta women (alas!), no warriors, no beasts. They are exaggerations of the "real" creations from his fertile mind. Once you have seen a Frazetta masterpiece, though, it will not leave your psyche. The sales into the hundreds of thousands of his three volumes of art from Peacock Press attest to this fact. Frank Frazetta most deservedly won the 1976 World Fantasy Award for Best Artist.

ROGER DEAN

Roger Dean is very much an opposite of Frank Frazetta. In his highly successful book, *Views,* Dean shows how he carefully plans his artwork through mountains of sketches and preliminaries. Frazetta does not. Dean basically works realistically in a fantasy world. Frazetta is exaggeration. Dean works with reproduction in mind while Frazetta produces a painting and lets the publisher worry about how to reproduce it. Yet, both Dean and Frazetta are at the top of their fields, Roger mostly with his record album covers, Frank with his book covers. Dean's *Views* must be highly recommended to the reader not only for the excellence of its art, but for the marvelous insight as to how these masterworks were conceived and executed. Dean is an *architect,* both literally (it is, says Donald Lehmkuhl in *Views,* "his principal concern") and figuratively. His designs are truly intended to be utilized. Until our science creates the proper mode of travel, we will have to be stunned by these creations vicariously through the brilliance of Roger Dean's work in volumes such as *Views* (which, by the way, may be ordered through *Whispers*). The 1977 World Fantasy Award for Best Artist went to Roger Dean.

AFTERWORD

While most artists work in both black and white and color, it is far from unusual for one area to be better known than another. This book could not have interior color art, and we decided against inadequately reproducing color work in black and white. We have, though, been able to reprint some black and white artwork by some of the World Fantasy Award-nominated artists whose fame lies in that area.

Most important to note is our full-color cover from Roger Dean. Dean gets thousands of dollars for his record album covers and would obviously be far beyond the budget of an anthology such as this; however, through his great generosity and as a result of his admiration of the World Fantasy Award, we have been allowed to reprint a full color painting for our cover. Obviously our great thanks cannot come close to repaying our debt to Roger's thoughtfulness to us and the award, but thank you, Roger, nonetheless.

This Russell Kirk novelette is the last of the trio nominated for a World Fantasy Award from Kirby McCauley's *Frights*. It won the 1977 award in the Short Fiction category. Russell Kirk is, of course, best known for his classic books on political thought including *The Conservative Mind, Eliot and His Age,* and *The Roots of American Order*. It is a tribute to his genius that such serious volumes have sold over *one million* copies. It is no less surprising that his supernatural fiction, while traditional in the purest sense, is also full of insight and commentary. After reading this treasure from the literary hoard of Dr. Kirk, you will be pleased to know he has recently written several more stories that will shortly see print and very well may find their way into a future World Fantasy Awards' book.

There's a Long, Long Trail A-Winding

by RUSSELL KIRK

Then he said unto the disciples, It is impossible but that offences will come; but woe unto him, through whom they come!

It were better for him that a millstone were hanged about his neck, and he cast into the sea, than that he should offend one of these little ones.

—Luke 17: 1,2

Along the empty six-lane highway, the blizzard swept as if it meant to swallow all the sensual world. Frank Sarsfield, massive though he was, scudded like a heavy kite before that overwhelming wind. On his thick white hair the snow clotted and tried to form a cap; the big flakes so swirled round his Viking face that he scarcely could make out the barren country on either side of the road.

Somehow he must get indoors. Racing for sanctuary, the last automobile had swept unheeding past his thumb two hours ago, bound doubtless for the county town some twenty miles eastward. Westward among the hills, the highway must be blocked by snowdrifts now. This was an unkind twelfth of January. "Blow, blow, thou Winter wind!" Twilight being almost upon him, soon he must find lodging or else freeze stiff by the roadside.

He had walked more than thirty miles that day. Having in his pocket the sum of twenty-nine dollars and thirty cents, he could have put up at either of the two motels he had passed—had they not been closed for the winter. Well, as always, he was decently dressed—a good wash-and-wear suit and a neat black overcoat. As always, he was shaven and clean and civil-spoken. Surely some farmer or villager would take him in, if he knocked with a ten-dollar bill in his fist. People sometimes mistook him for a stranded well-to-do motorist, and sometimes he took the trouble to undeceive them.

But where to apply? This was depopulated country, its forests gone to the sawmills long before, its mines worked out. The freeway ran through the abomination of desolation. He did not prefer to walk the freeways, but on such a day as this there were no cars on the lesser roads.

He had run away from a hardscrabble New Hampshire farm when he was fourteen, and ever since then, except for brief working intervals, he had been either on the roads or in the jails. Now his sixtieth birthday was imminent. There were few men bigger than Frank Sarsfield, and none more solitary. Where was a friendly house?

For a few moments, the rage of the snow slackened; he stared about. Away to the left, almost a mile distant, he made out a grim high clump of buildings on rising ground, a wall enclosing them; the roof of the central building was gone. Sarsfield grinned, knowing what that complex must be: a derelict prison. He had lodged in prisons altogether too many nights.

His hand sheltering his eyes from the north wind, he looked to his left. Down in a snug valley, beside a narrow river and broad marshes, he could perceive a village or hamlet: a white church tower, three or four commercial buildings, some little houses, beyond them a park of bare maple trees. The old highway must have run through or near this forgotten place, but the new freeway had sealed it off. There was no sign of a freeway exit to the settlement; probably it could be reached by car only along some detouring country lane. In such a little decayed town there would be folk willing to accept him for the sake of his proffered ten dollars—or, better, simply for charity's sake and talk with an amusing stranger who could recite every kind of poetry.

He scrambled heavily down the embankment. At this point, praise be, no tremendous wire fence kept the haughty new highway inviolable. His powerful thighs took him through the swelling drifts, though his heart pounded as the storm burst upon him afresh.

The village was more distant than he had thought. He passed panting through old fields half grown up to poplar and birch. A little to the west he noticed what seemed to be old mine-workings, with fragments of brick buildings. He clambered upon an old railroad bed, its rails and ties taken up; perhaps the new freeway had dealt the final blow to the rails. Here the going was somewhat easier.

Mingled with the wind's shriek, did he hear a church bell now? Could they be holding services at the village in this weather? Presently he came to a burnt-out little railway depot, on its platform signboard still the name "Anthonyville." Now he walked on a street of sorts, but no car-tracks or footprints sullying the snow.

Anthonyville Free Methodist Church hulked before him. Indeed the bell was swinging, and now and again faintly ringing in the steeple; but it was the wind's mockery, a knell for the derelict town of Anthonyville. The church door was slamming in the high wind, flying open again, and slamming once more, like a perpetual-motion machine, the glass being gone from the church windows. Sarsfield trudged past the skeletal church.

The front of Emmons's General Store was boarded up, and so was the front of what might have been a drugstore. The village hall was a wreck. The school might have stood upon those scanty foundations which protruded from the snow. And from no chimney of the decrepit cottages and cabins along Main Street—the only street—did any smoke rise.

Sarsfield never had seen a deader village. In an upper window of what looked like a livery stable converted into a garage, a faded cardboard sign could be read—

REMEMBER YOUR FUTURE
BACK THE TOWNSEND PLAN

Was no one at all left here—not even some gaunt old couple managing on Social Security? He might force his way into one of the stores or cottages—though on principle and prudence he generally steered clear of possible charges of breaking and entering—but that would be cold comfort. In poor Anthonyville there must remain some living soul.

His mittened hands clutching his red ears, Sarsfield had plodded nearly to the end of Main Street. Anthonyville was Endsville, he saw now: river and swamp and new highway cut it off altogether from the rest of the frozen world, except for the drift-obliterated country road that twisted southward, Lord knew whither. He might count himself lucky to find a stove, left behind in some shack, that he could feed with boards ripped from walls.

Main Street ended at that grove or park of old maples. Just a sugarbush, like those he had tapped in his boyhood under his father's rough command? No: had the trees not been leafless, he might not have discerned the big stone house among the trees, the only substantial building remaining to Anthonyville. But see it he did for one moment, before the blizzard veiled it from him. There were stone gateposts, too, and a bronze tablet set into one of them. Sarsfield brushed the snowflakes from the inscription: "Tamarack House."

Stumbling among the maples toward this promise, he almost collided with a tall glacial boulder. A similar boulder rose a few feet to his right, the pair of them halfway between gateposts and house. There was a bronze tablet on this boulder, too, and he paused to read it:

Sacred to the memory of
JEROME ANTHONY
July 4, 1836–January 14, 1915
Brigadier-General in the Corps of Engineers,
Army of the Republic
founder of this town
architect of Anthonyville State Prison
who died as he had lived, with honor

"And there will I keep you forever,
Yes, forever and a day,
Till the wall shall crumble in ruin,
And moulder in dust away."

There's an epitaph for a prison architect, Sarsfield thought. It was too bitter an evening for inspecting the other boulder, and he hurried toward the portice of Tamarack House. This was a very big house indeed, a bracketed house, built all of squared field-stone with beautiful glints to the masonry. A cupola topped it.

Once, come out of the cold into a public library, Sarsfield had pored over a picture book about American architectural styles. There was a word for this sort of house. Was it "Italianate"? Yes, it rose in his memory—he took pride in no quality except his power of recollection. Yes, that was the word. Had he visited this house before? He could not account for a vague familiarity. Perhaps there had been a photograph of this particular house in that library book.

Every window was heavily shuttered, and no smoke rose from any of the several chimneys. Sarsfield went up the stone steps to confront the oaken front door.

It was a formidable door, but it seemed as if at some time it had been broken open, for long ago a square of oak with a different grain had been mortised into the area round lock and keyhole. There was a gigantic knocker with a strange face worked upon it. Sarsfield knocked repeatedly.

No one answered. Conceivably the storm might have made his pounding inaudible to any occupants, but who could spend the winter in a shuttered house without fires? Another bronze plaque was screwed to the door:

TAMARACK HOUSE
Property of the Anthony Family Trust
Guarded by Protective Service

Sarsfield doubted the veracity of the last line. He made his way round to the back. No one answered those back doors, either, and they too were locked.

But presently he found what he had hoped for: an oldfangled slanting cellar door, set into the foundations. It was not wise to enter without permission, but at least he might accomplish it without breaking. His fingers, though clumsy, were strong as the rest of him. After much trouble and with help from the Boy Scout knife that he carried, he pulled the pins out of the cellar door's three hinges and scrambled down into the darkness. With the passing of the years, he had become something of a jailhouse lawyer—though those young inmates bored him with their endless chatter about Miranda and Escobedo. And now he thought of the doctrine called "defense of necessity." If caught, he could say that self-preservation from freezing is the first necessity; besides, they might not take him for a bum.

Faint light down the cellar steps—he would replace the hinge pins later—showed him an inner door at the foot. That door was hooked, though hooked only. With a sigh, Sarsfield put his shoulder to the door; the hook clattered to the stone floor inside; and he was master of all he surveyed.

In that black cellar he found no light switch. Though he never smoked, he carried matches for such emergencies. Having lit one, he discovered a providential kerosene lamp on a table, with enough kerosene still in it. Sarsfield went lamplit through the cellars and up more stone stairs into a pantry. "Anybody home?" he called. It was an eerie echo.

He would make sure before exploring, for he dreaded shotguns. How about a cheerful song? In that chill pantry, Sarsfield bellowed a tune formerly beloved at Rotary Clubs. Once a waggish Rotarian, after half an hour's talk with the hobo extraordinary, had taken him to Rotary for lunch and commanded him to tell tales of the road and to sing the members a song. Frank Sarsfield's untutored voice was loud enough when he wanted it to be, and he sang the song he had sung to Rotary:

> *"There's a long, long trail a-winding into the land of*
> *   my dreams,*
> *Where the nightingale is singing and the white moon beams;*
> *There's a long, long night of waiting until my dreams all*
> *   come true,*
> *Till the day when I'll be walking down that long, long*
> *   trail to you!"*

No response: no cry, no footstep, not a rustle. Even in so big a house, they couldn't have failed to hear his song, sung in a voice fit to wake the dead. Father O'Malley had called Frank's voice "stentorian"—a good word, though he was not just sure what it meant. He liked that last line, though he'd no one to walk to; he'd repeat it:

> *"Till the day when I'll be walking down that long,*
> *   long trail to you!"*

It was all right. Sarsfield went into the dining room, where he found a splendid long walnut table, chairs with embroidered seats, a fine sideboard and china cabinet, and a high Venetian chandelier. The china was in that cabinet, and the silverware was in that sideboard. But in no room of Tamarack House was any living soul.

Sprawled in a big chair before the fireplace in the Sunday parlor, Sarsfield took the chill out of his bones. The woodshed, connected with the main house by a passage from the kitchen, was half filled with logs—not first-rate fuel, true, for they had been stacked there three or four years ago, to judge by the fungi upon them, but burnable after he had collected old newspapers and chopped kindling. He had crisscrossed elm and birch to make a noble fire.

It was not very risky to let white woodsmoke eddy from the

chimneys, for it would blend with the driving snow and the blast would dissipate it at once. Besides, Anthonyville's population was zero. From the cupola atop the house, in another lull of the blizzard, he had looked over the icy countryside and had seen no inhabited farmhouse up the forgotten dirt road—which, anyway, was hopelessly blocked by drifts today. There was no approach for vehicles from the freeway, while river and marsh protected the rear. He speculated that Tamarack House might be inhabited summers, though not in any very recent summer. The "Protective Service" probably consisted of a farmer who made a fortnightly inspection in fair weather.

It was good to hole up in a remote county where burglars seemed unknown as yet. Frank Sarsfield restricted his own depredations to church poor boxes (Catholic, preferably, he being no Protestant) and then under defense of necessity, after a run of unsuccessful mendicancy. He feared and detested strong thieves, so numerous nowadays; to avoid them and worse than thieves, he steered clear of the cities, roving to little places which still kept crime in the family, where it belonged.

He had dined, and then washed the dishes dutifully. The kitchen wood range still functioned, and so did the hard-water and soft-water hand pumps in the scullery. As for food, there was enough to feed a good-sized prison: the shelves of the deep cellar cold room threatened to collapse under the weight of glass jars full of jams, jellies, preserved peaches, apricots, applesauce, pickled pork, pickled trout, and many more good things, all redolent of his New England youth. Most of the jars had neat paper labels, all giving the year of canning, some the name of the canner; on the front shelves, the most recent date he had found was 1968, on a little pot of strawberry jam, and below it was the name "Allegra" in a feminine hand.

Everything in this house lay in apple-pie order—though Sarsfield wondered how long the plaster would keep from cracking, with Tamarack House unheated in winter. He felt positively virtuous for lighting fires, one here in the Sunday parlor, another in the little antique iron stove in the bedroom he had chosen for himself at the top of the house.

He had poked into every handsome room of Tamarack House, with the intense pleasure of a small boy who had found his way into an enchanted castle. Every room was satisfying, well furnished (he was warming by the fire two sheets from the linen closet, for his bed), and wondrously old-fashioned. There was no electric light, no central heating, no bathroom; there was an indoor privy, at the back of the woodshed, but no running water unless one counted the hand pumps. There was an oldfangled wall telephone: Frank tried, greatly daring, for the operator, but it was dead. He had found a crystal-set radio that didn't work. This was an old lady's house, surely, and the old lady hadn't visited it for some years, but perhaps her relatives kept it in order as a "holiday home" or in hope of selling it—at ruined Anthonyville, a forlorn hope. He had discovered two canisters of tea, a jar full of coffee beans, and ten gallons of kerosene. How thoughtful!

Perhaps the old lady was dead, buried under that other boulder among the maples in front of the house. Perhaps she had been the General's daughter—but no, not if the General had been born in 1836. Why those graves in the lawn? Sarsfield had heard of farm families, near medical schools in the old days, who had buried their dead by the house for fear of body-snatchers; but that couldn't apply at Anthonyville. Well, there were family graveyards, but this must be one of the smallest.

The old General who built this house had died on January 14. Day after tomorrow, January 14 would come round again, and it would be Frank Sarsfield's sixtieth birthday. "I drink your health in water, General," Sarsfield said aloud, raising his cut-glass goblet taken from the china cabinet. There was no strong drink in the house, but that didn't distress Sarsfield, for he never touched it. His mother had warned him against it—and sure enough, the one time he had drunk a good deal of wine, when he was new to the road, he had got sick. "Thanks, General, for your hospitality." Nobody responded to his toast.

His mother had been a saint, the neighbors had said, and his father a drunken devil. He had seen neither of them after he ran away. He had missed his mother's funeral because he hadn't known of her death until months after; he had missed his father's, long later, because he chose to miss it, though that omission cost him sleepless nights now. Sarsfield slept poorly at best. Almost always there were nightmares.

Yet perhaps he would sleep well enough tonight in that little garret room near the cupola. He had found that several of the bedrooms in Tamarack House had little metal plates over their doorways. There were "The General's Room" and "Father's Room" and "Mama's Room" and "Alice's Room" and "Allegra's Room" and "Edith's Room." By a happy coincidence, the little room at the top of the back stair, on the garret floor of the house, was labeled "Frank's Room." But he'd not chosen it for that only. At the top of the house, one was safer from sheriffs or burglars. And through the skylight—there was only a frieze window —a man could get to the roof of the main block. From that roof, one could descend to the woodshed roof by a fire escape of iron rungs fixed in the stone outer wall; and from the woodshed, it was an easy drop to the ground. After that, the chief difficulty would be to run down Main Street and then get across the freeway without being detected, while people searched the house for you. Talk of Goldilocks and the Three Bears! Much experience had taught Sarsfield such forethought.

Had that other Frank, so commemorated over the bedroom door, been a son or a servant? Presumably a son—though Sarsfield had found no pictures of boys in the old velvet-covered album in the Sunday parlor, nor any of manservants. There were many pictures of the General, a little roosterlike man with a beard; and of Father, portly and pleasant-faced; and of Mama, elegant; and of three small girls, who must be Alice and Allegra and Edith. He had liked especially the photographs of Allegra, since he had tasted her strawberry jam. All the girls were pretty, but Allegra—who must be about seven in most of the pictures— was really charming, with long ringlets and kind eyes and a delicate mouth that curved upward at its corners.

Sarsfield adored little girls and distrusted big girls. His mother had cautioned him against bad women, so he had kept away from such. Because he liked peace, he never had married—not that he could have married anyway, because that would have tied him to one place, and he was too clumsy to earn money at practically anything except dishwashing for summer hotels. Not marrying had meant that he could have no little daughters like Allegra.

Sometimes he had puzzled the prison psychiatrists. In prison it was well to play stupid. He had refrained cunningly from reciting poetry to the psychiatrists. So after testing them they wrote him down as "dull normal" and he was assigned to labor as "gardener"—which meant going round the prison yards picking up trash by a stick with a nail in the end of it. That was easy work, and he detested hard work. Yet when there was truly heavy work to be done in prison, sometimes he would come forward to shovel tons of coal or carry hods of brick or lift big blocks into place. That, too, was his cunning: it impressed the other jailbirds with his enormous strength, so that the gangs left him alone.

"Yes, you're a loner, Frank Sarsfield," he said to himself, aloud. He looked at himself in that splendid Sunday-parlor mirror, which stretched from floor to ceiling. He saw a man overweight but lean enough of face, standing six feet six, built like a bear, a strong nose, some teeth missing, a strong chin, and rather wild light-blue eyes. He was an uncommon sort of bum. Deliberately he looked at his image out of the corners of his eyes—as was his way, because he was non-violent, and eye contact might mean trouble.

"You look like a Viking, Frank," old Father O'Malley had told him once, "but you ought to have been a monk."

"Oh, Father," he had answered, "I'm too much of a fool for a monk."

"Well," said Father O'Malley, "you're no more fool than many a brother, and you're celibate, and continent, I take it. Yet it's late for that now. Look out you don't turn berserker, Frank. Go to confession, sometime, to a priest that doesn't know you, if you'll not go to me. If you'd confess, you'd not be haunted."

But he seldom went to mass, and never to confession. All those church boxes pilfered, his mother and father abandoned, his sister neglected, all the ghastly humbling of himself before policemen, all the horror and shame of the prisons! There could be no grace for him now. *"There's a long, long trail a-winding into the land of my dreams . . ."* What dreams! He had looked up "berserker" in Webster. But he wouldn't ever do that sort of thing: a man had to keep a control upon himself, and besides he was a coward, and he loved peace.

Nearly all the other prisoners had been brutes, guilty as sin, guilty as Miranda or Escobedo. Once, sentenced for rifling a church safe, he had been put into the same cell with a man who had murdered his wife by taking off her head. The head never had been found. Sarsfield had dreamed of that head in such short intervals of sleep as he had enjoyed while the wife-killer was his cellmate. Nearly all night, every night, he had lain awake surreptitiously watching the murderer in the opposite bunk, and feeling his own neck now and again. He had been surprised and pleased when eventually the wife-killer had gone hysterical and obtained assignment to another cell. The murderer had told the guards that he just couldn't stand being watched all night by that terrible giant who never talked.

Only one of the prison psychiatrists had been pleasant or bright, and that had been the old doctor born in Vienna who went round from penitentiary to penitentiary checking on the psychiatric staffs. The old doctor had taken a liking to him, and had written a report to accompany Frank's petition for parole. Three months later, in a parole office, the parole officer had gone out hurriedly for a quarter of an hour, and Sarsfield had taken the chance to read his own file that the parole man had left in a folder on his desk.

"Francis Sarsfield has a memory that almost can be described as photographic"—so had run one line in the Vienna doctor's report. When he read that, Sarsfield had known that the doctor was a clever doctor. "He suffers chiefly from an arrest of emotional development, and may be regarded as a rather bright small boy in some respects. His three temporarily successful escapes from prison suggest that his intelligence has been much underrated. On at least one of those occasions, he could have eluded the arresting officer had he been willing to resort to violence. Sarsfield repeatedly describes himself as non-violent and has no record of aggression while confined, nor in connection with any of the offenses for which he was arrested. On the contrary, he seems timid and withdrawn, and might become a victim of assaults in prison, were it not for his size, strength, and power of voice."

Sarsfield had been pleased enough by that paragraph, but a little puzzled by what followed:

"In general, Sarsfield is one of those recidivicists who ought not to be confined, were any alternative method now available for restraining them from petty offenses against property. Not only does he lack belligerence against men, but apparently he is quite clean of any record against women and children. It seems that he does not indulge in autoeroticism, either—perhaps because of strict instruction by his R.C. mother during his formative years.

"I add, however, that conceivably Sarsfield is not fundamentally so gentle as his record indicates. He can be energetic in self-defense when pushed to the wall. In his youth occasionally he was induced, for the promise of $5 or $10, to stand up as an amateur against some traveling professional boxer. He admits that he did not fight hard, and cried when he was badly beaten. Nevertheless, I am inclined to suspect a potentiality for violence, long repressed but not totally extinguished by years of 'humbling himself,' in his phrase. This possibility is not so certain as to warrant additional detention, even though three years of Sarsfield's sentence remain unexpired."

Yes, he had memorized nearly the whole of that old doctor's analysis, which had got his parole for him. There had been the concluding paragraphs:

"Francis Sarsfield is oppressed by a haunting sense of personal guilt. He is religious to the point of superstition, an R.C., and appears to believe himself damned. Although worldly-wise in a number of respects, he retains an almost unique innocence in others. His frequent humor and candor account for his success, much of the time, at begging. He has read much during his wanderings and terms of confinement. He has a strong taste for good poetry of the popular sort, and has accumulated a mass of miscellaneous information, much of it irrelevant to the life he leads.

"Although occasionally moody and even surly, most of the time he subjects himself to authority, and will work fairly well if closely supervised. He possesses no skills of any sort, unless some knack for woodchopping, acquired while he was enrolled in the Civilian Conservation Corps, can be considered a marketable skill. He appears to be incorrigibly footloose, and therefore confinement is more unpleasant to him than to most prisoners. It is truly remarkable that he continues to be rational enough, his isolation and heavy guilt-complex considered.

"Sometimes evasive when he does not desire to answer questions, nevertheless he rarely utters a direct lie. His personal modesty may be described as excessive. His habits of cleanliness are commendable, if perhaps of origins like Lady Macbeth's.

"Despite his strength, he is a diabetic and suffers from a heart-murmur, sometimes painful.

"Only in circumstances so favorable as to be virtually unobtainable could Sarsfield succeed in abstaining from the behavior-pattern that has led to his repeated prosecution and imprisonment. The excessive crowding of this penitentiary considered, however, I strongly recommend that he be released upon parole. Previous psychiatric reports concerning this inmate have been shallow and erroneous, I regret to note. Perhaps Sarsfield's chief psychological difficulty is that, from obscure causes, he lacks emotional communication with other adults, although able to maintain cordial and healthy relations with small children. He is very nearly a solipsist, which in large part may account for his inability to make firm decisions or pursue any regular occupation. In contradiction of previous analyses of Sarsfield, he should not be described as 'dull normal' intellectually. Francis Sarsfield distinctly is neither dull nor normal."

Sarsfield had looked up "solipsist," but hadn't found himself much the wiser. He didn't think himself the only existent thing— not most of the time, anyway. He wasn't sure that the old doctor had been real, but he knew that his mother had been real before she went straight to Heaven. He knew that his nightmares probably weren't real; but sometimes, while awake, he could see things that other men couldn't. In a house like this, he could glimpse little unaccountable movements out of the corners of his eyes, but it wouldn't do to worry about those. He was afraid of those things which other people couldn't see, yet not so frightened of them as most people were. Some of the other inmates had called him Crazy Frank, and it had been hard to keep down his temper. If you could perceive *more* existent things, though not flesh-and-blood things, than psychiatrists or convicts could—why, were you a solipsist?

There was no point in puzzling over it. Dad had taken him out of school to work on the farm when he hadn't yet finished the fourth grade, so words like "solipsist" didn't mean much to him. Poets' words, though, he mostly understood. He had picked up a rhyme that made children laugh when he told it to them:

> *"Though you don't know it,*
> *You're a poet.*
> *Your feet show it:*
> *They're Longfellows."*

That wasn't very good poetry, but Henry Wadsworth Longfellow was a good poet. They must have loved Henry Wadsworth
Longfellow in this house, and especially *The Children's Hour*, because of those three little girls named Alice, Allegra, and Edith,
and those lines on the general's boulder. Allegra: that's the pret-
tiest of all names ever, and it meant "merry," someone had told
him.

He looked at the cheap wrist watch he had bought, besides the
wash-and-wear suit, with his last dishwashing money from that
Lake Superior summer hotel. Well, midnight! It's up the wooden
hill for you, Frank Sarsfield, to your snug little room under the
rafters. If anybody comes to Tamarack House tonight, it's out the
skylight and through the snow for you, Frank, my boy—and no
tiny reindeer. If you want to survive, in prison or out of it, you
stick to your own business and let other folks stew in their own
juice.

Before he closed his eyes, he would pray for Mother's soul—
not that she really needed it—and then say the little Scottish
prayer he had found in a children's book:

"From ghosties and ghoulies, long-leggitie beasties, and things
that go bump in the night, good Lord deliver us!"

The next morning, the morning before his birthday, Frank
Sarsfield went up the circular stair to the cupola, even before
making his breakfast of pickled trout and peaches and strong
coffee. The wind had gone down, and it was snowing only lightly
now, but the drifts were immense. Nobody would make his way
to Anthonyville and Tamarack House this day; the snowplows
would be busy elsewhere.

From this height he could see the freeway, and nothing seemed
to be moving along it. The dead village lay to the north of him.
To the east were river and swamp, the shores lined with those

handsome tamaracks, the green gone out of them, which had given this house its name. Everything in sight belonged to Frank.

He had dreamed during the night, the wind howling and whining round the top of the house, and he had known he was dreaming, but it had been even stranger than usual, if less horrible.

In his dream, he had found himself in the dining room of Tamarack House. He had not been alone. The General and Father and Mama and the three little girls had been dining happily at the long table, and he had waited on them. In the kitchen an old woman who was the cook, and a girl who cleaned, had eaten by themselves. But when he had finished filling the family's plates, he had sat down at the end of the table, as if he had been expected to do that.

The family had talked among themselves and even to him as he ate, but somehow he had not been able to hear what they said to him. Suddenly he had pricked up his ears, though, because Allegra had spoken to him.

"Frank," she had said, all mischief, "why do they call you Punkinhead?"

The old General had frowned at the head of the table, and Mama had said, "Allegra, don't speak that way to Frank!"

But he had grinned at Allegra, if a little hurt, and had told the little girl, "Because some men think I've got a head like a jack-o-lantern's and not even seeds inside it."

"Nonsense, Frank," Mama had put in, "you have a very handsome head."

"You've got a pretty head, Frank," the three little girls had told him then, almost in chorus, placatingly. Allegra had come round the table to make her peace. "There's going to be a big surprise for you tomorrow, Frank," she had whispered to him. And then she had kissed him on the cheek.

That had waked him. Most of the rest of that howling night he had lain awake trying to make sense of his dream, but he couldn't. The people in it had been more real than the people he met on the long, long trail.

Now he strolled through the house again, admiring everything. It was almost as if he had seen the furniture and the pictures and the carpets long, long ago. The house must be over a century old, and many of the good things in it must go back to the beginning. He would have two or three more days here until the roads were cleared. There were no newspapers to tell him about the great storm, of course, and no radio that worked; but that didn't matter.

He found a great big handsome *Complete Works of Henry Wadsworth Longfellow,* in red morocco, and an illustrated copy of the *Rubaiyat.* He didn't need to read it, because he had memorized all the quatrains once. There was a black silk ribbon as marker between the pages, and he opened it there—at Quatrain 44, it turned out:

> *"Why, if the Soul can fling the Dust aside,*
> *And naked on the Air of Heaven ride,*
> *Were't not a Shame—were't not a Shame for him*
> *In this clay carcass crippled to abide?"*

That old Vienna doctor, Frank suspected, hadn't believed in immortal souls. Frank Sarsfield knew better. But also Frank suspected that his soul never would ride, naked or clothed, on the Air of Heaven. Souls! That put him in mind of his sister, a living soul that he had forsaken. He ought to write her a letter on this eve of his sixtieth birthday.

Frank traveled light, his luggage being mostly a safety razor, a hairbrush, and a comb; he washed his shirt and socks and underclothes every night, and often his wash-and-wear suit, too. But he did carry with him a few sheets of paper and a ballpoint pen. Sitting down at the library table—he had built a fire in the library stove also, there being no lack of logs—he began to write to Mary Sarsfield, alone in the rotting farmhouse in New Hampshire. His spelling wasn't good, he knew, but today he was careful at his birthday letter, using the big old dictionary with the General's bookplate in it.

To write that letter took most of the day. Two versions were discarded. At last Frank had done the best he could.

Dearest Mary my sister,
     Its been nearly 9 years since I came to visit you and borrowed the $78 from you and went away again and never paid

it back. I guess you dont want to see your brother Frank again after what I did that time and other times but the Ethiopian can not change his skin nor the leopard his spots and when some man like a Jehovahs Witness or that rancher with all the cash gives me quite a lot of money I mean to send you what I owe but the post office isnt handy at the time and so I spend it on presents for little kids I meet and buying new clothes and such so I never get around to sending you that $78 Mary. Right now I have $29 and more but the post office at this place is folded up and by the time I get to the next town the money will be mostly gone and so it goes. I guess probably you need the money and Im sorry Mary but maybe some day I will win in the lottery and then Ill give you all the thousands of dollars I win.

Well Mary its been 41 years and 183 days since Mother passed away and here I am 60 years old tomorrow and you getting on toward 56. I pray that your cough is better and that your son and my nephew Jack is doing better than he was in Tallahassee Florida. Some time Mary if you would write to me c/o Father Justin O'Malley in Albatross Michigan where he is pastor now I would stop by his rectory and get your letter and read it with joy. But I know Ive been a very bad brother and I dont blame you Mary if you never get around to writing your brother Frank.

Mary Ive been staying out of jails and working a little here and there along the road. Now Mary do you know what I hate most about those prisons? Why not being on the road you will say. No Mary the worst thing is the foul language the convicts use from morning till night. Taking the name of their Lord in vain is the least they do. There is a foul curse word in their every sentence. I wasnt brought up that way any more than you Mary and I will not revile woman or child. It is like being in H———— to hear it.

Im not in bad shape except the diabetes is no better but I take my pills for it when I can buy them and dont have to take needles for it and my heart hurts me dreadfully bad sometimes when I lift heavy things hours on end and sometimes it hurts me worse at night when Ive been just lying there thinking of the life Ive led and how I ought to pay you

the $78 and pay back other folks that helped me too. I owe
Father O'Malley $497.11 now altogether and I keep track of
it in my head and when the lottery ticket wins he will not be
forgot.

Some people have been quite good to me and I still can
make them laugh and I recite to them and generally I start
my reciting with what No Person of Quality wrote hundreds
of years ago

Seven wealthy towns contend for Homer dead
Through which the living Homer begged his bread.

They like that and also usually they like Thomas Grays
Elegy in a Country Churchyard leaving the world to darkness
and to me and I recite all of that and sometimes some of the
Quatrains of Omar. At farms when they ask me I chop wood
for these folks and I help with the dishes but I still break a
good many as you learned Mary 9 years ago but I didnt
mean to do it Mary because I am just clumsy in all ways. Oh
yes I am good at reciting Frosts Stopping by Woods and his
poem about the Hired Man. I have been reading the poetical
works of Thomas Stearns Eliot so I can recite his The Hollow Men or much of it and also his Book of Practical Cats
which is comical when I come to college towns and some
professor or his wife gives me a sandwich and maybe $2 and
maybe a ride to the next town.

Where I am now Mary I ought to study the poems of John
Greenleaf Whittier because theres been a real blizzard maybe
the biggest in the state for many years and Im Snowbound.
Years ago I tried to memorize all that poem but I got only
part way for it is a whopper of a poem.

I dont hear much good Music Mary because of course at
the motels there isnt any phonograph or tape recorder. Id
like to hear some good string quartet or maybe old folk
songs well sung for music hath charms to soothe the savage
breast. Theres an old Edison at the house where Im staying
now and what do you know they have a record of a song you
and I used to sing together Theres a Long Long Trail A
Winding. Its about the newest record in this house. Ill play it
again soon thinking of you Mary my sister. O there is a long
long night of waiting.

Mary right now Im at a big fine house where the people have gone away for awhile and I watch the house for them and keep some of the rooms warm. Let me assure you Mary I wont take anything from this good old house when I go. These are nice people I know and I just came in out of the storm and Im very fond of their 3 sweet little girls. I remember what you looked like when I ran way first and you looked like one of them called Alice. The one I like best though is Allegra because she makes mischief and laughs a lot but is innocent.

I came here just yesterday but it seems as if Id lived in this house before but of course I couldnt have and I feel at home here. Nothing in this house could scare me much. You might not like it Mary because of little noises and glimpses you get but its a lovely house and as you know I like old places that have been lived in lots.

By the way Mary once upon a time Father O'Malley told me that to the Lord all time is eternally present. I think this means everything that happens in the world in any day goes on all at once. So God sees what went on in this house long ago and whats going on in this house today all at the same time. Its just as well we dont see through Gods eyes because then wed know everything thats going to happen to us and because Im such a sinner I dont want to know. Father O'Malley says that God may forgive me everything and have something special in store for me but I dont think so because why should He?

And Father O'Malley says that maybe some people work out their Purgatory here on earth and I might be one of these. He says we are spirits in the prisonhouse of the body which is like we were serving Time in the world here below and maybe God forgave me long ago and Im just waiting my time and paying for what I did and it will be alright in the end. Or maybe Im being given some second chance to set things right but as Father O'Malley put it to do that Id have to fortify my Will and do some Signal Act of contrition. Father O'Malley even says I might not have to do the Act actually if only I just made up my mind to do it really and truly because what God counts is the intention. But I think people who are in Purgatory must know they are climbing up and have hope and Mary I think Im going down down down even though Ive stayed out of prisons some time now.

Father O'Malley tells me that for everybody the battle is won or lost already in Gods sight and that though Satan thinks he has a good chance to conquer actually Satan has lost forever but doesnt know it. Mary I never did anybody any good but only harm to ones that loved me. If just once before I die I could do one Signal Act that was truly good then God might love me and let me have the Beatific Vision. Yet Mary I know Im weak of will and a coward and lazy and Ive missed my chance forever.

Well Mary my only sister Ive bored you long enough and I just wanted to say hello and tell you to be of good cheer. Im sorry I whined and complained like a little boy about my health because Im still strong and deserve all the pain I get. Mary if you can forgive your big brother who never grew up please pray for me sometime because nobody else does except possibly Father O'Malley when he isnt busy with other prayers. I pray for Mother every night and every other night for you and once a month for Dad. You were a good little girl and sweet. Now I will say good bye and ask your pardon for bothering you with my foolishness. Also Im sorry your friends found out I was just a hobo when I was with you 9 years ago and I dont blame you for being angry with me then for talking too much and I know I wasnt fit to lodge in your house. There arent many of us old real hobos left only beatniks and such that cant walk or chop wood and I guess that is just as well. It is a degrading life Mary but I cant stop walking down that long long trail not knowing where it ends.

Your Loving Brother

Francis (Frank)

P.S.: I dont wish to mislead so I will add Mary that the people who own this house didnt exactly ask me in but its all right because I wont do any harm here but a little good if I can. Good night again Mary.

Now he needed an envelope, but he had forgotten to take one from the last motel, where the Presbyterian minister had put him up. There must be some in Tamarack House, and one would not be missed, and that would not be very wrong because he would take nothing else. He found no envelopes in the drawer of the library table: so he went up the stairs and almost knocked at the closed door of Allegra's Room. Foolish! He opened the door gently.

He had admired Allegra's small rosewood desk. In its drawer was a leather letter-folder, the kind with a blotter, he found, and in the folder were several yellowed envelopes. Also lying face up in the folder was a letter of several small pages, in a woman's hand, a trifle shaky. He started to sit down to read Allegra's letter that never was sent to anybody, but it passed through his mind that his great body might break the delicate rosewood chair that belonged to Allegra, so he read the letter standing. It was dated January 14, 1969. On that birthday of his, he had been in Joliet prison.

How beautifully Allegra wrote!

Darling Celia,

This is a lonely day at Tamarack House, just fifty-four years after your great-grandfather the General died, so I am writing to my grand-niece to tell you how much I hope you will be able to come up to Anthonyville and stay with me next summer—if I still am here. The doctor says that only God knows whether I will be. Your grandmother wants me to come down your way to stay with her for the rest of this winter, but I can't bear to leave Tamarack House at my age, for they might have to put me in a rest-home down there and then I wouldn't see this old house again.

I am all right, really, because kind Mr. Connor looks in every day, and Mrs. Williams comes every other day to clean. I am not sick, my little girl, but simply older than my years, and running down. When you come up next summer, God willing, I will make you that soft toast you like, and perhaps Mr. Connor will turn the crank for the ice-cream, and I may try to make some preserves with you to help me.

You weren't lonely, were you, when you stayed with me last summer for a whole month? Of course there are fewer than a hundred people left in Anthonyville now, and most of those are old. They say that there will be practically nobody living in the town a few years from now, when the new highway is completed and the old one is abandoned. There were more than two thousand people here in town and roundabout, a few years after the General built Tamarack House! But first the lumber industry gave out, and then the mines were exhausted, and the prison-break in 1915 scared many away forever. There are no passenger trains now, and they say the railway line will be pulled out altogether when the new freeway—they have just begun building it to the east—is ready for traffic. But we still have the maples and the tamaracks, and there are ever so many raccoons and possums and squirrels for you to watch—and a lynx, I think, and an otter or two, and many deer.

Celia, last summer you asked me about the General's death and all the things that happened then, because you had heard something of them from your Grandmother Edith. But I didn't wish to frighten you, so I didn't tell you everything. You are older now, and you have a right to know, because when you grow up you will be one of the trustees of the Anthony Family Trust, and then this old house will be in your charge when I am gone. Tamarack House is not at all frightening, except a little in the morning on every January 14. I do hope that you and the other trustees will keep the house always, with the money that Father left to me—he was good at making money, even though the forests vanished and the mines failed, by his investments in Chicago—and which I am leaving to the Family Trust. I've kept the house just as it was, for the sake of the General's memory and because I love it that way.

You asked just what happened on January 14, 1915. There were seven people who slept in the house that month —not counting Cook and Cynthia (who was a kind of nannie to us girls and also cleaned), because they slept at their houses in the village. In the house, of course, was the General, my grandfather, your great-grandfather, who was nearly

eighty years old. Then there were Father and Mama, and the
three of us little sisters, and dear Frank.

Alice and sometimes even that baby Edith used to tease
me in those days by screaming, "Frank's Allegra's sweetheart! Frank's Allegra's sweetheart!" I used to chase them,
but I suppose it was true: he liked me best. Of course he was
about sixty years old, though not so old as I am now, and I
was a little thing. He used to take me through the swamps
and show me the muskrats' houses. The first time he took me
on such a trip, Mama raised her eyebrows when he was out
of the room, but the General said, "I'll warrant Frank: I
have his papers." Alice and Edith might just as well have
shouted, "Frank's Allegra's slave!" He read to me—oh, Robert Louis Stevenson's poems and all sorts of books. I never
had another sweetheart, partly because almost all the young
men left Anthonyville as I grew up when there was no work
for them here, and the ones that remained didn't please
Mama.

We three sisters used to play Creepmouse with Frank, I
remember well. We would be the Creepmice, and would
sneak up and scare him when he wasn't watching, and he
would pretend to be terrified. He made up a little song for us
—or, rather, he put words to some tune he had borrowed:

> *"Down, down, down in Creepmouse Town*
> *All the lamps are low,*
> *And the little rodent feet*
> *Softly come and go*
>
> *"There's a rat in Creepmouse Town*
> *And a bat or two:*
> *Everything in Creepmouse Town*
> *Would swiftly frighten you!"*

Do you remember, Celia, that the General was State Supervisor of Prisons and Reformatories for time out of mind?
He was a good architect, too, and designed Anthonyville
State Prison, without taking any fee for himself, as a model
prison. Some people in the capital said that he did it to give

employment to his county, but really it was because the site was so isolated that it would be difficult for convicts to escape.

The General knew Frank's last name, but he never told the rest of us. Frank had been in Anthonyville State Prison at one time, and later in other prisons, and the General had taken him out of one of those other prisons on parole, having known Frank when he was locked up at Anthonyville. I never learned what Frank had done to be sentenced to prison, but he was gentle with me and everybody else, until that early morning of January 14.

The General was amused by Frank, and said that Frank would be better off with us than anywhere else. So Frank became our hired man, and chopped the firewood for us, and kept the fires going in the stoves and fireplaces, and sometimes served at dinner. In summer he was supposed to scythe the lawns, but of course summer didn't come. Frank arrived by train at Anthonyville Station in October, and we gave him the little room at the top of the house.

Well, on January 12 Father went off to Chicago on business. We still had the General. Every night he barred the shutters on the ground floor, going round to all the rooms by himself. Mama knew he did it because there was a rumor that some life convicts at the Prison "had it in" for the Supervisor of Prisons, although the General had retired five years earlier. Also they may have thought he kept a lot of money in the house—when actually, what with the timber gone and the mines going, in those times we were rather hard pressed and certainly kept our money in the bank at Duluth. But we girls didn't know why the General closed the shutters, except that it was one of the General's rituals. Besides, Anthonyville State Prison was supposed to be escape-proof. It was just that the General always took precautions, though ever so brave.

Just before dawn, Celia, on the cold morning of January 14, 1915, we all were waked by the siren of the Prison, and we all rushed downstairs in our nightclothes, and we could see that part of the Prison was afire. O, the sky was red! The General tried to telephone the Prison, but he couldn't get through, and later it turned out that the lines had been cut.

Next—it all happened so swiftly—we heard shouting somewhere down Main Street, and then guns went off. The General knew what that meant. He had got his trousers and his boots on, and now he struggled with his old military overcoat, and he took his old army revolver. "Lock the door behind me, girl," he told Mama. She cried and tried to pull him back inside, but he went down into the snow, nearly eighty though he was.

Only three or four minutes later, we heard the shots. The General had met the convicts at the gate. It was still dark, and the General had cataracts on his eyes. They say he fired first, and missed. Those bad men had broken into Mr. Emmons's store and taken guns and axes and whiskey. They shot the General—shot him again and again and again.

The next thing we knew, they were chopping at our front door with axes. Mama hugged us

Celia dear, writing all this has made me so silly! I feel a little odd, so I must go lie down for an hour or two before telling you the rest. Celia, I do hope you will love this old house as much as I have. If I'm not here when you come up, remember that where I have gone I will know the General and Father and Mama and Alice and poor dear Frank, and will be ever so happy with them. Be a good little girl, my Celia.

The letter ended there, unsigned.

Frank clumped downstairs to the Sunday parlor. He was crying, for the first time since he had fought that professional heavyweight on October 19, 1943. Allegra's letter—if only she'd finished it! What had happened to those little girls, and Mama, and that other Frank? He thought of something from the Holy Bible: "It were better for him that a millstone were hanged about his neck, and he cast into the sea, than that he should offend one of these little ones."

Already it was almost evening. He lit the wick in the cranberry-glass lamp that hung from the middle of the parlor ceiling, standing on a chair to reach it. Why not enjoy more light? On a whim, he arranged upon the round table four silver candlesticks that had rested above the fireplace. He needed three more, and those he fetched from the dining room. He lit every candle in the circle: one for the General, one for Father, one for Mama, one for Alice, one for Allegra, one for Edith—one for Frank.

The dear names of those little girls! He might as well recite aloud, it being good practice for the approaching days on the long, long trail:

> *I hear in the chamber above me*
> *The patter of little feet,*
> *The sound of a door that is opened,*
> *And voices soft and sweet. . . .*

Here he ceased. Had he heard something in the passage—or "descending the broad hall stair"? Because of the wind outside, he could not be certain. It cost him a gritting of his teeth to rise and open the parlor door. Of course no one could be seen in the hall or on the stair. "Crazy Frank," men had called him at Joliet and other prisons: he had clenched his fists, but had kept a check upon himself. Didn't Saint Paul say that the violent take Heaven by storm? Perhaps he had barked up the wrong tree; perhaps he would be spewed out of His mouth for being too peaceful.

Shutting the door, he went back to the fireside. Those lines of Longfellow had been no evocation. He put "The Long, Long Trail" on the old phonograph again, strolling about the room until the record ran out. There was an old print of a Great Lakes schooner on one wall that he liked. Beside it, he noticed, there seemed to be some pellets embedded in a closet door-jamb, but painted over, as if someone had fired a shotgun in the parlor in the old days. "The violent take it by storm. . . ." He admired the grand piano; perhaps Allegra had learnt to play it. There were one or two big notches or gashes along one edge of the piano, varnished over, hard though that wood was. Then Frank sank into the big chair again and stared at the burning logs.

Just how long he had dozed, he did not know. He woke abruptly. Had he heard a whisper, the faintest whisper? He tensed to spring up. But before he could move, he saw reflections in the tall mirror.

Something had moved in the corner by the bookcase. No doubt about it: that small something had stirred again. Also something crept behind one of the satin sofas, and something else lurked near the piano. All these were at his back: he saw the reflections in the glass, as in a glass darkly, more alarming than physical forms. In this high shadowy room, the light of the kerosene lamp and of the seven candles did not suffice.

From near the bookcase, the first of them emerged into candle-light; then came the second, and the third. They were giggling, but he could not hear them—only see their faces, and those not clearly. He was unable to stir, and the gooseflesh prickled all over him, and his hair rose at the back of his big head.

They were three little girls, barefoot, in their long muslin night-gowns, ready for bed. One may have been as much as twelve years old, and the smallest was little more than a baby. The middle one was Allegra, tiny even for her tender years, and a little imp: he knew, he knew! They were playing Creepmouse.

The three of them stole forward, Allegra in the lead, her eyes alight. He could see them plain now, and the dread was ebbing out of him. He might have risen and turned to greet them across the great gulf of time, but any action—why, what might it do to these little ones? Frank sat frozen in his chair, looking at the nimble reflections in the mirror, and nearer they came, perfectly silent. Allegra vanished from the glass, which meant that she must be standing just behind him.

He must please them. Could he speak? He tried, and the lines came out hoarsely:

> *"Down, down, down in Creepmouse Town*
> *All the lamps are low,*
> *And the little rodent feet. . . ."*

He was not permitted to finish. Wow! There came a light tug at the curly white hair on the back of his head. Oh to talk with Allegra, the imp! Reckless, he heaved his bulk out of the chair, and swung round—too late.

The parlor door was closing. But from the hall came another whisper, ever so faint, ever so unmistakable: "Good night, Frank!" There followed subdued giggles, scampering, and then the silence once more.

He strode to the parlor door. The hall was empty again, and the broad stair. Should he follow them up? No, all three would be abed now. Should he knock at Mama's Room, muttering, "Mrs. Anthony, are the children all right?" No, he hadn't the nerve for that, and it would be presumptuous. He had been given one moment of perception, and no more.

Somehow he knew that they would not go so far as the garret floor. Ah, he needed fresh air! He snuffed out lamp and candles, except for one candlestick—Allegra's—that he took with him. Out into the hall he went. He unfastened the front door with that oaken patch about the middle of it, and stepped upon the porch, leaving the burning candle just within the hall. The wind had risen again, bringing still more snow. It was black as sin outside, and the temperature must be thirty below.

To him the wind bore one erratic peal of the desolate church bell of Anthonyville, and then another. How strong the blast must be through that belfry! Frank retreated inside from that unfathomable darkness and that sepulchral bell which seemed to toll for him. He locked the thick door behind him and screwed up his courage for the expedition to his room at the top of the old house.

But why shudder? He loved them now, Allegra most of all. Up the broad stairs to the second floor he went, hearing only his own clumsy footfalls, and past the clay-sealed doors of the General and Father and Mama and Alice and Allegra and Edith. No one whispered, no one scampered.

In Frank's Room, he rolled himself in his blankets and quilt (had Allegra helped stitch the patchwork?), and almost at once the consciousness went out of him, and he must have slept dreamless for the first night since he was a farm boy.

So profound had been his sleep, deep almost as death, that the siren might have been wailing for some minutes before at last it roused him. Frank knew that horrid sound: it had called for him thrice before, as he fled from prisons. Who wanted him now? He heaved his ponderous body out of the warm bed. The candle that he had brought up from the Sunday parlor and left burning all night was flickering in its socket, but by that flame he could see the hour on his watch: seven o'clock, too soon for dawn.

Through the narrow skylight, as he flung on his clothes, the sky glowed an unnatural red, though it was long before sunup. The prison siren ceased to wail, as if choked off. Frank lumbered to the little frieze window, and saw to the north, perhaps two miles distant, a monstrous mass of flame shooting high into the air. The prison was afire.

Then came shots outside: first the bark of a heavy revolver, followed irregularly by blasts of shotguns or rifles. Frank was lacing his boots with a swiftness uncongenial to him. He got into his overcoat as there came a crashing and battering down below. That sound, too, he recognized, woodchopper that he had been: axes shattering the front door.

Amid this pandemonium, Frank was too bewildered to grasp altogether where he was or even how this catastrophe might be fitted into the pattern of time. All that mattered was flight; the scheme of his escape remained clear in his mind. Pull up the chair below the skylight, heave yourself out to the upper roof, descend those iron rungs to the woodshed roof, make for the other side of the freeway, then—why, then you must trust to circumstance, Frank. It's that long, long trail a-winding for you.

Now he heard a woman screaming within the house, and slipped and fumbled in his alarm. He had got upon the chair, opened the skylight, and was trying to obtain a good grip on the icy outer edge of the skylight-frame, when someone knocked and kicked at the door of Frank's Room.

Yet those were puny knocks and kicks. He was about to heave himself upward when, in a relative quiet—the screaming had ceased for a moment—he heard a little shrill voice outside his door, urgently pleading: "Frank, Frank, let me in!"

He was arrested in flight as if great weights had been clamped to his ankles. That little voice he knew, as if it were part of him: Allegra's voice.

For a brief moment he still meant to scramble out the skylight. But the sweet little voice was begging. He stumbled off the chair, upset it, and was at the door in one stride.

"Is that you, Allegra?"

"Open it, Frank, *please* open it!"

He turned the key and pulled the bolt. On the threshold the little girl stood, indistinct by the dying candlelight, terribly pale, all tears, frantic.

Frank snatched her up. Ah, this was the dear real Allegra Anthony, all warm and soft and sobbing, flesh and blood! He kissed her cheek gently.

She clung to him in terror, and them squirmed loose, tugging at his heavy hand: "Oh, Frank, come on! Come downstairs! They're hurting Mama!"

"Who is, little girl?" He held her tiny hand, his body quivering with dread and indecision. "Who's down there, Allegra?"

"The bad men! *Come on,* Frank!" Braver than he, the little thing plunged back down the garret stair into the blackness below.

"Allegra! Come back here—come back now!" He bellowed it, but she was gone.

Up two flights of stairs, there poured to him a tumult of shrieks, curses, laughter, breaking noises. Several men were below, their speech slurred and raucous. He did not need Allegra to tell him what kind of men they were, for he heard prison slang and prison foulness, and he shook all over. There still was the skylight.

He would have turned back to that hole in the roof, had not Allegra squealed in pain somewhere on the second floor. Dazed, trembling, unarmed, Frank went three steps down the garret staircase. "Allegra! Little girl! What is it, Allegra?"

Someone was charging up the stair toward him. It was a burly man in the prison uniform, a lighted lantern in one hand and a glittering ax in the other. Frank had no time to turn. The man screeched obscenely at him, and swung that ax.

In those close quarters, wielded by a drunken man, it was a chancy weapon. The edge shattered the plaster wall; the flat of the blade thumped upon Frank's shoulder. Frank, lurching forward, took the man by the throat with a mighty grip. They all tumbled pell-mell down the steep stairs—the two men, the ax, the lantern.

Frank's ursine bulk landed atop the stranger's body, and Frank heard his adversary's bones crunch. The lantern had broken and gone out. The convict's head hung loose on his shoulders, Frank found as he groped for the ax. Then he trampled over the fallen man and flung himself along the corridor, gripping the ax helve. "Allegra! Allegra girl!"

From the head of the main stair, he could see that the lamps and candles were burning in the hall and in the rooms of the ground floor. All three children were down there, wailing, and above their noise rose Mama's shrieks again. A mob of men were stamping, breaking things, roaring with amusement and desire, shouting filth. A bottle shattered.

His heart pounding as if it would burst out of his chest, Frank hurried rashly down that stair and went, all crimson with fury, into the Sunday parlor, the double-bladed ax swinging in his hand. They all were there: the little girls, Mama, and five wild men. "Stop that!" Frank roared with all the power of his lungs. "You let them go!"

Everyone in the parlor stood transfixed at that summons like the Last Trump. Allegra had been tugging pathetically at the leg of a dark man who gripped her mother's waist, and the other girls sputtered and sobbed, cornered, as a tall man poured a bottle of whiskey over them. Mrs. Anthony's gown was ripped nearly its whole length, and a third man was bending her backward by her long hair, as if he would snap her spine. Near the hall door stood a man like a long lean rat, the Rat of Creepmouse Town, a shotgun on his arm, gape-jawed at Frank's intervention. Guns and axes lay scattered about the Turkey carpet. By the fireplace, a fifth man had been heating the poker in the flames.

For that tableau moment, they all stared astonished at the raving giant who had burst upon them; and the giant, puffing, stared back with his strange blue eyes. "O, Frank!" Allegra sobbed: it was more command than entreaty—as if, Frank thought in a flash of insane mirth, he were like the boy in the fairy tale who could cry confidently "All heads off but mine!"

He knew what these men were, the rats and bats of Creepmouse Town: the worst men in any prison, lifers who had made their hell upon earth, killers all of them and worse than killers. The rotten damnation showed in all those flushed and drunken faces. Then the dark man let go of Mama and said in relief, with a coughing laugh, "Hell, it's only old Punkinhead Frank, clowning again! Have some fun for yourself, Frank boy!"

"Hey, Frank," Ratface asked, his shotgun crooked under his arm, "where'd the old man keep his money?"

Frank towered there perplexed, the berserker-lust draining out of him, almost bashful—and frightened worse than ever before in all his years on the trail. What should he shout now? What should he do? Who was he to resist such perfect evil? They were five to one, and those five were fiends from down under, and that one a coward. Long ago he had been weighed in the balance and found wanting.

Mama was the first to break the tableau. Her second captor had relaxed his clutch upon her hair, and she prodded the little girls before her, and she leaped for the door.

The hair-puller was after her at once, but she bounded past Ratface's shotgun, which had wavered toward Frank, and Alice and Edith were ahead of her. Allegra, her eyes wide and desperate, tripped over the rung of a broken chair. Everything happened in half a second. The hair-puller caught Allegra by her little ankle.

Then Frank bellowed again, loudest in all his life, and he swung his ax high above his head and downward, a skillful dreadful stroke, catching the hair-puller's arm just below the shoulder. At once the man began to scream and spout, while Allegra fled after her mother.

Falling, the hair-puller collided with Ratface, spoiling his aim, but one barrel of the shotgun fired, and Frank felt pain in his side. His bloody ax on high, he hulked between the five men and the door.

All the men's faces were glaring at Frank incredulously, as if demanding how he dared stir against them. Three convicts were scrabbling tipsily for weapons on the floor. As Frank strode among them, he saw the expression on those faces change from gloating to desperation. Just as his second blow descended, there passed through his mind a kind of fleshly collage of death he had seen once at a farmyard gate: the corpses of five weasels nailed to a gatepost by the farmer, their frozen open jaws agape as if they were damned souls in Hell.

"All heads off but mine!" Frank heard himself braying. "All

heads off but mine!" He hacked and hewed, his own screams of lunatic fury drowning their screams of terror.

For less than three minutes, shots, thuds, shrieks, crashes, terrible wailing. They could not get past him to the doorway.

"Come on!" Frank was raging as he stood in the middle of the parlor. "Come on, who's next? All heads off but mine! Who's next?"

There came no answer but a ghastly rattle from one of the five heaps that littered the carpet. Bloodsoaked from hair to boots, the berserker towered alone, swaying where he stood.

His mind began to clear. He had been shot twice, Frank guessed, and the pain at his heart was frightful. Into his frantic consciousness burst all the glory of what he had done, and all the horror.

He became almost rational: he must count the dead. One upstairs, five here. One, two, three, four, five heaps. That was correct: all present and accounted for, Frank boy, Punkinhead Frank, Crazy Frank: all dead and accounted for. Had he thought that thought before? Had he taken that mock roll before? Had he wrought this slaughter twice over, twice in this same old room?

But where were Mama and the little girls? They mustn't see this blood-splashed inferno of a parlor. He was looking at himself in the tall mirror, and he saw a bear-man loathsome with his own blood and others' blood. He looked like the Wild Man of Borneo. In abhorrence he flung his ax aside. Behind him sprawled the reflections of the hacked dead.

Fighting down his heart pain, he reeled into the hall. "Little girls! Mrs. Anthony! Allegra, Oh, Allegra!" His voice was less strong. "Where are you? It's safe now!"

They did not call back. He labored up the main stair, clutching his side. "Allegra, speak to your Frank!" They were in none of the bedrooms.

He went up the garret stair, then, whatever the agony, and beyond Frank's Room to the cupola stair, and ascended that slowly, gasping hard. They were not in the cupola. Might they have run out among the trees? In that cold dawn, he stared on every side; he thought his sight was beginning to fail.

He could see no one outside the house. The drifts still choked the street beyond the gateposts, and those two boulders protruded impassive from untrodden snow. Back down the flights of stairs he made his way, clutching at the rail, at the wall. Surely the little girls hadn't strayed into that parlor butcher shop? He bit his lip and peered into the Sunday parlor.

The bodies all were gone. The splashes and ropy strands of blood all were gone. Everything stood in perfect order, as if violence never had touched Tamarack House. The sun was rising, and sunlight filtered through the shutters. Within fifteen minutes, the trophies of his savage victory had disappeared.

It was like the recurrent dream which had tormented Frank when he was little: he separated from Mother in the dark, wandering solitary in empty lanes, no soul alive in all the universe but little Frank. Yet those tremendous ax blows had severed living flesh and blood, and for one moment, there on the stairs, he had held in his arms a tiny quick Allegra; of that reality he did not doubt at all.

Wonder subduing pain, he staggered to the front door. It stood unshattered. He drew the bar and turned the key, and went down the stone steps into the snow. He was weak now, and did not know where he was going. Had he done a Signal Act? Might the Lord give him one parting glimpse of little Allegra, somewhere among these trees? He slipped in a drift, half rose, sank again, crawled. He found himself at the foot of one of those boulders— the farther one, the stone he had not inspected.

The snow had fallen away from the face of the bronze tablet. Clutching the boulder, Frank drew himself up. By bringing his eyes very close to the tablet, he could read the words, a dying man panting against deathless bronze:

In loving memory of
FRANK
a spirit in prison, made for eternity
who saved us and died for us
January 14, 1915

"Why, if the Soul can fling the Dust aside,
And naked on the Air of Heaven ride,
    Were't not a Shame—were't not a Shame for him
In this clay carcass crippled to abide?"

APPENDIX

World Fantasy Awards—1973–76

The First World Fantasy Awards were given in 1975 to honor material first published in the English language during 1973 *and* 1974. The awards committee initially did both the nominating and voting, although they welcomed direction from anybody wishing to alert them to good material. All of the judges removed themselves from award consideration for the period covered. The first awards committee consisted of:

Ramsey Campbell—Author and editor
Edward L. Ferman—Editor and publisher
David G. Hartwell—Editor and publisher
Fritz Leiber—Author and critic
Gahan Wilson—Artist and author

The votes were tabulated by the convention committee and checked by *Analog* editor Ben Bova. The winners were announced at the First World Fantasy Convention held at Providence, Rhode Island, on Halloween weekend, 1975. The winners are listed below with the runners-up following in alphabetical order.

BEST NOVEL: The Forgotten Beasts of Eld by Patricia McKillip (Avon)

Runners-up:

A Midsummer Tempest by Poul Anderson (Ballantine)
Merlin's Ring by H. Warner Munn (Ballantine)

BEST SHORT FICTION: "Pages from a Young Girl's Journal" by Robert Aickman (*The Magazine of Fantasy and Science Fiction*)

Runners-up:

"The Events at Poroth Farm" by T. E. D. Klein (*Year's Best Horror ⚹2*)
"A Father's Tale" by Sterling Lanier (*The Magazine of Fantasy and Science Fiction*)
"Sticks" by Karl Edward Wagner (*Whispers* magazine)

BEST SINGLE AUTHOR COLLECTION: *Worse Things Waiting* by Manly Wade Wellman (Carcosa)

Runner-up:

From Evil's Pillow by Basil Copper (Arkham House)

SPECIAL AWARD—PROFESSIONAL: Ian and Betty Ballantine

Runner-up:

Donald A. Wollheim

SPECIAL AWARD—NON-PROFESSIONAL: Stuart David Schiff (*Whispers* magazine)

Runners-up:

Harry O. Morris, Jr.
Roy A. Squires

BEST ARTIST: Lee Brown Coye

Runners-up:

Stephen Fabian
Gervasio Gallardo
Jeff Jones
Tim Kirk

LIFE ACHIEVEMENT AWARD: Robert Bloch

Runners-up:

Robert Aickman
Frank Belknap Long
Donald Wandrei
Manly Wade Wellman

The Second World Fantasy Awards were given in 1976 for material first published in the English language during 1975. Again the judges did both the nominating and voting. As usual, the judges removed themselves from award consideration. It should also be noted that the Special Award winners of the previous year are ineligible to receive back-to-back awards, one may win the Life Achievement Award only once, and only people living at the time of the nominations are eligible. The second awards committee consisted of:

Charles Collins—Publisher and editor
Basil A. Copper—Author
Gordon R. Dickson—Author and editor
Stuart David Schiff—Editor and publisher
Gahan Wilson—Artist and author

The votes were tabulated by David G. Hartwell and the winners announced at the Second World Fantasy Convention held in

Manhattan, New York over 1976's Halloween weekend. The winners are listed below with the runners-up following in alphabetical order.

BEST NOVEL: *Bid Time Return* by Richard Matheson (Viking/Ballantine)

Runner-up:

Salem's Lot by Stephen King (Doubleday/NAL)

BEST SHORT FICTION: "Belsen Express" by Fritz Leiber (*The Second Book of Fritz Leiber* [DAW])

Runners-up:

"The Barrow Troll" by David Drake (*Whispers* magazine)
"Born of the Winds" by Brian Lumley (*The Magazine of Fantasy and Science Fiction*)
"The Ghastly Priest Doth Reign" by Manly Wade Wellman (*The Magazine of Fantasy and Science Fiction*)

BEST SINGLE AUTHOR COLLECTION: *The Enquiries of Dr. Eszterhazy* by Avram Davidson (Warner)

Runners-up:

Deathbird Stories by Harlan Ellison (Harper and Row/Dell)
The Early Long by Frank Belknap Long (Doubleday)
Far Lands, Other Days by E. Hoffmann Price (Carcosa)

SPECIAL AWARD—PROFESSIONAL: Donald M. Grant (Publisher)

Runners-up:

Arkham House (Publisher)
Willis Conover (Author-publisher of *Lovecraft at Last*)

L. Sprague de Camp (Author of *Lovecraft: A Biography* [Doubleday])

Frank Belknap Long (Author of *Howard Phillips Lovecraft: Dreamer on the Nightside* [Arkham House])

Donald A. Wollheim (Publisher-editor)

SPECIAL AWARD—NON-PROFESSIONAL: Carcosa (Publisher: editor Karl Edward Wagner; Associates—David Drake and James Groce)

Runners-up:

Gerry de la Ree (Publisher-editor)
Harry A. Morris, Jr. (Publisher-editor)
George Scithers (Publisher-editor)
Roy A. Squires (Publisher-editor)
Robert Weinberg (Publisher-editor)

BEST ARTIST: Frank Frazetta

Runners-up:

George Barr
Stephen Fabian
Edward Gorey
Tim Kirk

LIFE ACHIEVEMENT AWARD: Fritz Leiber

Runners-up:

Ray Bradbury
Frank Belknap Long
Manly Wade Wellman

The Third World Fantasy Awards were given in 1977 for work first published in the English language during 1976. This was the initial year the fans were given the opportunity to nominate. A ballot was sent to all members of the previous conventions and the items in each category garnering the two highest amounts of votes were automatically placed on the final ballot. The judges were then allowed to add additional nominations and selected the winners from the joint compilation. As per the rules, none of the judges were eligible for the awards and previous Life Achievement Award-winners and the previous year's Special Award winners were not eligible. The third awards committee was composed of:

Robert Bloch—Author
David Drake—Author and publisher
Harlan Ellison—Author and editor
Charles L. Grant—Author and editor
Robert Weinberg—Publisher and editor

The votes were tabulated by David G. Hartwell and the judges' decisions announced at the Third Annual World Fantasy Convention held in Los Angeles, California over 1977's Halloween weekend. The winners are listed below with the runners-up following in alphabetical order.

BEST NOVEL: *Doctor Rat* by William Kotzwinkle (Knopf)

Runners-up:

The Doll Who Ate His Mother by Ramsey Campbell (Bobbs-Merrill)
The Dragon and the George by Gordon R. Dickson (Ballantine)
The Sailor on the Seas of Fate by Michael Moorcock (Quartet/DAW)
The Acts of King Arthur and His Noble Knights by John Steinbeck (Farrar, Straus, and Giroux)
Dark Crusade by Karl Edward Wagner (Warner)

BEST SHORT FICTION: "There's a Long, Long Trail A-Winding" by Russell Kirk (*Frights*—Kirby McCauley, editor [St. Martin's Press])

Runners-up:

"The Companion" by Ramsey Campbell (*Frights*)
"It Only Comes Out at Night" by Dennis Etchison (*Frights*)
"Dark Wings" by Fritz Leiber (*Superhorror*—Ramsey Campbell, editor [St. Martin's Press and W. H. Allen and Company, Ltd.])
"What is Life" by Robert Sheckley (*Playboy*)
"Two Suns Setting" by Karl Edward Wagner (*Fantastic*)

BEST COLLECTION or *ANTHOLOGY: Frights*—Kirby McCauley, editor (St. Martin's Press)

Runners-up:

Long After Midnight by Ray Bradbury (Knopf)
Cinnabar by Edward Bryant (Macmillan)
Superhorror—Ramsey Campbell, editor (St. Martin's Press and W. H. Allen and Company, Ltd.)
The Height of the Scream by Ramsey Campbell (Arkham House)
Flashing Swords ⅓—Lin Carter, editor (Dell)

SPECIAL AWARD—PROFESSIONAL: Alternate World Recording, Inc. (Record Publishers, Shelley and Roy Torgeson, directors)

Runners-up:

Arkham House (Publisher)
Ballantine Books (Publisher)
DAW Books (Publisher)
Edward L. Ferman (Editor-Publisher, *The Magazine of Fantasy and Science Fiction*)

SPECIAL AWARD—NON-PROFESSIONAL: Stuart David Schiff (Editor-publisher of *Whispers* magazine)

Runners-up:

Jonathan Bacon (Editor-publisher)
Arnie Fenner (Editor-publisher of *Chacal*)
Nils Hardin (Publisher-editor of *Xenophile*)
Gary Hoppenstand (Publisher-editor of *Midnight Sun*)
Harry O. Morris, Jr. (Editor-publisher)

BEST ARTIST: Roger Dean

Runners-up:

George Barr
Stephen Fabian
Tim Kirk
Michael Whelan

LIFE ACHIEVEMENT AWARD: Ray Bradbury

Runners-up:

Jorge Luis Borges
L. Sprague de Camp
Frank Belknap Long
H. Warner Munn
E. Hoffmann Price
Manly Wade Wellman